GW01418687

Khamsin

— A Thriller —

By
MARKO PERKO
AND
HRAYR SHAHINIAN

iUniverse, Inc.
New York   Bloomington

Khamsin
A Thriller

Copyright © 2010 Marko Perko and Hrayr Shahinian

All rights reserved. No part of this book may be used or reproduced by any means, graphic, electronic, or mechanical, including photocopying, recording, taping or by any information storage retrieval system without the written permission of the publisher except in the case of brief quotations embodied in critical articles and reviews.

This is a work of fiction. All of the characters, names, incidents, organizations, and dialogue in this novel are either the products of the authors' imaginations or are used fictitiously.

iUniverse books may be ordered through booksellers or by contacting:

iUniverse
1663 Liberty Drive
Bloomington, IN 47403
www.iuniverse.com
1-800-Authors (1-800-288-4677)

Because of the dynamic nature of the Internet, any Web addresses or links contained in this book may have changed since publication and may no longer be valid. The views expressed in this work are solely those of the authors' and do not necessarily reflect the views of the publisher, and the publisher hereby disclaims any responsibility for them.

ISBN: 978-1-4502-3888-5 (pbk)
ISBN: 978-1-4502-3889-2 (cloth)
ISBN: 978-1-4502-3890-8 (ebk)

Library of Congress Control Number: 2010909148

Printed in the United States of America

iUniverse rev. date: 11/5/10

MARKO PERKO:

As always, to my beautiful wife Heather,
my wonderful son, *the Bruin*, Marko III,
and my darling daughter, *the Little Rocker*, Skye Mackay.

HRAYR SHAHINIAN:

To my "Hamov" wife Leslie,
and my two treasures, Alexander and Karina,
who everyday make me appreciate the significance and rewards of
fatherhood.

Before all else, be armed.

—Niccolò di Bernardo dei Machiavelli (1469-1527)

Acknowledgments

M.P. & H.S.

To U.S. Air Force Brigadier General Robert L. Tate (Ret.), for his eagle eye on technical aspects of the story.

To U.S. Army Major Charles Wilbourn (Military Intelligence/Ret.) for his knowledge of terrorist organizations worldwide.

To those who unknowingly inspired us to write this book.

To the members of the United States military…we all sleep peacefully because of you.

M.P.

To my dearest mother Darinka T. Perko, who often wonders what a writer does, nonetheless, she always gives me her unwavering support.

To my father Mike Perko, who passed too soon, for teaching me to be curious.

To my sister Jeanette Risher, who shares my age for eleven days each year.

To Natalija Nogulich, Robert Vaughn, Dave Gotta, Peter Sainato, and Gary Higa.

H.S.

To my grandparents, survivors of the first genocide of the twentieth century, for teaching me the good and evil in mankind.

To my parents, Karnig and Maro Shahinian, for my education and all the sacrifices in making me who I am.

To my sisters Houry and Lara for all the great childhood memories.

To my ancestral and adopted countries of Armenia and Lebanon for giving me my "DNA."

To Rudyard Kipling for the poem *IF–*.

To America, the greatest nation on earth, for granting me the honor and privilege of citizenship. No matter what I achieve in this lifetime, I will never be able to repay that "debt."

Khamsin

PROLOGUE

Operating room three on the eighth floor of the Southern California General Medical Center was a place where miracles large and small occurred routinely, and today, February 17, a rather somber day, was no exception. There was an eerie quietness punctuated by two distinct, rhythmic sounds: one, a heart beating at 130 beats per minute, the other, yet another heart beating at 68 beats per minute.

Huddled in a corner around the large, secondary gas plasma-viewing screen were two high-risk obstetrical gynecological specialists and the circulating nurse. The primary gas plasma screen hovered just centimeters above the head of the patient. Opposite the screen, one could see the masked face of the lead surgeon, Dr. Alexander Hakimian, standing resolutely at the back of the operating room. His eyes were all that were visible on his shrouded face. They radiated extreme focus and intensity.

Dr. Hakimian, a world-renowned skull-base brain surgeon of rare talents, adored by his patients, admired by others, yet vilified by many of his peers, was in his element. He had turned the medical community on its head by shunning the traditional craniotomy, a profoundly medieval procedure that involved making an incision from ear to ear, after which the skin was pulled back to expose the skull. Next, the procedure required sawing off the top portion of the skull to reach the brain in order to access the abnormality.

Dr. Hakimian's approach was dramatically different and simply revolutionary. He promoted the use of minimally invasive techniques, principally micro-endoscopy and micro-instrumentation, to access the problem area either through a natural pathway such as the nostril, or via minute, millimeter incisions made in the eyebrow or behind the ear.

The results of Dr. Hakimian's approach were nothing short of miraculous, with patients enjoying shorter hospital stays, reduced recovery times, decreased overall risks, and fewer post-operative complications. It was a fundamental shift in the field of cranial surgery, and Dr. Hakimian had put the old school practitioners on notice.

This morning Dr. Hakimian was attempting to perform what others believed to be a miracle on Meghan Minson. She was a twenty-two-year-old woman who had only last year completed her bachelor's degree in broadcast communications at the University of Southern California. Moreover, the year before she had married, in Newport Beach, California, Silver Star recipient Lieutenant Commander Martin Minson, a graduate of the United States Naval Academy.

It was while the two were on their honeymoon in Prague that Meghan felt the first sudden, ripping pain in her head, followed by yet another pain radiating downward into her neck. At the time, she pushed the pain to the back of her mind. She was in love and nothing was going to get between her and the man in her life. However, the agonizing pain returned with greater intensity a few more times over the next six months. By then, she was finally pregnant and very happy.

Meghan suffered from Ehlers-Danlos syndrome, an inherited connective tissue disorder. Because of EDS, she had already had open-heart surgery at the tender age of six to repair leaky heart valves. Then, when she entered college, she was advised not to become pregnant because it would most assuredly result in severe health risks to both her and her fetus.

Despite the medical warning, Meghan was insistent upon having a child, even if that child might grow up without a mother. Her husband Martin was hesitant about the pregnancy, but Meghan could be very persuasive.

During her pregnancy, their worst fears came true. Meghan was diagnosed with two separate cerebral aneurysms. One was located near the optic nerves arising from the anterior communicating artery, and a second, more problematic aneurysm was situated in the posterior fossa arising from the posterior inferior cerebellar artery.

In spite of attempts to wait until the pregnancy was over, the aneurysm of the anterior communicating artery was on the verge of rupturing, and if it did, Meghan's dream of giving her husband a child would never happen. Delaying treatment was not a viable option.

In time, the two were directed to Dr. Hakimian, who built his reputation on the successes he had had operating on patients whom other doctors would turn away as inoperable.

After careful consideration, Dr. Hakimian, along with Meghan's high-risk OB-GYN specialist, opted to perform the first of two lifesaving surgeries during her third trimester. He would clip the anterior communicating artery aneurysm in an endoscopic approach through her right eyebrow; then, after the delivery of her baby girl months later, a second procedure behind her left ear would allow a clipping of the posterior inferior cerebellar artery aneurysm.

At precisely six o'clock in the morning, Dr. Hakimian indicated that he was ready. He began with an eyebrow incision followed by a one-centimeter keyhole opening in the right supraorbital area. He then introduced a 2.7 mm fiber-optic neuroendoscope into the cranial cavity and deftly advanced the scope along the floor of the anterior skull base and underneath the frontal lobe, all the while imminently aware that an ever so slight move of the scope left or right of the determined path would end the young woman's life instantly. It was like a game of high stakes poker, with everything riding in the hands of Dr. Hakimian.

"Richard, I need you to keep the blood pressure in the 90s."

"Yes, doctor," came back loud and clear.

Dr. Richard Kamen, the neuroanesthesiologist, was a longtime member of Dr. Hakimian's handpicked operating team.

Focusing tightly on the culprit, Dr. Hakimian uttered emphatically, "There it is." The aneurysm was completely exposed. One wrong move and it would rupture, leading to brain death in seconds.

Dr. Hakimian liked to compare his job to that of a bomb squad leader…one slight misstep and boom!

With rupture imminent, Dr. Hakimian had to move fast. "Gentlemen, let's do it. Alejandro, give me the clip."

Alejandro, Dr. Hakimian's personal scrub nurse, worked with robotic precision.

"Alejandro, the number four curved Penfield." Alejandro slapped the exact instrument into Dr. Hakimian's left hand. Dr. Hakimian introduced it alongside the endoscope. He gently used the Penfield to reveal the neck of the aneurysm, ever mindful that over clipping it would result in a massive stroke.

"Richard, drop the blood pressure to seventy systolic ASAP. This damn aneurysm is about to rupture."

Raising his head up for a moment, he quickly surveyed the immediate area. "Jerry, let me know how the fetus is doing. I want to save them both, but if it's not possible with this bleeding, then the mother lives," he said emphatically.

Suddenly, like a dam that breaks, pulsatile bright red blood started flowing out of control. "Suction," came out quickly from Dr. Hakimian, his hands moving with faultless precision. His eyes focused like a blue laser.

Over the next two minutes both the mother's and baby's heart rates continued to plummet to life-threatening levels. Dr. Hakimian, feeling the pressure to do what he does best, welcomed the challenge…it was his *raison d'etre*.

"Curved aneurysm clip," commanded Dr. Hakimian. Without looking in his hand, confident that Alejandro never missed a call, he advanced the aneurysm clip, avoiding the optic nerves and the optic chiasm.

"How's the fetus doing?" Dr. Hakimian asked without a scintilla of emotion. He was in control.

"You have maybe sixty seconds," answered Dr. Jerry Topalian, the lead high-risk OB-GYN. He refrained from discussing the obvious danger at hand.

Under magnification, Dr. Hakimian positioned the clip at the neck of the aneurysm. Once he was certain that no other vessels were cut or trapped on the backside of the aneurysm, he released the clip. Taking a deep breath, he paused, then looked at the monitors. Slowly, like an Italian opera in full voice, the two heartbeats started picking up speed and reached their previous base levels. It was music to his ears.

The most delicate and dangerous aspect of the procedure was now complete. Faces smiled underneath sterile, blue masks. The relief in operating room three was palpable.

Looking up for a moment, Dr. Hakimian asked, "Give me the vitals."

"Everything's fine, doctor," Dr. Kamen said. "Maybe after today we have all earned our places in heaven," he added. "We managed to save two lives at the very same time."

Dr. Hakimian gently withdrew the endoscope as the ceiling lights in the operating room turned on and the theme from *Mission Impossible* began to play. It was Dr. Kamen's way of stating the obvious.

Dr. Hakimian looked down at Meghan, nodded his head in the affirmative and then said, "Dr. Javahi, do your thing and make sure the final eyebrow closure is subcuticular. We have a beautiful wife and young mother to be. I want absolutely no evidence that she ever had an operation."

"Yes, doctor," exclaimed Dr. Reza Javahi, an associate of Dr. Hakimian's.

Unexpectedly, the phone in the operating room rang. Dr. Hakimian did not like to be disturbed while he worked his medical magic and the slight scowl on his face made the point.

"Operating room three," said Nicole Williams, the circulating nurse. Listening for a moment, she turned around and said to Dr. Hakimian, who was preparing to leave, "Doctor, you are wanted immediately in your office."

Dr. Hakimian quickly walked out of the operating room and headed to the physicians' locker room, wondering who would need him just now. After all, he had no appointments scheduled until the late afternoon.

Once inside the locker room he stepped in front of his personal locker. He opened the tall metal door and retrieved his white, starched doctor's coat with his name and title embroidered in burgundy thread above the left breast pocket. He slowly eased his arms through the sleeve openings. After adjusting his coat, he began to walk toward the exit when suddenly he stopped. His eyes darted about as if he had heard something odd, then he sat down on a bench near the door. *Damn it*, he said to himself. He was exhausted, truly exhausted; not from the long surgery, he was used to that; not from rising before the sun did, he had done that for years. No, his recurring nightmares exhausted him. Terrible nightmares that he used to be able to push aside for months and sometimes even for years at a time. *What was going on?* he had asked himself far too many times. *That was a lifetime ago, forget it*, he would tell himself. *Move on*, came another self-admonition.

Something was brewing in the deep recesses of his complex mind. It had all ended too fast. One day she was cocooned in his embrace and the next, she was gone. Disappeared. But he continued to ransack his memory in search of an answer. He could not help it. *Would he ever again know the magic that was her obsidian-colored eyes, eyes that pierced his very soul?* He wanted to know. He needed to know, but it seemed that it was not to be.

He rose from the bench and marched out of the locker room. His pace increased as he made his way through the lunch crowd moving about the complex of buildings in the warm Southern California sunshine. Approaching the main building, he crossed over the bridge that connected the hospital with the adjacent eleven-story structure that housed the offices of staff doctors. Once inside his well-appointed suite of offices Dr. Hakimian glanced at his institute's logo emblazoned on the glass-enclosed conference room door. It read: "Skull Base and Brain Institute." Every day he looked at it, he was filled with pride. However, this time a second look through the conference room's glass partition turned his facial expression from one of pride to one of consternation. It revealed three men in nondescript, dark suits talking intently. He did not know any of them, but their attire and mien clearly signaled *United States Government Agents*.

Annoyed, yet mildly curious, Dr. Hakimian entered his conference room and said without preamble, "Gentlemen, can I be of assistance to you?" He eyed each of them with a hard look and waited for a response.

A man in his late fifties, who easily carried thirty-five pounds of extra flesh and facial skin that shouted "too much sun," immediately approached him. "Dr. Hakimian, I am Senior Operations Officer John Barker from the National Security Agency and these are agents Roberts and Johnson. We're honored to meet you."

Dr. Hakimian just looked at him dispassionately, and then nodded curtly to the other two agents.

The NSA, the most shadowy of intelligence agencies, was born on the morning of November 4, 1952, in Washington, D.C. At the time, there was no fanfare, no press, no Congressional debates, not even a whisper of a rumor that it existed. There was never an official record of its creation in any of the federal government publications.

Harry S Truman had signed the presidential directive and the new agency was classified top-secret, branded with a code name that had never been made public. Some said its acronym stood for *No Such Agency* or *Never Say Anything*. To this very day, it has remained the most invisible and mysterious of intelligence agencies.

"Dr. Hakimian, we are here on behalf of Director Caccavale who wishes to speak with you."

Dr. Hakimian knew of Anthony Caccavale, director of an agency that was larger, more powerful, and infinitely more shadowy than the FBI, CIA, ATF, and DEA combined. He became a member of its inner-circle after having served for thirty-five years in the U.S. Air Force, retiring with the rank of lieutenant general. Three years ago, the president appointed him its director. Since then, he has been a man often embroiled with the press in pitch battles over what the American public had the right to know and what it did not. In addition, the issue of eavesdropping on American citizens believed to be communicating with terrorists always proved problematic, if not political quicksand.

"Does he? About what?" a physically and emotionally spent Dr. Hakimian asked flatly.

"He'd like to tell you himself, Dr. Hakimian," Senior Operations Office Barker stated emphatically.

"One moment doctor, we have an encrypted phone ready for you," agent Johnson interrupted. He removed the phone from the black government-issue briefcase set atop the conference table and handed it to him.

SOO Barker added, "Doctor, the director...."

Dr. Hakimian reluctantly placed the phone to his ear. After a series of whooshing sounds and a ping indicating that the two secure-phones had synchronized, Director Caccavale's raspy voice, the result of a bout with throat cancer a decade ago, came through as loud and clear as could be expected. "Dr. Hakimian, this is Director Anthony Caccavale of the National Security Agency. This call is at the request of the President of the United States."

That got Dr. Hakimian's attention. He had met the president in the Oval Office two years earlier, and had always been impressed by his unwavering commitment to the *war on terror*, no matter what it might do to his legacy.

"The NSA is on a vital mission central to the eventual success of the president's global war on terror, and based on your background and previous incursions into the Middle East, you have been selected to lead that mission."

Dr. Hakimian felt his brain slow to a stop, then shift into overdrive. Removing his right hand from his coat pocket, he slowly scratched his brow, staring impassively at the agents sitting silently in the room now looking like plaster-of-Paris statues.

"Doctor, I am aware that you have a very successful medical practice, and that you have a beautiful wife and young daughter and that your life is just where you want it," the director added.

Dr. Hakimian focused on the words *just where you want it*, as the director continued.

"I can't make you take this assignment, but what I can say is that the *clock is ticking*, Dr. Hakimian. I can't stress enough that should we as a nation fail in our pursuit to defeat those who seek to do us harm, we will cease to exist as a free people. In the final analysis, doctor, it is a very simple premise: *good versus evil*."

Dr. Hakimian held his breath for a beat before he finally responded. "Director, I have always believed that our course as a nation is righteous, just, and necessary." He paused, then added with great emphasis, "I, like most Americans, want the war on terror to succeed. But it has gone on for far too long because we have never had the real will to win the war for a host of reasons, beginning with the lack of political will. And now Afghanistan is another albatross around the neck of the American people." Dr. Hakimian could have said more, but held his fire.

"Excuse me, Dr. Hakimian," Director Caccavale interrupted, his raspy voice making it difficult at times to hear clearly over the secure phone transmission. "I certainly understand your apprehension, but your unique talents and belief in what America stands for make you the obvious choice. Quite frankly, doctor, the only choice." The emphasis on *only* was apparent.

Glancing into the reception area where a wheelchair-bound patient was nervously waiting for him, Dr. Hakimian said, "If you'll permit me to be blunt, Director Caccavale. I've done my time. I've violated my oath to heal more times than I'd like to remember. If you are as familiar with my previous incursions into the Middle East as you say you are, then you are well aware that I've had friends die terrible deaths because of a cause that many believe has long since lost its purpose. I've killed more men than I'm willing to admit to anyone, including myself." Pausing for another beat, he added, "And now director, the president is asking me to do it again...for the cause!"

Dr. Hakimian handed the phone to SOO Barker, effectively ending the conversation. With a look of disquiet on his face, he excused himself, and exited the room, leaving the three men behind, dumbstruck.

CHAPTER ONE

BEL-AIR, CALIFORNIA

Alec held the yellowed newspaper clipping in his left hand. He reached with his right hand for a cup of steaming Yame Gyokuro green tea sitting on the large glass tabletop in the French-windowed reading room just off his grand home's main dining area. He began to read quietly: "Arlington National Cemetery, whose motto is 'In Honored Glory, Our Heroes Rest,' is the final resting place for thousands upon thousands of America's bravest souls."

Taking another slow sip of the precious Japanese green tea, savoring its reputed healing powers, he continued reading, "The famed cemetery, whose origins reach back to the nation's first president as well as the great Civil War General Robert E. Lee, holds many secrets, and one of them is the unsung hero buried in Section 59."

The next paragraph followed with, "The final remains of William Francis, a highly-decorated U.S. Army Lieutenant Colonel and later the Central Intelligence Agency's principal operative in Lebanon, who was rumored to have been also working undercover as the political officer and station chief at the U.S. Embassy in Beirut, is marked by a simple white headstone."

Alec's dark eyes steadied on the next paragraph. "Francis's remains were discovered on December 27, 1992, after he had been taken hostage by a group calling itself Hezbollah or 'party of God' in March 1989. He was savagely tortured and summarily killed the next year."

Hezbollah, a Shi'a Islamist political and paramilitary organization, first showed its face in 1982 during the Israeli invasion of Lebanon at the time of the Lebanese civil war and has since become a powerful resistance movement throughout the Arab world.

Alec felt a deep sadness grip his thoughts. His eyes threatened to tear-up, but he resisted the urge. The article finished by saying that "a public service was held with full military honors on May 13, 1993, some four years after his death."

Alec knew about the memorial service…he was there.

As he reached for the large manila envelope on the table that had held the newspaper clipping, the phone rang. Ignoring its summons, he stared at the return address. *Whom did he know in Wolf Laurel, North Carolina?* he asked himself. He racked his brain. *No, he knew no one that he could remember,* he reasoned. Then, without deliberation or cause, he looked inside the envelope. There, tucked in a bottom corner he saw a once-folded piece of off-white notepaper. He hesitated at first, but then reached in and removed it. Unfolding the notepaper, he began to read the words scribbled in an unsteady hand in red ink.

Dear Alec, I know I probably shouldn't have done this, but you are the only one who understands my loss. Bill has been gone longer than I want to admit and I still miss his warm smile and the way he said my name. His memory tears at my soul every day and I know it does the same to you. Alec, you know that Bill would have wanted to be alive today to see that his work meant something; that he fought the good fight; and that terrorism would be eliminated in our time. It was his dream. But Alec, today very few people understand what Bill was trying to do. He knew that this day would come. He knew that we would be fighting for our lives in a world ripped apart by people who want to kill us in the name of their god. Alec, if Bill's death is to have any meaning, any meaning at all, then the fight to rid the world of the scourge of Islamic fundamentalism must continue. No one is better able to lead that fight than you Alec, and you know that Bill would have wanted you to. He trusted you and said that you were the best.

Love, Rachel Medford.

Alec's first thought was *the last he'd heard, she was very ill and in a convalescent home.* Followed by *he hadn't spoken to her in at least twenty years.* Then came *goddamn Caccavale. The son of a bitch got to her. He couldn't leave it alone. Since he couldn't make the case for my joining the president's crusade again, he had to go and pressure Bill's girlfriend to try.*

The cup of green tea was now empty, but the thought of Francis's memory filled his mind to overflowing. His emotions began to swing like a pendulum from thoughts of the good times with Bill to the time that Bill had saved his life just days before the kidnapping.

◆ ◆ ◆

The two first met in the spring of 1985 in a popular Beirut café one evening after Alec had finished class at the American University of Beirut. Alec often enjoyed eating dinner by himself and reading one of the latest American car magazines. That night he had been reading *Road & Track* as Francis casually walked by and sat down at the table next to him. Peering over his shoulder, Francis said, "Excuse me, but I couldn't help but see that you are reading my favorite magazine."

At first, Alec looked at him with suspicion, but then, as Francis cracked a smile, Alec said emphatically, "The new Corvette," pointing to the picture in the magazine. "It's one amazing car."

Francis slid his chair closer to Alec's table. Trying to be heard over the din of noise, he raised his voice about twenty decibels and said, "I had a '68 L-88 in bright red." Waiving off the waitress with his right hand, he continued, "And let me tell you, it blew the doors off of the Ferrari." His pride was visible. He added proudly, "From a dead stop, it was a hell of a ride."

The image of a bright red Corvette drew Alec into the conversation. He had always wanted a Corvette…it was American and he liked America. The thought of the massive horsepower its aluminum V-8 engine pumped out made him want it even more.

Francis continued, "Those rich old Bostonian farts who could afford to buy a Ferrari thought that because it was made in Italy, no American car could beat it. They were always shocked when I waved as I blew by them in third gear with lots of ponies and another gear left."

As the conversation continued, Alec's brashness and knowledge of American culture amused Francis. Detecting an accent that he knew was local Lebanese, he said, "You speak English rather well, Mr.—"

"Alexander Hakimian," he fired back instantly.

"Well, Alexander—"

"You can call me Alec."

"Then Alec it is," Francis replied. "And you can call me Bill. So tell me Alec, have you ever been to the U.S.?"

"No. Not yet. But after my training, I plan to start a practice in America on the West Coast, probably Southern California. I also read the *Wall Street Journal*, the *New York Times*, and *People Magazine*."

Francis was impressed, but he thought, the *New York Times*.... "So you're a doctor, are you?"

"I'm interning now, but it won't be too long before I'm finished."

"So what kind of doctor are you?"

"I'm going to specialize in brain surgery."

"So, a brain surgeon. Sounds very important."

Soon the meeting by chance on a warm spring evening led to a friendship that grew over time. The two talked cars, politics, and even played for the same local soccer club, Alec as a forward and Francis as the goalie.

At first, Francis posed as a businessman from Grand Rapids, Michigan, selling computer hardware and installation services to Middle Eastern companies. Yet, Alec sensed instinctively that he was anything but.... Occasionally Francis would broach the subject of democracy; what it meant to be free; and the price of freedom. Especially the price of freedom, for it always came at the cost of human lives. Francis impressed upon Alec that it was unavoidable; that the loss of lives was the price that had to be paid; and that men would always do what had to be done to be free. It was human nature at its most primal.

Alec fought the notion of killing for any reason, for it was his lifelong dream that he would one day become a doctor whose charge it was to save lives, not take them. As a Lebanese, he had seen too much death up close and it made no sense to him.

As the months ticked by, and with the deftness that was the hallmark of a man of Francis's ilk, meetings with Alec began to yield results. Francis, a CIA operative trained in the fine art of persuasion, could sense that Alec's head was filling with the ideals of democracy and of self-determination.

He was grooming Alec for....

Then, on a warm summer afternoon in late August 1987, Francis asked Alec to accompany him to his favorite restaurant in the coastal city of Jounieh, fifteen kilometers north of Beirut. It was famous for local Lebanese cuisine. Alec knew of the city, but not the reason he was going there.

Simple, meaningless banter filled the time as the two men drove up the eastern Mediterranean coastline to the restaurant in Francis's sleek, fire-engine red Lotus Europa. The whining sound of its race-bred, twin-cam engine was music to Alec's ears.

Soon the very picturesque, out-of-the-way restaurant called al-Bustan, or the Garden, came into view. It was sited on a bluff some one hundred meters above the undulating Mediterranean coastline. Once inside, Alec felt in a time warp of sorts, taken back to the time of the Crusades, as an elderly woman, her hands and slow gate evidence of a hard life, seated the two at a heavy wooden table with an unobstructed view of the sea below. Francis immediately ordered drinks. He then turned to Alec and said straightaway, his voice's timbre steady but somewhat muted, "Alec, in a few moments a gray-bearded man in his late-fifties will be walking through the door followed by two other men who are his body guards."

Alec returned Francis's look, but said nothing.

Francis scanned the small room filled with an odd collection of tables, most of them empty. The smell of the very distinctive Latakia tobacco smoke laid heavily on the air and caused his eyes to water a bit. Wiping them, he continued, "The man will ask me when the new Windows operating system will be released. I'll answer the question, then ask him to sit with us, and we'll order more drinks. He'll then ask me a very specific question."

"Excuse me Bill, but what the hell are you talking about, he'll ask you a very specific question? Who? What kind of question? And bodyguards. For what?" Alec asked point-blank.

"Alec, how long have we been friends? A few years now. In that time have I ever given you cause not to trust me?"

"No," he said instantly, his face punctuated by a look of consternation.

"Then know that you have no reason to now," Francis said, with a tone of reassurance.

Just then, a flash of bright sunlight and a warm breeze poured in through the opened door as a large man entered the restaurant, followed by two dark-blue suited younger men looking blank-faced, yet very alert and very capable.

Alec stared at the bearded man's face as he moved across the room, the man's eyes darting back-and-forth like a hawk searching for its prey.

Passing by their table, the man stopped and asked Francis, "So, when does the new *Windows* come out?"

Francis answered, "Arrowhead will be out next year. That's what I hear."

The restaurant's long family table in the back was now full of people feasting on its famous shish kabob, tabbouleh, and humus dishes. They were obviously celebrating something that required large carafes of red wine fit for a Roman bacchanalia. With no one paying any particular attention, the large man sat down with Alec and Francis as his bodyguards took their seats about three meters away near the kitchen, but facing the front door.

A man of few words, CIA Deputy Director for Operations Bishop Axelrod placed his elbows on the end of the table, clasped his hands, and fired away in his baritone voice. "Mr. Hakimian, I'm Bishop Axelrod, Deputy Director for Operations for the Central Intelligence Agency. Yesterday I attended a meeting of intelligence czars from various Middle Eastern and European countries in Athens." Glancing at Francis momentarily, he continued, "I received a call from Bill asking me to meet with him, because he was adamant that I talk to you. He insisted that you were the kind of individual who could work well in our company."

Francis and the DDO looked at Alec. They waited to see a reaction on his face. Even though he was seated across from one of the world's most secretive men, Alec said nothing. He always had a sixth sense and that sixth sense had told him some time ago that his friend William Francis was hiding something, something he felt would be revealed to him in due course.

"Francis speaks very highly of you, Mr. Hakimian. He believes that you have special skills that can be useful to us. I'm aware that you are a surgical intern, and a very talented one at that. First in your class I hear."

Alec said nothing.

"Let me be straight with you Alec. May I call you Alec?"

Alec nodded once.

Taking a deep breath that seemed to fill his rather significant girth, he continued, "What we do sometimes requires us to employ unique individuals such as you. I don't have to tell you that the Middle East is a tinderbox filled with very dangerous people. We and our allies are working to make it safer for everyone by stopping the growing Islamic fundamentalist threat. That threat, fueled by a very radical element of Islam, forces us to make decisions and to take actions that many would perceive as overly aggressive. But they simply don't appreciate nor understand the full extent of what we are up against. Alec, we believe that it is better to be pro-active. To take the fight to the enemy."

Francis kept his eyes on Alec, waiting for a sign that he was interested, or at least that he was listening. He gave no such sign.

Alec looked out the window, his chin resting on his clenched fist. He appeared to be staring into space as the roiling waves of the Mediterranean Sea pounded the jagged rocks below. Turning back to both men, he reached for his mineral water and lemon. After taking a long swallow, he locked eyes with DDO Axelrod, and blurted out under his breath, "I am a surgical intern who wants to help people live, not die. After all, you're the goddamn CIA."

Sensing Alec was agitated, DDO Axelrod inserted, "If you'll permit me, Alec. I understand your position, your philosophy. I have a son who's a cardiologist in Maryland. I also understand that doctors believe in 'first do no harm.' But I say, 'first *do harm to those who wish to do you harm'.*"

The DDO's last words resonated with Alec at some molecular level, but he remained stoical, needing to hear more. "So just what are my special skills or talents that you find so invaluable?"

DDO Axelrod paused for a beat, looked to Francis, then back to Alec. "Alec, what I'm asking you to do is help us get inside the minds of various anti-American fundamentalist groups. You have lived your life in this land. Even though we have highly-trained agents already in the Middle East, a native is far more attuned to the subtle beliefs and habits of these groups."

"Director, are you asking me to kill people…to assassinate them in cold blood? Is that what this is all about? Tell me," he insisted.

Sensing Alec's growing concern and obvious state of agitation, Francis tried to allay his suspicions. "Alec, the director is not asking you to kill anyone. What he's asking you to do is to join us. To help us learn their ways, to help us stop them before they stop us."

"So what is it that you want me to do?" Alec fired back.

Just then, a middle-aged waitress approached and in passable English, she asked politely, "Gentlemen, is there anything else I can get you? More drinks perhaps?"

Francis waived her off and leaned in closer to Alec as DDO Axelrod listened intently.

"Alec," said Francis. "I'm not going to bullshit you."

Alec stared at Francis, as a serious look crawled across his face.

"Alec, I am aware of your personal losses. I know that your mother and sister were killed in the '81 Beirut bombings. I know that you were injured. I know your family was devastated. Nothing can replace what you've lost. But you can help us make sure that others do not become victims. The fact that you are a native Lebanese, that you know how they think, how they feel, these are invaluable assets to us. Your language skills and quick mental reflexes make you just what we're looking for. We need you to give us that look inside certain terrorist organizations that are operating in the area. These fringe groups I'm talking about have taken one of the great religions of the world hostage. It can only lead to world chaos if not checked."

"But," Alec interrupted, "I am not one of them. I am an Armenian. I don't hold to their beliefs in any way. I do however have many decent and moderate Muslim friends, both Sunni and Shi'ite, and even Druze." Looking intently at Francis, he added, "But that doesn't make me one of them."

"Alec," Francis said, as the DDO looked on intently. "That is exactly why we believe you would be the perfect NOC. You have the instincts of an Arab. You speak the language that an Arab speaks, better than most Arabs speak it. After all, you have been inseparable from Sahar, a Palestinian-Arab woman for more than three years. I saw you with her. I saw you interact with her." Francis stopped just long enough to take a deep breath and a drink of his mineral water and lime and then he continued in his most convincing style. "They believe you. They embrace you as one of their own." Francis readjusted himself in the old wooden chair and waited for Alec's reaction.

Alec fought the urge to say *yes*. He knew Francis was right, but he had other plans. Yet, something far more powerful was sucking him into its maw. He was visibly torn. He remembered the bombings in his beloved city of Beirut, once called the Paris of the Middle East. Images of the lives lost, his mother, his sister, at the hands of indiscriminate, fanatical killers posing as so-called messengers of Allah blanketed his mind's view. Ironically, at times he would find himself empathizing with their cause but not their methods…killing innocents was not the answer. He knew the killings had to stop, but to do so, would by definition, involve killing. It was a Faustian bargain to be sure.

"Alec," DDO Axelrod interjected. "There is no guarantee here. Francis will train you, but it's up to you. If he tells me that you are not working out, then we'll just say good-bye to each other and call it a day. There's no coercion here. In a strange and twisted way you would be helping all those decent Muslims you call your friends."

The meeting in Jounieh ended with Alec realizing that the fight for freedom was far more important than any personal dream, and that a young man with his talents should be a part of something bigger than any personal desire.

The next eighteen months saw Alec's mentor, William Francis, instruct him on tradecraft and the finer points of covert operations. He learned human intelligence techniques and how the local terrorist groups operated. He studied the *Qur'an* and *Sunnah* and how to pray the obligatory five times per day in Arabic, from the first prayer of *Fajr* to the last, the *Isha*. As the weeks, then months wore on, Alec and Francis became ever closer, and Alec learned to trust Francis implicitly. It was at that time that Francis began to change the focus of the training. He started to instruct Alec in the finer points of hand-to-hand combat and the handling of small arms. Alec became a crack shot and actually enjoyed firing the various weapons at his disposal.

On several occasions, Francis asked Alec questions about how to kill someone using drugs, poisons, or even a surgeon's scalpel. Alec obliged him, for he knew where the questions were heading, and at that point, he also knew that he was well past the point of no return. He was in it now, and as was his nature, he was determined to become the best, the most *cunning assassin* the CIA had ever produced.

Until Francis's murder in 1989, and Alec's subsequent exposure as a Non Official Cover, Alec worked as a contract agent. He was singularly responsible for a menu of assassinations. Two Russian military officers in Afghanistan, an East German Stassi officer in Iran, two Arab terror merchants in Beirut, a Hamas operative, and a Venezuelan OPEC oil minister in Cairo all fell prey to his expertise as a skilled killer, an assassin of the first order. He further enhanced his agent profile by delivering human intelligence of critical import to CIA operations in the greater theater of operations that stretched from Tangiers to Baghdad. His codename was "The Doctor."

◆ ◆ ◆

The phone rang again, bringing Alec back to the present. It was six-thirty on a windy Friday morning and his scheduling nurse had phoned to remind him that he needed to be in the office by eight o'clock to consult with a Taiwanese family. The parents' eleven-year-old daughter had received an earlier diagnosis of an inoperable brain tumor.

The drive to the office took about fifteen minutes in his tungsten-gray colored Aston-Martin DB9. It had been a gift to himself for his many years of laboring endless hours in operating rooms to give others a second chance. The drive also gave him enough time to decide. He wanted revenge for his friend's death at the hands of ruthless terrorists who sought to impose their will on innocent people everywhere. It was a memory that had inhabited his psyche since that fateful day in 1989. He had spent too many years wondering if it would ever happen because he had spent far too many years hiding from his demons. He purposely put the death of his friend Francis in a deep, dark recess of his mind. He wanted to avenge Francis's death, but he had not. *Was he afraid?* he had asked himself countless times. He did not want to know. He did not want to find out. After he was exposed as a CIA agent of NOC status, something changed inside of him and he moved on. He did a year of research at Vanderbilt, followed by a surgical residency and fellowship. He then went on to setup his surgical practice in Los Angeles, California.

Alec brought the Aston-Martin to an instantaneous stop just feet from the doctors' entrance to the hospital's parking structure. The car's silky smooth 450 horsepower all-alloy V-12 engine idled as his mind raced. He held his hands tightly to the leather-covered steering wheel, as he scanned the car's luxurious interior. Then...it all coalesced in a nanosecond.

He had decided that he would take up *the gauntlet*.

CHAPTER TWO

The dimly lit and chilly United States Air Force C-17 Globemaster III *MilAir* transport, code name Palmetto 76, turned to take up an east-southeast heading out of Andrews Air Force Base. Stuffed with pallets of Pentagon classified cargo bound for Iraq, the aircraft lumbered toward the ancient city of Baghdad. It was not what Dr. Alexander Hakimian called flying in style, nor was it one of his trips to the Mariana Trench to free dive or to Zermatt to whoosh and schuss with the Continent's glitterati.

No. Alec was called to serve again, but at what cost this time? he asked himself. He remembered his daughter's last words to him before his departure. As an endless stream of tears rolled down her rosy cheeks, she said, "Daddy, stay." Her words were like a dagger to his heart. He sensed his wife's anger because of their emotional separation. He knew they had issues to resolve.

Trying as best he could to get comfortable on what had already been a very long and tiresome flight, Alec attempted to stretch out his long, athletic frame on a short, palletized VIP seat and started to drift off into a semi-conscious state. It was a place where he could get away, if only for a fleeting moment, from the emotional scene he had left at home. At that moment, a junior flight officer tapped him on the shoulder. Somewhat annoyed, Alec glanced up and then closed his eyes again, trying to find a dream that would pass the time.

"Dr. Hakimian, this is for you," the junior flight officer said in a low and respectful voice, as he reached out to hand Alec a collated stack of

twenty sheets of paper handed to him by a flight officer in the plane's
cockpit.

Alec looked up again, reluctantly took the sheaf of papers, and
nodded a thank-you. At first, his tired eyes refused to focus, but
in seconds, the words on the title page brought his entire body to
attention.

T-H-R-E-A-T M-A-T-R-I-X.

Every morning the President of the United States and his intimates
were given the Threat Matrix, and considering the present temper of the
time, it always contained alarming and perilous information.

The Threat Matrix was composed by as many as a dozen various
intelligence agencies that ascertained the latest threats and plots against
the United States, its protectorates, and allies. It was the daily by-
product of the Terrorist Threat Integration Center, whose charge it was
to assist habitually antagonistic agencies such as the CIA, FBI, and the
NSA in working together.

Alec thumbed through the report, memorizing every line, every
startling revelation. Familiar words hit him as he read...Teheran,
Islamabad, Riyadh, Kabul, and Damascus. All were capitals of Islamic
Fundamentalist States. Yet, he could not help but think about his youth
in a once peaceful Lebanon and his subsequent years as a medical
student, and now he was heading back to the khaki-colored sands of
the Middle East, not to see family, not for a college reunion, but to meet
with Task Force 121 and the NSA's operative.

Alec knew TF 121 was comprised of the CIA's Special Activities
Division, together with DEVGRU or the United States Naval Special
Warfare Development Group, formerly known as Navy SEAL Team 6,
and the U.S. Army's Delta Force, to create an intelligence and operations
unit unmatched anywhere. It excited him.

Alec's ability to analyze voluminous streams of data had served him
well. Nevertheless, his most valuable quality was that when faced with a
life or death situation, he jumped into the fray with what his detractors
thought to be reckless abandon. But just ask his confederates and they
would say that they wanted Alec on their side, every time.

In truth, Alec was *not* a team player and his outbursts were legendary
within the intelligence community. That had troubled Bishop Axelrod,
by then promoted to DCI, or Director of Central Intelligence. As such,

it was his decision to bring Alec *in* some years ago. His departure from the agency was said to have been to the mutual benefit of itself and Alec, but Alec knew otherwise.

When Beirut CIA station chief William Francis was kidnapped in 1989 and subsequently tortured and eliminated in 1990, Alec's world was shattered. He had warned Director Axelrod and his minions of analysts for months that his friend Francis was on the hit list of numerous Islamic extremist groups. His pleadings fell on deaf ears. Then it happened. Francis was gone, and his own cover in Beirut was blown. It was always Alec's suspicion that Director Axelrod had deemed him a liability. As such, Director Axelrod feared he would become a rogue agent, determined to find out how and why his friend Francis was murdered. He knew that Alec would not let the incident go unanswered, so he had to take him out of the equation.

At 1903 hours local time, the *MilAir* transport, call sign "Big Bird," began its slow descent as the intercom belched, squealed, and then "Buckle up gentlemen, it's Baghdad International a few klicks away, and please bring your seats to the upright position," came out with a harshness that could trigger a migraine headache.

The blue sky was clear on that late April afternoon, as the sun began its slow glide below the horizon. The ambient temperature was a barely tolerable 29° Celsius. The city appeared quiet, but Alec knew that in a terrorist zone nothing was what it appeared to be. Although U.S. military presence had been drastically reduced, inasmuch as the major focus had shifted a few years ago to Afghanistan, greater violence had inevitably returned to the cities of Iraq.

Others onboard were quickly moving their seats into the upright position while Alec still remained seated at a reclined angle, consumed by the words on page after page of the Threat Matrix.

Just minutes from touchdown the junior flight officer approached Alec with a secure cell phone. "Doctor, it's Ambassador Harris calling," he said.

Alec reached for the phone.

Looking at Alec, he added, "We're synced, sir."

Alec quickly grasped the secure cell phone with his left hand and raised it to his ear, all the while balancing the report on his right knee as he continued to peruse it. "Yes, Sean," Alec said, his eyes still on the report.

"Alec, we got him. We got the bastard," Ambassador F. Sean Harris said with a sense of relief and great pride.

"Got whom?" Alec responded, as he placed the report on the seat next to him.

"Al-Tamimi. Kamal al-Tamimi," he said loud and clear, with a detectable chuckle in his voice.

"Sean, where? When?" Alec asked, with astonishment in his voice. He was not sure if al-Tamimi, one of bin Laden's first lieutenants, would ever be caught. Al-Tamimi had a reputation for evading even the most determined of pursuers for more than fifteen years.

"In a spider hole outside of Ad Dawr. Just like our boys bagged Saddam years ago. What's the chance of that?" he asked. Pausing to catch his breath, he continued, "TF 121 moved in on two sites, Wolverine One and Two. They did a quick cordon-and-search and bingo, Wolverine Two came up aces."

"Sean, were there any other HVT's?"

"No other High Value Targets, but two garden variety Saddam Baath Party loyalists with AK-47s were bagged a couple of hundred meters from where we fished al-Tamimi out of the hole," Harris answered. "Who thought these guys were still around? Anyway, I'll fill you in with all the details when you land."

Suddenly, before Alec could reply, the military transport, buffeted by strong winds, hit the runway hard as the landing gear strained to keep it upright. The report suddenly slid off his right knee and onto the floor. Alec immediately set the cell phone on the adjoining seat and bent over to retrieve the papers when the aircraft jerked and shuttered violently, knocking him out of his seat and into a bulkhead. He tried to regain his balance, but the aircraft jerked again. The motion thrust him forward into a skein of telecommunication wires exposed on the bulkhead.

Slowly retracting his left hand, he winced noticeably. His first thought was, *if it's cut, I can't operate.* Fortunately, his hand had just missed a razor-sharp piece of metal hidden between the wires. He breathed a sigh of relief as he rotated it in every direction, examining it closely. It hurt, but he was confident that everything was okay.

The mighty C-17 Globemaster III finally screeched to an abrupt halt before the airport's main terminal of pre-cast concrete, glass, and steel. U.S. soldiers were everywhere, like worker bees busying themselves in their hive. Two armored personnel carriers came roaring passed the aircraft. Seeing armored personal carriers, or APCs, running about was still de rigueur in Baghdad.

The junior officer came rushing up to Alec and queried, "Dr. Hakimian, are you all right?"

"Yes. Didn't fasten my seatbelt," Alec said in jocular fashion, despite knowing that it was no joking matter. His day job was that of a world-class brain surgeon. His hands were his tools.

"May I get you something, sir?" came out with a Southern kindness and concern.

Alec pondered the suggestion and then said, "No. I'm just fine, but thanks anyway."

Once back in his, seat Alec searched for the cell phone. He found it in pieces beneath his feet. He thought about the U.S. Ambassador to Iraq's call to him aboard the C-17. *Ambassador Harris had called to tell him that another of the human "weapons of mass destruction" was now in custody. Saddam and the likes of men such as al-Tamimi had exterminated upwards of two million innocent people. They certainly qualified as weapons of mass destruction, he reasoned. There was no doubt about it. And he hoped that the people of Iraq would continue to mete out swift justice to every terrorist in their midst, just as they had to Saddam and his hirelings several years ago.*

The thought continued, *so what were people talking about? He never understood why Americans let the press feed them propaganda at such an unrelenting rate. Never thinking for themselves. Never challenging the established mainstream media. Never understanding that national security trumped one's personal concerns...any time, every time.* He thought... *Machiavelli clearly knew it nearly five centuries ago. Why didn't every American know it? It was not quantum physics.*

Alec checked his left hand again by moving it in every direction. It was fine, a little sore, but otherwise fine. Now he was anxious to get out of the fourth-class plane seat he had been riding in for what seemed like days and find a quiet place to clean up.

As the C-17's passenger door opened, Alec was quick to move.

Grabbing his valise, he debouched, taking his first step on to the tarmac. Images of his days in the Levant came rushing back at warp speed, like an Alpine avalanche in deep winter.

The first image hit him between his sore eyes, as gusts of coarse sand came out of nowhere and slapped him in the face. As he wiped away the bits of sand, the sting still apparent, he began to walk toward the terminal.

Sahar. The exotic Sahar. The Palestinian Sahar. He had lost count of the years it had been since they had last spent time together, first in Lebanon, then later in Syria. Alec wanted to remember, but for now he continued to move toward the terminal's entrance about fifty meters away, yet the images continued to come at him, ever faster and ever more intense.

The picture of his friend Francis amongst his brutal captors, knowing that the end of his life was imminent, both saddened and angered Alec. Every time he thought about it *he became enraged.* Every time he thought about *the CIA, no, that fat ass Director Axelrod giving him bogus information about his friend's murderers,* he wanted to know why.

The phony information had caused him to hunt down and eliminate two supposed members of Hezbollah, yet they turned out to be nothing more than Syrian day laborers who had been working as stone masons on a new administration building in the city of Beirut.

He wanted to face-off with Axelrod, but he had suffered a massive heart attack and died seven years ago while traveling to his summer home in Connecticut. There would be no revenge when it came to Axelrod. However, revenge there would be for his friend. Of this, he was most certain.

Alec continued to walk toward the massive terminal complex, struggling to rid himself of the idea that he had needlessly killed two men, possibly fathers just like himself. He could not shake the thought. The Agency had to cover up its mistake and Alec was the scapegoat.

"Dr. Hakimian. Dr. Hakimian," shouted an army captain, motioning to Alec with his right hand. Startled, Alec looked toward the sound that disturbed his possessed state.

"Yes," Alec said, trying to shout back above the sound of an F-18 fighter jet flying low overhead, its afterburners glowing a brilliant crimson.

The two walked toward each other as if by echolation. Alec was dressed in a light brown Polo shirt, Zegna olive-drab colored linen pants, and chestnut hued Cole-Haan loafers. His black rip-stop nylon Tumi valise was casually slung over his right shoulder. The captain, replete in well-worn military issue fatigues, a sun-parched face set-off by pearl-black colored aviator sunglasses, walked briskly, with a slight hop in his step, toward Alec. His P-92 9mm parabellum Beretta army issue sidearm hung in plain view.

CHAPTER THREE

Baghdad, once caught in a whirlpool of endless sectarian violence that radiated some thirty miles out in every direction and accounted for eighty percent of the country's dead and wounded, was changing. Since "The Surge" of 2007, violence was almost nonexistent at times, and the democratic government was taking root, albeit in fits-and-starts. The Sunni Awakening Councils had been a great success.

Similar to neighborhood watch groups in the U.S., these councils kept tabs on al-Qaeda terrorists and assisted U.S. and Iraqi forces in ridding them from the country. Many of the councils' leaders were former members of al-Qaeda who had tired of the endless fighting. Alec knew that although the Iraqis still had no concept of *real peace*, the military "surge" did much to increase the chances that it would eventually take root and the country would become a viable democracy.

Military vehicles moved quickly about, soldiers heavily armed and suspicious looked around every corner, locals scurried to and fro, some carrying what essentials they could to their war-ravaged homes, others putting what gas they could find into their dilapidated cars, while babies screamed for milk. Still others were in constant search of clean water and day jobs, as foreign journalists tried to make their deadlines via intermittent wireless communication. And yet, the city was rebuilding itself at an astonishing rate. Apartments and single-family dwellings were popping up like weeds in a dirt field.

Iraq was now under the control of the democratically elected government that struggled to keep sectarian interests at bay. Not unlike the early years after the American Revolution, disparate forces sought to undermine Iraq's government at every turn. But make no mistake about it, United States military forces still held sway over various areas of the country, determined to make democracy work for the Iraqis.

Present-day Iraqis prayed that their country would once again return to its former greatness: a place where eminent minds such as the eleventh century optician Al Hazen, a true Mesopotamian, whose brilliance had solved the greatest scientific conundrum of the previous eight millennia…the mystery of vision, would once again thrive.

"Doctor Hakimian, I'm Captain Maya," the thirty-something captain said, his facial features giving away his Middle Eastern ethnicity. Alec extended his right hand to him.

The captain then motioned for Alec to jump into the shotgun seat of the bullet-riddled HMMWV–High-Mobility Multipurpose Wheeled Vehicle or Humvee, originally designed for policing and light action.

The look of the vehicle seemed almost prehistoric to Alec. Its stark, linear lines certainly did not say low-drag coefficient. Its up-armored outside skin gave one the feeling that the triceratops of the Jurassic Period inspired its design. "How was your flight, sir?" the captain said, as he looked at Alec out of the corner of his eye.

"Let's just say that it was not what I'm used to, Captain Maya." Alec continued without a pause as he scanned the immediate area out of habit, "How long will it take us to get to CENTCOM-Baghdad?"

"Sir, about twenty minutes through town," the captain replied. "Actually, it's only about eleven kilometers from here to CENTCOM-Baghdad in the Green Zone, and it was once the deadliest eleven kilometers in the world. Even though the additional troops have worked wonders and there have been fewer deaths, I ask you to please put on the flack vest and the helmet, sir," he added, as he handed the protective gear to Alec. "By the way, I thought you should know that we still call it 'running the gauntlet' every time we make the run."

The words *the gauntlet* resonated in Alec's mind. As he adjusted his helmet and interceptor flack vest stuffed with bulletproof porcelain plates, he just listened. The captain appeared to enjoy hearing himself speak. With the two of them now seated inside the Humvee, the captain continued, "We're lucky today, sir."

"How's that captain?" Alec questioned flatly.

"We only have to make this trip once and in daylight. Nighttime can still be a real crapshoot. Some say that going to the airport is a little bit safer than coming from the airport to the city, but I don't see the difference. Anyway, we have a chase car following us."

"What's that behind us, our backup?" Alec queried.

The captain glanced in the rearview mirror, then said, "Oh that, sir. Yes. It's the MRAP-ATV."

"Looks like a Humvee on steroids," Alec remarked.

"It is, sir. Kind of. It's V-shaped steel body works great when it rolls over a live IED. The explosion is directed to the sides and away from the men inside. Works great. It's saving lives every day, but I think it's a little tough to drive at times because it's about twice the size of the vehicle we're in now. I've heard we're getting the very new ECV3. They already have it in Afghanistan."

"What's the ECV3?" he queried.

"Sir, it's technical name is the Expanded Capacity Vehicle version three. It's supposed to be the *luxe* type of what we're in. It's even painted in a nicer looking olive drab color, if you can consider olive drab nice looking." The captain held tight to the steering wheel. He kept his eyes focused on what was in front of him, all the while wearing a broad smile, yet giving no indication of what he was really thinking.

Alec looked around at the Humvee he was in and wondered why he was not at least in the MRAP, if not the ECV3. He reluctantly held the thought to himself.

"No worries, sir. We're in a Full-up Frag 5. You know, this is the Humvee with all the extra armor shit bolted on," the captain said with a constant smile painted across his tanned face.

Alec was not amused nor convinced.

As the Humvee and MRAP slowly pulled away from the tarmac, Alec began to think about the mission ahead. Suddenly, he spotted a mosque off to his left. "Captain, what's the name of the mosque?"

"Sir, that's the Ibn Taymiyah mosque. It's where many of the insurgents used to gather to plan their attacks on us. We cleared it of munitions and weapons a long time ago. It's fairly quiet now. The locals see to it. However, the pricks seem to replicate like amoebas and every so often they try to hit us."

"Are those a flock of Blackwater's white-striped *Little Bird* black choppers off to our left?" Alec asked, pointing to the shimmering sky.

"Yes, sir. As you know, since early 2009, Blackwater Worldwide no longer had a contract to work in Iraq. But there's still a small number of their operatives working under what is now called Xe Services. Some like what they do, others don't. For me, we need every private security contractor we can get. They help keep the peace in different ways than the military. Numerous private construction firms hire them to protect their personnel and property across the whole of Iraq and Afghanistan." He continued, "Most of their personnel are ex-military, but some say they are nothing more than soldiers of fortune. In recent years, they've had some really bad press and big problems. Today they're still around, but not so obvious."

A warm smile came over Alec's face when he thought about Saddam, the number one of the infamous "fifty-five," swinging from the hangman's rope in a dank room designed just for such a purpose. The delicious irony was not lost on Alec, for he thought, *what better way for the monster to have died than by hanging, a method of killing that over his despotic reign he had raised to an art form. And to think, he had been caught cowering like a frightened child in a hole and the Iraqis, after a lengthy and democratic trial, returned him to a hole, only dead.*

The "fifty-five" was the initial list of the highest value targets determined by the president and military officials at the beginning of the war in March 2003. These targets were Saddam Hussein and his subordinates, whom the U.S. Administration wanted captured, *dead or alive.* Thankfully, most of them were now dead.

Alec liked the "dead or alive" choice. It was a belief that he had kept tucked away deep in his psyche for decades. He was convinced that *dead was a good thing when it came to terrorists.*

CHAPTER FOUR

As a self-prescribed, momentary distraction, Alec took a long look at his Vacheron Constantin skeleton wristwatch. It brought back memories, for the costly and rare watch was a gift from the King of Spain five years ago after he had performed a life-saving surgery on the king's ailing wife. *He wondered why he even brought it, for he knew it did not belong in this place.*

The time was fast approaching 1955 hours and Baghdad was not looking any better to him. Living in the International Zone, formerly known as the Green Zone, created by the Coalition Provisional Authority at the war's outset gave a false sense of sanctuary from the realities of war. The zone was designated the most secure area of the city, but every time an explosive was set-off inside it, everyone realized that nothing in Baghdad was ever secure.

The Muslim call to *Isha*, the nighttime prayer, tempered the moment as it reverberated across the city's skyline, heralding the first hint of darkness.

Thoughts of the exotic Sahar caromed about his mind again. He was haunted by her. Her caress, an elixir. Her image, constant now that he was back in the Levant. He wanted to know the real truth. He had been told by his friend Dr. Raymond Raissi that she died in a car accident on her way to warn him after his covert agent cover was blown, but he never saw her body. There was no funeral, and her family never spoke about her again. To him, *nothing added up*. He had real doubts.

The battle-tried Humvee thudded along on well-worn, over-inflated all-terrain tires as the passenger seat pinched and poked at Alec's posterior. The ride was made even more ponderous by the need to put armor plating on a vehicle that was never designed to carry it.

The heavily traveled road of ruts and bumps took its toll on both vehicles and their occupants. Dodging the occasional blown-up car, ubiquitous pothole, or pile of rubble was commonplace in the land of terror and turmoil. It made Alec thankful that the Humvee he was riding in was somewhat bombproof, inasmuch he had heard that many were not, and that angered him.

As the Humvee and MRAP approached the first checkpoint cordoned off by a large redoubt formed out of twelve-foot high concrete T-Wall blast walls covered with murals painted by local children, Alec realized caution was still mission critical. The colorfully painted walls did not ease his mind, nor did the Hesco barriers made of cardboard and wire frames filled with sand.

The U.S. military moved the checkpoints and flash checkpoints along the route on a regular basis so that it made it more difficult for the insurgents to target potential victims. Even then, primitive IEDs, or improvised explosive devices, and VBIEDs, or vehicle-borne improvised explosive devices, were widespread methods used by insurgents to inflict death and destruction. They were highly effective, could be made on the cheap with little technical expertise required, and nearly impossible to defend against.

Flash checkpoints occurred at nighttime when very cautious, very nervous soldiers pointed flashlights at oncoming vehicles, signaling that they must come to a complete stop before the barricades.

The protocol at every checkpoint along the six-lane *highway of death* was the same. Slow down as one approached the soldiers. When told to stop, *stop!* After having the vehicle checked, leave when told to leave. Any slight movement not ordered by a soldier would most likely get one shot…dead!

Off to his left Alec sighted a platoon of British soldiers moving in tight formation as they prepared to head to Southern Iraq while the 1ˢᵗ Iraqi Commando Battalion was readying for an afternoon incursion north of Baghdad. Captain Maya had his military radio tuned to the Al-Arabiya radio station. It was established in March 2003 by the

Coalition Provisional Authority to assist in giving the Iraqis the truth about the military action in their country. Four times as many Iraqis listened to the Dubai-based broadcasting company as compared to the Qatar-based and Arab-financed Al-Jazeera, which many believed was a political organ of Islamic extremists and a powerful force for advancing their agenda of terror since its inception in 1996.

Alec knew that there was no other choice but to fight for freedom. Despotism had to be excised, wherever it raised its ugly head. And America was the surgeon. *Who else would do it?* Certainly not the French. After their histrionics at the United Nations and elsewhere, they could not even be counted on to deliver fresh bread to the corner market, let alone engage *the enemies of freedom*. And in recent years their very own country had felt the deleterious effects of turning a blind eye to the worldwide war on terror as French-born Muslim extremists burned city after city in a violent revolt against the establishment.

Bomb attacks from insurgents, both domestic and foreign, were still a fact of life in Iraq now that U.S. military forces had a greatly reduced presence in the cities. Everyone knew it. Everyone feared it. Everyone lived with it, for freedom's price was very high. After all, the United States has had troops on the border between South and North Korea since the 1950s. Moreover, it was only after President Reagan forced the Soviets' hand that the U.S.S.R. was no more.

CHAPTER FIVE

Al-Tamimi was chambered in an undisclosed place not far from where Saddam Hussein was imprisoned until his hanging back in December 2006 at Camp Justice. His recent capture silenced some detractors, yet still others continued to carp that enough had not been done. Why had bin Laden not been captured or al-Zawahiri? Alec always believed that the Americans had the distinct advantage…*money and might…now if they could just follow it up with unrelenting resolve, success would be a fait accompli…at least in terms of the physical war…yet winning the political war at home was always a different matter in a politically correct world.*

"Son of a bitch," Alec said with a tight voice, as he quickly grabbed his left forearm just below the shirt line. "What the…!" his thought momentarily distracted by the piercing sound of two U.S. F-18 fighter jets taking off from Baghdad International.

"Just one of those sand bugs, sir. We have to deal with them out here all of the time," came a response from the captain.

Alec's mind floated back to his youth in Lebanon and the barghash mosquitoes. He remembered they were always an annoyance, especially in the summer when the blistering heat caused them to multiply exponentially.

"It seems that sometimes the local critters we confront out here can be as troublesome as the insurgents," the captain said light heartedly. "By the way," he added, fighting back a laugh at Alec's expense, "in a few days the bite will start to ulcerate."

"Thanks captain, that's most reassuring," Alec rejoined. "But I have an all too intimate familiarity with the barghash, or critter as you say."

The ride across the city was troubling to Alec. He inventoried the immediate area as best he could. Falafel shops peppered the roadside and served the locals a very inexpensive dish that did little more than temporarily fill their bellies. The elderly struggled to survive in a city of survivors. For centuries, the Iraqis had been tested, and now their greatest test was still ahead. The United States' plan was to help them put in place a *real* democracy in a country that had never known democracy. In fact, Alec thought for a moment and then realized that *there has never existed an Islamic country that was truly democratic.* Yet there was hope, because in 2005, seventy percent of Iraqi voters dipped their fingers in purple ink, signifying their desire to live in a free country...*and democracy was on the march.*

The resurrection of Iraq was in full force, as American know-how flexed its mighty muscles. From large U.S. companies to smaller business concerns from yet smaller countries that supported the war, they were all thanked with contracts that would in time yield significant profits. Such was the way of the world.

Office buildings were growing out of the sands of Iraq at an impressive rate. Economic prosperity was growing; schools opened to all; women permitted access to every area of Iraqi society; and newspapers free to print what they wanted without fear of reprisals.

As Alec and the captain approached their destination, two U.S. Marine FAST Company guards clenching M9 firearms in their gloved hands waived them on through the Republic Palace's gated entrance, home to Central Command, Baghdad. Security personnel were everywhere, as heavily armed soldiers stood sentry at every turn. Numerous personal security-detail employees loitered about coddling an array of weaponry that included Glock semi-automatics, Bushmaster sniper rifles, and Beretta M9s. U.S. Army Criminal Investigative Command sported the much-prized M11s, as did U.S. Navy Criminal Investigative Service officers. APCs flitted about crazily like insects feeding on a carcass as U.S. fighter aircraft screamed overhead like flying predators showing no mercy. Strykers used to run critical-man missions were also present, as was the Terra Max, the U.S. military's newest "warbot." It was an autonomous version of the MTVR, or medium tactical replacement vehicle, designed to run supply missions about the environs of Baghdad without the need of a driver. It utilized LDR, or light detection and ranging, to see where it was going with great accuracy.

The immense, grotesquely ornate palace, just one of dozens Saddam Hussein had built over the many years while he financially, emotionally, and physically raped and murdered countless citizens of Iraq, was a fitting place for Central Command. After all, it said in simplest of terms to the last Saddam Hussein loyalists... *you lost, we, the citizens of Iraq, won.*

Although Alec was used to the finer things in life, even he was awestruck as he looked up at the palace's overwhelming size. It was beyond large. It was colossal. The grounds and outbuildings that had not been bombed during *"shock and awe"* gave voice to a place that at one time must have been spectacular, something that would have made the Roman emperors Diocletian and Caligula feel impotent. Off to the left the ocean-sized swimming pool was a favorite place for soldiers and Marines to spend their off hours during the nasty heat of the day.

Alec walked up the long steps to the palace's main entrance. He stood before doors that seemed to reach to the heavens. Two soldiers standing post quickly examined each man's credentials and handed them CENTCOM-Baghdad ID badges, thus permitting them to enter the inner sanctum of the base. The immense doors opened to let Alec and the captain enter. Their massiveness reminded Alec of the great Gatun Locks of the Panama Canal.

The foyer was at least fifty feet high and set off by four grand staircases and enormous chandeliers. The multi-colored marble walls, wainscoting, and base-relief designs were embellished by twenty-two carat gold leaf that appeared to go on forever. Massive, stuffed sofa chairs filled the distant corners of the foyer. Voices echoed, as if in the depths of the Grand Canyon.

Everywhere Alec looked, it was gold, gold, and more gold. He thought *it tacky.* To him it was the sign of a man who was very insecure. He thought, *a man who needed to show such ostentatious wealth and power by despotic means had to know that the end would inevitably come at the hands of U.S. military forces and the Iraqi people.*

It did.

It was as it should be, Alec believed.

Unexpectedly, a voice came from behind and caught his attention. "Dr. Hakimian, I am General Sherman Meade," the general said, with a robust tone emanating from his barrel chest. "I trust that your trip here was pleasant," he added, reaching to shake Alec's hand vigorously.

"Well, general, it was first cabin," Alec said, with a wry smile and a touch of sarcasm in his voice.

The general sized Alec up, then asked him to follow him and his aides across the gargantuan foyer and down one of the many hallways that led to what seemed like endless rooms. The ubiquitous pictures of Saddam Hussein in manifold poses had been removed long ago. Many local Iraqis were employed as maintenance workers who labored to turn the palace into an efficient command center for U.S. forces.

As the two walked, Alec and the general were quiet for a moment. Then Alec stopped, turned and faced the general as he said, "The Threat Matrix was given to me on the flight here, general. It states that Saddam had stockpiled untold tons of VX nerve gas and that the Fedayin Saddam transported the weapons to Syria. Even the Syrians have not attempted to really deny it," Alec added. "Moreover, the Khamsin is without question at the center of this intricate web of terrorism with all other terrorist organizations taking their marching orders from it. General, there's no question that the Khamsin is our primary target."

"Dr. Hakimian," the general interrupted, "I couldn't agree with you more. But we must be ever aware that the biological and nuclear components of the WMD issue are always credible threats that cannot be put on the back burner and forgotten as if they never existed. I won't lie to you doctor, finding WMD would be a real coup for us. It would take a lot of pressure off our presence here. It would cool many hotheads in Congress. But despite the Hezbollah having VX that they obviously plan to fit onto Katyusha rockets, eliminating the Khamsin's threat is paramount to our success in the war on terror," the general said, with certainty. "Let me add that the NSA representative you are about to meet will give us the latest details, so we'll both be learning together what she knows and has in mind," he concluded, his voice trailing off, as he looked to his right at an approaching aide waving a communiqué in his hand.

The room was at least thirty-five meters by forty-five meters. *There was that gold again*, Alec thought. An oversized wet-bar made of highly polished French black walnut, inlaid with Oriental mother-of-pearl, was lost in one corner of the room.

It must have been a grand time for Saddam and his cadre of killers. A real den of insidious iniquity, Alec imagined.

Oversized black leather sofas that rested on immense, thick Persian carpets, dotted the central area. Haphazardly nailed on one of the elaborately decorated walls were various maps of Iraq, and especially the city of Baghdad. One map indicated the locations of safe areas in Baghdad, a city of seven million people. Other maps further demonstrated the overall success of the pacification of the country in most of its provinces. Phones rang off the hook incessantly as aides, secretaries, and the like were peripatetically moving about in what could have been under different circumstances a modern ballet.

All of a sudden, the door opened and, "Dr. Hakimian, this is Mica Seddons, our NSA chief operative in Iraq," the general intoned with noticeable pleasure as he motioned for her to enter.

Alec's look was telltale. He was smitten at first sight. He did his best to maintain his composure, not wanting to seem obvious, but he thought her bewitching. Wide-set sea-blue eyes, flaxen hair, and a sylph body painted with porcelain white skin were simply alluring. He figured she was thirty-four, maybe thirty-five years old, but everything was in the right place and in ample proportions.

She was a tall glass of water, he quipped to himself.

Mica Seddons walked deliberately toward him and stopped a handshake away. Her liquid lips formed Alec's name in a most suggestive manner. "Dr. Hakimian, we've been waiting for you," she said in her sultry tone, as she extended a soft hand, set off by French-tipped, finely manicured nails.

Alec knew that he had to keep his focus. "Miss Seddons, it is Miss Seddons, isn't it?" Alec queried. He needed to know.

"Yes, it is doctor, but please call me Mica," she replied coyly.

Mica Seddons had always known she was a distraction to men. From her days as a teenager growing up in San Francisco, she knew her physical characteristics drew most everyone into her orbit. Once she had even flirted with the idea of becoming an actress after starring in two high school plays and later dating several of Hollywood's young leading men. Fortunately, with the guidance of her father, a former deputy director of the NSA in the 1980s, who realized early on his daughter's uncanny ability to process copious amounts of information and arrive at the right answer, she was pointed in the direction of college. Ultimately, she received a full scholarship to the California Institute of Technology, graduating with a degree in computer science.

Mica Seddons spent about eighteen somewhat exciting months at the Jet Propulsion Laboratory's Deep Space Network as an analyst before boredom set in. It was something that always plagued her. As she liked to tell it, the intrigues of the NSA came to her rescue while she was sipping a chai latté at a local Starbucks near the JPL facility in Pasadena, California.

In time, it was Seddons who had earned the opportunity to be the NSA operative tasked to bring Alec up-to-speed and to set the stage for his mission. Now seated comfortably in an executive-style leather chair, she crossed her legs, getting Alec's immediate attention, and said straightaway, "Dr. Hakimian, let's talk about the reason why you are here. As you are aware, we are convinced that Hezbollah possesses enough VX to annihilate much of the Middle East." She paused for a moment, sliding her tongue slowly across her bottom lip, then continued, "Syria is the crucible in which they foment and carry out their plans. We believe that Iran is ironically the recipient of Saddam's nuclear hardware, but we need confirmation, real confirmation, eyes on the ground. Our latest information received from human intelligence, electronic surveillance, and DOCEX analysis tells us that this was orchestrated by the Khamsin."

Alec just looked and listened.

She continued, "The primary task of your mission is to first find the source of the Khamsin and the links to its primary sleeper cells. These cells are a complex network of jihadist units that function throughout the world, from where we are right now to as far as Indonesia." Staring at Alec, she crossed her legs again, the black stiletto high heels provoking his prurient sense, and added, "We need to reach the top of this pyramid of terrorism. We need to cut-off the head of its leader, the one who decides whom gets attacked, by what means, and when." As she leaned closer, Alec could feel her sweet breath on his face. "Finding the source of the Khamsin won't eliminate every terrorist cell, but doctor, it will go a long way to slowing them down."

Struggling to maintain her composure, she felt a surge of power course through her as she spoke with such authority and conviction.

Alec's concentration drifted off for a second as he reflected on the young Iraqi family he had read about the day before. The story in the *The Times* of London reported that the family had been returning from the funeral of a family member in Tikrit. Like a shepherd leading his flock, the father crossed a street in northwest Baghdad, his seven children and wife followed in lockstep. A crazed homicide bomber came out of nowhere, and in the blink-of-an-eye, they were gone. Gone like they had never existed, except for the walls of a nearby building that were painted with their burning, bloody flesh and seared bone fragments.

The city was uneasy…again.

The journalist ended the cautionary tale by saying that this was Baghdad, an ancient city still under siege at times and living with grinding poverty.

Alec scratched the barghash mosquito's festering bite on his arm, then asked rhetorically, "Mica, I assume that southern Lebanon figures into the equation?"

"Yes. Southern Lebanon is a hotbed of insurgent activity. Our local intel informs us that the Khamsin has a heavily-armed training camp in the area that supplies Hamas with members of the Izz ad-Din al-Qassam Brigade to attack Israel," she responded with a friendly voice. Continuing, "Doctor, permit me to put a fine point on this. To be very frank, this whole sandbox called the Middle East is our target area. We now know that the IAEA has announced that Iran has an advanced version of IR2 centrifuges that replaced their older P-1 models. The IR2 is designed to enrich uranium at a faster rate, and they are doing just that. They have thousands of them, acting as if they are breeding some rare animal. I guess you could say that enriched uranium is a rare animal in this part of the world. Most of the centrifuges are at Natanz and they want more, tens of thousands more. Maybe even a hundred thousand. Experts tell me that just nine thousand centrifuges operating at full capacity and without errors could produce enough fissile material to make a nuke in just four months. As I'm sure you are aware, only days ago the DIA DOCEX Project translated tapes confirming that WMD were transported to Syria only months before the war broke out. DIA also learned that Tarik Aziz might have used proxies to deliver nuclear, biological, or chemical WMD to the U.S. in very small quantities. He even had moles within the United Nations telling him where the inspectors would go before they got there, and that's also why they never found WMD. By the way, UVA recon photos from the remote piloted aircraft called the Bell *Eagle Eye II* also confirmed such movements and the chatter is constant. Now the question is, how did all this come to be? Answer…the Khamsin."

Alec let Seddons continue her thoughts as he watched intently.

"Well doctor, as the Threat Matrix indicated today, the DIA's DOCEX Project has exploited additional material that is overwhelming. Many believe that years ago the Project was discontinued, but in truth, it still minds valuable data. To date, some 2,290,000 documents have been exploited. They have yielded a treasure trove of new information that focuses primarily on the Khamsin, and its powerful influence over much of the Muslim jihadist organizations as well as its unique ability to unite Sunnis and Shi'ites. We also know from these exploited files that the Khamsin is planning an attack somewhere in the U.S. that will utilize nuclear material, so we can't waste any time. You and your team must find the source of the Khamsin. You must find its leader and stop him." Her conviction was contagious.

In 1961, the DIA, or the Defense Intelligence Agency was formed after the Defense Reorganization Act of 1958 mandated that changes in the methods of intelligence gathering had to be made more efficient. In 1986, the DIA was designated a United States Department of Defense combat support intelligence agency. Since the Iraq War, it has been tasked, to large measure, with the ongoing DOCEX Project.

The Project ran twenty-four hours a day translating millions of documents retrieved from the invasion. They represented documents that Saddam Hussein and his generals and minions were not able to destroy as American and Coalition Forces marched virtually unmolested into Baghdad in 2003. The speed of exploitation was paramount to the Project's success if the information was to be of any value.

These documents comprised extremely valuable information gathered from handwritten and typewritten papers, video and audio tapes, computer hard drives and floppy discs, as well as photographs, satellite images, and CDs.

Alec seemed to hold his breath for a long beat. His mind grinding away, assimilating Seddons's every word.

Seddons methodically continued, as her voice grew stronger. "Doctor, you will be working with several freedom fighters that you'll meet soon." She turned around her comely silhouette dressed in black gabardine, as the ampleness of her breasts was in full view.

Alec was paying attention.

Seddons took a long breath and then continued, as she locked eyes with Alec, "Dr. Hakimian, the war here is a volatile mix of variables that makes for a level of instability unknown to most Washington hacks and wonks. Every time I read an article in an American or European newspaper droning on about why we are here, I wish I could just tell them what's really happening. The press's relentless attacks on our purpose here demonstrates a level of ignorance that's oftentimes incomprehensible to me." She slammed her small hand defiantly on the table to emphasize her sense of frustration.

Surprised by her openness, Alec found it both refreshing and provocative. He knew that America's purpose in Iraq, Afghanistan, and wherever else terrorism surfaced to work its evil had to be confronted and eliminated. As Machiavelli would counsel, answer with force, for *liberty needs an army.*

Despite the recurring thoughts of his wife and daughter safe at home, and confronted with the present temptation, he knew now more than ever before that he was where he should be, in the *maw of the tiger.*

If freedom didn't win, nothing else mattered, he reasoned. *And Francis's murder would be made right,* he swore to himself.

"Doctor, we both need a little shut-eye," she said to Alec. Not disagreeing, Alec stood up and was about to speak when, "How about we meet back here in five hours? At that time your team will be here and I can fill you in more."

Pausing a beat, he said, "Mica, sounds great to me. My flight over here was longer than I had imagined."

"All right then, back here in five hours it is. And thank-you General Meade."

The general nodded as he pointed to the door.

CHAPTER SIX

Alec fell off into a dream state and remembered that only days ago he was happily cuddling his daughter Karina and talking about the future with his wife Leyla. Tomorrow Karina would be two, and he would not be there. His wife of four years, a former college Fine Arts professor, and now a doting mother, was his connection to a reality he rarely experienced, and he knew she would not be happy.

As a renowned brain surgeon, Alec lived in two worlds. He often thought of himself as two people in one body. One moment, he would be in his spectacular Italianate-style estate atop the hills of Bel-Air, California, eating, laughing, and playing with his wife and daughter. They were his anchor to the real world. The cherub-faced Karina reminded him that love and innocence did exist, even in a world torn asunder by racial, social, and religious strife. As for Leyla, she got as close to him as anyone, but never close enough to really know him. And the next, the Sunday evening news would remind him that tomorrow's weather in Southern California would be the same as usual, clear and warm, even in April. Then, without warning, his mind would shift into combat mode. It was at that moment that his wife would lose him, completely. Two lifesaving surgeries scheduled for the next morning were now his focus.

One surgery involved the removal of a large tumor that had invaded the optic nerve and would eventually blind the patient if left alone. The other was an aberrant blood vessel pressing on the brainstem and adjoining cranial nerves and surgery was the only answer. Alec would run through endless *what-if* scenarios, always wanting to get it perfect.

When asked by family and friends alike how he did what he did, how he was able to toggle between hugging his daughter in the evening and by morning having the laser focus to perform a delicate brain surgery, he would answer casually, as he gestured with his arms spread wide and eyes looking upward, "It's a Zen thing."

Alec always sweated the details. He understood that in the small, delicate world of the brain, dealing with minutiae was part-and-parcel to the success of a surgery.

Yet, he knew nothing was ever for sure.

The thoughts continued.

There were days when he just wanted it all to stop. No surgeries, no constant thinking at the speed of light, no having to be *on* all of the time. He just wanted to be. But now, he was thousands of miles away in a land that was once the center of the civilized world, yet unfortunately today the AK-47 was its unofficial national symbol.

Alec always harbored the feeling that when he came to the United States, he had left a part of his life behind, a part of his soul buried in the hot sands of the Middle East. *And Sahar. His lovely Sahar. Why did she have to die?* He struggled with the why. It tormented him.

Then, there was the thought of William Francis. The torture and murder of his friend and the subsequent assassinations by his own hands of two men falsely accused of the murder bludgeoned his psyche. Alec had always suspected that Director Axelrod was at the root of it all. *If he didn't outright set him up,* Alec was convinced, *he certainly made no effort to protect him.* He could not escape the thought.

Alec always believed that because of his fierce independence, unwavering confidence, and success as a NOC, Director Axelrod had it in for him. He knew that the director had been a mediocre field agent consumed with a malignant envy of people such as Alec.

He remembered heading for the Bristol, his favorite local restaurant, on Verdun Street in Beirut late one spring night to meet with Francis and discuss details of a planned mission he was about to undertake when his friend Mahmoud quickly approached him on foot yelling his name. Once upon him, Mahmoud told him in a frantic tone that he had just heard that his friend William Francis had been kidnapped

before dawn from his apartment in the center of the city. He told Alec
that three men armed with AK-47 machine guns pulled up in front of
Francis's three-story apartment building complex in a white van and
stormed his apartment, knocking the door down and physically forcing
him into the van. As they sped off, several people looked out their
windows, but said nothing. The fear of local terrorists seeking revenge
made most mute in such circumstances.

Alec recalled feeling helpless when he heard the news. He always
understood the danger of such an action by terrorists under the banner
of Islamic fundamentalism was simply a basic reality in the Middle East,
but he never thought it would happen to Francis. After all, he was too
good, too quick, and he was the best at covering his tracks. *Did Francis
get careless? Were his kidnappers men he knew? Was he set-up, and if so,
who did it?* These were questions for which Alec had no answers, but
he had suspicions.

As he rolled over, his face now buried in an oversized pillow,
his fatigued body was drenched in perspiration brought on by the
nightmares. The demons of his past were looming large once again,
and he just wanted them to let him go, to release him. He had paid the
price and now sought redemption through his life as a surgeon, but that
would have to wait, again.

Damn Director Axelrod, Alec said to himself. *Damn him.*

Despite his dream of becoming a doctor in America, Alec sometimes
thought *that the "real" story of his life had been cut short by his leaving
his homeland.* He remembered the many pleasantries he experienced
there, the many friendships he built, and Sahar, who was now lost to
him forever.

"Dr. Hakimian, it's Mica. Mica Seddons," she said rather loudly,
while knocking on the door of his room in the officers' quarters.

Alec rolled over again in his bed, pulling the covers on top of
himself. Four hours sleep normally worked for him, but not this time.
He needed to rest his entire being. The long flight, the sensory overload,
and flashbacks had put his body in a state of deep discharge.

"Dr. Hakimian, sorry to disturb you, but Task Force 121 intercepted
two al-Qaeda couriers carrying a communiqué from Fadeel al-Khalayleh
to Usama bin Laden," Seddons shouted through the door, as she
continued to knock loudly. "We need to go, sir."

Alec tried to crawl farther under the covers, but Seddons was persistent.

It was a very exhausting series of dreams, *no*, very exhausting nightmares.

"All right, all right," Alec said, with great reluctance. He wanted to sleep. "Wait a minute." Alec thought, *goddamn al-Khalayleh. After al-Zarqawi's death at the hands of U.S. Special Forces, with the assistance of both Iraqi and Jordanian intel, in June of 2006, al-Khalayleh became his replacement and continued to be very active in the cause of Islamic fundamentalism.*

Alec staggered before the dressing mirror in what must have been one of Saddam's suites that quartered one of his stable of pleasure women. The garishness of the large bedroom and adjoining dressing and bathing area could not be overstated. It was vulgarity raised to a bizarre art form.

Pulling from his "go bag" a pair of khaki pants, he put them on, one leg at a time. Next, a hunter green pullover Polo shirt, and then a pair of barely worn Merrell jungle mocs. He replaced his Vacheron wristwatch with a more practical timepiece, a Panerai "Radiomir Rattrapante" chronograph. It also held sentimental value, for it was a gift from his friend William Francis. His hair did not need to be coiffed; it always seemed to be in place. A two-day growth of beard was apparent, but a dab of Creed cologne, a couple of breath mints, and he was ready.

Reaching for the heavy mahogany door, he stopped, turned, and walked back to his toiletry bag sitting on the black marble sink top. Quickly retrieving his deodorant, he pulled his shirt up and painted each underarm with short strokes. Taking a few deep breaths, he stole one last look at the mirror and then glimpsed out the large window as military vehicles of the 3rd Battalion, 7th Marines headed out in the darkness just before dawn on their way to a four-hour patrol fifty klicks south of the city.

Alec opened the door to an anxious Seddons. "Sorry doctor, but we need to get to the briefing room, please." She motioned for Alec to move forward; she did not.

Their eyes locked onto each other like the laser guidance system of a Tomahawk missile. Alec knew that what was about to happen was not what should happen, and she did too, but —

She stepped back just in time, Alec thought to himself. He was not sure he would have done the same.

Brushing his hands through his thick mane, he said, "So what is it, Mica?" Alec was denying to himself what almost happened.

Seddons took another step back as she balanced delicately on her black leather high heels and said, "Task Force 121 has captured two al-Qaeda couriers that are being interrogated as we speak. Something about al-Khalayleh asking bin Laden for help to gin up hostilities between Shi'ites, Sunnis, and Kurds in the hopes of an all out civil war." Catching her breath, she continued, "If we don't get a handle on this, the fragile new Parliament will go up in flames," she said, as they hurried down the long hallway to the CENTCOM briefing room.

CHAPTER SEVEN

Activity in CENTCOM-Baghdad headquarters was 24/7. It never stopped, for the war on terror never stopped, nor did the Tigris River, as it meandered quietly by.

Created in 1983, U.S. Central Command, a theatre-level unified combat command, was charged with the responsibility of keeping watch over troublesome and rogue countries between the Eastern and Pacific Commands. USCENTCOM's home base was at McDill Air Force Base located in Tampa, Florida. Presently, it was tasked to maintain U.S. security interests in the formal Area of Responsibility that comprised twenty-seven nations. It specifically represented areas that reached from the Horn of Africa, across the Arabian Gulf region, and into Central Asia. The Middle Eastern theatre had always proven to be the most problematic.

"Once at CENTCOM, you'll meet the members of your team," Seddons said categorically, as they walked quickly down the long, marbled hallway.

Activity at CENTCOM-Baghdad or CENTCOM-Forward never changed. It was a beehive of endless critical decision-making on a level that made the New York Stock Exchange seem like a prayer meeting for monks. Nevertheless, Alec had never before seen more brass in one room other than when his wife dragged him along to a large plumbing fixtures outlet to purchase hardware for their recently renovated vacation home in Sun Valley, Idaho.

Without warning, a serious and amazingly fit fifty-four-year-old General Meade entered the cavernous, highly secure space reserved for CENTCOM-Baghdad communications, as officers and noncoms turned to salute. He acknowledged them with a "gentlemen take your seats."

Alec and Seddons were standing at the long end of a dark oak conference table when the general said, "Doctor. Miss Seddons. We are about to launch a super black ops, code named *Operation Star 9*. Now it's time that we get on with it." Turning directly to Seddons, "Miss Seddons, please ask our other team members to come in."

Seddons reached for the heavily carved mahogany door depicting scenes of Muhammad speaking to his flock in the ancient city of Mecca. The twenty-two carat gold doorknob was too large for her small hand. Forced to use two hands, she pulled it open with the help of an aide, revealing an adjoining room populated with eight men, some attired in camouflage gear, others in native Iraqi outfits, right down to the *abaye*, the ethnic male Iraqi garb.

Ranging in age from twenty-six to thirty-five, these modern-day freedom fighters and defenders of democracy were prepared to go anywhere, anytime, and do anything for the cause of freedom. Written on their weatherworn and scarred faces were the costs of freedom. Seddons motioned for the team to enter.

Looking to Alec, "These are your men of Operation Star 9," Seddons said.

Alec sat up in his seat as she began.

"Here, first up doctor, is Robert Tishermann."

Tishermann turned his head in Alec's direction and nodded. Alec returned the gesture.

"Robert has qualities that make him an excellent choice for the op. He has a good deal of intimacy with the region, speaks fluent Arabic, has distinguished himself in service to the CIA's Special Activities Division for many years now, and is fiercely dedicated to the war on terror."

The Special Activities Division of the CIA's National Clandestine Service has been responsible at times for covert operations on a paramilitary basis. If a member of SAD were compromised during a mission, the U.S. government would deny all knowledge of the operative and the covert mission.

Alec slid his chair in a bit closer, his face showing no expression. He slowly rubbed his two-day growth of beard, as if he were pondering something. He knew that obviously there were those who respected Tishermann's talents as a field operative, but he was troubled by the thought of having to be in congress with anyone who knew CIA Director Axelrod. To him Director Axelrod was still a bastard, even though he had died years ago.

"Next, meet communications expert Steve 'Wireless' Pratt. He can get you connected with just two tin cans and a string if need be."

Pratt attended Carnegie Mellon University for two years before joining the U.S. Army to serve his country just as his brother did in Gulf War I. A corporal in the exclusive Army Rangers, he stood an impressive six-foot-five. His close-cut black hair revealed a perfectly shaped skull, accented by a nasty scar reaching from an inch above his right ear down to the base of his neck…a Taliban fighter had tried his best, but Pratt survived, the fighter did not.

"And here we have Mr. Bobby 'Sureshot' Roberts." Delta Force Sergeant Bobby Roberts hit Alec with a snow-white, Tom Cruise-style smile that was infectious. "Bobby can put lead between two veins in a tree leaf at fifteen hundred meters. As one of the best snipers around, he's got 116 confirmed kills."

Bobby acted as if he was clearing his throat and then piped in proudly, his Southern drawl apparent, "Ma'am. That's 117."

"Sorry, Bobby," she said, giving him a soft smile. "And Sergeant Manuel Alvarado here is his eyes," she added with a smile directed at Alvarado.

Alvarado tipped his head in acknowledgment.

Spotter Manuel Alvarado hailed from East Los Angeles, by way of UCLA, where he had been a starting running back on the football team for two years. Manuel had the look of confidence hardened by years as a veteran of many a Middle East tour. He loved the challenge, but when he retired, he planned on being a hunting guide on the Kenai Peninsula in Alaska.

Seddons took a half turn, pursed her liquid-red painted lips, and introduced two Navy DEVGRU Team Specialists, Frank Nutworth and

Bernard Riemann. "Dr. Hakimian, specialists Nutworth and Riemann will be your demo dudes on the ground." Seddons enjoyed her own alliterations, even when they fell flat.

Bobby mumbled under his breath, "How come the squids get to blow shit up?"

Nutworth and Riemann were joined at the hip. They had been working together for more years than each man wanted to admit. From bridges and barracks to dams and depots, their abilities as masters of mayhem were unchallenged. They met when they were members of the 2000 U.S. Summer Olympic Shooting Team in Sydney, Australia. Their expertise, even in hand weapons, was unchallenged and today their choice of personal protection was M4s with M203 grenade launchers and Aimpoint M68 scopes modified to their liking. They also kept P226s within a few inches reach. The two were walking arsenals and loved it.

Nutworth was the more intense of the two, as many Navy SEALs tended to be, while Riemann had a mind that embraced the most nuanced aspects of life. He was the team's Spartan warrior, possessed of sinewy muscle, a finely chiseled facial bone structure, and a look that said, "Don't stand in my way."

Alec sat silently digesting Seddons's every word.

"Any questions, Dr. Hakimian?" she asked, as General Meade stood quietly in the background.

Alec just moved his head from side to side in answer to her question. He would ask his questions when he was ready.

On the far side of the briefing room the activity never stopped. Officers and noncoms were answering phones and plotting points of attack on large, colored wall maps. Images on organic light emitting diode (OLED), flat-panel computer displays changed at a rapid rate as hard drives hummed, printers spit out page after page of data, and analysts scrutinized it all.

Off in the distance intermittent automatic gunfire riddled the air as a pumpkin sun was barely peeking out of the night, signaling another day was upon the Levant, while it began to paint the sands with shimmering shafts of light. The city was in the throes of awakening, as the call to *Fajr*, the pre-sunrise prayer, rang out again.

The room continued to bother Alec. He wondered what had gone on there before U.S. forces liberated the Iraqis from the madman; what unspeakable acts of vulgarity and violence had happened in the room in the name of amusement for its former resident.

Seddons continued, "And here is your field medic and recon expert Sergeant Cameron Mackay. You'll get used to his Scottish brogue, hopefully." Marine reconnaissance expert Sergeant Mackay had also doubled as a medic for special ops teams on three previous tours of the Middle East. As a naturalized citizen for some twenty years, Sergeant Mackay would do anything for his adopted home.

"And bringing up the rear, linguist extraordinaire, the man of many tongues and other talents, Josiah Darwin," Seddons said, half out of breath, as an audible chuckle reverberated throughout the room. She blushed openly.

Green Beret Sergeant Josiah Darwin had an uncanny ability to speak a number of languages with the believability and argot of a native. Be it Euskara of the Basques or a spate of Slavic tongues, he had no trouble being understood. Moreover, he was a master of disguise who could blend in wherever he traveled. Josiah rounded out his show with advanced small arms weaponry capabilities.

Tishermann looked on with tangible indifference, as he lounged in a slovenly, sybaritic-like manner in one of palace's deep, leather sofas.

Seddons finished with a flurry by adding that Operation Star 9 would do what no other black ops anti-terrorism team had ever done. She was convinced that the team she had assembled with the assistance of General Meade and NSA Director Caccavale under the panoply of Task Force 121 would help make her mark, and with that, land a top job in Washington.

Alec sat quietly.

Seddons then walked deliberately in front of the men and said, "Gentlemen, before we get into the meat of it all, let me introduce the man who is about to lead you."

The members of Operation Star 9 looked on with slack-jawed gazes, still not knowing who Alec really was or why he was now their intrepid leader.

"Miss Seddons, if I might," General Meade interrupted, as the military members of Operation Star 9 stood at attention.

Seddons quickly stepped aside.

"Boys," the general began. "Our business of covert black ops has always been one that does not permit us to speak publicly about our successes, yet our failures, though rare as they are, are always in the press." The members were still at attention. "So, make me proud. That means I do not want to read about you in the papers. Ever." He was about to salute and leave the room when a thought grabbed him. "By the way, if any of you are wondering why your code name is Operation Star 9, I'll tell you."

Each man in the room looked straight at the general and waited.

"You are nine of America's best and bravest. Each of you represents a star in your country's flag."

There was an aura of real pride in the room.

Continuing, the general said, with a sense of showmanship, "Now, I might as well tell you about the man who is to lead you to hell-and-back."

Seddons was not expecting the general to steal her thunder, but after all, he was the general.

"Who of you has not heard of the CIA's deepest NOC? The 'non-official cover' who acts with the precision of a surgeon. The man who is a legend to some, a myth to others, and feared by all. The man they called 'The Doctor' during his years of service to the Agency." He paused for emphasis, then, as if he were a presenter at the Oscars, he looked to Alec, and said, "Gentlemen, I give you 'The Doctor,' Dr. Alexander Hakimian." The room fell silent.

Everyone within earshot of the general's voice looked at Alec with a curiosity often reserved for children viewing a rare animal padding across the Serengeti on a National Geographic television special. Alec was used to such a reaction, but never accepted it easily.

"By the way, The Doctor is your XO. You're to salute your executive officer whenever it is appropriate. That is all," the general said flatly, then stepped back.

"Thank-you, general," Alec said, as he stood up. Now front-and-center he began. "Gentlemen. The fact that none of you has ever heard of me, other than by my moniker, is one of the reasons why I am here. Now, why are you here? Because there are those who think you are the best at what you do. We shall see." He moved slowly about the room, eyeing each man individually.

Alec began to present the particulars. "At the top of our agenda is the Khamsin." Alec scanned the faces of each man as he continued, "Have any of you men heard of the *Khamsin*, the master terrorist network the likes of which has never been known before? It's thought to be funded by a radical Arab billionaire that to date has not been identified, other than to say that he has assembled a cartel of terrorist organizations and a war chest that make bin Laden and his boys look like nothing more than common street thugs. The Khamsin's funding is in the billions of dollars. But it's not so much its money that troubles me, but rather its means, measured in the level of its worldwide contacts. The Khamsin's purpose is to breed, spread, and perpetuate the ultimate form of transnational terror. The Khamsin has successfully been able to do what no Arab nation has for centuries. It has unified Arabs and Muslims, both Sunni and Shi'a, from the Middle East and Africa to the South Pacific and the United States under a pseudo-religious caliphate aimed at world domination at all cost."

Alec was now making his point very clear. "It is tied into the boardrooms of corporate America. It has unfettered access to the heads-of-state in just about every country worth counting. It is known that even Presidents of the United States have welcomed the leader of the Khamsin into the Oval Office, never knowing who he was or his real intentions." Alec turned for a moment to look out the window at a battalion of soldiers moving stealthily through the growing dawn.

He continued, "The majority of the Khamsin's financing is derived from oil. What's very troubling, what gives me great pause, is that the leader of this fanatical organization is also bent on controlling the world's oil supply and will stop at nothing to achieve his stated goals. That includes the annihilation of the infidels. Gentlemen, you know who the infidels are, don't you?" Alec made it a point to stare directly into the eyes of every man now under his aegis. He paused just long enough to give those in the room time to digest his monologue. "They are you, your families, and everyone who loves freedom."

Bobby Roberts waived his hand. "Sir."

"Yes, Bobby," Alec remarked.

Hitting Alec again with his megawatt smile, he asked, "Dr. Hakimian. This Hamstring, I mean *Kamsin*. What is it supposed to be?"

"Bobby, it's Khamsin with an 'h', and the 'K' is silent," he replied. "As for what it is, it's the namesake of the vicious, cyclonic, hot desert wind that blows across the Middle East, connecting the sands of Arab and Muslim countries. It represents the unity that every imam and mullah dreams of. The unity that will bring all of Allah's true believers into a cohesive force. A force so ominous that it makes the Crusades little more than a computer strategy game that any ten year old can master in a weekend. It is a force so menacing that it will bring about the fall of western civilization if left to its own devices. Even al-Qaeda, Hamas, Hezbollah, and Abu Sayyaf in the Philippines pay homage to the Khamsin and its leader, *al-Ankabut*. Saddam himself treaded lightly when it came to the Ankabut. He was and is the cause's éminence grise. He conceived of its manifesto, requiring nothing less than total victory over the infidels," he added, with measured intensity. "And much like the hydra that never dies, the Ankabut has demonstrated his ability to survive under any circumstance. But we, Operation Star 9, are about to change all of that." Self-doubt was never an affliction of Alec's. He ended with, "Gentlemen, this is the ultimate clash of civilizations. The gravity of the situation cannot be overstated. It's for all the marbles this time."

At this point, only a cacophony of ringing phones, beeping computers, and faxes could be heard in the background. Alec had their full attention. He had made his point perfectly clear.

"Sir. I mean, Doc," Bobby blurted out innocently.

"Yes, Bobby. What is it?" Alec responded.

"I know you probably think this is a stupid question, but...."

"And the question is?" Alec asked immediately.

"What kind of doctor are you, sir?"

Alec hesitated, then said, with Seddons and General Meade focused on him, "Bobby, I explore people's skulls to see if they have anything in them."

Everyone tilted his head somewhat quizzically.

"Specifically, I specialize in an area of the brain that until recently was considered hidden from view, and thus, inoperable by conventional means in many cases. But now with fiber optics and new techniques, I can remove tumors from the base of the skull without trauma to the area and without any sign of surgery," he said rather pedantically. "Now does that answer your question?"

"Thanks. Yes it does, sir," Bobby replied respectfully, but still wasn't sure that he understood what Alec had just said.

"Any other questions about my medical skills? Fine, then it's our job to accomplish our mission quickly and with as little fanfare as possible," Alec said flatly.

General Meade chimed in. "Remember, Operation Star 9 does not exist outside this room."

CHAPTER EIGHT

BRENTWOOD, CALIFORNIA

Several conspicuous characteristics served to identify Dr. Raymond Raissi. His round, russet-skinned face, framed neatly by coiffed and thinning, black-dyed hair, was what one noticed at first blush. His unrelenting perseverance, a certain embonpoint, and most importantly, great wealth, also served to make him one of the most recognizable and powerful men in the world.

Raissi could be seen some mornings in his Brentwood mansion, replete with two guardhouses, twenty-four hour room service, a staff of eighteen, and eleven acres of meticulously manicured landscaping and pools, perusing many of the world's major newspapers. His thirst for news was unquenchable.

The mansion was of such extravagance that his friends often referred to it as the Ritz Raissi. Nervous servants scurried about fulfilling his most insignificant demands. He was certainly king of his own castle, and he had many castles, and many treasures to fill them.

This morning he found *The Times* of London amusing. On its front-page, it reported that he would soon be enjoying a night at the opera with Her Majesty, the Queen of England. It was something he never took pleasure in other than to say that he always knew that the political benefits of such an occasion were incalculable. And the *New York Times* reported that the President of the United States was about to undergo his yearly two-day physical.

Raissi remembered his years at Yale University and the fact that both he and the president had been members of its super-secret Skull and Bones Society. The two had met on several occasions since their time at Yale. On occasion, Raissi's philanthropic efforts crossed paths with the president's need to raise campaign funds. Politicians always sought out Dr. Raymond Raissi to fill their political war chests with cash.

His present lifestyle was light years from the tent cities he lived in that dotted the Levant. Born to Muslim Bedouin parents sixty-four years ago, Raissi was short in physical stature and Napoleonic by nature. Some said he had survived with the skills of a professional conman. Cunning, striking swiftly at every opportunity that came his way, he was at the same time most personable.

Raissi was destined to be famous, if not infamous, and he knew it.

In time, he made his way to New York City, where the world of capitalism shined brightly. He had no problem marrying money and Muhammad. He was convinced capitalism could very easily be an instrument of influence and that great good would come of it. He knew what it was like to want for the simplest things in life. He knew what it was like to see those around him live hopeless lives. Bettering himself would advance his personal agenda.

Ever the optimist, as a young college student on scholarship, his keen intellect worked its magic. In time, many of the sons and daughters of New England's most prominent families befriended him.

Little more than two years after graduating from Yale, Raissi received his doctorate in chemical engineering from the Massachusetts Institute of Technology. Not yet twenty-five, he was asked to work in the research department for Global Petroleum Resources.

Raissi knew oil was his future. He knew that it was power. Limitless power.

He had plans.

CHAPTER NINE

Damascus, mostly Roman built, was the oldest continuously occupied city in the world, dating back to pre-historic times. It was an archive of much of the history of early mankind.

The city, known to its intimates as Sham, was once the home to Babylonians, Persians, Greeks, and Romans. It was also the scene of many a bloody battle for religious supremacy during the Crusades of the late eleventh to thirteenth centuries.

To Muslim fanatical fundamentalists the Crusades have never ended, they have simply been in hibernation, until now. The extreme hatred these fanatics have held for the infidels has fermented over the centuries. They felt the West had attempted to vanquish their cherished Islam. All the while, the West of today found Islam's lack of women's rights, theocratic governments, and resistance to any semblance of modernity simply out-of-sync with twenty-first century society.

The continued hatred had now reached a boil in the crucible called the Middle East. It was fueled by the vitriol of such despotic demagogues as Usama bin Laden, the Saudi royal family, Ayman al-Zawahiri, Mahmoud Ahmadinejad, and their countless minions and hirelings. For the past twenty-five plus years, the Khamsin has held sway over many of the thoughts and emotions of Muslims across the globe.

The maniacal followers of the Khamsin have sought redemption for their perceived brutality of Muslims at the hands of the West. Inspired by the teachings of the Prophet, they also found refuge in the admonitions of the faith's twelfth century Turkish imam al-Farabi, who professed the importance of politicizing the faith. Unable to answer the success of democracy and liberty in the United States and Western Europe, the faithful have been asked to give their lives willingly for the good of Allah and the Brotherhood of Islam.

The legend of the Ankabut has ridden on the wind of the Khamsin across the sands of the Middle East and throughout the world for years. It has made millions shutter and quiver while still millions more have been whipped into a frenzy at the thought of his name. In Arabic, it meant the *spider*, the spider that weaved its evil web to capture and consume its prey.

Like the spider that ruled over the insect world, the Ankabut sought to rule over mankind's world. Said to be ruthless, scheming, fearless, messianic, and yet at times personable, and even affable, the Ankabut has been the driving force behind the Khamsin terrorist cartel that has effectively merged the two major sects of Islam, the Sunni and Shi'ites, to serve its needs.

Though the actual place of his birth was unknown, the Ankabut called Damascus home. There as a youth, he began his climb up the ladder of crime by trading in black-market small weaponry in its seedy back streets. Flush with enough U.S. dollars by his late teens, he formed his first mafia-style organization.

In time, the young man who would become the Ankabut engaged in the theft of munitions from U.S. and British military bases throughout the Middle East and Europe and sold them to Islamic fundamentalists. At first, he was merely a sympathizer of their plight, but in time he became a true believer, a fanatic.

As the Ankabut's power and influence grew, so did his ever-expanding network of Islamists dedicated to the word of Allah. Then he just *disappeared*. No one ever knew why or how, he was simply gone. Just like that. Then without preamble he reappeared, and has since spread his web of death and destruction worldwide with far greater force.

The Khamsin's every aspect had been carefully orchestrated with great thought and even greater patience, for the Ankabut knew that patience was the most valuable asset in the war against the West. Patience, as taught by the Qur'an.

The Ankabut would eventually attract the sympathies of some of the power merchants of capitalism in the United States and Western

Europe. These individuals would clandestinely provide money and means for the cause. They were the fuel and their aberrant Qur'an was the engine that carried the Khamsin and the Ankabut on their epic journey to worldwide Islamic hegemony. Wherever the Khamsin's wind blew, it left behind a scorched earth...death, destruction, and domination were its calling cards.

CHAPTER TEN

The variegated, mosaic bell tower above the foyer of the luxuriously decorated Italianate-style hilltop estate rang loudly, signaling the presence of someone at the front gate. The guard had the day off for personal reasons.

The elaborately manicured grounds seemed to go on forever. They were secured by a ten-foot high wrought-iron fence, whose workmanship was reminiscent of the highly talented Chalybian metal smiths of ancient Armenia circa 1300 B.C. It was said that the Chalybes held the secret to the art of metallurgy and fine ironwork.

Inasmuch as Hampton, the residence's major domo, was detained in town on an important errand, the daytime maid answered the call at the front gate.

"Yes, who is it please?" she asked inquisitively.

"I'm from Universal Messenger Service, and I have a delivery from Dr. Raymond Raissi."

The maid was familiar with the name but needed to check with the lady of the house before she could let him enter the grounds.

Picking up the in-house phone, she buzzed the breakfast room. Leyla Hakimian grabbed the phone from a small Chinese-lacquered end table to her right and answered, "Yes."

"Mrs. Hakimian, there is a man from the Universal Messenger Service, and he has a delivery from Dr. Raissi."

Leyla paused a moment, glanced at the LED flat-panel screen positioned on the opposite wall that displayed images from ten video cameras placed strategically around the estate and said, "Fine, let him in Dalia."

In moments, a messenger dressed in white-tie-and-tails delivered a large, eggshell colored envelope with calligraphy gracing its front side. Dalia examined the delivery, signed for it, and said thank-you. Closing one side of the intricately carved front doors fashioned from dark-stained Japanese cherry wood, she marched immediately through a maze of rooms feathered with the finest of furnishings and directly to the breakfast room. There, she found Leyla seated with her young daughter Karina.

"Milk," bright-eyed Karina demanded, as she pointed to her sippy cup.

"Just a minute, dear," her mother responded, as she first looked out of the corner of her eye at the impressive envelope Dalia held in her hand, then glanced over to her daughter Karina as she was about to toss her breakfast plate.

"No, Karina," she said quickly. "Please finish it for mommy."

Karina went back to playing with her crème of wheat and milk.

The maid reached across the table and handed Leyla the oversized envelope. "Here, Mrs. Hakimian," she said politely, as Leyla put her hand out.

"Thank-you, Dalia."

The dark-eyed beauty, Dalia Sarkisian, was rescued by Leyla about two years ago from a God Love's You homeless shelter for wayward teenagers and young adults that was one of Leyla's special charities. She often spent time working in soup kitchens on holidays and had a real affection for children forced to leave home or orphaned by a parent because of alcohol, physical abuse, or drugs. Dalia had been pressed into prostitution in the Ukraine after leaving her homeland of Armenia at the age of seventeen. Now twenty-two, she was living a happy life working for the Hakimian family while attending a local city college to better her English.

Leyla looked up at the surveillance monitor and saw the messenger walking away from the front gate toward a blue courier van. She then stared for a moment at the envelope. It was addressed to Dr. and Mrs. Alexander Hakimian.

"Milkie," Karina demanded again, swinging her sippy cup in protest. Dalia quickly filled it.

"Thank-you, Dalia."

Leyla turned to Karina and smiled. Gently opening the envelope with a sterling silver filigree letter opener, she slowly slid out the finely engraved invitation. She noticed it was made of Crane paper, and remembered Alec once telling her that Crane also made the paper for U.S. currency. She always found Alec's limitless fount of knowledge fascinating and wished he were here *with her now*, but she had trained herself to dismiss that thought out of personal survival.

Leyla, in her mid-thirties and of slender build, was energetic and friendly. She was blessed with a quick mind and her time at Colgate University was well spent. Her smile radiated across a room and made everyone in her presence feel relaxed. She had a particularly calming effect on Alec, especially when he was in one of his intense modes, which was often. It was often difficult on their marriage, but she tried to be understanding, even though in her loneliest hours she often wondered if she had married the right man.

The invitation said that their presence was requested at the Beverly Hills Hotel to honor Raymond Raissi, PhD., for his endless philanthropy and civic work. It was given by the Arab-American League, the Center for American Philanthropy, and the Council on American-Islamic Relations. It went on to say the evening was formal attire and that transportation would be provided for those who desired it. The time, seven-thirty in the evening. The date, May 16th.

Leyla reminded herself that she had not heard from Alec in nearly three weeks. She was saddened because her daughter missed him. For herself, she was forlorn, desperate for his touch. She hoped she would not have to attend the event without him. Unfortunately, she was all too unwillingly accustomed to such situations. Alec would be saving a life one day and gone the next. It was a lifestyle she thought would end some day. "Mrs. Hakimian, you have a call from Dr. Hakimian," Dalia said, as she interrupted Leyla's thoughts.

Leyla's face turned happy as she grabbed for the phone. An operator said in a faint voice, "Please hold for Dr. Hakimian."

"Hello, hello. Leyla," Alec said with great anticipation.

"Yes, yes dear. *Hamov*, my delicious one," she said with a gasping breath. "How are you? Where are you? I love you and Karina misses her father."

"I'm fine. I can't say exactly where I am because our line is not secure. How's Karina? Is she there?"

"Yes, here she is."

"Karina, it's your daddy. It's your daddy, darling."

Karina's face was flush with excitement as she struggled to grab the phone with her small hand. "Da da," she blurted out with great joy and surprise.

"Karina, my little girl. It's daddy," Alec said with excitement and love in his voice. "How's daddy's little goodness girl? I love you so much."

"Home. Da da?" Karina said, as she shook her sippy cup from side to side with milk spraying everywhere.

"Daddy will be home soon my love. I'll bring you a present and we'll go to the park. I love you. Bye-bye, goodness girl. Give the phone to mommy," Alec said, his jaw tightening in an effort to hold his emotions in check.

"Bye-bye, da da. Love you," Karina said, as she dropped the phone on the table while trying to hand it back to her mother.

Alec heard a series of thuds as Leyla grappled for the phone. He thought he had lost the connection.

"Darling, I miss you so. When will you be home? I worry about you every waking moment. Everyone is asking about you. Margaret is still not out of the hospital and Bob Higgins passed away yesterday. The funeral is not set yet."

Alec felt his body tighten up as he processed the words about his accountant's death and his former secretary's hospitalization. "Bob was a great guy, but his cardio problems were serious for years. Please extend my condolences to his family and tell them when I return I'll pay my respects. And do the same with Margaret."

"Fine. Alec. You sound different. Is everything okay?" she said, with concern and alarm in her voice.

"Yes, yes. Just tired."

"If you say so. But are you really okay?" she asked insistently.

"Yes. Yes, Leyla. You don't need to worry," said Alec.

"You don't have some cutie with you, now do you?" Leyla questioned somewhat laughingly.

"Sure I do," he said facetiously. "Her name is Nefertiti."

"Alec. You remember the last time you were away? You had a hard time getting back to how we like you."

"Leyla," he said sternly, "don't worry. It'll all be okay."

Pretending to be satisfied with Alec's answer, she said, "By the way, we received this very fancy invitation today." Staring at the invitation in her hand, she continued in her usual soft voice, "It was delivered by a messenger in white tie and tails. Imagine that, white tie and tails at nine in the morning. Anyway, we're invited to the Beverly Hills Hotel to honor Dr. Raymond Raissi," she added with an undertone of disdain in her voice. "It says for all his philanthropy and civic mindedness. Please." The sarcasm was evident in her tone.

"Now, Leyla. When is it?" Alec asked nonchalantly.

"May 16th. Will you be back by then?"

"Hopefully, but if I'm not, take your father, unless he received an invitation too. If so, then take your brother. He likes fancy soirees."

"I'm not going if you can't," she said emphatically. "When was the last time you saw him?"

"Remember when we were in Sveti Stefan before Karina was born? We ran into him and his brother Raja at the casino. He invited us to spend a few days on his 190 foot felucca moored in Monaco, but we were leaving the next day," Alec recalled with precision.

Alec remembered that when his *cover* was blown in Beirut after Francis was killed, he needed to get out. For still unknown reasons, the CIA had no defined exit strategy. Raissi's private Boeing 727 jet was at Beirut International Airport at the time and through a mutual friend, he was spirited out of the Middle East in the dead of night. It was Alec's only option, and it was then that he knew he could not rely on the Agency anymore and Raissi became his friend.

"Yes, I just loved that week in Sveti Stefan. Our room had the best view of the Adriatic Sea. The food was magical. We should go back sometime with Karina. The Montenegrin locals were so kind and the men were so tall and handsome. Anyway, do I really need to go if you don't get back in time?"

"Yes. He helped me get to America and out of respect for his generosity, you need to go even if I don't get back in time. Tell him that I was called unexpectedly to Antwerp to perform an emergency operation and deeply regret that I was not able to attend, but I'm thinking of him."

Reluctantly, "Okay, *hamov*." The two had always used the Armenian shorthand *hamov* as an expression of love they felt for each other.

"Don't you remember his older brother?" Alec asked. "Raja was kind of strange, I'll admit that."

"Oh, yes." Leyla said sarcastically. "Wasn't he the one who would always push people out of the way wherever we went? Then he'd rub that big, ugly scar on the right side of his neck as he laughed. He was weird," Leyla remarked. Leyla never felt comfortable around Raja and never wanted him to think they were close.

"Yes, that's him. But I think Raja's just protective of his brother," Alec remarked.

"Well, I didn't like him. He was rude and crude," Leyla countered.

Not wanting to belabor the point that he was sure he could not win, he said, "So, will you do it? Will you go, for us?"

Reluctantly, Leyla said, "Okay. Okay, but you owe me, big time."

"I'll bring you back an hourglass with real desert sand in it or a snow-glow," Alec said laughingly.

"Cartier is more my style, but then again, you know that," she said, as she looked at her platinum Cartier pavé Panther wristwatch Alec had given her after Karina's birth.

"I've got to go now. I have a very important meeting," he said, not wanting to be specific. "I love you very much and give Karina a big kiss from her daddy. Say hi to your father and brother, and tell my parents I'll see them soon. Don't worry about me. I'll be okay."

"Alec. Listen to me. You come home soon and don't be a hero. We need you," she said plaintively, as she began to weep silently.

"Leyla, until then *hamov*," he said, then closed the connection.

Leyla paused a moment as she stared out at the rippling blue water of the long, serpentine pool at the back of the residence. She then looked across the oval glass breakfast table and gave Karina a bright smile that covered a deep sadness. Calling for Dalia, she said, "Dalia dear, please take Karina to her room and get her dressed for our mommy and me class. We need to leave in about twenty minutes."

"Surely, ma'am. How about the blue dress that Dr. Hakimian bought her for Christmas when you were in St. Barts?"

"Perfect. She'll like that. It'll remind her of her daddy," Leyla added softly.

As Karina and Dalia left the breakfast room, Leyla closed her tired eyes and drifted off. Instantly, the white clouds began to appear again and old thoughts that she managed to keep at bay most of the time raced toward her from all angles. She had held it in for years now and Alec knew it. There was even a tacit understanding between the two of them that they would never talk about it because he had assured her that it was over, but she knew otherwise.

She recalled that no sooner had the two of them married that Alec had received a call and before she knew it her honeymoon was over and he was gone. To where she didn't know, she never knew, but she did know that every time he left, the strain on their marriage grew ever greater…the rift between them grew ever wider. And, just when she thought that the distance between them had become insurmountable, along came their beautiful daughter Karina and things seemed to work out and Alec became the doting father and attentive husband, for a while.

In times of sadness and insecurity, Leyla would compare herself to what many would call the "other woman." Yet, her family and friends looked at her and were envious. Married to a successful doctor, living in a dream house, and the mother of a young, healthy daughter seemed like the life anyone would want. However, she never imagined that her "perfect" life would come with conditions that she had not counted on. It was the memory of the other woman Alec loved in Beirut that brought her to this point. A woman that she felt had been passionate and exotic in a way that she was not. True, she was a lover to Alec without limits, but it did not govern her life. After all, discretion and priorities were part of her upbringing and as such, she lacked the spontaneity that Alec wanted, and she knew it.

While Alec was indeed drawn to her classic, elegant beauty, Leyla knew that an unbridled animal magnetism was what the other woman must have had…it was a chemical reaction between the two. While she had a burning desire to be a wife and mother, she recognized that the other woman must have represented the unpredictable, and Alec liked that unpredictability from time-to-time since his every day life had to be very predictable or people died.

In all fairness, she had admitted to herself many times over the years of her marriage to Alec, that he had never spoken explicitly about the other woman except to say that she died many years ago…but a wife always knew when things were not right, when another woman inhabited her husband's mind.

While Leyla thought she brought out the Dr. Jekyll in Alec, she was convinced that the other woman had brought out the Mr. Hyde in him.

CHAPTER ELEVEN

LONDON, ENGLAND

The meeting was set for 10:30 in the morning at Brown's Hotel, one of London's finest old-world haunts for the well-heeled.

Dr. Raymond Raissi awoke from a deep sleep as the bright sun crept through the hand-embroidered, floor-to-ceiling silk shears. It was a quarter past eight, London time. His wife was back home in Los Angeles, but he was not alone.

A clear spring day in the city on the Thames was hard to come by, but it would not be unusual for Raissi to have ordered it, because he could. Raissi called his eighteenth century four-story Lowndes Square mansion his home while in London. Quartered between Knightsbridge and Belgravia, Lowndes Square was home to many of the world's rich and famous.

Raissi had purchased it from a princely member of the Saud family five years ago for nineteen million pounds sterling. Although his wife never liked it, he found it most convenient. He spent a great deal of time at his company's European headquarters in London, so having a place to call home was a necessity.

Raissi never trusted the staff or security at any hotel, no matter where it was. His natural inclination to be suspicious made staying for even a night at a publicly trafficked hotel out of the question.

A man of unlimited means, Raissi had never disclosed his actual wealth, but last year Forbes put it at 22.3 billion U.S. dollars. Not quite Gates or Saudi money, but Raissi only saw it as a challenge, for money was his oxygen and the acquisition of power was his lifeblood.

Upstairs in the second-floor master suite a long, slender outline of a body rustled a bit under the sheets, but managed to stay asleep. Raissi was in his dressing room with Baker, his personal bodyguard, helping him select his suit, shoes, shirt, and tie.

The powerful looking Mick Baker was a former British SAS covert ops specialist that attracted the eye of Raissi in Saudi Arabia three years ago. While Raissi was at a meeting of American-Arab oil executives in Riyadh, he was introduced to him. Baker was looking for a way out of the service and Raissi managed to open the door.

It was not the first time Raissi helped a man in need.

Baker owed him. Raissi knew it.

Saville Row bespoke suits were standard attire for a man who was always in the limelight. Raissi often recalled his years of abject poverty in the deserts of the Middle East and vowed he would never live that life again. He had an image to preserve and project.

The phone rang in the next room. Baker quickly reached for it on the Brazilian rosewood end table. "Yes, half past nine it is. Right," Baker answered.

"Dr. Raissi, your car will arrive from the storage facility at half past the hour," Baker informed in his distinctly serious voice.

Raissi was busy staring in the floor to ceiling Venetian mirror at his stocky, yet relatively fit body now swathed in the finest of fabrics. He knew money hid most imperfections. Adjusting his tie, he combed his black-dyed eyebrows and turned to walk slowly into the cavernous bedroom. He picked up his gold-filigree Patek Phillipe wristwatch, checked the time, and then placed it on his left wrist. He then walked over to the opposite side of the bed, reached down and slapped the bare ass under the Pratesi silk sheets. It jumped and a sleepy voice meowed, "Leave me alone. I'm tired."

With a Cheshire cat grin on his face, his commanding voice stated, "You should be. You asked for it. I'll be back later today. Harrods is waiting for you. Tonight I have an early engagement at the Royal Albert with the Queen, but after that we'll do a late dinner at Toto's." He then motioned for Baker to get the door.

"Wait," came a sultry voice from under the silk sheets. "I would like to go with you tonight. I've never been to the Royal Albert Hall, and

I've never met the Queen of England," she said pleadingly. "I heard she can be funny at times."

Raissi paused. He in no way thought the queen was ever funny. Looking down at the large bed, he said with detectable irritation in his voice, "My dear, that isn't possible right now. You know that. And furthermore, she is not funny at all."

"But —" she countered.

"Please, not now," he insisted. "We'll talk about it at dinner. Buy a nice dress for tonight and go to Cartier or Bulgari and have fun if you must," he said. "Good-bye, my dear."

A soft moan emanated from under the silk sheets.

Raissi quickly left his spacious master bedroom suite and walked down the long hall dotted with Rembrandts, Titians, and Vermeers. They spoke to him. They said that *he had indeed arrived.* As he stepped into the elevator, he padded the left side of his coat. It was there. It made him feel secure.

The cobalt blue, ultra-luxury long-wheelbase Rolls-Royce Phantom Centenary limousine idled quietly on the drive. Sporting a solid sterling silver Spirit of Ecstasy mascot that retracted into the grill when parked, the bullet-proof behemoth of a passenger car awaited its owner. Kamil, Raissi's chauffeur, would willingly give his life for him. He stood taller than two meters, was heavily muscled and dark skinned, indicating his northern Syrian roots.

The CIA had unsuccessfully targeted Kamil's father for elimination nearly two decades ago, and then a few years later the Mossad also failed in their attempt. Subsequently, Kamil's father orchestrated several successful attacks on Coalition Forces during the First Gulf War. He later died at the hands of Israeli police during a raid that killed thirteen Palestinians...three were children.

Raissi exited a side entrance and stopped to speak to the gardeners working next to the porte-cochere. He then stepped into the car's immense rear seating area through one of the suicide doors. They facilitated easier ingress and egress for passengers.

The interior was swathed in the finest matching cobalt blue Connolly leather and rare Carcassian walnut embellishments. The Phantom Rolls, now produced buy BMW, had lost some of its classical appeal, but at over £350,000, it made a statement that spoke to everyone who saw it.

It said, "Look at me. I'm one of the few 'haves' and you are one of the many 'have nots'."

Raissi loved what it said.

Baker eased himself into the front passenger seat to ride shotgun next to Kamil.

The leviathan of an automobile sped away into the Tuesday morning traffic of Brompton Road as if it were Moses parting the Red Sea. Raissi immediately picked up the gold-plated secure cell phone and placed a call. No connection.

The Rolls continued to Knightsbridge Road then west to the Royal Geographical Society at Exhibition Road. While it rolled along effortlessly, Baker turned to Kamil and the two began to chat about whether David Beckham or Pelé was the greatest soccer player. Not interested in the least, Raissi finally made use of the optional divider window. Picking up his secure cell phone again, he re-dialed the number. He never used speed dial. His mistrust ran deep, very deep. Waiting impatiently, the connection was made and a voice was heard. Raissi said quickly, "*Marhaba, ya Ali.* Hello, Ali. Is everything ready? This must go without any mistakes. The queen herself will be there. The hospital means a great deal to me, Marbah," he added.

"We are prepared," said Marbah with solicitude.

"I am pleased," Raissi said with contained force, ending the call. He set the secure cell phone on the seat next to him and looked out the window. He appeared to be in deep thought. The television in front of him had the sound muted, but the images told the story with the closed caption turned on. The Palestinian Authority was still in a state of chaos and the United States stock market was iffy at best. Political machinations in the Middle East always made markets nervous. Then BBC One's medical reporter announced that Dr. Raymond Raissi was in London today to dedicate a new hospital wing that he had donated for the research of childhood diseases.

A smile grew on his round, full face, for he had lost a sister to cancer as a young boy.

He shut off the squawk box and let his head fall back onto the soft leather headrest embroidered with the Raissi family crest depicting a black raven in flight that he had commissioned some twenty years ago. Without prelude, he drifted off for a long moment.

The miles raced effortlessly by. Baker and Kamil continued their discussion about soccer. Raissi heard nothing through the glass divider.

"Look. Watch out!" shouted Baker. "Kamil. He's heading right for us!" he shouted again.

Kamil swerved to avoid a lorry that had crossed over the divider line into oncoming traffic. The sudden lateral movement rocked Raissi in the backseat.

Kamil quickly looked in the rear view mirror and caught a glimpse of his boss. He hoped he had not upset him. He saw Raissi intently speaking on the cell phone again and appeared to be agitated. *Hopefully not by the sudden movement of the car,* he thought to himself quietly.

CHAPTER TWELVE

The President's Daily Brief, often referred to as the PDB, was delivered to Walter Reed Military Hospital in Bethesda, Maryland. The president was enduring his yearly physical that took two days to complete, and he was not very happy about it.

He never understood the yearly physical anyway. He was aware that there had never been a credible study showing that people who had yearly check ups lived longer than those who did not. It was one of the great conspiracies of retail medicine. However, he was the president and people wanted to know that their president was healthy.

Seated in an upright position in bed, the president perused the PDB in earnest while a nurse checked his vitals: pulse, temperature, blood pressure. Seated at a mahogany table near a large window were the Secretaries of Defense and Homeland Security, along with the NSA director. Two assistants were seated at an adjoining table. Also, in the large hospital suite two Secret Service agents stood rod-straight on each side of the door. "Gentlemen," pointing to the two agents in the room, "would you please step outside," the president ordered in a pleasant enough voice. Both men gave a respectful nod and exited.

Post 9/11, the then president established the Office of Homeland Security, also known as the Department of Homeland Security, to coordinate all homeland security efforts. Homeland Security answered to the president and it implemented the executive branch's plans to keep the nation safe and secure. However, the truth was that it was ineffective because the turf wars between intelligence agencies who constantly vied for increased appropriations was ever constant. That was the game.

"And nurse Carol, please," the president said as he looked toward the door.

"Certainly, Mr. President. Dr. North will be in to speak to you shortly." She quickly released the blood-pressure cuff, made some notes, and left the room.

"Damn doctors. They always think they have something important to say. Now, this PDB, let's get to it," the president said directly.

"Mr. President, the PDB is very telling today. There is still chatter in Basra pointing to a possible attack on the oil facilities there. Things are no better in North Korea, while Iran's nuclear facilities are nearly rebuilt only two years after the Israelis destroyed them again for the umpteenth time. Also, the U.N. has once again turned a blind eye to the looming problem. But what's new," Walter Trucker, the Secretary of Defense, said jokingly. The president was not amused. "Oh yes, Mr. President, you asked last week about Mick Dornan's whereabouts."

"You mean the NFL linebacker for the Seattle Seahawks who left to join the Army Rangers?" the president asked rhetorically.

"Yes sir, he left millions of dollars behind to serve his country."

Harper C. Drummond, the Secretary of Homeland Security, added with enthusiasm, "Great guy. A true American hero. At twenty-seven, and with his life going perfectly, he decides to leave it all behind because he says he needs to pay back the country for all of his good fortune. We need more like him."

Looking to the SecDef, the president added, "Damn right, and keep me in the loop on Dornan."

"Will do, Mr. President," the secretary answered.

"Where's he at now?" the president asked.

"He's in Afghanistan and his brother's with him."

"I want to know what that boy's doing. He's why we can't be beat," the president said with detectable grit.

"Mr. President, now that we're on the topic of the American spirit, inline with the likes of Mick Dornan, I need to brief you on the Operation Star 9 mission," Secretary Trucker said directly.

"So what do you have for me? You have the team that's going to execute my *Executive Order 331*," he stated.

Executive orders were the outgrowth of the United States Constitution's Article II that in 1789 granted vague "executive power" or plenary power to the president to issue special orders that he deemed necessary to carry out his duties as the country's chief executive. He issued most orders to United States executive officers to help direct their operations. Failing to follow an executive order resulted in removal from office.

"Most certainly, Mr. President," the secretary answered.

"Then let's hear it," the president insisted.

"We have assembled a team of specialists with the assistance of Miss Mica Seddons, the chief NSA operative in Baghdad as well as General Meade. Called Operation Star 9, this team is comprised of seven men from various branches of the military, all special ops, and one spook from the Company. The ninth is from the private sector. These are the best of the best, Mr. President. The man in charge of this NSA black ops unit is none other than 'The Doctor'."

"I assume he's the one from the private sector," the president remarked.

The secretary paused, "Yes he is, Mr. President."

"What's his real name?" asked the president.

"Dr. Hakimian, Dr. Alexander Hakimian," Secretary of Defense Trucker answered.

The president paused for a long moment, glanced out the large-paned window in contemplation, and then said slowly, "Dr. Hakimian, I know that name." He continued to think out loud saying, "Hakimian. Hakimian. Dr. Hakimian." He said to himself as he scratched his chin, *I've heard that name before.*

"Well, Mr. President. Dr. Alexander Hakimian is a world-renowned brain surgeon. Just a few years ago, he saved the life of the King of Spain's wife. In the world of medicine, he is regarded as a genius. This man has been known to take on patients after all other possibilities have been exhausted and after these patients have been told to go home and die." He paused to let the president take a sip of chilled water.

"If I recall, my predecessor nominated his father-in-law Judge Robert H. Vanley to the federal bench. I met Dr. Hakimian once at a benefit for this very hospital a few years ago. So he's The Doctor? Brilliant. Who would have ever thought! Just brilliant. But what are his qualifications for this op?"

"Mr. President, his talent as a doctor is not the reason he was chosen to lead this elite group of men. He was chosen because he is a true patriot, and he was the most brilliant of our assassins. He was the National Clandestine Service's most effective NOC. He does not crack, he does not make a mistake, and he does not flinch. His psychological profile is bulletproof, the result of many hard years spent in the Middle East before coming to the states. Dr. Hakimian is a very different kind of patriot. As a naturalized citizen who previously called Lebanon home, he exemplifies the best of America, a country built upon the hard work and dedication of immigrants. Besides, Dr. Hakimian has an endless capacity for gathering information, processing it in a nanosecond, and acting on it without second-guessing himself. He is multi-lingual and knows the ways of those in the Middle East. His skill set is unmatched for this mission."

The president took another sip of chilled water. He reveled in the jingoism of the moment.

"But Mr. President, I know you have to rest, so if you will permit, let me ask Director Caccavale to fill you in on the particulars."

"Very well."

"Mr. President." Director Caccavale waited for recognition by the president. He then began in his signature raspy voice. It was the result of chemotherapy and radiation treatments after his surgery to remove a squamous-cell throat cancer ten years ago. "Operation Star 9 is tasked to go after and capture the leader of the Khamsin, his lieutenants, and the WMD that we know Hussein possessed after he sent it to Syria just before we hit him back in 2003. Mr. President, as you are now aware, Dr. Hakimian's code name during his years as the CIA's deepest deep cover operative was The Doctor. During that time, he accomplished things that still amaze and impress even us. Mr. President, the eight other members of Operation Star 9 were chosen to work seamlessly with Dr. Hakimian. These highly-trained soldiers respect only a leader who has, how should I say it…been there, done that, got the t-shirt, if you know what I mean, Mr. President," Caccavale said, as a smile appeared on his round, olive-skinned face.

Director Caccavale continued, with the president looking on

intently. "Mr. President, you have charged Operation Star 9 with a mission far greater than any mission we have ever undertaken in special ops. Dr. Hakimian and his team are good-to-go, sir," Caccavale said with visible intensity as he thrummed his fingers on the table in front of him.

On occasion Director Caccavale applied histrionics to make his point. In this case, the president knew that he was not overstating the severity of the situation. The survival of western civilization was surely at stake.

"Director, I appreciate your view. Our survival and the survival of those nations that value freedom are in peril if we do not eradicate the Khamsin. I pray for the success of Operation Star 9. And Anthony, make sure that they get the support they need," the president said with emphasis, as he looked to the director, then to the other men. "Anthony," the president added with greater emphasis, "all the support they need." Then, staring directly into the eyes of Director Caccavale and then Secretaries Trucker and Drummond, he asked in jest, "So gentlemen, anyone of you want to join me? I've got to get my ass reamed with a twenty-five foot garden hose and then some guy's going to do it again with a gloved finger." A sadistic laugh exploded from his barrel chest.

CHAPTER THIRTEEN

Operation Star 9 needed time to prepare. Their digs were far better than they were normally accustomed to on a daily basis. Given that most of the men drew about thirty-six thousand dollars US in yearly pay, significantly less than their peers in the civilian world, and slept all too often in holes or on cold ground, the rooms in the Republican Palace were a nice change. Many had a clear view of the Tigris River, and together with the Euphrates, the two formed the lifeblood of modern-day Iraq.

Reinforced, bombproof T-Walls and Hesco barriers protected the Republican Palace's position in the International Zone. Coils of surgically sharp razor wire, earthen berms, and high chain-link fences also kept it somewhat safe. M1A3 Abrams tanks, MRAPs, and Bradley fighting vehicles constantly roamed the borders of the zone, while aircraft strafed the area. The occasional T-55 tank rolled by with a full compliment of newly minted Iraqi Army forces eager to enforce the law. The ubiquitous white-striped Little Bird black helicopters from the Xe private security firm were ever-present.

Those who lived and worked within the zone, together with the camp's hundreds of soldiers-in-residence, thought it the safest area in Baghdad. Yet, constant vigilance was the order of the day.

"Dr. Hakimian," General Meade said, "good morning."

"Good morning, general," Alec responded, as he rubbed his now ulcerating bite, courtesy of one nasty barghash mosquito.

"Doctor," Seddons said laughingly, "you should have that checked out by a doctor." Staring at Alec's arm she added, looking a bit squeamish, "Looks like it's painful." Seddons had nerves of steel, except when it came to spiders. As a young child her older brother would put harmless spiders in her bed at night...she never slept much until she left home.

Alec seemed to accept the advice with no comment.

"And that doctor, brings me to the next point," said Seddons, simultaneously launching a big smile his way.

Alec leaned back in the soft leather chair and breathed deeply several times. He found such a practice helpful under times of stress.

"If you'll permit me, general," Seddons said. "Both the NSA and CIA have supplied intel from our covert Mossad agent. His name is Bilal Noureddine. He poses as a Syrian customs agent on the border between Syria and Iraq. He was an eyewitness to the WMD that entered Syria back in 2003 at the start of the war."

Alec interrupted, "This Noureddine. Is he reliable?"

"Yes, doctor. His past performance gives me every reason to trust his word. Noureddine's intel has been spot on. By the way, he's a member of the Druze...very loyal, very secretive," she added.

Seddons walked slowly around the conference table and continued her thoughts as she faced Alec. "The Druze began as a sect of Shi'ite Islam in Eleventh Century Egypt. They call themselves Mowahhidoon. It means monotheistic. They draw their beliefs from the Bible, Qur'an, and Sufi parables. Because they feel a loyalty to the country they live in, the Druze are found in the Israeli, Lebanese, and Syrian militaries," she said, still looking at Alec's tired eyes, hoping to get a reaction from him.

"Fine," Alec said as he shifted in his seat. He was getting bored with the briefing inasmuch as he had once lived with the Druze for several months before the Francis incident.

Seddons was not finished yet. Reaching into her Il Bisonte soft-shell, black-leather briefcase, she retrieved a dossier and slapped it down on the table before Alec. Opening it slowly, she began, "Doctor, we know that a Syrian named Habib Hassim, who tends a butcher shop in Damascus, is the leader of the Khamsin cell there."

Habib Hassim never thought of himself as a devout Muslim. Yes, he prayed to the great Allah, his most merciful, whenever anyone was watching, but within his own mind, he knew Allah as the one who never showed him mercy. U.S. aircraft fired on his family when they lived in Najaf and killed two of his children. Only months before their death, he lost his wife after a painful fight to overcome ovarian cancer. Work paid even less, and his future looked pointless. Then on the first day of Ramadan three years ago Hassim shook the hand of a stranger introduced to him in the local mosque and his life changed forever; he had become a soldier for Allah.

Pointing to the 8" X 10" color glossy photo obviously taken with a high-resolution digital camera, Seddons pushed her finger into the likeness of Hassim's weatherworn face. "This Hassim is a fanatic. He's the type of fanatic that the Khamsin seriously recruits. He spent five months in a training camp in northern Syria. We've known about the existence of the training camp, but its location moves from time to time so it makes it difficult to keep tabs on all the comings and goings. The CIA's local snoop, who had made friends with the camp's second-in-command, was beheaded only two weeks ago after he slipped up and shot his mouth off to his mistress."

Alec stood up and began to walk around the table...he had been sitting too long. Reaching to pick up the photo of Hassim, he said casually, "So tell me Mica, this Hassim fellow. Where's he now?"

Her delicate hands, with fingers flared out, pressed on the table top as she stood bent over, looking at additional photos and data. "Not sure," came out instantly.

"Not sure?"

Standing upright, she said, "That's right." Looking to Alec's hand that held the photo of the bearded, middle-aged, shabbily dressed man with dark, sorrowful eyes, she added, "He's a lot smarter than he looks. The last we knew he was in southern Lebanon. Anyway, he's a problem that must be dealt with."

Seddons reached for a bottle of Pellegrino mineral water. Filling a glass halfway, she continued, "By 2200 hours Operation Star 9 will head for an unmanned crossing at the Syrian border near Abu Kamal, about 400 kilometers from here. It's located opposite the wild-west Iraqi town of Husaybah. Your transportation there will be aboard the Army Fourth ID's Chenoweth "Fast Attack" Desert Patrol Vehicles. These dune buggies have electric drives for stealth movement and are equipped with two 2.75" Hydra-70 pod rocket families." Seddons paused to enjoy how good it felt to demonstrate her technical skills, then continued with greater emphasis. "Doctor, I won't attempt to make this operation anything but what it is, supremely necessary and very dangerous. We need to stop the Khamsin, the Ankabut, and we need to prove that WMD went to Syria and that nuclear hardware ended up in Iran. I know it's a tall order, but it is the war on terror that we are fighting." She paused to see her last words register with Alec. Then she moved on. "Your crossing from Abu Kamal to Tadmur won't be easy nor probably without incident. Anyway, from there Noureddine will provide your transportation and disguises. You will travel as Bedouins west to Tadmur. There you will be introduced to his superior, the Mossad's chief agent in Syria."

Alec remembered Tadmur, also known by the pre-Semitic name of Palmyra, "the bride of the desert." Historians said it was more glorious than Damascus. In ancient times, Palmyra was a major point on the caravan route from the city of Homs to the Euphrates River.

The ancient Romans found the Palmyrenes, led by their Queen Zanubia, a mighty opposition force. Although the Romans lost to the queen in an earlier battle, they defeated her and the Palmyrenes in AD 272. Today, evidence of the Roman invasion still existed in a series of elaborate temples and outbuildings that reminded one of ancient Rome.

Palmyra possessed the famous Afka spring that was the lifesaver of the desert. Its sulfuric water, the cure for any number of illnesses, also gave life to the plantations and nurseries that contained the spectacular array of palm trees so precious to desert dwellers.

Alec had been there with Sahar, the stunning Palestinian beauty that he met while at the American University of Beirut. She studied political science and Eastern philosophy, and he was a second-year medical student.

One long weekend during their school break, the two had stopped at the Hotel Palmyra on their way home to Beirut after a pilgrimage to Dayr az Zawr. They had journeyed to Dayr az Zawr, some two hundred kilometers from Tadmur, to pay homage to Alec's Armenian ancestors who had been massacred by the Ottoman Turks in 1915. This heinous act represented the first genocide of the twentieth century that cost 1.5 million blameless Armenian lives.

Alec also remembered with fondness that Sahar sympathized with his loss. It was then that they became true soul mates. She had even accompanied him to a monastery in the area where he prayed for the fallen. Alec's uncle had donated the funds for the monastery several years before. Sahar was also with him on his visit to the local caves where countless Armenians met their fate and the only sign of their former existence was a sea of sadly decayed bones.

Alec's time in Dayr az Zawr constantly reminded him that the evil of some men knew no bounds. With a finely tuned moral compass, Alec left Palmyra determined to do what he could to see that justice was meted out to the world's evildoers.

Their love for each other was the envy of friends and family alike, despite their coming from two different worlds. Alec, the Christian Armenian, and Sahar, the Muslim Palestinian were inseparable. He felt their bond was forever. She felt the same. He now wondered if the hotel where they made wild love was still standing. The thought of it precipitated an avalanche of emotions. To this day, his busy life with a loving wife and daughter in Los Angeles was punctuated by her essence whenever he was emotionally spent; whenever he let his mind wander off, even for a brief moment. He had asked himself many times, *how could a dead woman still be so much alive in his mind?* She inhabited his thoughts like nothing he could have ever imagined.

The bright sunlight outside the large window made Alec massage his eyes with the palms of his hands. He needed more sleep.

"Doctor, we have knowledge that the Syrians treat this area as very special. Syrian border patrols are everywhere, 24/7," Seddons added, as she pointed to Tadmur on the large wall map. "The secret Matar Tadmur al-Askari military airport is off limits to all but those with the highest security clearances."

Alec just looked on, taking it all in.

"Now, there's something they don't want anyone to see, and we want to know what it is. It's overrun with security, lots of it," she cautioned.

"Miss Seddons," the general said, gesturing to her, then to Alec. "Doctor, know that you and your team will be behind enemy lines and there's no way we can get to you in time, should it go south on you in the Syrian Desert. So, between now and 2200 hours, whatever you need, just let me know. My men are preparing the Chenoweths and support to the border."

"Miss Seddons, I think the Dr. Hakimian needs a little more shut-eye," the general said without preamble. "He's got a lot to do."

"Yes, general, you're probably right," Seddons added, turning to smile at Alec.

"General, Miss Seddons," Alec said mildly. "My men are resting now, and we'll do a *realization* in about three, maybe four hours."

A realization was a mind technique that both battle-hardened soldiers and elite athletes went through before they took on their adversaries. It meant that every soldier or athlete ran through the preset scenario in his mind, as if it were in real time. It proved effective in preparing for battle or an athletic competition. It helped anticipate situations before they occurred. It also reduced the level of uncertainty that accompanied any engagement.

CHAPTER FOURTEEN

A supernatural, vespertine stillness made sleep impossible. The time was nearing and Alec just sat in the chair facing the immense window in his room. The sun had long since dropped below the horizon and Baghdad seemed to settle down for the night, but the temperature was still in the high 20's Celsius. Alec could hear in the background the military television report the weather tomorrow would reach into the high 30's Celsius and the humidity would be near one-hundred percent. He had hoped for cooler temperatures, since his team would be moving across the barren sands without cover, but furnace days and blow-dryer nights were what it was.

Suddenly, much like bomb flashes off in the distance that disturbed the darkness in the city, the darkness in Alec's mind was disturbed by thoughts of his wife and daughter back in California without him. Suddenly, he had a sinking feeling in his stomach. *Was he getting too close to Mica or was it an innocent flirtation?*

The witching hour was approaching.

Alec had tried to nod off for a short moment, but a ringing phone caused him to jump out of his resting position. "Hakimian here," he answered, without listening for who it was.

"Doctor, it's Bobby."

"Yes. Bobby," Alec said, somewhat reluctantly, running his fingers through his hair.

"I need to talk to you," Bobby pleaded subtly.

"Can't it wait until we all meet at 2200 hours?"

"Well Doc, not really."

Relinquishing his position, Alec said, "All right. Meet me in the commons area in twenty."

"Okay. Thanks."

Alec could not imagine what was so important that Bobby needed to meet before the prescribed time when the entire team would gather for the briefing.

The commons area at CENTCOM-Baghdad was a series of ornately decorated rooms connected by large doorways where commissioned officers and members of the Coalition often ate and relaxed. It featured fresco-lined walls and garish, gold-painted furniture. When one asked what the previous occupant had done with his money, one could see it in the commons area and everywhere else. It was difficult to get one's arms around the idea that Saddam's main palace in Baghdad was now the home of the United States' Central Command for Iraqi operations. What was more mind boggling was the idea that this madman had more than fifty other such palaces scattered throughout the countryside, and all at the expense of his once caged citizens.

Alec was seated at a small table that featured an inlaid chessboard made of rare woods. He was staring down at it when Bobby Roberts walked in.

"Doc, great game. The Persians invented it, so they say."

Looking up from his seat, "Do you play?" Alec asked, never figuring that Bobby would have an interest in anything beyond video games.

"Checkers mostly, Doc. Don't forget, I'm an Alabama boy. But I've been known to dabble a bit," Bobby said with a grin.

"Sit down, Bobby. It's your move."

Bobby sat down, stared at the board, and then moved his knight to B3.

"So Bobby, what's so urgent that we have to talk now? We've only a few hours before the team's briefed." Alec contemplated his next move.

"That's why I need to talk to you, Doc. Now," Bobby said somewhat forebodingly.

"Go on," Alec insisted.

"Well, it may seem like it's nothing, but when we got to our quarters,

Tishermann went off quickly and didn't say where he was going. When he returned, he looked different. I mean he acted different. Then he got a call on his cell and quickly left again. As he walked across the area in front of the wing of the palace that we're in, he seemed nervous, very nervous. I can read body language, sir. I couldn't hear what he was saying, but I could see that he was alarmed or bothered about something."

"Bobby, Tishermann's CIA," he intoned, yet held his own doubts about him.

"Right, Doc. I know that he's CIA, but it's what he said when he came back and started to walk down the hallway to his room. He thought he was still alone because everyone else had gone to chow. He had even seen me leave, but I returned immediately through a rear door to get my iPod Touch."

"So what did he say?" Alec questioned.

"He was still on his cell when he said, 'They will not make it.' Then he ended by whispering *Allahu Akbar*! Why would he say that? He's supposed to be one of us. Isn't he?" Bobby said in a concerned voice.

Alec had to admit to himself that the actions of Tishermann gave him pause. But then again, he thought he should heed his own advice and remember that Tishermann was indeed CIA. Because of that, things were not always what they seemed. Moreover, he believed Seddons had thoroughly vetted him.

"Bobby, I understand your concern," Alec said, as he made his next move, pawn to E5.

Bobby stood up from the table and said, "I guess I should get ready, sir."

"Right, Bobby. Right," Alec responded, then looked down at the chess board.

CHAPTER FIFTEEN

2100 hours came too quickly for OS9. Several of the men were roused from a state of deep sleep by Alec walking down the hallway pounding on each door and exclaiming much like a town crier in Medieval Britain, "Five minutes 'till the briefing, gentlemen."

Riemann, the "Viking" as he was nicknamed by his OS9 peers, was the first out. Tishermann exited his room looking as if he had been ready for days. He just did not look right in his "new" fatigues. Josiah was the next to show up in the briefing room. Then Nutworth, Mackay, Pratt, and Alvarado wandered in, almost in lockstep, all still seemingly half asleep. Alec then appeared through the adjoining doorway and called the men to attention.

Nutworth took a simple head count and said, "Where the hell's Bobby?"

At first blush, Alec thought the question somewhat ironic, but then added, "Riemann, get Bobby."

Just then, Bobby walked in sporting a shaved head and eating a hamburger. "So let's go get the bastards."

"Where'd you get the burgerrr," Mackay asked, rolling the second "r" in burger.

Taking another bite, he smiled, then, "I met a babe named Lisa in the commissary," came out muffled.

Alec stared at him, then said, "Gentlemen, very soon we will be making our way to the Syrian border at an unmanned crossing near Abu Kamal."

"How are we getting there, by helo?" Nutworth asked.

"Chenoweth Fast Attack Vehicles," came back instantly.

"Cool. I love dune buggies," Bobby mumbled through a mouthful of hamburger.

"You love anything that isn't bolted down," said Alvarado, as he polished his spotting binoculars.

"These dune buggies," Alec said with humorless emphasis, "have electric drives and advanced solar power supplies that meet EPA standards." Designing a military vehicle to meet EPA standards infuriated him, *but even the military had its limits in this age of political correctness.* "We need to be as stealth as possible. They will allow us to do that, but the trade-off is that the exposed roll cages mean that an artillery shell that comes even close will end it all. And rifle fire.... You figure that one out."

"How fast do they go?" Bobby interrupted with childlike enthusiasm.

"Sergeant Roberts, they'll travel at freeway speed, but it's not speed that we're concerned about. We need to get to the rendezvous point without any hitches. Now, once at the crossing we'll be met by our contact Bilal Noureddine. Noureddine is a Mossad agent working as a Syrian border guard. This guy's our lifeline, so listen to him," Alec admonished the team.

"So what's the mission, Boss?" Riemann asked.

"Terrorists, boys," Alec answered. "Terrorists, and WMD, if we're lucky. But first we're to find the top-secret Matar Tadmur al-Askari military airport in the Syrian Desert and gather intel on the nuclear centrifuges that we know have been heading to Iran for years."

"Didn't the Dems say that they don't exist, and that we're still in this 'mother of all sandpits' without a real reason except for the oil?" Bobby fired back. "I don't know what they're talking about. Between Afghanistan and Iraq, we've liberated fifty million people. Isn't that reason enough? And the oil. If we wanted their oil we could just take it from them, or anyone else, and that includes the Saudis, and the other terrorist bastards, and that Khamsin dude." Bobby finished with a flurry. "And my mother wants to know that if we're here for oil, why is she paying $3.50 a gallon to fill up her Honda?"

Alec knew that Bobby was right. He also knew that the deeper purpose of OS9 was to go beyond the issue of WMD and to find the Khamsin and its leader, and now was not the time to get political. "I empathize with your politics Bobby, but tonight we are not Republicans or Democrats. We are Americans highly trained to do a job. All right, check your gear and in about fifteen minutes APVs and heavy-equipment transporters will take us and the buggies to the western outskirts of town. From there we'll head toward Abu Kamal some four hundred kilometers due west. Once there Noureddine will brief us and then on to Tadmur." Taking a breath, he continued, "Tadmur used to be called Palmyra, or the city of palms. It was the capital of Syria at the time of Christ. The Romans conquered the land around AD 272. When they left, evidence of their time, influence, and greatness can still be seen in archaeological wonders such as ornate temples, a theatre, and a Roman-type senate building. The ancient part of the city is near Tadmur."

"Sounds like we'll be on a group tour and you're the travel guide," Bobby said in a muffled chuckle as he inventoried the room looking for approval. "Say, what's playing tonight at the theatre?" he added, to draw attention away from his previous remark.

Alec was not in the mood. "So, any real questions?"

Pratt said, "Anything else we should know, sir?"

"The Ankabut and his Khamsin have been moving all types of WMD. Intel has it that there's a plan to blow a U.S. city with a suitcase nuke or a dirty bomb. Like I said before, Noureddine will brief us when we arrive at the border. He'll have the latest intel."

"So where's the Ankabut? Does anyone know? And what about the WMD? Are they in Syria for sure?" Riemann asked.

"Some in Syria, others possibly elsewhere," Alec said tersely. "Noureddine's station chief will bring us up to speed once we make Tadmur."

"So when do we ride?" Bobby asked eagerly.

"The buggies are ready to roll," Alec answered. "Remember to make sure that your weapons and gear are in order. We can't take a full compliment because of the limited space in the buggies. We also need to be prepared to change our mode of transportation if necessary, so traveling light is paramount to making this mission work. Remember, you'll be changing into native garb, so you won't be able to have firearms in plain view."

"What about *One Shot*? I can just slip her under my t-shirt," Bobby commented, with a slight smile on his youthful face, but he was serious. After all, One Shot was his favorite collapsible sniper rifle. To date, it had dropped fifty-three men in their tracks.

"Bobby, just make it work. Improvise."

Bobby figured that if he had to, he could scope a .50 caliber Desert Eagle, the most powerful production semiautomatic pistol ever made. *The range wouldn't be close*, he reasoned, *but it would be fairly accurate. Maybe even an M-4 Maverick re-configured with an Aimpoint sight. Maybe both.*

The staging area behind the main building on the palace grounds was tented and lit with low-emission lighting to avoid attracting any needless attention.

At 2230 hours, the three dune buggies in camouflage paint, alloy roll cages, and aggressive sand tires were at the ready. Lightweight titanium shielded the electric drives and the carbon-fiber seating area was modified to carry three soldiers and gear.

The temperature was now at about 25° Celsius and the air was still for a May night. It was unnervingly still, given the circumstances. The moon was not bright enough to travel without visual aide, so the dune buggies were outfitted with infrared lighting, while Hydra rocket pods sat atop the roll cages, just in case. Alec was concerned about the range of the electric drives, but there was no time to second-guess anything now. When it came to a time-sensitive military operation, you went with what you had.

"Gentlemen," General Meade said, "you'll be tracked by satellite and you'll be given all available intel from our end," as he looked first at Alec and then to Bobby and on down the line. Everyone stared at Pratt; after all, he was the communications man.

Seddons was somewhat nervous and just stood silent. As much as she was integral to the assembly of Operation Star 9, she had no concept of what was about to happen. She knew it and thought it best to observe.

There was a palpable tension amongst the members of OS9. The diesel-powered transporters were idling close by, waiting for their cargo. Last minute details were completed and the dune buggies, gear, and weapons were loaded into canvas-covered M1070 Heavy Equipment Transporters.

The men climbed into three Humvees as the transporters moved out first. "Gentlemen," Alec said, speaking into his wireless lip mike attached to his collar. "Everyone check communications," he ordered, as he adjusted his earpiece. "Do you have earbuds? And Pratt, do you have the sat phone, etc?" he snapped.

Each man instantly began checking his gear.

The Humvees quickly followed close behind in caravan fashion.

Two hundred meters down the road, Riemann spotted a regiment of the Ohio Army National Guard. They roamed the military convoy routes in Buffaloes searching for improvised explosive devices.

The Buffalo, originally designed and built in South Africa, where landmines were commonplace, was the answer to IEDs. The prehistoric looking, heavily armored, all-terrain monster was fitted with a remote-control arm that reached out sixteen feet. The end of its arm was fitted with a pushing and grabbing device that unearthed IEDs with little problem. The Buffalo's success record was perfect. None had been put out-of-commission nor had any of its operators ever been injured or killed. No matter what the insurgents threw at it, the Buffalo was undaunted and a real lifesaver.

About fifty klicks out of Baghdad the lights of the desert metropolis began to fade, save an occasional firefight that sparked on the horizon. Dimly lit concrete huts, each with a television satellite dish mounted atop its flat roof, dotted the sides of the road. The inhabitants in each hut usually counted a dozen or more and lived each day just to fight for another day of survival. Life, even after liberation, was hard. However, hope had displaced despair.

Soon the transporters and Humvees pulled to the side of the road in a clearing where there were no buildings or people. The moon shone lightly, and the wind was blowing SSW at about twenty knots per hour.

Without delay, several equipment operators backed the Chenoweth Fast Attack Vehicles out of the transporters. Alec, Nutworth, and Riemann got into the first military-grade dune buggy. Pratt, who had raced dune buggies in the Nevada Desert, would drive number two, and Bobby, a former Alabama state motocross champion, would do the same in number three. The fact that the buggies made no sound beyond a low hum as they began to roll off across the desert added an additional eeriness to the night.

It was now 0150 hours and the three Chenoweths were throwing up plumes of sand as they hightailed it across the desert floor, guided only by infrared light, a very dim moonlight, and GPS. Alec led, followed by Bobby, with Pratt's vehicle trailing some twenty meters behind.

Alec had calculated that by traveling flat-out OS9 would arrive at the rendezvous point near Abu Kamal around 0330 hours. The cloak of night would still be in effect, thus, they would have some degree of anonymity as they met up with Noureddine at the border.

All was quiet as they continued down the route, each driver's hands tightly gripping the thick steering wheel. They passed one hovel of a home after another, with Alec ever mindful that the people of Iraq deserved a better life. *Nothing else need be said*, he thought. *Just get the job done.*

The desert was soon clear of ramshackle abodes and Abu Kamal waited across a long stretch of warming sand. As the kilometers rolled by, the men inside the dune buggies tried their best to relax, but the thought of entering into truly hostile territory with absolutely no backup was always cause for pause. Yet, every one of them knew that this was what they had trained for years; this was *special ops.*

By 0215 hours, the road had long played out. By 0335 hours, OS9 had arrived at a clearing in the desert that looked like any other, save a pair of palm trees standing like sentinels in the middle of nowhere. In the vicinity, Bobby spotted small plant growths about the size of golf balls popping out of the sand. He would later learn they were desert truffles. Although the haughty French would most certainly turn up their noses at them, they were very much a regional delicacy.

All of a sudden off to the southeast at about two kilometers out something was moving their way. Alec tried to use his infrared binoculars, but the sand swirls made it difficult to identify specific objects. Whatever it was, it was moving slowly. As the minutes ticked by, the men walked about looking for anything other than sand. They found more sand.

"I sure hope that this guy shows up," Bobby said, as he jumped off the buggy.

"Yeah, this is not the place to be just hanging out," added Nutworth.

Pratt attempted to make contact with CENTCOM-Baghdad. After a few tries he was able to get an uplink to one of the communications satellites serving CENTCOM worldwide.

Alec could now faintly make out images as they made their way closer. Suddenly, he could not believe his eyes. He kind of chuckled at the sight of a lonely Bedouin herding about a dozen horses in the middle of the Syrian Desert.

"Doctor," Pratt said, as he called for Alec. "I have CENTCOM-Baghdad on the sat, sir. It's General Meade," he continued, as he handed the encrypted Iridium satellite phone to Alec.

The latest version of the Iridium satellite phone system, unlike others, was comprised of sixty-six satellites orbiting in crisscrossing paths at 480 miles above the earth. This system delivered unparalleled voice and data communications virtually anywhere in the world.

"Yes, general. We're here at the rendezvous point. We'll do, general," Alec finished, as he ended the call.

Bobby and Riemann played poker with a deck of hand-painted playing cards depicting scenes of Muhammad's struggle in the seventh century. The cards were lifted from Saddam's palace in Takrit by one of Riemann's buddies in the 4th ID. Bobby did not have a chance, for Riemann was a master of numbers and card counting was a simple task for him.

Mackay sat alone inventorying his medical supplies for the second time in the past half day. He was edgy.

Alec could now make out the distinct figure of a man dressed in classical Bedouin garb with eleven horses in tow. Two of them carried cargo, the others just plodded along in lockstep.

"What the fuck is that?" Bobby shouted, as the man and his horses, some white, others gray and even black, entered the area near where the dune buggies were parked. The other men whipped their heads around to see a heavily clothed man with a quizical look on his face ragged face. His thick black beard was speckled with white grains of sand. The contrast was eye-catching.

"*Maraheb*. Greetings," Alec said, as he gestured to the team to gather near the man and his spectacular Arabian horses. Alec held on to his P99 just in case.

"*Marhaba*, Al-Khamsa awaits," the man said. He possessed a very noticeable, yet clearly understandable Middle Eastern accent and his English sounded schooled.

Al-Khamsa, meaning *the five*, was the name given by Muhammad to his five finest mares that would comprise the foundation of the Arabian breed. It was the *word* Alec needed to hear to confirm his contact.

Alec sized Noureddine up. Time would tell if he was what Seddons had said he was.

"Where's the engine?" Noureddine asked jokingly and rhetorically as he stared at the dune buggies.

"They're electric," Nutworth answered.

"What you mean, electric?" Noureddine said, having fun with Nutworth.

"They make no sound, so that we can travel in stealth mode. You can't hear us coming," Nutworth answered.

"Is that like your stealth fighter shot down in your war with the Serbs?"

"Not quite," Riemann answered with a scornful look on his face.

"What is the amperage and total voltage output? And the horsepower?" Noureddine asked, as he walked around one of the buggies slowly passing his hand over its skeleton-like frame. He was particularly enamored of the solar cell power supplies. "I like this," he added, running his hand over the solar cell unit.

"How do you know so much about these rigs?" Bobby asked, looking him straight in the eye.

"Virginia Tech," he said, pointing to himself. "Don't let the clothes fool you. I majored in electrical engineering, then did two years at General Motors working in their alternative drive train division," Noureddine announced proudly. "I was also embedded with the Fourth ID during the First Gulf War. They had some interesting equipment. These look like the latest version," he said.

Bobby and the others were nonplussed. Alec was simply amused.

"Gentlemen, we must move on before the sun rises," Noureddine exhorted. "Here," as he pointed to one of the two Arabians carrying cargo, "put these on."

Bobby held up a large tent-like garment and laughed, "Not me."

"What you are wearing will most certainly get you killed," Noureddine cautioned.

Bobby's eyes rolled in his head as he reluctantly took the garment. The others got the message and in no-time-at-all OS9 looked more like a family of goat herders than a crack special ops unit, and that was the idea. With some ingenuity, they were able to stuff most of their weapons under the loose-fitting garments. Even Pratt's communication equipment managed to fit in the satchels of one of the horses rigged with cargo carriers.

Admittedly, no one liked the head garb, *but better that than dead*, most thought. Besides, it did serve a purpose, for protection was needed from the pounding heat and blowing sands of the vicious Khamsin. As for traveling on horseback, it was different, but they were prepared.

When the men of Operation Star 9 were candidates in the final selection process, a prerequisite was that they all had to be experienced horsemen. It was always known that the uncertainty of the feral deserts of the Middle East required anyone who wished to survive its hardships to have skills beyond the obvious.

With everyone costumed, Alec ordered the dune buggies to be buried in a sand dune about fifty meters from the palm trees. He also ordered the batteries to be removed and buried separately at least fifty meters from the buggies.

"Doc, what do you mean bury the buggies? How are we to get to Tadmur?" Bobby asked with an astonished look on his face.

Alec focused his eyes on the horses feeding on the few patches of grass under the palm trees. One had left a puddle of noxious smelling piss beneath its belly. "Horses, boys, horses. Get in the cowboy spirit. Remember, many of our presidents used to ride horses."

The others looked on incredulously as Bobby retorted, "But horses! Camels maybe, but horses?"

"Camels are very unusual in Syria. Horses, mules, and donkeys are the most common modes of transportation. In fact, you won't find camels at all in Lebanon. Bobby, you've been watching too many old movies," Alec said a little pedantically.

"Shit, it'll take days, and where's the food? I'll even eat MREs?" Bobby fired back.

Noureddine proudly held up a side of roasted lamb in one hand and a sack made of goat's hide that contained some sort of mysterious liquid in the other. He offered Bobby a drink.

"Not me," Bobby said defiantly. "Smells toxic."

"It's so goddamn dangerous out there that you won't have time to think about eating," Alec said laughingly.

Just in case they were needed later, the Chenoweth's were sealed in military-grade Mylar to preserve their viability before they were buried in a massive sand dune.

A bright pumpkin-colored sun began to creep up over the horizon.

OS9 headed toward Tadmur.

CHAPTER SIXTEEN

OCEAN OF FIRE, SYRIA

The warm, bright sun made its presence known quietly. As it rose in the east, the men of OS9 wondered why they had to carry all their gear and weaponry on the back of horses. The answer would come soon.

"Doctor," Noureddine proclaimed. "You are much smaller than your reputation," he chuckled, as the team moved out.

It was Noureddine's way of letting Alec know that he was aware of *The Doctor* through his own handlers. The knowledge of Alec's first CIA mission to eliminate a Hamas operative in Dubai had impressed Noureddine.

"That's what everyone tells me," Alec said with a wolfish grin.

"Perhaps you are not The Doctor," Noureddine retorted jokingly.

"Perhaps. Perhaps."

"Doc," Pratt said from behind.

The sands began to stir as a venomous viper scudded across the path in front of Pratt's horse. Pratt was motionless, then hollered out, "Snake. Snake," as he pointed nervously to the lethal reptile. Hurriedly, he kicked his horse, and moved out of its way.

"Sir," Noureddine said, "it's only dangerous if it bites you."

Pratt and the others found no comfort in Noureddine's comment and quickly lifted their feet off the stirrups.

The encounter with the viper reminded Alec of the invention of the stirrup around 500 B.C. It had dramatically changed the course of history. From that time onward warriors on horseback could more effectively direct their mighty steeds with their feet while both hands were free to wield weapons of war.

As the caravan of special ops soldiers and operatives continued to move slowly toward Tadmur, the rolling sands of the eastern Syrian Desert began to take their toll. The eyes burned from the salt released because of constant perspiration and the sandblasting winds of the Khamsin made the exposed skin of each man burn as if on fire. In addition, much like the snow blindness encountered by skiers, traveling endless kilometer after kilometer on the sands of an almost featureless desert could turn the sighted into the purblind.

"Doctor, so you still speak Arabic?" Noureddine asked somewhat sarcastically.

"*Naam*, yes," answered Alec.

"*Naam*, yes," Noureddine said, with a smile painted itself across his sun-scared, bearded face. "I thought your years as a doctor in America made you forget," Noureddine added laughingly. "Good. Very good," Noureddine replied, as he encouraged his horse to move along with a couple of swift kicks to her sides.

"How long before we arrive in Tadmur?" Bobby asked Noureddine.

"Not too long. Maybe by this time tomorrow."

"What, tomorrow this time." Bobby remarked, with disappointment in his now dry voice. He rubbed his chapped lips with water, but nothing would help. To make matters worse, bits of hot sand had embedded themselves in his skin. He thought, *how much worse could this get?*

Alec looked at his watch. It was nearing 1100 hours, and it did not appear that the team, feeling it was held hostage on horseback, was making very much headway. The now ulcerated barghash mosquito bite on his left forearm was worsening. He tried to squeeze the pus out of it, but the result was more pain. The flecks of sand imbedded in the ulcer exacerbated the problem and the topical antibiotic just was not doing the trick.

Noureddine motioned to the caravan to dismount several hours into the tortuous journey. At that moment, all the men could think about was food and liquids. Bobby quickly grabbed for an MRE—a meal ready to eat—and a candy bar that he had hidden in his abaye, a loose-fitting tunic worn by most Bedouins of the desert. Pratt and Nutworth, along with Mackay and Alvarado did the same. Noureddine reached into a bag tied to one of the packhorses and pulled out a jar of hummus paste, pita bread, and a plastic bottle of mineral water. The bottled mineral water was his way of reminding himself that there was a modern world that had a few things of value.

Alec walked around the bivouac area slapping a couple of horses on their hindquarters as if he were on a cattle drive somewhere along the Chisholm Trail. Small, sandy specks of dust rose off the horses' parched hides and a few parasites fluttered their wings but stayed put. His thoughts wandered off to his daughter and wife and what he was doing out in the middle of a godforsaken land that was once part of history's great Fertile Crescent. Ironically, it was now more reminiscent of the Middle Ages and represented what had become for the entire world, a battleground for the ultimate clash of civilizations.

Some of the men ate quietly, slowly. While picking sand from their teeth, food soon lost its importance. Riemann cleaned his weapons, as did some of the others. Their concern now was the damage that would be done by the sand that was everywhere. They needed to protect their weapons. It even managed to make its way into the creases of everyman's buttocks, crotch, and ears. And as much as guns did not like moisture, they also found sand anathema to their very existence as functioning weapons of war.

The sun was hot and bothersome. The clothes did not help. Their morale, though not flagging, was being seriously tested. They wanted action.

Noureddine looked to Alec. "From this point on we must watch the horizon for soldiers. The Syrians patrol this area on a regular basis. We know that they are still hiding something out here. I must tell you that I saw large transport vehicles pass through the border into Syria prior to your country attacking Iraq. These heavily guarded vehicles were not carrying sacks of flour. That's for sure," Noureddine said.

Alec pondered the seriousness of what Noureddine was saying as he continued to poke at his meager food.

"So you are saying that the weapons came through Abu Kamal?" Alec queried.

"Most certainly," Noureddine fired back quickly. "My cousin works undercover in the transport division of the Syrian Army. I have been a border guard for nearly eleven years. The movement of weapons from Iraq did indeed take place at the beginning of the war. Many of your people think that your president was wrong, but he was right. He was very right. Just ask me, Noureddine, I tell the truth." He finished the sentence with a gesturing of his hands toward the unblemished sky above.

Noureddine was the offspring of a Jewish mother and a Druze Muslim father. He grew up in Tel Aviv. There, his father labored as an auto mechanic and his mother in a hospital. Because of his heritage, Noureddine was imbued with respect for both sides of the Jewish and Arab dilemma. He had always believed in Israel's right to coexist in peace with all Arab nations. He also held dear the Arab qualities of hospitality and generosity that he learned from his father, while at the same time his mother gave him the Jewish qualities of survival and family loyalty. At least on an abstract level, Noureddine always looked to bridge the gap between Jews and Arabs.

Noureddine fed the horses with a paltry few handfuls of grain and then called for the team to mount up. Nutworth and Riemann checked their weapons and explosives kept on one of the packhorses. Pratt made a last minute communication attempt to CENTCOM-Baghdad before they left, but to no avail. Each of the other men made sure that his weapons were functioning properly. Each steeled himself mentally for what he knew was about to happen out in the savage desert where the top-secret airport was located, and where nuclear hardware was making its way to Iran.

The mighty Khamsin began to rise as it sculpted the sand dunes with the fine hand of a Michelangelo. The uneventful day seemed too perfect. How was it that they had not seen a soul? Not a traveler, not a even a Bedouin, no flora nor fauna, save a deadly snake and desert truffles. No airplane surveillance, no land patrols. And the sand and sun…relentless. Although sand was granular in nature, the intense heat at times seemed to impart a parched look to its surface. The men started to feel not only the monotony of the ride, but the heat and dryness that were part of desert life.

Sergeant Alvarado, who had grown up on a rancho in Durango, Mexico, could not help but marvel at the beauty of the Arabian horse. The mighty Arabian horse had made its presence known some time between 5000 B.C. and 3500 B.C., yet in truth, its beginnings were as mysterious as the horse itself.

The Arabian was a wild horse of the northern reaches of Syria, the steppes above the coast, and southern Turkey. Inasmuch as the Arabian Peninsula has been arid for most of the last ten millennia, the likelihood of the Arabian originating there bordered on the impossible. In fact, the origin of the word "Arab" was just as difficult to ascertain. It was said that it derived from the Hebrew *Arabha*, or steppe land. "Arab" was a Semitic word meaning "desert," or a denizen of the area, making no inference as to a specific nationality.

The Arabian horse was responsible for changing the course of history on many an occasion. It was because of the majestic and powerful Arabian that the Egyptians explored regions beyond their borders, thus extending their empire. The Arabian was also responsible for shortening the communication times between vast distances because of its speed and endurance.

The uniqueness of the Arabian horse has been preserved throughout history on stone pillars, hieroglyphics, and seal rings. Even King Solomon paid homage to the Arabian in 900 B.C., calling it the horse of the Egyptian Kings. Throughout the Old Testament, other references to the breed could be found.

Bedouin tribesmen, who have treasured the Arabian equine over the centuries, have always considered it their most valuable possession. They have kept the breed pure over the ages and to this day its confirmation, confidence, and uniqueness were unequalled amongst all equines. The ability to run like the desert wind, each step, poetry in motion, was the mark of an Arabian.

Alec's ears strained to hear it. Riemann knew that something was different. Pratt held out a listening device and watched the meter register intermittent input. At first, it sounded like nothing more than a low hum in the distance. Then it was gone, then back, then gone again.

"What was that?" Riemann and Bobby asked.

"Nothing, just the Khamsin letting us know that she is here," Noureddine answered with hesitation in his voice. He knew otherwise. He sensed they were not alone.

1800 hours came and went without incident. The landscape had changed to reflect the dominance of sand dunes in the area. Some were unusually high.

"Goddamn, look at that," Nutworth said to Bobby as he pointed to the rising sand dunes.

"Look at what?" Bobby asked, as the others turned to the sound of his voice.

"The sand dunes. Humongous mothers. Where'd they come from?" Nutworth asked with incredulity.

Noureddine responded, "As we approach Tadmur, you will see many changes. The sand dunes, as you say, will become hills that reach up hundreds of meters. Many of the Roman ruins of Tadmur rest in a valley surrounded by sand hills colored with the blood of its enemies. It is the only refuge against the mighty Khamsin when she is angry."

Pratt's sensor registered again. It was able to detect motion or sound at fifty kilometers. The human ear wasn't quiet so capable. This time it was more consistent. Noureddine reached for his Kalishnikov tucked in his cargo bag. He removed the safety, tapped the ammo clip, and chambered a round. Alec and Bobby watched.

"Doc," Pratt said in a rush. "I've got something here, sir. Now the sound is approaching from the northwest."

"What is it?" Alec asked.

"I don't know sir, but its signal is increasing," Pratt said rapidly. "I'll try to grab one of our Enhanced Crystal satellites. Maybe it'll tell us what's coming," Pratt said hurriedly.

Alec turned to Noureddine, waiting for a response. Noureddine looked to the northwest, his ears reaching for a sound, for a clue. The others were vigilant.

The horses began to act up as they were spurred on toward Tadmur. It had always been known that animals possessed a keener sense of impending danger than humans. Reading the environment, they picked up the nuances of change long before they were apparent to humans.

"Pratt, are you linked?" said Alec.

"No sir. I can't find the hook, but I'll keep trying."

Alec was not satisfied, but he knew the limitations of being deep in enemy territory. During his years as a CIA NOC, he experienced a complete disconnect from all U.S. officials. It was now, as the nineteenth century naturalist Hebert Spencer first stated, *survival of the fittest.*

The sand dunes and hills became more common, as the city of Tadmur came into focus through the setting sun. Noureddine looked toward one of them, as if trying to get his bearings. "Doctor, Matar Tadmur al-Askari, the top-secret military airport, is northeast of the city. It's best that we follow the sinking sun to our northwest around the city."

Alec recalled that during the French mandate of Syria in the first half of the twentieth century, they used the very same airport for military operations because of its remoteness.

The long day was becoming night, as the moon, nowhere to be found, gave no assistance. Infrared vision was necessary. Each man pulled off his headwear and attached infrared binoculars. Nutworth and Riemann held lightweight M-16 rifles outfitted with Aimpoint sights. Bobby switched to his sniper rifle outfitted with a US Optics SN3 T-Pal 3.2-17x44mm scope that had night-sighting capabilities. He kept it close to his chest.

Puff! Puff! Puff! Both Alec and Noureddine looked down to their right. Three puffs of dust appeared above the sand, then two more in front of them.

Taking cover behind a low sand hill, spotter Alvarado trained his binoculars on the distant hill in front of him. Scanning the terrain, he sighted a sniper lodged between two large, unusual rock outcroppings, firing from a 7.62mm Dragunov sniper rifle, the weapon of choice for Syrian snipers. He knew the Dragunov had an effective range of 1,300 meters.

"Bobby, there he is," Alvarado said. He had spotted the camouflaged sniper about six hundred meters out at one o'clock. The instant reflection of his optics was telltale.

Bobby looked in the direction that Alvarado had indicated. "I can drop him." Bobby said confidently.

"Sight him in. Wind's from left-to-right at three knots," Alvarado advised Bobby.

Bobby sighted him in through his US Optics SN3 T-Pal 3.2-17x44mm scope and slowly squeezed the trigger. "Like ducks in a pond, baby. Just like ducks in a pond."

The bullet hit the sniper in the left eye and he went down without a fight.

A slight sound in the distance became a roar of machines approaching quickly behind the hill some fifteen hundred meters to OS9's left.

"Move behind the hill over there," Noureddine directed, as he pulled the horses behind a high rise of sand.

Alec waived his hand, motioning in the same direction.

The whirring roar was closing in. Then there it was, a large Soviet BTR-50P Amphibious Personnel Carrier, with its steel tracks spewing up rooster tails of sand three to four meters in the air as it ate its way across the burning desert. It was capable of carrying up to twenty infantrymen equipped with AK-47 7.62mm assault rifles. The BTR-50P itself was fitted with an 85mm D-44 division gun and fired from the rear deck, while the front carried a spindle-mounted 7.62mm SGMB machine gun.

The personnel carrier was flanked on one side by a BTR-80K commander's rubber-tired vehicle that was equipped with an eleven-meter telescope mast and a full compliment of communication and navigational devices. Just meters to the left of the BTR-50P, a two-man recon jeep-style vehicle moved cautiously. Each man carried the ubiquitous and highly reliable AK-47.

Bobby and Alvarado found a high position about hundred meters from the main group. Alvarado quickly spotted the APC again and as quickly gave Bobby the coordinates and windage numbers. "Bobby, take him."

One squeeze of the trigger and splat…the driver of the BTR-80K was hit square between the eyes. It made Bobby smile.

All of a sudden, a shot came out of nowhere and found Pratt's left shoulder, taking him to the ground. He was bleeding profusely. Mackay hurried over to his position and began triage. Alec, Noureddine, and Tishermann fanned out in the hopes of making themselves more difficult to hit. In the middle of a desert, hiding was not usually an option.

The BTR-50P armored personnel carrier began firing its spindle-mounted 7.62mm SGMB machine gun. One of the packhorses was struck directly in the chest and died before it hit the ground. The ammo it carried cooked off, with one strafing Nutworth's lower right leg. With Pratt now stabilized, Mackay, under furious fire, made his way over to aid Nutworth, whose injury would later prove to be a deep bullet laceration requiring eleven sutures. Since suturing on the battlefield often proved difficult, he temporarily closed the long wound with medical skin glue.

The soldier commanding the D-44 division gun met the same fate as did the driver of the BTR-80K. It was a Bobby "Sureshot" Roberts *kill-shot* to the mid throat area. Both vehicles were now motionless as infantrymen scurried off, taking cover behind a series of small rises in the rolling sand dunes.

Riemann grabbed Bobby's M60E3 and leveled it at yet another incoming vehicle some fifty meters out. Squeezing off two long bursts of rounds, the engine compartment and front tires took direct hits. Rolling to a halt, the Syrian soldiers bailed out as Bobby began picking them off, one at a time.

Absent the faint moon and save the weapons' fire, it was now complete darkness…advantage Operation Star 9, for infrared dominated the night. The BTR-50P personnel carrier stopped and troops exited and spread out, taking cover behind two small sand hills. By now Alec, Riemann, and Tishermann had flanked them on the right. Josiah and Noureddine stayed with the remaining horses to prevent them from bolting, all the while firing a shot here and there in an effort to keep the Syrians at bay.

Now with Alec, Riemann, and Tishermann behind the Syrian troops from the personnel carrier, they were able to force them to defend their position from multiple angles.

Mackay was able to make both Nutworth and Pratt somewhat comfortable. He then took up a position that now had the Syrians boxed in on all sides. The Syrians repeatedly fired rounds in frustration, searching for a target. Every shot fired enabled Alec's team to determine each soldier's exact location.

"Noureddine, will they surrender?" Alec asked.

"No. To surrender would guarantee execution if they ever got back to Tadmur. No, they won't surrender."

Alec needed to get his psychological bearings and make decisions that would immediately impact the success of the mission. *Does he force a surrender, even if it resulted in the killing of many, if not all of the Syrians? Did the Syrians send for other troops? If OS9's position was now compromised, what were its options?* The questions kept coming.

By 0410 hours, the firefight had slowed to a shot-here-and-there from the Syrians. Alec's decision needed to come soon. Turning to Noureddine, he said with resolve, "I must get my men out of here and on to Tadmur."

"We must move far away from our present position and let the darkness work for us. Heading directly for Tadmur could prove the wrong move," said Noureddine.

Alec knew that Noureddine was right, but he also knew that he had two wounded men. Although Nutworth and Pratt had relatively minor wounds, they needed some time to heal. If only they could make Tadmur soon. Nevertheless, Pratt had to keep communications alive.

"How far from Tadmur are we?" Alec asked Noureddine.

Within earshot, Pratt preempted Noureddine and said that he had hoped he could get a GPS satellite link connection in a few minutes. Pratt was aware that out in the depths of the Ocean of Fire reliable communications were never a certainty. Alec would take what he could get, even from a wounded soldier. "Doc, we are seventeen kilometers northwest of Tadmur," Pratt said with certainty, staring at the screen of his GPS. His shoulder ached from the gunshot, but Mackay had worked his medical magic, and he knew he could continue to Tadmur.

Gunfire from the Syrians had now slowed to an occasional round sent in the direction of OS9, but never hitting its mark. Alec ordered Mackay, Alvarado, and Bobby to move in and recon the situation. He and Riemann would follow.

In just seconds, Alec and Riemann moved on horseback from the left to a point within thirty meters of the five remaining Syrians. They appeared to be wandering aimlessly in the dark, in a state of confusion. Riemann performed a sentry takeout on the closest one with surgical precision. The soldier was quickly cut from carotid artery to carotid artery, spurting blood more than ten meters out. As his blood hit the warm sand, it formed puddles of plum-red liquid that quickly percolated beneath the surface. Another soldier charged Alec, firing his AK-74, a later Chinese variant of the AK-47. Alec swiftly jumped behind a small hill to take cover. With one shot from his P-92 9mm Beretta semiautomatic, lead found its way into the heart of the enemy. Riemann's flash grenade cleared the area of any remaining threats.

The dawn slowly began to illuminate the now blooded desert sand. Carnage carpeted the area. Military vehicles were reduced to nothing more than metal carcasses and bodies would soon become putrefying carrion. The Khamsin's powerful wind would soon erase all evidence of the nighttime mêlée. Alec knew that time was not on his side. Mackay gave last minute medical attention to Pratt and Nutworth, making sure that the dressings covering their wounds were tight enough to not loosen or fall off during their ride.

Alec paused before he mounted his horse and seemed to be in a state of contemplation.

"Boss, let's go," said Bobby.

Alec didn't move. There were those times, those trying times when he needed to focus deeply on something, and in order for him to do that he would focus on nothing for a moment. It would clear his mind. It was his way of meditating.

The others just watched.

Alec rubbed his eyes, looked in the direction of Tadmur, and then urged his horse to move out, saying nothing.

"What the hell was that?" Bobby whispered to Mackay.

Nutworth and Pratt slowly mounted their weary steeds.

Noureddine took a gulp of tea blended with honey and lemon from his goat sack and looked at Alec.

Tadmur was in front of them.

CHAPTER SEVENTEEN

The ostentatious Rolls-Royce Phantom arrived at the Royal Albert Hall just seconds behind the queen's very own glass-roofed Bentley limousine. Raissi had orchestrated it that way. It made for a grand entrance and an opportunity for him to upstage the Queen of England. It wasn't the first time.

The Royal Albert Hall, planned by Queen Victoria's prince consort Albert and completed in 1871 as his memorial, was to host an evening concert honoring Dr. Raymond Raissi's continuing philanthropy in the United Kingdom. The unique oval concert hall, located on Kensington Gore, adjacent to Hyde Park, had been the chosen venue for some of the musical arts most historic moments.

At precisely 7:45 P.M., seated next to the queen in the Royal Box were Raissi and several members of the royal family. Their gratitude for his philanthropy expressed itself by inviting him to myriad formal occasions at Buckingham Palace, Sandringham Castle, Highgrove, and even the British monarchy's ancestral home of Balmoral Castle in the famed Scottish Highlands.

Raissi, as many of the London tattler rags had often reported, was an interloper amongst British royalty. He knew he had bought his way in by virtue of his endless donations to hospitals, civic organizations, building funds, and restoration projects throughout the whole of Great Britain from the Isle of Man to the Scottish Orkney Islands, but it never bothered him.

Raissi was a man with a plan.

The Vienna Philharmonic's rendition of Dvorak's *Slavonic Dances* was one of Raissi's most beloved pieces of classical music. The Royal Box was always the most inviting place to listen to such pleasing sounds that made love to the ears.

Just after an intermission that involved small talk with the queen and her consort in a private room off the main foyer, Raissi returned to his seat next to her. He always felt comfortable around royalty, but he was not sure if they felt the same. Once again, as a devout follower of the Prophet, it did not matter to him, for in his mind he truly disdained monarchies, even Arab monarchies.

Suddenly, Baker approached the entrance to the box and asked the usher to get Raissi's attention. Raissi turned and motioned to Baker to enter.

Baker walked quietly but dilberately, his steely-blue eyes constantly darting back-and-forth, as he updated his surroundings in his computer-like mind, to Raissi and leaned down over his right shoulder. He then whispered, "Sir, a U.S. State Department officer is waiting in the foyer office for you."

Raissi, perturbed by the disturbance, excused himself from the Royal Box and walked briskly out of the hall and into the foyer. There, an agent escorted him to an oak-paneled office. It had the tang of centuries-old pipe smoke; DSS Agent Joe Muldoon was waiting.

The DSS agent instantly reached out his hand and said, "Dr. Raissi, sorry to disturb you like this, but I have been directed to take you to the U.S. Embassy immediately."

"What's this all about," Raissi demanded, his voice raising several decibels.

"I'm not at liberty to say Dr. Raissi, just that we must get to the embassy now," an overweight but seemingly fit DSS Agent Muldoon responded.

Raissi found the request outlandish. "I'm sitting with the Queen of England enjoying a symphony that honors me tonight, and you're telling me that I have to leave now," he said coldly, his dark eyes steeled on the agent.

"Dr. Raissi, please allow me to take you to the embassy where you will be briefed."

"Briefed," he fired back.

"Yes, briefed. I can't say more than that, sir." He politely motioned with his hand for Raissi to exit the room with him.

"Very well then, permit me," Raissi said with mocking emphasis, "to extend my apologies to the queen and her family before you drag me out of here."

"Fine, sir."

Moments later Raissi expressed his apologies to the queen and was escorted from the Royal Albert Hall. He was then immediately ushered into a bulletproof black Chevrolet Suburban for the short ride to the United States Chancery on posh Grosvenor Square between Hyde Park and North Audley Street.

The embassy itself was a pre-cast concrete, Portland stone and gold-anodized aluminum structure that featured a bronze American eagle whose wingspan reached fifteen meters. Several of its floors were underground in order to abide by the building standards that governed Grosvenor Square's architectural requirements.

Raissi had been to the U.S. Embassy on several occasions for affairs that included the presentation of the most recent ambassador to the Court of St. James as well as the welcoming of U.S. corporate executives to London. This time was not what he had expected.

Raissi entered through the large embassy doors as two Marines stood sentry, flanked by a special detail of two Diplomatic Security Service agents ordered by the Secretary of State.

The chargé d'affaires immediately greeted a perturbed Raissi and led him into the ambassador's office.

The DSS, formed in 1985, was the federal law enforcement arm of the United States Department of State. Mandated to protect foreign dignitaries on United States soil as well as certain U.S. Ambassadors overseas, the service was important to international diplomatic relations.

The ambassador's office was overwhelming to most, for it was large by any measure. The attention to every detail, from the elaborate wainscoting and Persian carpets to the ancient Chinese vases framing the large stone fireplace and an oil painting of the President of the United States, was to be expected.

"Please have a seat, Dr. Raissi," the chargé d'affaires said in a very measured tone. "Ambassador Timberton has already left Heathrow and should arrive any minute now. He just returned from Washington, sir."

"You mean he is not here?" Raissi questioned with an edge in his voice. He did not like waiting for anyone or anything, not even friends or ambassadors.

Ambassador Timberton suddenly charged in from an adjoining office. He was a little out of sorts. "Excuse me Ray, so sorry for inconveniencing you," he said apologetically, as he reached to shake hands.

Raissi looked at the ambassador and offered his hand. "Good to see you, Bill. How was Washington?" his asked, his sarcastic tone evident.

"You know, Ray. Too much political correctness for me," he answered.

"So, can you tell me what this is all about?" Raissi demanded to know.

"Ray, please, sit down," the ambassador requested, as he gestured to a very large sitting area with an ornately carved mahogany coffee table as its centerpiece. A towering Waterford crystal flower vase full of long-stemmed red roses provided the final accent.

The two walked over with the ambassador's left hand placed lightly on Raissi's right shoulder. They sat across from each other in identical French black oak chairs upholstered in deep burgundy leather and finished with fine brass, metalwork studs. The moonlight streaming through the tinted windows illuminated the exquisitely woven carpet.

"Can I offer you a drink, Ray?"

"Mineral water," Raissi requested.

"Perrier, fine?"

"I'd prefer Pellegrino, thank-you. You can never trust the French, not even their water," he said with a smile.

The ambassador pressed a button on a console set on a side table. An aide entered. "Charles, two Pellegrinos please."

"Yes, sir," said Charles. "Ice, sir?"

The ambassador looked at Raissi, who nodded a yes. "Yes, Charles, that'll be fine."

Raissi looked around at the ambassador's office, not because the décor impressed him, but because he appreciated the manifold ways power and influence manifested itself. He knew that the United States Ambassador was an extension of the most powerful man on the planet, the president.

"Ray," the ambassador said, looking directly at him, as he proceeded to explain, "two days ago in Nottingham a terrorist cell was infiltrated by MI5. Agents killed two Yemenis who had fired on them. It's been kept from the press until tomorrow. We and the Brits needed time to assess the situation." The ambassador paused to take a sip of his Pellegrino. Raissi appeared to show an indifference to the initial news. "Ray, what the Brits found in the bedroom of the apartment in Nottingham they had penetrated was a series of newspaper clippings and photographs taped on a wall. One of those photographs was of you at a public function we think was back during Christmas time. Several of the newspaper clippings featured stories on you as well."

Interrupting, Raissi asked, "So you think what about this?"

Hesitating a beat, the ambassador continued, "We've had one of the best FBI profilers from our London office take a look at it, and it is his professional opinion that you are a target of these terrorists, two of whom MI5 still believes are somewhere in the Nottingham area. They hope that several leads they have received in the past few days will lead to their capture. And not soon enough, I assure you, Ray."

MI5 or Military Intelligence section 5, the United Kingdom's national security service version of the FBI, was established in 1909 to fight German espionage efforts. Since then, it had morphed into a highly secretive organization whose charge was to thwart terrorism, espionage, and subversion *in-country*.

Raissi feigned concern about the ambassador's remarks. He reached for another drink of Pellegrino and then asked, "Bill, so what am I supposed to do? I certainly won't go into hiding or even look over my shoulder. And I certainly won't let MI5 run my life."

Raissi stood up and extended his hand to the ambassador, "I must go, Bill. Thank-you for the briefing, and I'll be careful," he said somewhat flippantly.

"Ray, MI5 and our FBI will keep in touch with me, and should you need any assistance while you are in London, just call. You have my direct number?" the ambassador queried, as he shook Raissi's hand. "My driver will return you to the Royal Albert. By the way, give my regards to your charming wife and the children. Ray," he paused, "so sorry for any inconvenience."

Raissi paused for a moment as an image of his wife appeared before his mind, only to be replaced by an image of his waiting dinner guest. "I will, Bill. And my best to Natalija and the boys."

Two DSS agents met Raissi as he left the ambassador's office and escorted him to the awaiting Suburban. He returned to the Royal Albert Hall, courtesy of the U.S. Chancery.

CHAPTER EIGHTEEN

TADMUR, SYRIA

The sun continued its journey up from behind the horizon in the east as OS9 licked its wounds. Nutworth and Pratt were able to keep moving, although both would agree that they could have used a day of rest.

The sands of the central Syrian Desert gave no warning of what was to come.

The team moved deliberately toward Tadmur, ever vigilant of potential threats from other Syrian military units.

It was early morning when the first hint of the famous Roman ruins of Palmyra came into view. The magnificent remains of a once grand city, built in the third century A.D., still had a presence that took one's breath away. Nestled in a valley of light colored, seemingly undisturbed ancient sand, the simple obelisks and heavily colonnaded buildings appeared to be saying *tread lightly*. Just one look at the ruins and one was instantly transported back to the ancient Roman Empire. Palmyra was renowned throughout the Middle East as an example of what antiquity had to offer archaeologists and tourists alike.

Noureddine was careful not to have the team enter the ancient city located about ten kilometers from Tadmur, for it was imperative to keep out of sight of the morning tourist buses stampeding into the area.

The horses were tired and the heat of Syria was relentless. Dry mouths and little food made the journey evermore taxing. The team hungered for a warm meal and a place to clean up.

As the kilometers passed under the hooves of their horses, Alec was struggling with the thought of what went down last night. Having so easily, and without a scintilla of remorse, taken the lives of Syrian soldiers now caused him great angst. After all, he was a trained physician whose first charge was to *do no harm*, yet the struggle had always been with him. From one of his early kills years before in Cairo as a medical student employed by the CIA to last night's bloodletting, Alec was never comfortable with the act of killing, yet he knew it was inevitable if freedom was to survive.

By 0800 hours, Tadmur had come into view. From a distance, OS9 espied cars, trucks, and buses pregnant with eager tourists traveling to and from the city by way of the main highway.

"Doctor," said Noureddine. "Our contact awaits us at the Palmyra Cham Palace. It is best that we leave the rest of your men just outside the city until we meet with him."

Alec was not prepared to leave his men in the middle of the Syrian Desert. "No," Alec fired back emphatically, "the team stays together."

Noureddine just shook his head, buried his heels into his horse's flanks, and urged him on.

As Alec and his team came upon the city from the northeast, feelings of years ago came rushing back as a cataract of emotions hit him from every angle. This was where he and Sahar had vowed their love for each other and their desire never to be apart, and now he knew the painful truth, that she had died trying to save him.

After quartering their horses on a rise flush with date trees and a freshwater spring, the faux Bedouins approached the Palmyra Cham Palace, an oasis with several hundred rooms and suites, eateries, and the local "Oasis" discotheque.

Alec decided to acquiesce to Noureddine's request and left Mackay and Tishermann behind.

"Pratt, link us up with CENTCOM-Baghdad," Alec ordered. "They need to know our location. Ask about the resupply."

"Yes, sir. Will do," Pratt answered.

Alec thought it best to enter the hotel by way of the parking lot entrance, thus hoping not to attract too much attention. The men moved quickly, finding an out-of-the way area in the bar just off the pool. Despite being dressed as Bedouins, they felt out of place.

"*Shlonak*, how are you?" Noureddine asked the bartender. "Hot tea for my men," he said with a smile.

Bobby shot him a look of incredulity. "Tea?"

Alec scanned the area, trying to find anything that he could hitch his memory to…nothing. The hotel had changed from a small, neglected hideaway for young lovers and weary travelers on the cheap, to a five star hotel for sheiks, well-heeled entrepreneurs, and raconteurs. *Where was Sahar?* he asked himself. He had imagined she would be right beside him. *What a ridiculous notion*, he thought.

"Doctor, I'll return in a few minutes." Noureddine rubbed his weathered beard and cautioned, "Please stay here."

"I could get used to this," Bobby remarked, as he ogled two bikini clad young maidens sashaying across the pool deck in front of them. "Look like Swedes to me," he said to Alvarado quietly, all the while glancing over his shoulder to make sure the Syrian military or local police were not loitering about.

"Yeah, Swedes," Alvarado said *sotto voce,* as he sat up in his chair, hoping to get a better view.

The others were too busy replenishing lost liquids. Nutworth admitted to feeling better, but still favored his wound hidden beneath his dirty garments.

The unrelenting heat never waned and the Khamsin continued to blow sand as if it were a category five tornado bifurcating the American Midwest. No amount of training ever seemed to be sufficient when one had to move about in such a feral environment. Even Alec, native to the Levant, did not remember the desert heat to be so unforgiving.

A teenage waiter, dressed in ancient Roman garb for the benefit of tourists, arrived with a large pot of steaming tea and cups for everyone. Bobby just sat back and looked as the waiter filled the cups with steaming tea. "Where the hell's the Bud? I want beer, not colored water."

"Bobby, just drink the goddamn tea and when we get back stateside, I'll buy you a friggin' keg of Bud," Alvarado said flatly. The strain of the heat and the mission were beginning to show again, but he knew now was not the time to feel anything of a personal nature.

About fifteen minutes later Noureddine came walking back across the narrow area that separated the main bar from the restaurant. A man whom Alec immediately recognized as Barslan followed him. Alec left his bar stool and walked over to Noureddine.

A very thick, well-groomed gray and white beard protected the hearty Fadi Barslan's aging face. His deep blue eyes and skin, sandblasted by the desert winds, indicated that he was no one's fool. Fadi Barslan held his head high. He exuded confidence.

At nearly two meters, Barslan was taller than most Semites. He was three years into his fifth decade. Dressed in modern clothing one could purchase in any resort hotel, he looked more like a tourist than the chief Mossad agent in Syria.

Extending his hand to Alec, "*Ihtiramat*, my respects. Dr. Alexander Hakimian," he said, gesturing with his four-fingered right hand.

"*Marhaba*, hello, Mr. Barslan," Alec continued.

"No, no, please Fadi. My name is Fadi. Remember?" he insisted.

"Fadi, okay. Fadi it is," Alec smiled. "In Amman it was Avi, the Sidewinder."

Alec first met Fadi when he was assigned to a two-man assassination team and Fadi was the CIA's primary contact in Tel Aviv during a mission to neutralize a KBG field officer in 1988. Alec had never imagined a time when he and Fadi's paths would ever again cross after he left the CIA, but he knew that the intelligence community was very small.

"We need to discuss where they are," Alec said, alluding to WMD. "I need answers to questions that have haunted the U.S. for years now. I need to prove their existence, and I need to know what you know about the Khamsin's latest movements." Alec finished without moving his eyes from an attentive Fadi.

The teenage waiter approached Alec and Fadi again. Fadi waived him off with a *tsk-tsking* sound from his mouth full of yellow teeth; a mouth framed by permanently chapped lips. "Funny to me, you know. A young Muslim boy serves liquor to you in a bar today, yet he will kill you tomorrow," Fadi said in a conversational manner. Looking at Alec, he continued, "Yes, I'm a Jew, and I've read the Holy Qur'an. One must know what fanatical misinterpretations drive those who want us dead," he said with detectable concern and resolve.

Alec and Noureddine just listened as Fadi was obviously used to an audience. Alec knew Fadi to be a moral man. He also knew it was Fadi who had warned Francis in 1982 of the impending attacks on both the Sabra and Chatila Palestinian refugee camps in Lebanon.

"So, you've come to hear where they are?" Fadi asked rhetorically.

His accent carried a friendly flavor. "Well," he continued, as he peered through the blinds that shielded him from the hot piercing sun fighting to light the dark, tranquil bar area. "The Syrian government's very own is connected to the Khamsin. This man is Syrian himself," he added, as he showed small pictures of the man to Alec and Noureddine. He's a mole. He is the defense minister's son, Mahmoud Taher. He is the liaison between Hamas, Hezbollah, and the Iranian government and he takes his marching orders from the Ankabut. He is a venomous snake. A snake whose head I will cut-off," he added with a residue of unalloyed disgust. "*Il doit être mort*, he should be dead."

"*Votre Francais est passable*, I see your French is still passable," Alec said with a Cheshire-like grin.

Fadi smiled and scratched his curly hair.

Continuing, Alec added, "So Hezbollah and Hamas received WMD from Iraq? When?" Alec asked.

"Yes, from Saddam before the war with America," he answered. "The weapons were of three types…nuclear, biological, and chemical. Hezbollah received large quantities of Saddam's VX for their use in World War II vintage Soviet Katyusha rockets. As you know, they have an effective range of some 20 kilometers, if not more. They can be fired from almost any place within that distance, usually via mobile ZiS-6 truck launchers. The Khamsin delivered chemical agents to Hamas operatives in the Gaza Strip via Amman, Jordan. Then they were transported through the Egyptian border town of Sharm El-Sheikh, where the Palestinians have dug underground tunnels that stretch all the way to the Gaza Strip refugee camp of Rafah." Fadi paused, drawing a deep breath. "The Matar Tadmur al-Askari military airport has been the staging area for flights to the Iranian nuclear facilities at Natanz, Ardakan, and Isfahan since before the war. Thousands of centrifuges, nuclear fuel, and other nuclear apparatuses are now in Iran. We believe that the Khamsin is responsible for the dissemination of this aspect of the NBCs as well. My sources tell me that the Ankabut himself is personally involved in these transactions," Fadi added, trying to draw another deep breath after such a long monologue.

"Is there any proof beyond what you've seen or heard?" Alec asked pragmatically.

"Certainly. Photos, radioactive readings, my word. I know that

Francis told you my word is good. And that intelligence sharing put me personally at odds with our most popular tank general," Fadi said fiercely.

"I do trust you and have for a long time, but we must be certain that what you saw are indeed weapons. Don't jazz the intel. Is it the 'high-grade' nuclear material? I'm not interested in the low grade nuclear waste that the Syrians buried out here years ago."

"It's the heavy stuff, the 'high-grade' as you say," Fadi answered.

"The photos must demonstrate the same. I must see it for myself. We have only one opportunity to get this right, Fadi. There are forces who wish us to fail," Alec responded with *gravitas*.

In the past, various countries had bribed the Syrian government to accept the dumping of nuclear waste in the Palmyran Desert but that was not what OS9 was after. They had to make sure they found evidence of nuclear weapons or equipment necessary to produce them. Nothing less would do.

"There is still a great deal of activity at Matar Tadmur al-Askari," Fadi fired back.

"Fadi, we need to recon the airport and the area surrounding it."

"Very good. Noureddine will act as your guide. He knows the area."

1200 hours came and went.

The sun stayed high above the burning sands.

CHAPTER NINETEEN

JABAL AL HUSSEIN, JORDAN

The encrypted Iridium 9505A satellite phone transmission to Jabal Al Hussein, Jordan, was clear. The caller did not identify himself by name, yet the recipient, Fuad al-Akhdar, stood at attention the moment he heard the digitally altered voice. The voice, tinged with a palpable Middle Eastern accent, had an intonation that could mesmerize even the most resistant of individuals.

"*Salamat*, hello," the caller said softly.

"*Keef halak*, how are you doing, sir?" al-Akhdar responded. He then added, "I've been waiting for your call."

"Yes, indeed," the caller said.

Then a harsh sound of static interference was heard, then nothing. The caller was visibly upset, but knew he must wait for the re-connection. The falling of heavy rain outside the caller's window made listening even more difficult. He ordered it shut.

"Yes, Fuad. I hear you now," said the caller. "Anyway, we will have our day. *Allahu Akbar*, God is great."

"*Allahu Akbar*," Fuad responded instantly.

"Have you spoken to Hassim?" he asked flatly.

"Yes. He and Abdul Majid are on their way from Damascus with the material and should arrive tomorrow night. The trip is slow. They must be alert. The Jordanians watch the border, but I have fixed the Daraa crossing. There will be no problem," Fuad said with certainty.

"Very good, Fuad," said the caller.

"The Jordanians can be bought," Fuad said with glee. "They are friends of the United States, but they will do what we want when pushed hard. They know the consequences," Fuad added.

"Yes, Fuad. We cannot fail. We must not fail," the caller said. "The Khamsin is not to be trifled with. Its enemies will be drowned in its violent whirlwind of hot sand and curdled blood, for Allah wills it," the caller continued with messianic fervor. "In time my work in America will come to an end, and then we will all do Allah's work together, for the Qur'an tells us it will be so," he added.

"*Allahu Akbar, Allahu Akbar,*" Fuad retorted.

CHAPTER TWENTY

LONDON, ENGLAND

Raissi returned to the Royal Albert Hall as the concert was moments from ending. The queen had left earlier due to a flare up of her much-publicized gastrointestinal problem. That was the official word. Nevertheless, the gossip columnists' useless banter often speculated as to what her real ailment was. Some hinted that she had terminal ovarian cancer; others believed that it was a sexually transmitted disease contracted while on an extended trip to visit former British colonies on the Dark Continent a decade before. Her paramour was said to be a cousin thrice removed.

Baker was waiting inside the hall's entrance for his master. As Raissi approached, flanked by two DSS agents, finely attired concert attendees were making their way out through the great doors. Many were commenting on the performance while still others chatted about what they had in mind for dinner at any one of London's many posh eateries. Baker's powerful torso forced its way toward Raissi as the agents physically cordoned off a small area surrounding their charge.

"Dr. Raissi, this way," Baker said, as he gestured in the direction of an alternate exit.

The agents moved ahead of Baker and Raissi and led them to the exit. They opened the doors and waited until Raissi and Baker moved down the steps toward the bulletproof Rolls-Royce Phantom. Baker held an oversized Burberry plaid umbrella over Raissi as a heavy mist wet the concrete steps. With his other hand, he reached into his pocket and pulled out the car keys. Pushing a button on the ignition key, he remotely started the car's engine. Since Kamil was ill, it was the only way to be sure that while the car was left unattended, no one had the opportunity to attach an explosive device to it.

Raissi did have his enemies, the knowledge of which never escaped his thoughts.

"Thank-you, gentlemen. I'll be fine from here," Raissi said to the DSS agents, dismissing them with a sneering smile.

The agents nodded in the affirmative and disappeared back into the hall.

The misting turned again to gentle rain as the custom Roller made its way along the Kensington Gore that quickly became Kensington Road and headed for Lowndes Square. On the left, Hyde Park appeared quite foreboding in the damp darkness. Raissi fell back into the deep, lush Connolly leather seat and took a long, deep breath. With the divider window half raised, he made a call to his residence. A woman's voice, one that could bring any man to his knees under certain circumstances, greeted him. "My dear, I'll be there very soon," he said, with a raised sense of affection. "The concert was a true bore."

"I had fun today. The man at Bulgari was very nice. He showed me a ring, a one-of-a-kind diamond ring. You'll just love it. Lots of D-Flawless carats," she giggled softly. "And I'm hungrrry," she purred.

"What, no Cartier?" he said casually, although he was imminently aware that D-Flawless carats amounted to a large sum of money. *She was very high maintenance*, he thought as he smiled to himself.

"No, just Bulgari this time, dear," she said with the smile of an ingénue rising across her softly defined face set-off by high cheekbones.

Moments later the car turned onto Lowndes Street. Several hundred meters ahead appeared the Raissi residence. The multi-storied, chalk-white Georgian mansion seemed to shimmer in London's gently falling rain. Baker negotiated the Phantom Rolls through the gates and under the two-story high porte-cochere. Raissi could see lights on in the master bedroom. A wide smile came over his face again.

Baker quickly jumped out of his seat and raced around the car to open Raissi's door. At the same time, the butler opened the west side entrance of the palatial residence and greeted Raissi, "Good evening, sir. May I take your coat?"

"Yes, Harris," he said.

Raissi walked through the side entrance and handed Harris the butler his black-cashmere overcoat and then immediately took the elevator to the second-floor master suite. Relaxing his Asprey tie, he opened the right side of the double-doors and entered a lavishly appointed sleeping area that made the presidential suite at any five star hotel seem like Motel 6 in comparison. It even contained its own completely outfitted fitness area that was accessed through an adjoining set of pocket doors. The bed, with a view of the manicured gardens and the front yard fountain, was not a king size. No, that was far too small for a man such as Dr. Raymond Raissi. It was Raissi size…more like a small soccer pitch covered in Pratesi linens.

The bathing area was equally up to Raissi's standard of excess. The bathtub itself could easily occupy half a dozen individuals with adult beverages. Instead, its marbled surfaces and the room's lavish interior were complimented by the presence of just one ravishingly stunning woman.

"*Habibti*, my darling. You are supposed to be ready for dinner," Raissi said, as he stared at the woman's long, wet, deep ebony hair. Her eyes, shaded by perfectly groomed eyebrows and long, curled eyelashes, shown like those of an Abyssinian cat. A flawless skin recently colored by a trip to the Bahamas enhanced a delicately defined bone structure. Her smile radiated with the purity of perfectly positioned porcelain white teeth. Her hands were long and slender and finished off by a well-applied manicure.

Purring her words like Eartha Kitt, she said slowly, "Come in, it's warm."

"I'd love to, but I thought you were hungry," he responded.

"I am hungrrry," she purred again, while undressing him with her eyes.

"Perhaps later, but I'm feeling like Italian. Let's go, we've reservations at Toto's."

She raised herself from the bubbly water to reveal a body so comely that Raissi was having second thoughts. "Please hand me the towel," she requested coyly.

Raissi did so and then walked over to the large Venetian mirror embellished with gold-leaf filigree. He gave himself a once over look, rubbed his full face and wished he were ten kilos lighter. The woman's reflection in the mirror served to remind him that in his own world of deceit, destruction, and dollars, there was one thing that was indescribably more enticing, if only for a brief moment.

"Come here," she commanded from her dressing area.

The in-house phone rang. "Doctor, the kitchen would like to know if you will be dining in tonight?" came the question from Harris.

"No, we'll be leaving for dinner. Please have Baker ready the Bugatti," he ordered. Turning to her, "*Habibti*, you look as bright and stunning as the stars that hang over the Arabian Sea on a warm summer evening."

"My love, you are my world," she said, as she delicately slipped into a ruby-red, Valentino strapless dress, sans any hint of under garments. Her bountiful breasts, still somewhat damp, needed no assistance. Charles Jourdain high heels raised her several centimeters above an already statuesque height. "Please," she said, as she picked up the gold Bulgari, double-hinged jewelry box from atop the cherry wood end table and handed it to him. "Go ahead, open it."

Raissi hesitated for a moment as he visually undressed her yet again. At times she was tempting to the point of absolute distraction, when he would feel out of control, and he did not like being out of control. Raissi slowly opened the box to reveal a sparkling twelve-carat, D-flawless diamond dinner ring flagged by ten Brazilian emeralds. "It's superb," he said. "My money has such wonderful taste," he added laughingly. "It's big enough to ice skate on, isn't it?"

Smiling, she extended her left hand and spread her long, slender fingers, teasingly wiggling her ring finger. Raissi slid the rock on, smiled, and kissed the fullness of her left breast. "Dear, please get me the lynx from the other closet. The long one. It's so *au courant*. Don't you think?"

Raissi walked over to the specially refrigerated closet designed for fur coats. There was his wife's white-mink windbreaker, an ermine trench coat, and a full-length Russian lynx coat hanging from the rack. *Tonight*, he thought, *was a night for the ultimate statement of wealth and conspicuous consumption*. He slowly pulled the floor-length Russian lynx coat off its hanger and carried it over to her. Placing it gently across her lean shoulders, he kissed her regal neck. Turning around, she answered with a long, passionate embrace. He buried his hand between her legs until she moaned and then said with a sly grin, "Let us go have something to eat, shall we?"

The rain had stopped. Baker had the Bugatti Veyron EB 16.4 Fbg par Hermes idling at the south entrance. With a stratospheric price tag of £1,500,000, the rarity of this automobile was beyond words. It was handmade from a secret recipe that included carbon fiber, scarce alloys, and the finest leathers and woods. It had supplanted the McLaren F1 as the world's fastest production car the moment it debuted. The Veyron even required a special key to activate its special *top speed* mode. It was unquestionably an F-35 stealth fighter jet on four wheels, and Raissi liked that.

Not only rare, but also mechanically complex and temperamental, the Veyron was capable of true speeds in excess of 470 kilometers per hour.

With the two secured in their five-point belted racing seats, Raissi gently prompted the car to roll down the long driveway and out on to the pavement. Like kicking a thoroughbred in its hindquarters, he stomped on the drilled aluminum throttle without hesitation. The Veyron rocketed from a dead stop to over 185 kph as Knightsbridge Road to Sloane Street came and went in a flash. Like a wisp of smoke, it was there, then gone…roaring passed block after block with its two occupants shielded from the din of night by the symphonic sound of its engine, effortlessly pounding out 1,001 unbridled horsepower from a W16 configured 8.0 liter, sixteen cylinder all-alloy engine cooled by ten radiators. Lights went on in many a residence, as the car made its presence known. It was thunderous in sight and sound, just like Raissi.

The destination was Walton Street, home to some of the city's better-known restaurants. Toto's, the choice for the evening, was fine Italian cuisine, as the film director Fellini would have envisioned it. The patrons were many of London's most influential. From opera and moviegoers to beautiful women and rich male prowlers of the night, Toto's appealed to glitterati of all stripes.

The Veyron snarled and hissed as it rolled to an abrupt "look-at-me" stop before the front door. Valets scurried from every corner to assist. They knew that Raissi was a big tipper. Rumor had it that one night after dinner with friends, he ordered his chauffeur to tip the valet, who had not even parked his limousine, one thousand pounds sterling. Raissi's tipping had become legendary throughout the whole of London.

The Veyron's interior, drenched in special Hermes leathers and titanium accents, was accessed by a sculpted door handle blended elegantly into the exquisitely shaped aluminum door panel. If da Vinci were alive, he would have most assuredly designed the Veyron.

A smartly dressed valet helped the woman pour herself out onto the walkway as Raissi followed. Looking nervously at Raissi, the parking attendant did not know what to do next. His expression indicated that he had never driven one of these magnificent examples of the zenith of automotive art and science.

"Leave it where it is," Raissi commanded.

The parking attendant looked blankly at Raissi, then nodded in the affirmative.

Raissi's private corner table on the second floor overlooked the main room. From his vantage point, he was removed from the fray, yet he could take in the energy of the animated crowd whenever he so desired.

Once seated, the maitre d' rushed over with a bottle of Tattinger's finest champagne and two Baccarat crystal long-stem, fluted glasses. "Dr. Raissi, it's been some months since we last saw you," he said in a Neapolitan laden accent, as he poured the liquid effervescence ever so slowly for two. "And madam, so nice to see you again. You look lovely tonight," he said with expected politeness.

"Yes, Bartolo. It has," Raissi said mildly.

"Your usual, sir?" he queried.

Looking at her, Raissi said to the waiter, "Bartolo, some buffalo mozzarella and Capri tomatoes for now."

"Very good, sir. Very good," Bartolo said, as he bowed in an obsequious manner, backing away slowly.

As Bartolo left, Raissi sent a smile across the table. Reaching for her soft ring hand, he said, "My dearest, be patient. Our work is coming to an end and soon we will be together forever in Allah's Seventh Heaven."

"But when? But when?" she said with great frustration in her sultry voice. "I left a time and a place many years ago that I thought was all I needed. I left a man who was everything to me. He gave me true love and hope, but he didn't believe in our fight, the fight to free our people from the chains of the West and to serve Allah, his most merciful."

"Do you have regrets about leaving him?" Raissi asked with feigned interest.

She paused for a long instant, then answered, "In truth, yes. Yes, there are times I regret that we are no longer together, and I regret misleading him. Yes, it was an exciting life, but I always knew that he wanted something quite different. I tried to show him the way. To have him be part of it. Then he left and you appeared like a Greek god riding on the wind. And now we fight together."

For a moment Raissi looked blank-faced at her. A cacophony of sounds filled the air around them. Then he said, pronouncing each word very clearly, "*Habibti Sahar*, my darling Sahar. You are why I am." He held her hand tightly and the two exchanged a longing look.

CHAPTER TWENTY-ONE

The Beverly Hills Hotel, located on Sunset Boulevard in the heart of the city's ritziest homes, was a magnet that attracted the world's most celebrated individuals, especially those in the film industry.

Tonight the hotel, painted in its trademark pink color and green-leafed motif, was to play host to three hundred select individuals invited by the Arab-American League, the Center for American Philanthropy and the Council on American-Arab Relations to celebrate the myriad years of philanthropy that was associated with Dr. Raymond Raissi.

The limousines motored up the long serpentine drive to the hotel's main entrance like honeybees returning to their hive. Each vehicle released its special passengers, one after another, as valets scurried about in a well-orchestrated ballet...they were used to such happenings and never faltered.

The lovely Leyla Hakimian and her father, the patrician Judge Robert H. Vanley, were far down the drive in their Mercedes-Benz Maybach Zeppelin, awaiting their turn. Leyla always felt uncomfortable in such an ostentatious car, but Alec was an aficionado of the automotive industry's finest offerings, and the Maybach Zeppelin filled the bill.

Mercedes-Benz resurrected the famous automobile mark in the early 2000s as a handcrafted automobile to rival anything Rolls-Royce had to offer. Its flowing lines, distinctive interior, and overall craftsmanship were what set the Maybach apart from any other Mercedes-Benz. As for Leyla, her choice was a standard production Mercedes-Benz GL 550 SUV. She thought it functional, reasonably stylish, yet not too over-the-top, and its 4-Matic all-wheel drive system was certainly a safety feature she thought made sense.

Carlton, the chauffeur, negotiated the behemoth silver-over-black Maybach cautiously through the entrance and up the long drive to the hotel's main entrance. No sooner had it stopped than a female valet, smartly dressed, reached for the limousine's rear door. Leyla was the first to exit. Stepping very slowly out of the rear seating area, her Yves Saint Laurent designed silk-jersey dress in Diana Vreeland red clung to her athletic body like a second skin. Those who could wear YSL did so because of how someone like Leyla looked in one of his haute couture creations. Everyone within eyeshot stared at her as if a princess were in their midst. Her father followed and the two entered the hotel. There, a wedding coordinator directed them to the grand ballroom.

The grand ballroom was just that, grand by all measure. The multiple sets of French double doors that led to the main room were dressed in large bouquets of imported, fresh flowers intertwined with variegated strands of fine silk taffeta. Each table had as its centerpiece a tall vase of Lalique crystal stuffed with an abundance of fresh flowers. The hand-painted dinnerware was of the Old Imari pattern by Royal Crown Derby of England. Each place setting was setoff by Cristofle of France silver flatware. The glassware featured the same country's Baccarat craftsmanship in its Massena pattern. The wood-carved chairs by Pierre Deux were covered in a fine, deep green velvet brocade fabric. They cleverly utilized the Persian foot design that made for an easier exit at a crowded table when Mother Nature called.

The manager of the grand ballroom of the swank Beverly Hills Hotel had been preparing months for the epic event. After all, Dr. Raissi was a man larger than life and expected nothing less.

A tuxedo-attired usher seated them with a view of the large, center-stage podium.

Security was evident at every turn and rightly so, for Dr. Raissi was about to be feted by a room stuffed chock-a-block with very important dignitaries from corporate chiefs and maverick entrepreneurs to ambassadors and Washington insiders.

The grand ballroom, now filled to capacity, pensively awaited the guest of honor. Adiah Raissi, Dr. Raissi's wife of thirty-two years, arrived stylishly late with her two teenage children in tow. Her son

Tabar escorted her, dressed in a Balenciaga original, and his sister Ghotta to the center table. Also seated at the table were Governor Bellevue of the Great State of California and his wife; the President of the Arab-American League and his wife; as well as the Presidents of both the Center for American Philanthropy and the Council on American-Islamic Relations. Finally, seated at an adjoining table were Raissi's brother Raja and his companion, a young harpy from Lyon, France.

The price of admission to the gala was fifty thousand dollars per table, with the monies benefiting charities that Raissi supported.

The room waited. The air was thick with anticipation, but still no Dr. Raissi. His wife Adiah began to show worry, if not embarrassment, on her heavily made up face that had seen better times, for her husband was supposed to have landed at Los Angeles International Airport hours ago. The last she had heard from him, he was somewhere over the Great Divide a little after 5 P.M. Pacific Standard Time. He told her that he would meet her at the hotel around 7:30 P.M. It was now 8:10 P.M. Everyone, especially his wife, had anticipated his long overdue arrival.

Out of the corner of her eye, Adiah espied her personal secretary approaching the table, cell phone in hand and a wearing a bright smile on her face. Adiah took the cell phone from her and placed it slowly to her diamond-studded ear. "Hello," she said reflexively.

"Adiah, my sweet one. I beg your forgiveness for not being there yet. It won't be much longer. We had a headwind all the way from the Rockies. Long flight. See you very soon. Please give my apologies to everyone," he added, as melodic sounds from the forty-one piece orchestra simmered in the background. A medley of music from Bach to the Beatles seemed to please everyone.

"Please hurry, Ray. Everyone's here," she said with urgency in her voice, all the while nervously staring at the governor across the table. "Hurry," she exhorted.

"Governor, Ray will arrive shortly," Adiah said in her best socialite voice as she handed her assistant the cell phone. The governor smiled politely then continued with his conversation.

Adiah Raissi, now somewhat nervous, but not wanting to show it, because she was the perfect hostess, rose from her chair and walked deliberately over to Leyla's table and said, "Leyla. Judge." They all exchanged air kisses and then she continued, "Are you enjoying yourselves? So where is Alec?" Before Leyla could reply, she added. "I simply adore him. He's so brilliant."

"He was called to Antwerp for an emergency surgery. He thought he'd be back in time, but there were complications."

"Well, perhaps we can have the two of you over soon. In the meantime, I hope you will find the evening enjoyable, and I know Ray will be pleased to see you when he arrives." Touching Leyla gently on the shoulder, she smiled graciously to the two of them then returned to her table.

Attentive black-tie waiters looked to Mrs. Raissi for their cue to begin serving the first course after an earlier feast of hors d'oeuvres.

Suddenly, the orchestra began playing an introduction inspired by *Hail to the Chief.* The lights dimmed and then Dr. Raymond Raissi appeared from a side door flanked by two smartly dressed security guards. Waving with both hands held high, spotlights illuminating his tuxedoed presence, he smiled like a politician as he worked the room, pressing the flesh and exchanging cordialities along the way to his table.

Everyone stood to pay homage to one of the world's great givers.

Raissi was a past master of the well-orchestrated grand entrance and what better way to gin-up the anticipation than to be fashionably late, he often said, when asked about his legendary tardiness.

Finally, he took his seat next to his wife after kissing his children and giving apologies to those seated at his table.

"Ray," the governor said jokingly, "we thought you were going to phone it in."

"Never," Raissi said, "Never. Good to see you, governor. And Miriam, you look ravishing."

The room settled down as waiters began serving the first course, an Italian radicchio drenched in Beluga caviar flown in from Russia only hours before. Tattinger champagne continued to flow like the water at Niagara Falls into long-stemmed flutes that stood a foot high.

"Adiah my dear, forgive my tardiness," Raissi whispered into her ear, taking a deep smell of her Joy perfume. She shot him a look that feigned forgiveness.

Turning in Leyla's direction, Raissi walked over and kissed her on the cheek then shook Judge Vanley's hand. "Judge, Leyla my dear. So good to see you. And where's my dear friend Alec?"

"He sends his regards, but he was called away to Antwerp on an emergency surgery," answered Leyla, disappointment evident in her soft voice.

Somewhat crestfallen, Raissi remarked, "I see. The man's a genius. He's a lifesaver. We all know that. But I'm glad to see the both of you here tonight." Motioning to a passing waiter, Raissi ordered, "Please keep my guests' glasses full." The waiter immediately topped off everyone's champagne flute at the table. "Anyway, we'll talk later." Excusing himself, he said, "Please enjoy."

By nine o'clock many of those in attendance were already intoxicated by the food and drink that never stopped. Very much like Raissi himself, it was excessive, but it served his purpose.

Shortly after dessert and cappuccinos, the master of ceremonies for the night took to the stage. He was none other than Governor Bellevue himself. Standing before the ornate podium brought in just for the event, he began his remarks. "Ray, we are all very excited that you took time out from your very busy schedule to be with us tonight," he said with a big grin on his face as he looked to Raissi. "Ladies and gentlemen, as you all know, Dr. Raissi's a man of epic proportions. Why only hours ago he was in London being honored by the Queen of England for his generosity, and now he's here with us to celebrate his equally monumental contributions to American society. Dr. Raymond Raissi is a true rags-to-riches success story that should serve to be a paradigm for all American youth." Pausing for applause, he continued, as Raissi sat next to his wife, hand-in-hand. "Tonight ladies and gentlemen, you've been invited to celebrate the accomplishments of Dr. Raissi, whether through his own largesse or by his skill as a motivator of others, his work can been seen from coast to coast and around the world. Hospitals, schools, medical research facilities, and libraries have all benefited from Dr. Raissi's belief in giving back to the country that welcomed him with open arms. And now I'd like to introduce to you the President of the Arab-American League, Mr. Amir Muhaad."

Amir Muhaad, though slight in physical stature, walked to the podium with an air of confidence, for he too had made his way as an orphaned teenager from Syria to America twenty-five years ago. After a short stint working for a Boston-based high-tech firm he ended up in New Haven, Connecticut, where he founded a private computer chip company that he sold three years ago to the Intel Corporation for nearly two billion dollars. Since that time, he has devoted his efforts to the preservation of Arab culture in America.

With an oversized smile on his face, Muhaad held the mike somewhat nervously and began his paean to Raissi. "Ray, my dear friend. You are why I am here tonight," he declared, pointing to Raissi. "Not only have you made it possible for me to realize the dream of owning a company, but you have made it possible for many others to live their dreams as well. What makes you so extraordinary is that you've never asked for anything in return. Tonight we are all here to honor you for your philanthropic work. Praise long overdue. Ray, you are the philanthropist's philanthropist, and it is my esteem honor, on behalf of the Arab-American League, the Center for American Philanthropy and the Council on American-Arab Relations I present you with this plaque," Muhaad said proudly, as he raised a very large mahogany wood plaque with an engraved brass plate affixed to it.

Raissi simply tried his best to act modest, but inside he believed that he deserved every complimentary word said about him.

The orchestra began to play as Muhaad summoned Raissi to the podium. "Ray, come up here my dear friend," he said, as he motioned to Raissi.

Everyone stood and applauded loudly as Raissi walked to the podium. His wife and children joined him by his side.

"Ray," Muhaad said, as he handed Raissi the plaque. Raissi held the plaque as Muhaad read aloud the inscription, "Presented to Dr. Raymond Raissi for his endless philanthropic work over the years for the betterment of American society."

Raissi began his remarks by saying, "I am humbled by this award." Loud applause and cheering interrupted his words. Signaling for everyone to take their seats, he continued, "Everyone here tonight is my dear friend, for you are all members of that very select fraternity of givers. Givers that make a difference."

Applause broke his cadence again for a brief moment. Stepping away from the microphone for a beat, he feigned humility and then continued, "The world of today is in a turmoil the likes of which we have never experienced before. Nations are capable of eliminating other nations with the simple push of a button. Religions battle religions. Terrorists seek to uproot the very foundation of our civilization, and the poor are getting poorer."

After pausing for applause that again interrupted his words, he added with great conviction, "We are here tonight not to honor me, but to honor the act of giving. I am simply an example of that act. So I once again say that I am humbled by your presence here tonight, and that you seek to recognize me for the very same thing that you do," Raissi said, with contrived emotion seeming to supplant his cocky style.

The crowd stood and applauded raucously. Raissi raised the plaque over his head as if he had just won the "the men's singles title" at Wimbledon. He shook Muhaad's hand and then reached out for his wife and children to follow him back to his table. He gave the plaque to his son, who began reading the inscription to himself as he sat down.

"Well, I'd say that was well-deserved," Judge Vanley remarked aloud, as he reached for his champagne flute and quickly drained it.

"Yes, father. Dr. Raissi certainly is something," Leyla responded sarcastically. She never hid her dislike for Dr. Raissi or his swarthy and shifty brother.

Unexpectedly, Leyla's BlackBerry cell phone rang. She hastily fished in her small, red Bottega Veneta evening purse for it as the ringing attracted everyone's attention at the table. Finally, her small hand found it. Reading the screen, she recognized the caller's number as coming from her home. She wondered what Maria, the family's nighttime maid, who was caring for her daughter Karina, wanted at this hour. Always somewhat nervous when her daughter was out of her sight for even a moment, she said, while plugging her other ear with the palm of her hand in an effort to hear over the music from the orchestra, "Yes, Maria. What is it? Is Karina okay?" There was a long pause as she waited for Maria's response, then very impatiently she repeated, "Is Karina okay?"

Judge Vanley looked on with concern creasing his well-tanned face as the others at the table had already returned to their conversations and seemed not to pay attention.

A frightened Maria, manacled with plastic handcuffs, was forced to answer by the man who was holding the phone to her ear. With tears slowly running down her cheeks, and a cut lip caused by her resistance to him, she started to speak. In a state of true terror, she pushed out the words, "Miss Leyla. Karina is not well."

"What do you mean, not well?" Leyla asked instantly. "What's wrong, Maria? Tell me!"

There was no answer. The phone conversation had ended the moment the other man in the room clicked "the end" call button. Leyla instantly pressed the call-back button on her cell phone. It rang and rang. She waited for Maria to pick up. Thoughts started to flood her already frantic mind. She called back again. No reply. She tried the second number, the same. No reply.

Turning immediately to her father, who could read the undiluted concern on her face, he said, "What is it my dear? Is Karina all right?"

As her father reached to comfort her, she responded frantically, almost coughing her words out. "I must go. Something's wrong with Karina. I lost the connection with Maria, and now she doesn't answer."

"Then I'll go with you," her father insisted.

"No. Please stay. Enjoy the evening. You have a lot of friends here tonight that you haven't seen in some time, and I don't want to take you away from them."

"Nonsense, my dear."

As Judge Vanley started to stand up to go with her, Leyla put her hand on his shoulder and said insistently, "Father, I'm okay. It's probably nothing. When I get home I'll call you. So please stay."

"If you insist."

"I insist, and I'll leave the car for you," she added, as she picked up her purse and turned to march out of the ballroom.

"No, you take it. I can get a ride home," he said.

"It'll be faster for me if I take a cab. They're right outside the door." Glancing at her platinum Cartier pavé Panther wristwatch, she continued, "Carlton won't be back from his dinner with the car for at least an hour."

Believing she was probably right, he said, "Okay, but don't forget to call me the moment you arrive home."

She was already five steps away and did not answer.

CHAPTER TWENTY-TWO

One wave from Leyla's slender hand and a blue Beverly Hills Cab Company car pulled up. A valet quickly opened the door for her and before the door closed, she said, "Stone Canyon, and quickly please."

The cabbie knew of Stone Canyon Road. It was one of Bel-Air's most desirable residential streets.

"What address, miss?" he asked, as he eyed his fare. He could not help but ogle at Leyla. *She was stop-and-stare beautiful,* he thought. *She's poured into that bitchin' dress. Wow!*

"Miss, what address on Stone Canyon?" the cabbie asked again, as he rolled down the hotel's driveway and forced his cab into traffic, causing a commuter bus to swerve into the next lane. In moments, the cab had already passed the intersection at Sunset Boulevard and Whittier Drive and was rocketing west toward Bel-Air.

Her mind was swirling. She tried to call Maria again. Still no answer. And, as had happened many times before, whether in a crisis or a perceived crisis, she could not count on Alec. She could not call her husband who was supposed to protect her and their daughter from harm. *Why was he not with her?* she asked herself again. She had not spoken to him in weeks. The excuse government officials gave was that he was incommunicado and would contact her when he could. *He was out in the field as it were,* they told her. She had thought, *damn her life right now. She just wanted comfort. She needed the warmth of her husband's embrace. She wanted to be safe with her daughter.* Now her thoughts grew worse. Her mind was chaotic, but she knew she needed to focus, so she drew a few deep breaths and tried to relax for the short ride home.

As the taxicab approached Stone Canyon Road, the night air was warm and a gentle breeze wafted across the treetops. Under any other circumstance one would think it a harbinger of good things to come, but not this night, not for Leyla Hakimian, and she knew it.

The battered blue Beverly Hills cab took a hard ninety-degree right turn onto Stone Canyon. The overarching trees hid the moonlight above, while the green fairways of the Bel-Air Country Club passed on her left. The cabbie asked casually, "Are we close, miss?"

"Sir," she said in a tentative voice, "it's just up past Bellagio Road on the right. I'll show you, as we get closer. You'll see a light-colored stone guardhouse at the main entrance." Leyla knew that the gateman was off for the evening, something about a sick daughter. So the cabbie would have to stop at the entrance and she would have to get out and punch in the gate code to enter the grounds because the remote keypad was in the Maybach.

The cabbie drove slowly across the angled intersection of Bellagio and Stone Canyon, all the while peering out the window, looking for the gatehouse.

"There, turn right just past the ivy-covered stone wall."

It was too late. The cab rolled past the entrance. The cabbie immediately put the car into reverse and backed up. The cab triggered the security lighting that illuminated the guardhouse and driveway.

"Excuse me, but I'll have to get out and key-in the code," she said.

"All right, miss." The cabbie started to jump out and run around to the right rear door to let her out.

"Never mind. I'll open the door myself," Leyla said to the cabbie, who then returned to the driver's seat and reached for his ringing cell phone.

After keying-in the seven-digit alphanumeric code, she returned to the cab and said, "All right, let's go."

The cabbie mumbled something in Farsi into the cell phone then closed its clamshell. Putting the cab into gear, he looked somewhat overwhelmed by the endless cobblestone driveway that came into view behind the tall wrought iron gates setoff by two large golden "Hs." The driveway seemed to go on forever. Leyla looked at the cabbie's face in the rearview mirror and pointed ahead. Finally, they reached the summit of the long driveway. The thirty-one thousand square foot Italianate-style residence loomed large over the manicured grounds.

Unbeknownst to Leyla, as she exited the cab, she was being watched. The two heavily armed intruders were waiting. After paying the cabbie, she hurriedly half-ran to the front door and nervously punched in the access code.

As she entered the foyer, her worst suspicion was confirmed. The large, Fourteenth Century Ming vase, always on the center table, was now in a thousand pieces on the marble floor. Her first thought, *why hadn't the alarm gone off?* Then she screamed out, "Maria. Karina. Where are you?" Suddenly she heard a noise in the kitchen. She ran frantically, her high heels clattering on the cherry wood floor as she crossed through the den. When she reached the large kitchen area, she saw Maria seated next to the fireplace, a look of horror on her deeply lined face. "What's happening, Maria?" Maria's look to the side told her that someone else was in the room. One more step and she saw a tall, swarthy looking, bearded man with a semiautomatic handgun in his right hand and a cell phone in the other. He pointed the handgun straight at her as a second man, short, but heavily muscled, grabbed her from behind and forced her into a kitchen chair.

Without prelude, the bearded man with dark, recessed eyes stated in a well-spoken English tinged with a deep Middle Eastern edge, "You will come with us now. And please, for your daughter's sake, do not give us any problems."

Leyla, stunned for a moment, quickly gathered her thoughts and blurted out, "Where's my daughter? Where's Karina?" As she started to get up and search for Karina, she was forced back into her chair. She reflexively tried to fight off the second man, but to no avail.

With the gun still pointed at her, the two intruders spoke to each other in what she knew to be Arabic. Then the shorter man left the room.

Leyla, wanting to scratch out the eyes of her captor, glanced at a quivering Maria, her bloodied lip now severely swollen. She then turned to her captor and demanded, "Where's my daughter, you animal? What have you done with her? I demand to see her."

In an arrogant tone, the bearded man replied, "You are not in a position to demand anything. Do what I say Mrs. Hakimian and your daughter will not be hurt."

"Who are you? What do you want? Where's my daughter?"

"Who I am is not your business. As for what I want, I want you. And here is your daughter," he added, his eyes indicating that she was entering the kitchen.

Just then Leyla turned in her chair and saw her young daughter in the arms of the other man. "Give her to me," she ordered.

"Mommy, mommy," Karina yelled out, trying to free herself from the man's grip.

Leyla rushed to the two and pulled her daughter out of the man's arms. She tried to comfort her confused and crying young child, holding her close and hoping that it was all a terrible dream.

"Now, Mrs. Hakimian, here's what's expected of you."

Holding tightly to her daughter, she screamed, "What do you mean, what's expected of me?"

"You heard me. You will leave with us, and your daughter will not be harmed. I know that you have a safe room. We have deactivated all levels of your security system, as you might have suspected. I must admit that it's a nice system, well-designed to stop amateurs. When we leave, your daughter and this woman," he said, pointing his semiautomatic handgun at Maria, "will be placed in the safe-room. In time, someone will come looking for them and they will be found."

Leyla, consoling her daughter as best she could under the circumstance, looked directly at her captors and said loudly, "I'm not going to leave my daughter."

"You have no options, Mrs. Hakimian. Now say good-bye to your daughter."

"I will not leave her," she fired back again, now in a purple rage.

Levelly, with no vocal variation, he responded, "Yes. Yes, you will Mrs. Hakimian, or your daughter —"

"My daughter what?" she interrupted.

With his impatience growing, he said, "If you do not leave with us, then I will personally take great pleasure in first killing your daughter, then the woman, then you." Looking to the other man, he ordered him to take the maid and child to the safe room on the second floor.

As the man reached for Karina, Leyla resisted with all her might. "No. No. You can't take her," she pleaded.

Suddenly, a gunshot rang out that caused Leyla and Maria to shutter and Karina to become instantly inconsolable. Everyone looked at the bearded man with the gun. "That's enough. I told you. One more outburst and people start dying. Now let her go and she will be okay with the woman once we leave."

Minutes later the second man returned to the kitchen. There was a brief exchange of words between the two men. The shorter man then left the kitchen and exited out the back door.

"All right, let's go Mrs. Hakimian. Do I need to cuff you?"

She shook her head slowly, hoping to stall for time. "Can I at least change my clothes?"

"I said, let's go. That means, let's go. And besides," eyeing her lasciviously, "the red dress wears well on you. It's your color."

The two left by the back door and entered the black Audi A8L.

The blacked-out windows concealed the terrified, kidnapped victim inside.

CHAPTER TWENTY-THREE

PALMYRA, SYRIA

By 1940 hours OS9 had cleaned up, eaten, and prepared for the reconnoitering of the super top-secret, heavily guarded Syrian military airport. Palmyra at night presented a most compelling view of the sky above. Constellations seemed to jump out from deep space. The wind blew gently from the southeast as the day's heat slowly turned to a tolerable warmth that felt somewhat rehabilitating at times.

Everyone knew that the wind the Arabs called the mighty Khamsin was not far behind. Its power would scour their faces, causing them great pain, and turn fallow vehicles, homes, and even weapons.

Before the briefing, Josiah joined Mackay and Tishermann at the bivouac site. It was there that Josiah contacted CENTCOM-Baghdad to confirm the resupply of matériel delivered via a blind-man black drone from Baghdad. The resupply would include munitions, jet propulsion skis known as *SandJets*, and the latest version of the experimental *exoskeleton* body suit. It was also where Mackay would keep Tishermann in his sights as Alec had ordered.

"Gentlemen, tonight just four of us are headed for the military airport. Mackay, Nutworth, Riemann, Tishermann, and Josiah will stay behind at our bivouac and work the town with Fadi for any intel. I must tell you I anticipate new intel that points to the Khamsin. The nuclear, biological, and chemical weapons we've all heard about are out there. Fadi's seen several Khamsin and al-Qaeda operatives in town the past few weeks. And Pratt," he looked toward him, "I'll need to be able to talk to CENTCOM-Baghdad and even D.C. if necessary."

Pratt nodded in the affirmative. "Bobby, Alvarado. You two know that the area will be lousy with heavy security. Find your best vantage point and stand ready."

"Roger that, Doc," Bobby responded, grinning from ear to ear. He and Alvarado put on their combat, lightweight *exoskeleton* body suits required for the mission. The futuristic battle gear was made of a unique nanotechnology fabric that could be either as soft as velvet or turn as hard as armor when responding to a perceived threat such as a projectile or explosive device. Alec and Pratt did the same, then covered the suits with their loose-fitting abayes or tunics. They were good to go.

Those who wore the extraterrestrial-looking exoskeleton human performance augmentation (EHPA) suit were called "tin men." Powered by special fuel cells for remote area recon, extended mobility, and combat, the exoskeleton body suit was unmatched battlefield technology for the soldier. It also carried a global positioning system and the capability to close small to medium wounds by applying an integrated tourniquet when necessary. A compartment in the suit fed antibiotics to the injured or infected area. These wearable machines were only available to U.S. special ops team members working in the Middle East. Each exoskeleton suit equipped soldier was worth twenty normally equipped soldiers. Even the walking speed of an exoskeleton-equipped soldier was doubled, and the surmounting of walls as high as four meters proved no problem. The shoulder, arm, hip, and leg joints were amplified by electric micro-motors that dramatically increased the soldier's performance.

"Gentlemen, make sure that your communications are all functioning properly. We'll need night vision capabilities and full GPS," ordered Alec.

Matar Tadmur al-Askari Airport, about ten klicks outside of town, was well hidden from the untrained eye. It was home to the country's most clandestine operations. Several U.S. administrations had been convinced of it. NSA/NRO satellite recon confirmed it. Images showed that the Iraqi WMD ended up in Syria for dispersal. It was OS9's charge to verify the satellite images and to transmit such information back to CENTCOM-Baghdad, USCENTCOM, the National Security Council, and to the president himself.

Alec and his team, comprised of Pratt, Bobby, and Alvarado, headed for the airport with Noureddine. Some twenty-five minutes out they sighted an old Soviet made Mig-25 fighter jet that strafed the area for a few passes then turned to the secret airport.

The team proceeded without delay. The horses were more cooperative under the blanket of night, for the previous day's temperature had reached a stifling 40° Celsius. The nighttime sky was as clear as could be, making star gazing a means of passing the time.

Pratt was doing his best to make a connection with CENTCOM-Baghdad while his white Arabian padded across the tepid sands northeast of Palmyra. Alec, seemingly rapt in thought, guided the team toward its destination. Noureddine sat mute while Bobby, cradling his modified sniper rifle in the crease of his left arm, told bad jokes within earshot of Alvarado. Alvarado did his best to humor him. It was the only way to get Bobby to stop.

"Doc," Pratt said loudly, "I've got a sat connection. CENTCOM-Baghdad is aware of our position."

"Excellent," responded Alec. "Can you stay linked?" asked Alec.

Pratt returned a response, "As of now sir, yes, but the Syrians probably have some sort of dynamic diffusers that could make it more difficult. They may even be able to pick up our signal and zero-in on us. Remember, several years ago the French sold them highly advanced, military-grade communication systems, so who knows what they know, but I'll do my best."

Alec did not comment.

Gradually the airport came into view over the rise, and so did its many security towers that periodically broke the line of continuous fencing that encircled the airport, outbuildings, and hangars. The main gate was heavily fortified. The control tower, some five stories high, revealed at least six individuals inside. Former Soviet jet transports were taking off and landing at a steady rate. Large hangars, drenched in intense floodlights, were the centers of a great deal of activity. Long flatbed trucks laden with immense, bulky crates marked with the universal symbol for radioactive substances drove out of hangars at what seemed like an intricately choreographed dance. Bobby and Alvarado took a position behind a rise one hundred meters away and simply observed the ingress and egress of transport vehicles.

Alec was now in position. He raised his 16 megapixel digital Nikon SLR camera and began snapping high-resolution photos with a long-range lens and sending them via military Wi-Fi to Pratt's notebook computer. After about fifteen minutes, it was decided that Bobby and Alvarado would take a position nearer Alec, Pratt, and Noureddine.

All of a sudden, two Syrian guards appeared from behind a small, weather-beaten and poorly lit guardhouse just outside the gated entrance. They began walking slowly in the direction of the team. Alvarado spotted the target and quickly gave Bobby the coordinates, drift rate, and wind speed.

Bobby waited.

Noureddine moved back to watch OS9's six o'clock. Lying behind a small sand hill, Alec waited until the guards had passed. Alec then quickly shed his Bedouin garb that had hidden his exoskeleton suit, replete with thumbnail-sized computer chips that tracked everything from the body's vital statistics to responding to a medical trauma to the wearer within nanoseconds. Next, like a hungry tiger that had stealthily stalked his prey, Alec leaped on the first guard, taking him down and severing his carotid artery with his Ka-bar combat knife, all at the same time. Blood shot out and into Alec's eyes. The blood's viscosity blinded him momentarily. Then, before the second guard could raise his firearm or his voice, Alec wiped the blood from his eyes with one hand, and with the other plunged the Ka-Bar combat knife into the guard's sternum. He turned it, hearing the bone crunch, as he watched the guard hit the sand. The guard writhed in pain for a few seconds then was dead, blood leaking from his chest.

Killing the two men…it had to be done. Alec never took pleasure in ending a life, but it was necessary. From the time of the American Revolution to the winning of two world wars and the fighting of the war on terror, killing the enemy was the fundamental component of the *freedom equation* for America.

"Sir, we lost our link with CENTCOM-Baghdad," Pratt said to Alec.

"What? Did we send the photos?" Alec responded.

"I believe so, sir," Pratt answered. "Yes, I believe they received all of them before the link was lost, but no confirmation as of yet."

"CENTCOM-Baghdad needs them. Link up again and resend," Alec demanded with urgency in his voice.

"I'll try, sir," Pratt replied, "but I think that we are being jammed by the Syrians. The geo-sat has passed. We'll have to wait until the next one."

"Any way around it?" Alec asked, as he continued to snap digital shots of the movement of freight onto heavy transport aircraft.

"I'll give it another try. Maybe I can hook onto a private satellite through the backdoor and redirect. It'll be iffy though," said Pratt with concern.

Alec was grateful for the *exosuit*. It was working as designed, and sometimes he knew that was not the case with experimental technology. "Bobby, Alvarado. It's time to move in. Keep an eye on the lateral areas of the entrance. I need to go in," he ended.

Noureddine expressed immediate concern over Alec's decision. "Sir, too dangerous. If you are caught it is…," he said with a dire look.

"I understand, but I need to see the actual devices outside of the crates. I need proof that no one can deny. I need in-your-face photos. Big ass, clear photos of all the shit," Alec said confidently.

"But —" Noureddine was interrupted.

"There's no other way *ya sahibi*, my good friend," Alec said, with his dark eyes wide open, a furrowed brow now showing his consternation.

"But how will you get in?" asked Noureddine.

Alec did not have a plan, but that was not about to stop him. It never had before. Suddenly, a six-axle flatbed truck drove up to the entrance and the driver waited to be permitted passage. A second truck approached; it was a military truck carrying provisions. Chickens and goats could he heard in the truck's rear canvassed area. It was now time to move.

Alec silently crept up to the back of the second truck as the guards, some five meters away, jabbered with the driver up ahead. With a single vertical jump he landed inside the back of the truck. The chickens' squawking made his presence undetectable to the driver up front.

Without warning, the truck lurched forward, throwing Alec off balance. Regaining his balance, he found a place to hide under sacks marked garbanzo beans.

"*Salamat, keef el ahel.* Hello, how are the parents?" the guard asked the driver.

Alec hoped that the driver's familiarity with the guard would distract him from needing to check the cargo.

"*Hamdullah, keef el ayleh*? Fine, how is the family?" the driver fired back.

"Good," he answered.

"I've got chickens, goats, beans, lots of tea, and flour in the back," the driver announced.

Alec was silent.

"Very good," the guard said, as he motioned to the gate tender to let the truck pass.

"*Leyle saideh, ya sahibi.* Good night, my good friend," the driver said, as he put the old truck into gear. It sputtered briefly, then died. Alec's heart stopped. Bobby and Alvarado watched intently.

The driver turned the key and cranked the motor over again. Nothing. The guard began to walk back over to the truck as the driver tried again. Coughing and sputtering, the beater of a 1960s Mercedes-Benz transporter came to life. The driver put it into gear again and delicately feathered the throttle. He moved slowly through the gate and into the airport facility, as the guard hurriedly waved him on.

The powerful sounds of a 1970s Boeing 707 four-engine jet aircraft taking off put the chickens and goats into a state of agitation. Alec felt the truck stop. He then quickly pulled a portion of the canvas covering aside and peeked out. The driver was talking to a soldier outside a building with a sign that indicated in Arabic that it was the office of the airport's commander. Alec needed to get into one of the airport hangars and verify that the centrifuges and other materials did exist and that they were headed for Iran.

Bobby and Alvarado kept in communication with Alec via their exosuits' integrated communications. Noureddine watched intently as a military half-track with two soldiers roared across the desert about a klick southeast of the airport. Pratt attempted to sync-up again with CENTCOM-Baghdad. While the truck driver was still conversing with the soldier who shared his cigarettes, Alec made his move.

Slipping furtively out of the truck's back compartment, Alec quickly moved across a small dirt driveway and ended up behind the closest hangar. He could hear voices in Arabic saying that they were glad the cargo was leaving. They knew it was dangerous. One spoke of two soldiers who just last week had taken ill with undisclosed illnesses. They became weak, had vomited for days, and had blisters on their hands, legs, and forearms. Alec knew the signs…radiation poisoning.

Alec found a door ajar at the back end of the large steel-and-tin-sided hangar. Once inside, he saw them. There were thousands upon thousands of centrifuges, mostly crated and ready for shipment. Next to them were heavy, lead containers marked with the radioactive symbol. Click, click, click. He then clicked off at least two dozen more high-resolution shots of the contents inside the hangar. Verification was now just a couple of computer keystrokes away. "Pratt, I've got the real proof. The centrifuges and everything else. You should have them now," Alec said.

"Roger that, sir."

The photos would finally put to rest the issues surrounding the nexus between Iraq, Iran, and the war on terror. Despite the two countries' religious and historical differences, when it came to the war against the West, they were united by the Khamsin and the cause of Islamic fundamentalism.

Alec now had what he came for. Backing out of the door, he heard voices in a nearby office. Moving closer, the voices became more audible. With his ear next to a window that was ajar, he could hear the two men clearly, one an obvious military officer with the rank of colonel marking his epaulets, and the other, a well-dressed civilian man in his late thirties. The civilian, speaking with a stutter, was telling the colonel that the Khamsin always honored its promises and as soon as the last shipment left for Iran, he would receive the final payment.

Alec instantly snapped a couple of photos of the two men. As he did, the civilian happened to look in his direction. Alec instantly dropped from view, but it was too late. The civilian turned to the colonel and the two rushed outside. The colonel called for his guards to find the intruder and kill him. Alec had already moved to a covered place behind a storage shed.

The civilian abruptly left in a dusty, black Mercedes-Benz S63 AMG, while the colonel sounded the alarm signifying that an intruder was present. Alec quickly snapped a shot of the vehicle's rear license plate.

"Sir," came out of Alec's earpiece. "Get out of there now! Guards are coming from the far end of the airfield toward you. Get out of the gate before they close it." Pratt could see on his laptop the movements of bodies throughout the area.

As Alec adjusted his earpiece to hear Pratt more clearly, he felt a prod-like object in the back of his neck. It was the touch of cold steel. "*Quf, ma titharrak*. Halt, don't move." Alec turned around and was face-to-face with a young Syrian military guard holding a Chinese variant of the AK-47 called the AK-74. *He couldn't have been more than eighteen years old*, Alec told himself.

The soldier grabbed Alec by the arm and ordered him out from behind the storage shed and toward an open area in front of the commander's station. Alec knew that he could not let that happen.

"*Mat ouakhizni ya rayess*. Excuse me boss," Alec said facetiously, hoping to calm the guard long enough to take control of the situation. He suddenly snatched the automatic weapon out of the guard's hand with the speed of a prizefighter and knocked him out with the butt of the weapon. Instantly, he drew his Ka-Bar combat knife from the leg strap on his exosuit and reached down to plunge its surgically sharp blade into the young man's brain stem at the base of the neck, but hesitated. Instead, he pushed the knife's blade just far enough to draw a trickle of blood. Thinking a beat, he then knocked him out with a pressure point move.

Getting out of the airport would prove far more difficult than getting in, Alec realized. Several dozen soldiers continued to frantically search about as their commander barked orders to capture the intruder. Alec had the advantage of moving in the dark with his night-vision capabilities.

He moved to the corner of the hangar nearest the gate and crouched down, waiting. Two long-bed transporters rolled up to the exit and Alec seized the moment. He rolled under the closest one. The exoskeleton suit helped him hang on to the sub-frame by applying additional grip to his hands and legs.

It was not more than fifteen seconds before the transporter rolled passed the gate and headed for the main highway leading out of the area and toward Palmyra. Speaking into his lip mike, Alec warned, "Bobby, Alvarado, I'm under the truck that is leaving now."

As the driver shifted gears from low to second, Alec dropped down onto the road below and rolled off the blacktop and into a large cluster of dry brush. At the moment he hit the pavement, the exosuit filled with a cushioning air that absorbed the direct impact.

Picking himself up, Alec quickly made his way to Pratt several hundred meters southeast. "Sir, are you all right?" Pratt asked with concern.

Shaking himself off, he said, "Yeah, I'm all right." He then handed Pratt the backup sixty-four gigabyte flash memory card with additional shots of the nuclear components, materials brought from Iraq before the U.S. invasion, and the license plate of the Mercedes-Benz.

Pratt took the memory card, and inserted it in his Dell military model notebook computer and tried again to link up with CENTCOM-Baghdad. He was still hoping that the transfer via satellite of the earlier photos from Alec's camera had worked. But he had yet to receive confirmation, so he decided that redundancy was called for, just to be sure.

Alec looked on with great anticipation, for he knew that the photos were vital to proving the nuclear aspect of the WMD premise, particularly the last photos of countless centrifuges and nuclear material leaving for Iran.

A few beeps and screen flashes on Pratt's laptop resulted in a link up. Pratt executed a few keystrokes and nearly one hundred high-resolution digital photos were uploaded for analysis. Moments later CENTCOM-Baghdad confirmed receipt of the photos.

In just minutes, analysts at USCENTCOM and the NSA were able to identify the man leaving the airport in the Mercedes-Benz as the Syrian defense minister Mustapha Taher's son Mahmoud. Mahmoud Taher was indeed the Khamsin's man in Syria, and he took his marching orders directly from the Ankabut. It was also known that he was the instrument of communication between Hamas, Hezbollah, and the Iranian and Syrian governments.

Now well passed 0500 hours, it was time to meet up with the rest of OS9 in Palmyra. Alec called in Bobby and Alvarado and with Pratt and Noureddine the five men headed back across the desert sands, the very same sands that had been tread upon by the mighty Romans millennia before.

Chapter Twenty-Four

BAGHDAD, IRAQ

In the midst of a strong wind, Baghdad was struggling to awaken for another day of uncertainty while off in the distance the crackle of machine gun reports added to the tension of the day. The sun would soon be in full cry, and every denizen of the primeval city would once again be humbled by the crippling power of its heat.

The Khamsin lay in wait, ready to ambush unsuspecting citizens with a wind so ferocious that many fought to breathe when it was at its angriest.

"General Meade, please," pleaded a sleepy Seddons in her CENTCOM-Baghdad quarters.

General Meade's aide-de-camp, Lt. Marshall Tibbits, answered the phone saying that the general was still asleep.

Phone still in hand, Seddons looked out the window of her quarters at a small contingent of U.S. Marines, whose credo was "No better friend, No worse enemy." She took a deep breath and then, in an insistent voice, said, "This is Mica Seddons. Lieutenant Tibbits, please awaken the general. It's extremely urgent."

"One moment, I'll inquire, Miss Seddons," he said. The wait seemed forever, then, "Miss Seddons, the general will be with you shortly in the command ops center," he stated categorically.

"Thank-you, lieutenant," Seddons said, and clicked the phone.

Seddons rifled through picture after picture received from OS9. The findings were astonishing to be sure. Vindication was at hand for those who always knew the truth. And soon the naysayers would face a well-deserved public dressing down.

At 0520 hours, Seddons opened the large steel door leading to the COC and found a somewhat cranky General Meade examining the latest intel reports from a firefight that had just taken place between U.S. and Iraqi regulars against a rogue unit of insurgents in Takrit. Takrit still managed to maintain its reputation as one of the last holdouts for Saddam sympathizers and a point of the Sunni Triangle, but since the "surge," their influence had been severely limited.

"General Meade," Seddons said apologetically, as she walked toward her desk topped with piles of papers. "We just heard from OS9." General Meade was brought to attention as Seddons continued. "Dr. Hakimian was successful in finding evidence of WMD." She was pleased.

"Specifics please," General Meade said, cold and precise, as he looked over his reading glasses at Seddons.

"Of course, general. Of course," she replied rather acquiescently. "OS9 sent back undeniable proof of thousands of centrifuges being flown out of Syria to Iran. Here," she said, as she handed the general a large, high-resolution color photo of one of the hangars at Matar Tadmur al-Askari, the secret Tadmur Military Airport in Syria. "You can see here that nuclear centrifuges are being loaded on aircraft. And the U.N. just sits there and lets Iran violate their resolutions without any recourse. General, what more proof do they need?"

General Meade began to relax, as he held the photo in his large, scarred hands. "Miss Seddons, this is good. This is very good." He continued to persue the photos, then asked, "Do we have contact now with OS9?"

"Yes and no," she said seriously, waiting for his response.

"What the hell does that mean, Miss Seddons?" the general barked.

"Well, General Meade, it has been very difficult as of late to keep in communication, and we don't know why. We sent the resupply drone to the coordinates near Palmyra specified by OS9. Then we received these photos and this report, but nothing else. We are trying to re-link now," Seddons said with urgency.

The general carefully perused the report for vital details. They indicated that Mahmoud Taher, the son of Syrian Defense Minister

Mustapha Taher, had spoken to the commandant at Matar Tadmur al-Askari.

Looking at the general, Seddons said, "Dr. Hakimian heard Taher talking to the commandant. He indicated that the final payment for the shipments to Teheran would be forthcoming. We know it was Taher because Alec said that the man spoke with an intermittent stutter. General, Taher speaks with an intermittent stutter. There's no doubt it was Taher that Alec saw at Matar Tadmur al-Askari."

Thinking for a moment, he said, "Miss Seddons, OS9 must not engage anyone at the airport. My hands are tied on this one. The suits in D.C., want to deal with the situation through the diplomatic route involving the International Atomic Energy Administration." He added with sternness in his voice, "No war has ever been won with diplomacy, but what do I know. I'm only a general whose charge is to kill people and break things. At least that's what many people think we do in the military." He paused a beat, then continued, "Tell OS9 that they must apprehend Taher outside of the airport. So no diplomatic disaster, please."

"General Meade," Seddons remarked, "our embassy in Damascus will confer with Dr. Hakimian and OS9 when they arrive. Our CIA operative Fulbright Collins will meet them. He has already arranged for OS9's transportation to the embassy once they reach the outskirts of the city."

"Good," the general said, then scratched his forehead as he walked out of the situation room and back to his quarters for a little more shuteye.

CHAPTER TWENTY-FIVE

PALMYRA, SYRIA

Alec, Pratt, Noureddine, Bobby, and Alvarado had returned to Palmyra by morning. There, Fadi and the others had much to discuss with them.

"Fadi," Alec said, as he looked around the pool area of the hotel, "Taher's son was at the airport. He's the money man that's orchestrated the movement of the IR2 class centrifuges to Iran. I'm convinced that he's the link to the Khamsin. Mustapha Taher has always been a suspect and now his son is."

"Doctor, Taher will be in Damascus. His home is there and so is his snake of a father," Fadi said with heat in his voice. "I'll slit his throat," he added, as he motioned with his hand across his throat. "Bastard," he added, then mumbled something unintelligible in Hebrew.

The men cleaned up; took in some body fuel; then headed out with Alec to where Mackay, Josiah, and Tishermann were stationed with the remaining horses and supplies.

Fadi followed them out to the meeting point. Noureddine stayed back, knowing that in less than a day he had to be back at his post on the northeastern border of Syria at Abu Kamal or risk having his cover exposed. He would say his good-byes later.

The day was as it always was…hot and getting hotter.

By late morning, OS9 had accomplished the necessary rest and refit, and it was decided that the sooner the team left for Damascus the better, despite being physically spent by the hundreds of miles traveled and the tortuous heat.

As Alec sighted the encampment under the palm trees, he could not help but realize that what was about to happen in Damascus could be a turning point in OS9's efforts to track down the Ankabut and the Khamsin. He knew that the discovery of WMD would not be sufficient to satisfy the dedicated detractors, but it would go a long way in helping Americans find a reason to continue the support of the worldwide "war on terror." When the Ankabut was found, and Alec knew *he* would be, it will have all been worth the sacrifice; and he dreamed of avenging his friend's death with his own hands.

Bobby and Riemann were the first to test out the jet-powered SandJets that came in the resupply. Originally designed for special ops units working in northern climes, the skis were modified to glide effortlessly across desert sands. The power was drawn from a unique fuel cell that answered continuous power needs for long periods of time. The propulsion unit on each ski looked very much like a small jet engine, even down to the micro-turbine blades.

"Boss," Bobby yelled, as he sped across the sand waving to the men like a boy with his first bicycle.

Alec was not in a humorous mood, but he managed a slight nod of his head.

Josiah, Mackay, Tishermann, and the rest were soon gliding about as if they were in Sun Valley, Idaho, in the December snow. Alec proved the quickest study, for in just a few minutes he was moving across the sands at speeds approaching sixty kilometers per hour. At that speed, Damascus was just four hours away.

OS9 spent the next hour or so inspecting their gear, taking in more liquids and making certain that all weapons were functioning properly. Pratt worried about his communications equipment while Bobby found the need to fix a portion of the slide mechanism on his modified sniper rifle. It had been damaged when it fell from his horse on the return from the airport.

Each man adjusted his exoskeleton's cooling system. The cooling was accomplished by three kilometers of very fine polymer tubing woven into the fabric of each suit. The tubing, courtesy of NASA, carried in it a liquid similar to that used to keep an astronaut's ambient temperature at a comfortable level. The very loose fitting Bedouin garb allowed each man to conceal his weapons and exoskeleton suit from the unfriendly eye.

Turning to Fadi, "My friend, it's time that we leave," Alec said, patting him on the shoulder.

"Yes, it is indeed time," Fadi said reluctantly. "You accomplished much while you were in Palmyra. We are pleased that you found what we knew all along, and now the world will soon know. You must now find the Ankabut and cut his legs off. No, cut his heart out and feed it to the pigs," Fadi said with great feeling. "We must be free from his grip and the Khamsin must be no more," he added with conviction.

"Fadi," Alec said, "you understand what the world does not."

The two men exchanged a few words of gratitude.

Fadi stood as OS9 left their bivouac on SandJets.

It was a sight so futuristic, so surreal that it could have been the last flickering frames of a science fiction movie.

CHAPTER TWENTY-SIX

THE WHITE HOUSE, WASHINGTON. D.C.

The early morning sun sprinkled the air with brilliant light as the President of the United States and the First Lady waved gaily from the Truman Balcony of the White House to a throng of supporters, journalists, and photographers. He looked as fit as ever, having returned a few days ago from a two-day stay at Walter Reed Hospital for his yearly physical. His good medical report meant that he was still in control of the "*football.*"

For obvious reasons, the football was never more than a step or two away from the president at all times.

The suggestion of the football came about at the behest of President John F. Kennedy as a result of the Cuban Missile Crisis. Kennedy was concerned that the Soviets would launch nuclear missiles and there would be a slow U.S. response. A National Security Action Memorandum created the football.

Every military candidate of officer rank seeking to carry the football had to pass what was referred to as the "White Yankee" background check. He had to be as clean as the driven snow in every way to be accorded the top-secret job and honor of carrying the football for the president.

Carried in the form of a briefcase and chained to the wrist of the military officer responsible for its safekeeping, the football contained the SATCOM radio and handset, the nuclear launch codes dubbed the "Gold Codes," and the President's Decision Book.

It was the most important and expensive piece of luggage in the world.

In 1999, President Clinton was at a NATO meeting in the Reagan Building in Washington, D.C. At the end of the meeting, he ordered his motorcade to leave immediately for the White House. In doing so, he left behind the football and the military officer entrusted with it. The officer had to walk the half-mile back to the White House with the football chained to his wrist.

After some twenty minutes of cheers, cameras clicking, and journalists futilely asking questions that the president could neither hear or chose to ignore, he met in the Oval Office with the Secretaries of Defense and Homeland Security, as well as the Director of the NSA, to discuss today's President's Daily Brief.

The Oval Office was undoubtedly the center of the world, and on this day, those summoned by the president were three of the free world's most powerful individuals. Walter Trucker, the SecDef, was seated on one of the two opposing sofas embroidered with the Presidential Seal, as was the carpet under his feet. Homeland Secretary Harper C. Drummond and NSA Director Anthony Caccavale seated themselves quietly on the other sofa.

"Gentlemen, the president will be with you shortly," said Colleen Slaughter, the president's personal amanuensis.

The three men looked up from their conversation and smiled reverentially.

"Can I have Lisa Anne here," she said, turning to introduce a new, young staffer, "get you something to drink?"

Lisa Anne always got the same response when introduced...eyes zeroed in on her fulsome breasts, luscious-lipped smile revealing snow-white teeth, and legs that went on for days. Her perkiness was very alluring to the three middle-aged men seated in the Oval.

Giving her a long look, Director Caccavale said with a wide smile, "Thank-you, Lisa Anne. I'll have a mineral water with lime."

"I'll have the same," responded Secretary Drummond.

"Make that three," Secretary Trucker said. "It's a hot day," he added, adjusting his tie a bit as Director Caccavale stared at Lisa Anne's breasts out of the corner of his eye, all the while dreaming of what they looked like under her tight-fitting blouse.

"I'll be back shortly," young Lisa Anne said, as she backed out of the Oval Office, the three men staring somewhat furtively.

A white door, barely discernable in the curvature of the office's wall, opened. The president entered from his private office as the three men stood to greet him.

"Good to see you, Mr. President," Secretary Trucker stated politely.

"Yes, Mr. President, you look great," Director Caccavale said with his usual solicitude.

"I try, Cac. I try," the president said with a chuckle.

Secretary Drummond shook the president's hand as he said, "Mr. President, I'm pleased that you still have what it takes to play me. I miss my tennis partner."

Making a swinging motion with his right hand as if he were holding a tennis racket in it, he said, "Gentlemen, I'm still a little sore in my ass, but it could be worse. Ever try that garden hose up the ass game? It's real sexy," he said facetiously. The president then sat down behind Resolute, the gargantuan walnut and mahogany desk, a gift from Britain's Queen Victoria to the United States in 1880. He gazed out one of the many bulletproof windows at the crew of gardeners who maintained the eighteen acres of grounds that comprised the White House compound. Two twenty-something Marines stood sentinel just outside the exit to the Rose Garden. "Now, the PDB. Where are we?" he queried, as he continued to look out the window.

Director Caccavale began, "We have received word that Operation Star 9 was successful in obtaining photos of the Matar Tadmur al-Askari military airport in Syria." That got the president's immediate attention. Continuing, "Dr. Hakimian was able to see firsthand that the Iraqis, with the help of the Khamsin, had sent WMD to Syria before the invasion. He witnessed centrifuges, nuclear fuel, and other hardware being loaded into Iranian military air transports at the Matar Tadmur al-Askari military airport. He also overheard the Syrian Defense Minister's son concluding a monetary transaction for the shipments to Iran's Natanz facility."

A huge smile grew on his face. "Do we have the photos?" the president asked.

"Yes, Mr. President, we do," he answered, then handed the president a large, gray folder marked by two red stripes and a "top-secret" classification that contained the photographs. "Dr. Hakimian and his team are on their way to Damascus, where they will capture Taher and prove the link between him and the Ankabut. Intel points to Taher as the Ankabut's man in Syria."

"Remember, I want Dr. Hakimian to have whatever he and OS9 need. They have my mandate to move at their own speed," the president said, with a hint of impatience, as he scrutinized the photos. "If it weren't for the military engagement still burning hot in Afghanistan, and the fact that I'm in this office, I'd love to be there with them," the president, a former Navy SEAL, said excitedly.

Director Caccavale knew that woven within the president's words was an implied consent that OS9 had a presidential *get-out-of-jail free pass*. In effect, OS9 had carte blanche to do what they needed to do to get the mission accomplished, and if that required that people who were in the way would be eliminated, then so be it. "I understand, Mr. President. We understand," he said looking to Trucker and Drummond.

"Now, what else do we have?" the president asked.

SecDef Trucker piped up. "Mr. President, just hours ago we received word that Specialist Mick Dornan —"

Interrupting the SecDef, the president said in his commander-in-chief tone, "Yes, the Seattle Seahawks player who left to join the Army Rangers. What about him? Where is he?"

Drummond and Caccavale held their emotions in check, for they knew what SecDef Trucker was about to say. SecDef Trucker said with great reluctance, "Twenty-seven-year-old Specialist Dornan was killed in Afghanistan during a firefight with Taliban insurgents."

The president was visibly crestfallen. It was like a knife to his heart. Looking out the window again at a very rare blue rose, "Sons a bitches!" he said loudly, as he slammed his clenched fist on the wall next to him.

Waiting for the president's next word that did not come, Trucker continued, "His Ranger Regiment was ambushed near the city of Sperah, some forty-five kilometers southwest of the city of Khowst. He was the only American soldier killed in the firefight."

"Do we know who did it?" the president said in a solemn voice.

"No, sir. Not yet. But we're working on it."

"Working on it," the president said with white heat in his voice. "I want to know and know now. Dornan's the kind of hero that we need. His death cannot go unanswered. The bastards, find them. Operation Freedom for All will not fail. Not on my watch!"

The three men nodded in complete compliance. When the president spoke, they knew to listen. And when he spoke with such fervor, they knew to act, immediately.

"Gentlemen, we are finished for today," the president insisted as he rose from his chair.

"Mr. President, there's one more issue," Director Caccavale said.

"And that issue is…?" the president said, casting a strong eye on him.

"Dr. Hakimian sent a communiqué indicating that he has a strong reason to believe there is a mole in Operation Star 9."

"What do you mean a mole? Who?" the president said with an inflamed voice.

"Dr. Hakimian has for some time felt that one of his men has been communicating with jihadist sympathizers, if not Khamsin operatives."

"Has he given you any idea who it is?" the president asked.

"The CIA member. Although the agent has never before proven to be a problem, Dr. Hakimian feels that there is more to his story than meets the eye. His name is Robert Tishermann. He was a Palestinian child living in a Beirut refuge camp, who was adopted as a young boy by German missionaries during the Arab-Israeli War of 1973. Dr. Hakimian thinks that he's compromised. There were two instances in the last few weeks that have given him reason to suspect Tishermann," the director finished.

"What does he plan to do?"

"He's watching him but has made no decision as of yet."

"Keep me in the loop on this," the president insisted. He then rose from his chair, adjusted his bespoke dark-blue suit jacket and stepped toward the three men. Reaching out with his right hand, "Boys, we've got to win this one. The WMD Operation Star 9 found in Syria is a giant step, but we need more, we need to nail them all. I want the leader of the Khamsin *dead or alive*. Do I make myself clear?" Not waiting for an answer, he shook each of their hands, excused himself, and then disappeared out the same door he came in.

CHAPTER TWENTY-SEVEN

Dr. Alexander Hakimian's immediate plan was quite simple. He was to make his way to the world's oldest continually occupied city under the cloak of night by crossing a remote and foreboding desert all the while knowing that dark forces were gathering off in the distance to stop him.

Once Alec and OS9 succeeded in making Damascus, he would be briefed at the U.S. Embassy. There he would be told to kill one man, capture another, and find the biological and chemical aspects of the WMD that his president knew were still out there.

Getting used to the jet propulsion skis still took some doing for a few of the men. However, once they felt comfortable with them, the SandJets allowed OS9 to move at speeds approaching sixty kilometers per hour while wearing their Bedouin abayes that hid their exoskeleton suits and weapons.

"Whoa. Damn. This is cool, very cool," Bobby said, as he raced past Riemann and Mackay, his abaye fluttering in the wind. "This is really better than the bikes I used to race down South. I wonder how much these cost. Can I buy them at Sports Chalet?" he asked jokingly.

"Bobby," Josiah answered. "Try two hundred grand a copy. And no, you won't be able to buy them anytime soon at your local Sports Chalet or Wal-Mart."

Alec thought about the two hundred and forty kilometers southwest of Palmyra that the team had to travel to reach Damascus. From Abu Kamal to Palmyra they had the benefit of surprise, but now Alec was all too aware that OS9's presence, though not specific, was known to Syrian military intelligence. So, it was paramount to the success of the mission that they move with all due dispatch. However, the decision was made to wait until the night extinguished the light and use the darkness as protection on their journey across the sands to Damascus.

Some fifty kilometers into their journey, Riemann was the first to notice it. An undeniable humming sound caught his attention. Although the SandJets created their own irritating sounds, the humming off in the distance became ear piercing.

Riemann came to a stop, as did the others. The night was clear, the sky was filled with twinkling stars, and the temperature was unusually warm for 2040 hours. Riemann tried to zero in on the direction of the humming sound. The others did the same.

Nutworth stopped next to Pratt and nudged him. "Hey, what the hell is that?" he asked.

Pratt looked back over his shoulder and listened intently.

"What do you think, Pratt?" Alec asked.

The sound was wavering, then constant, then wavering. "Could be a small plane, sir," he answered, as he scanned the sky above.

"But way out here. Who's got a plane out here, if not the Syrian military?" Bobby chimed in.

By now, Alec was locked onto the humming sound. It was more like a buzz to him, but in the dark of night it proved more difficult to differentiate between sounds, because there was no reference to fix on. The sound kept moving in and out, in and out, as if zigzagging back and forth.

Josiah looked upward, "Where the hell's that coming from?" he asked.

Pratt tried to get a fix on it with his portable tracking device. "Now it's gone," Pratt said.

"Let's get going, boys," ordered Alec.

The team started off again, and again the sound returned. The humming, somewhere northeast of their position, was now closer. Then, over a small rise, it appeared. It was a black, pilotless aircraft commonly known as a UAV or unmanned aerial vehicle.

"What the hell," Bobby exclaimed.

Riemann was the first to see it clearly. A very small, black star was visible low on the rudder and next to it was a name…The *Nemesis.* The UAV *Nemesis* was a U.S. drone that had extraordinary capabilities. Besides being able to recon vast expanses of land for upwards of sixty continuous hours, it could also surgically strike targets with depleted uranium ordnances. "Must be from CENTCOM-Baghdad mapping our whereabouts again," Riemann said, with relief in his voice.

The pilotless drone plane, using low-observable technology, took off from somewhere in Iraq, but a military specialist stationed as far away as the United States usually flew it. It was often the case, inasmuch as information gathering by the military got its marching orders stateside.

The UAV, in all its iterations, was one of the U.S. military's most powerful tools of reconnaissance and first strike capabilities.

"Smile boys," yelled Bobby. "We're on Candid Camera," he said jokingly. He attempted to moon the camera, but his abaye and exosuit made it impossible, even for him, a self-admitted expert in the area of high school pranks.

The drone turned northeast and disappeared, leaving only a residue of the irritating sound in everyone's ears.

"Gentlemen, it's Damascus that's our goal before sunrise, so let's move," ordered Alec.

The small jet turbines spooled up and their whooshing sounds carried across the desert floor like a sea breeze rolling atop the Indian Ocean.

The hours ticked away. The men were tired but determined. Cars and trucks passed by from time to time at a distance on the main route from Palmyra to Damascus. The occasional lone traveler on his horse or donkey was a remarkable sight, even in the Syria of today.

Pratt soon had the flickering lights of Damascus in his sights. Once a vital center of trade during ancient times, ironically today it was a stronghold for the poor, terrorists, murderers, and human miscreants of the first order. Billboards scattered throughout the city advertised Hamas and Hezbollah's successes in ads designed to gain new recruits to jihad. And the country's leader, just like his father before him, deserved the contempt of the civilized world, while he appealed to the less civilized.

On the outskirts of the city, OS9 stopped behind a cluster of long-abandoned buildings to assess the situation and to do a cursory recon. The call to the Muslim presunrise prayer of *Fajr* had ended in the ancient city, as it began its struggle to come alive for another day. Travelers, merchants, and day-workers passed in and out in a frenzied manner. The open markets were abuzz with barters, beggars, and butchers. The underbelly of the city concealed the truth about Damascus. It was a city that had long since become anachronistic by any measure, so it was an open invitation to terror merchants of every stripe fueled by an interpretation of Islam unknown to the faith's more sensible believers. These barbaric hijackers of the faith desired to wreak death and destruction on all that did not abide by their tenets.

Before entering the northeastern most point of the city, OS9 disposed of their SandJets at the pre-determined point established before leaving and moved quickly to two nondescript 1980s style Toyota Land Cruisers supplied by a local asset. Alec knew that the Adnan Al-Malki District of Damascus was awash in wealth derived from sales by arms merchants and drug dealers to currency manipulators and outright thieves, not to mention those politicians who were adept at siphoning off vast amounts of cash payments from such international agencies as the United Nations and the World Bank. It was also the habitat of bottom-dwellers such as Mahmoud Taher.

Alec had actionable intelligence that Mahmoud Taher was last seen entering his home on Adnan Al-Malki Street late last night. Taher lived with his wife Abir and his brood of three children. Abir was previously the young mistress of the country's current president when he was still a medical doctor who specialized in ophthalmology. He had banished her from his inner circle of influence nearly a decade ago and married another woman whose pedigree was far more acceptable.

Taher, who had been acquainted with Abir a few years before, bumped into her one day on his way to the local *musjid*, or mosque. She now mothered his children and watched his back, for Mahmoud attracted enemies with uncanny regularity.

"Bobby, I want you, Alvarado, Riemann, and Pratt with me. Nutworth, Mackay, Tishermann, and Josiah, you get to the embassy at 2 Al Mansour Street to prep for our next move. It's not far from Taher's. And there's additional intel that's waiting for us."

"Doc, do I have to still wear this blanket," Bobby asked Alec with frustration in his voice.

"Nice try, Bobby."

"Josiah, if there's any contact with the locals, you handle it," Alec said, knowing that Josiah's fluent Arabic and darker appearance could be the difference between the men making it to the embassy or not. Everyone possessed a limited Arabic vocabulary, but to err on the side of caution, since Alec would not be there, Josiah would make himself the target of any attention that might come their way.

As Alec and his team approached the Taher residence in their beat-up Toyota Land Cruiser from Shukri al-Quatly Street, he lightly touched his Walther P99 9mm handgun. He had no doubt that it would be needed, and probably soon. As the large, gated residence came into view, Bobby and Alvarado jumped out and set up across the street on a small rise behind a large shade tree.

Three young children played in the side yard paved with green concrete. There was a small patch of grass next to a large fountain. The thirteen-room, three-story residence all but filled the entirety of the property. The main house was typical white walls; gold leaf accented ironwork on doors and windows; and etched glass everywhere. The outbuildings were no less garish. Every window in every room had steel, roll-down covers for security reasons. A nanny was sitting on a stone bench next to the children's play set while guards, two in number, walked aimlessly about the compound. At the rear was a helipad and a small fleet of luxury vehicles, one, the black Mercedes-Benz S63 AMG seen at the secret airport. Another, a Bentley Continental Flying Spur Speed with Iranian Embassy plates, was dressed out in the Middle Eastern choice of black-on-black with privacy curtains and parked next to the Mercedes-Benz.

"Bobby, what's your view?" Alec asked, as he and Riemann stood behind a garage at the corner of an alley some fifty meters from the Taher residence.

"Perfect, Doc," Bobby responded. "I've got a pretty good view of the main entrance and most of the front grounds."

"Pratt, are you linked up?"

"Roger that, Doc," Pratt answered, sitting at the far corner of the local park.

Suddenly, a man in his late thirties appeared at the front door. He seemed to be shouting to the children in the side yard. The nanny jumped up immediately and raced over to the children who were on the swings.

Alec knew it was Taher. His small, stocky stature was a giveaway. The balding head and ubiquitous moustache served to confirm it. "Bobby, Taher at the front door," he said, pointing toward the front door. "That's the man I saw at Matar Tadmur al-Askari."

"I can drop him now," Bobby said.

"Wait. Riemann and I'll enter the compound from the north side," Alec fired back instantly.

"Viking, let's move," Alec said to Riemann.

Six white, faux-stone pillars framed the immense, carved front door that Taher stood before with a cell phone in his hand. He looked like he was going to move off the wide porch area that ranged over half of the residence's front side.

"Doc, can you hear me?" Pratt asked.

Alec adjusted his integrated noise-canceling, wireless lip mike as Pratt's voice shot into his earpiece. Reception was crystal clear.

Pratt had intercepted an Iranian Embassy phone call to Taher. "Doc, Taher will be leaving for the Iranian Embassy very soon."

Alec and Riemann were now over the fence. "Riemann, you secure the corner," pointing to the right side of the residence. The house's landscapeing made it difficult to see anyone on the porch. Alec made his way closer to Taher, stopping first behind one of two fountains that were the focus of the front yard, a yard also paved with a hideous green concrete and dotted with a few sickly-looking palm trees. Grass never seemed to be a favorite with Middle Easterners, whether in Baghdad or Beverly Hills.

Taher was dressed in white linen pants and a black, opened silk shirt with gold jewelry adorning his hirsute chest. His stubby fingers were covered in high-roller style diamond rings, and his left wrist displayed a solid-gold Rolex Presidential model wristwatch also bathed in diamonds. He looked like a shifty Las Vegas gambler.

Taher reached into his right pant pocket and retrieved a ringing Vertu Signature II cell phone. Alec could barely hear him over the sound of falling water in the fountain. He was speaking in French to someone.

He was stuttering. Alec made out that there was to be a meeting at the embassy and a flight to Teheran.

As Alec crept closer, his abaye caught a sprinkler head that attracted the attention of Taher. Taher immediately barked out a command and two guards came running from behind the main house.

Taher was panicked, barking orders that startled his children as they came running toward him.

"Bobby," Alvarado warned, "two o'clock!" Alvarado's spotting was always right on, but this time he had no time to calculate wind speed and distance. Bobby was on his own.

Bobby sighted the guards and pop, pop. Both went down in slow motion. Taher turned to move back into the residence as his three children, chased by their nanny, rushed to his side, grabbing at his pant legs, causing him to lose his balance for a moment.

Alec raced toward him. Taher sensed his closeness. He pulled a light caliber semiautomatic handgun from the small of his back and was set to fire at Alec. Taher struggled to free himself from his children still clinging to his legs and crying uncontrollably. Bobby hesitated taking the shot, not wanting to take the chance of hitting one of the children.

The nanny fought to protect the children by pulling them away from their father. The moment Taher was free of his children he took a shot at Alec, but missed. Alec leaped directly at him, taking him down. The commotion further frightened the children and nanny who witnessed Alec wrestling Taher on the ground.

Riemann appeared from around the corner and looked directly into Taher's eyes. Taher, restrained on the ground by Alec's martial arts grip and shear strength, realized that he was no match for the two warriors before him.

"Pratt. Taher is down," Riemann yelled into his lip mike.

Pratt notified Bobby and Alvarado to stay put until the situation was completely neutralized.

Alec stood Taher up on his flat feet and shackled him with double-lock plastic Flexicuffs. Taher did not offer any resistance. "*Ma fik tiktol kelna.* You can't kill all of us. *Al-Ankabut* will free me. The Khamsin cannot be stopped," he continued in an incoherent manner, as Alec pulled the manacles tighter. "The mighty wind will cover all of the infidels with their own blood as Allah, our master, praises his followers," Taher said, with defiance in his voice.

Alec looked at Taher as if he had just heard the diatribe of a psycho. *"Hallak ana raissak, ya khara.* Right now I am your master, you piece of shit," Alec said. Riemann pulled up tighter on the Flexicuffs, causing Taher to flinch and moan from the instant pain to his wrists and shoulders.

Alec had come to a point in his life where his tolerance for religious fundamentalism of any kind in general and Islamic fundamentalism in particular was at its end. He wanted to eradicate all those who sought to harm him, his family, his countrymen, and civilization as we know it. He was more than willing to risk it all for the sake of liberty, for the sake of William Francis. *There was no alternative...jihad be damned!*

Alec ordered the horrified children and nanny to get into the house. Through the front door Alec could see movement in what he thought was part of the kitchen area. A figure flashed by. "Pratt, get the car," Alec ordered.

"Bobby, Alvarado, meet Pratt at the gate," said Alec, as Riemann hurriedly walked Taher down the steps toward the front gate.

Inside the large residence near the front door a shout was heard. All of a sudden, a short, well-fed woman came bounding out the door brandishing a large, unwieldy semiautomatic handgun in her small hands. The woman charged Alec, screaming, *"Allahu Akbar,* God is great." Riemann reached for his gun as the woman fired a shot that missed him. *"Allah natrak ya habibi.* God is waiting for you, my love," she shouted to Taher. With the two children and the nanny looking on through a tall window inside the living room, the woman fired a second shot that hit Taher directly on the side of the head. The bullet blew the opposite side of his head nearly clean off. Blood and bone splattered on Alec's left shoulder and face. Before Riemann could get a shot off, she fired a third. It went straight through her mouth and out the back of her head.

The nanny attempted to comfort the crying children, but to no avail. They came running out of the residence screaming and crying as Alec gazed down at a dead Taher and his wife.

Pratt rushed up to Alec. "Sir, we've got to get to the embassy," he said, "and fast."

Another guard appeared in the back of the compound. Neighbors looked on, but kept silent.

"Sir, there's one at your three o'clock about twenty meters out," Bobby said. "I can do it now."

Alvarado gave Bobby the distance and wind speed. Pop! The guard fell silent.

"Now, let's get out of here," Alec said quickly.

"Goddamn," Bobby said with a shortness of breath that was evident. "What the fuck was that? She blew him away, then *offed* herself. That's fucking crazy! Nuts, if you ask me. These people are psycho."

Alec was silent on the ride to the United States Embassy at Abou Roumaneh, 2 Al Mansour Street.

CHAPTER TWENTY-EIGHT

The United States Embassy in Damascus, Syria, was established as the result of a treaty of commerce and navigation with the Ottoman Empire in 1830. Within five years, the first consular representatives were sent to Syria. By 1847, a U.S. Consular Agency was set up in the city of Aleppo, and in 1941, Syria declared its independence from France. By 1952, the United States raised its Legation and Consular Office in Damascus to embassy status. Since that time, the two countries have had an ongoing adversarial relationship.

Alec thought Taher's death to be a great loss, for he knew he was a direct link to the Khamsin. He fought the feeling that killing had now come all too easy to him, a man sworn to save lives. However, such was the nature of war, the world war on terror.

OS9 was in hostile territory.

Pratt pulled the white 1985 Toyota Land Cruiser in front of the embassy gates on Al Mansour Street. A few words with the U.S. Marines standing guard and the team rolled past the gates and into the center of the vast compound. Alec exited and stood for a moment, then brushed himself off, since the abaye was a magnet for primordial dirt and debris. Riemann, Bobby, and Alvarado jumped out of the backseat and tried to brush themselves clean of what were thick layers of dirt and grime, but they soon learned that it was an exercise in futility.

"Jesus, so this is the best Damascus has to offer?" Bobby questioned with an astonished look, as he scanned the surrounding area like an eagle looking for its prey. "It looks so damn old, and smells like a pile of horse shit if you ask me," he added, still trying to shake himself clean from the long ride.

"Damn it, Bobby. Why can't you just appreciate it for what it is, real history, ancient history What did you expect, Vegas?" Riemann said pedantically.

Bobby stared at Riemann incredulously. "What the fuck, now you're a history teacher."

The Viking said nothing.

The men were edgy.

Alec walked toward the entrance to the main embassy building. Bobby and the boys were met outside by the other members of OS9 already quartered in a secondary building behind the main embassy building.

Two Marines holding forth at the entrance immediately opened the steel, wrought-iron security doors as Alec walked through, nodding to the guards, who gave him a head-to-toe once over. Once inside, he was immediately met by the operations officer for CIA station chief Fulbright Collins.

"Dr. Hakimian, Mr. Collins has been expecting you," Harry Marks, the embassy's public affairs officer, said with as much of a smile as he could muster. "This way, sir," he said, as he led Alec across an impressive foyer and into the CIA station chief's office that looked out onto Al Mansour Street and a green fragment of grass in a small park across the street. "Things have been very hectic around here. We heard that earlier today two U.S. Army soldiers of the 1st Cavalry near Basra were killed by an IED at a security checkpoint. One of the soldiers was the youngest son of Mr. Collins's closest friend," he said sympathetically. "There was also a soldier of the 4th Marines shot to death by a sniper in the northeast of the country while examining a car that was said to have contained several UXOs in transit. You'd think that these unexploded ordnances would be a thing of the past in Iraq today, but that's simply not the case. In fact, today Afghanistan is an even more dangerous situation," he added with a look of disquiet on his weary face.

Alec expressed his concern automatically, but had other things on his mind.

Suddenly, forty-three year-old Fulbright Collins entered the large, stately office. Collins was a Princeton educated political scientist who was recruited by the CIA right after graduation. His famous patrician father Worthington Collins also served in the Agency for a few years before he was tapped to be the ambassador to Syria some thirty years ago. Attired in a blue blazer, gray flannel pants, and an unkempt mop of brown hair with a hint of gray at the sides, reminiscent of an Oxonian scholar, Collins gladly reached his slight hand out to Alec, "Doctor, sorry we had to meet under such circumstances. I've always wanted to thank-you for saving my sister's life several years ago. You are famous in diplomatic circles, I'll have you know," he said chattily, removing his tortoise-shell eyeglasses as he wiped the tiredness from his eyes. Continuing, "You, sir, are a miracle worker."

"So she's okay," Alec remarked.

"She's fine. Just fine. In fact, she had two more children after your miraculous surgery, doctor," Collins said with a glimmer on his face. "Two lovely, twin girls. Tanya and Tia."

Wanting to get to the point, Alec said, "It is my understanding that you have intel for me."

"Certainly, Dr. Hakimian," he responded. "Just give me a moment," he added as he rose from his chair only to disappear into a small anteroom behind his desk. Moments later, he emerged with an oversized, brass-zippered black-leather diplomatic pouch. After he unlocked a four-number, solid brass combination lock that was attached to one end, he began rifling through its contents. Seconds later, he handed Alec transmissions from both the NSA and the CIA Directorate via USCENTCOM.

Alec reached for the papers across the ceremonial-size desk and began to peruse the contents. Using Echelon, the NSA eavesdroppers had obtained irrefutable evidence that Robert Tishermann, CIA operative and member of OS9, passed information to an Ankabut operative regarding OS9's mission. Countless calls made from Tishermann's cell phone, one that he thought was secure, had been intercepted several times over the past few weeks. The CIA's human intelligence operatives confirmed many of the NSA's findings of fact. Ali as-Saffah was the Ankabut's liaison and the link to Tishermann.

The documents further revealed that Tishermann had identified Alec as OS9's leader. Alec, though having suspected Tishermann for sometime, was nevertheless stunned to see it in print. There was no doubt now. Alec was certain of it. The report went on to show Tishermann, a Palestinian born CIA agent, had also been implicated in the execution of his dear friend William Francis in 1989.

Tishermann, secretly a lifelong Hamas and Hezbollah sympathizer, was stationed in Israel in late 1988; he passed valuable information to these Islamic terrorist organizations on a consistent basis. It was during that time he met Francis in Beirut.

Francis had become a serious problem for Hezbollah, the organization that paid strict adherence to a version of Sharia law created by Ayatollah Khomeini, founder of the Islamic Revolution in Iran. As a consequence, the Ayatollah Khomeini and his eventual successor Ayatollah Sayyid Ali Khamenei, had ordered Francis's capture, torture, and eventual assassination. Tishermann's information about Francis's whereabouts and actions had made the heinous act possible.

It all made sense now.

Looking up at Collins, Alec calmly set the papers down on the desk and walked about the room, thinking. *Tishermann had sold him out. He had sold out every man in OS9. He had sold out his country, Alec's country. He had sold out Francis, Alec's friend.* Now he had to answer Tishermann's unpardonable act of treason. Remembering that the United States Constitution enumerated only two specific crimes, one being treason, the decision had been made, and he knew the president would agree.

A white rage grew on Alec's face as Collins looked on with concern. "Doctor, is there something wrong?"

Alec did not respond at first. To him there was too much wrong. He walked over to Collins and said, "I need a secure phone."

"By all means, doctor," Collins answered, as he directed Alec to an interior room adjacent to his office full of electronic wizardry. A gaggle of LED computer screens, scramblers, scanners, ciphers, deciphers, encrypted Iridium satellite phones, and the like were all set-off by blinking red, blue, and green light emitting diodes.

Alec placed a secure call to CENTCOM-Baghdad. "This is Dr. Hakimian," Alec said to the young, female voice on the other end. "I need to speak to General Meade."

"Yes, Dr. Hakimian, right away," the voice said. "Please give me a moment," she said politely.

Alec waited for what seemed an eternity.

"Yes, doctor, General Meade here," the general responded.

Wasting no time, "General Meade, I've read all the intel, both electronic and humint. Do you confirm the findings?"

"Most certainly. Until now we've had only unconfirmed suspicions, but just didn't know who the mole was. The fact that Tishermann is the mole did catch us by surprise. His cell phone calls revealed his true agenda. What we don't know is the extent of the damage. What we do know is that OS9 has been compromised," the general said, then fell silent. He started again, "And Ali as-Saffah was recruiting in Aqabah the last we heard."

"Yes, general. We have been compromised," responded Alec. He felt a swift pang of disgust that quickly turned to white-hot hate for Tishermann.

"Dr. Hakimian, I know this is no consolation, but we're very proud of what you and OS9 have accomplished. We have been vindicated by your discoveries to date. This gives all of us greater reason to stay the course, to help the Iraqis rebuild their country into a democratic example in the region and to give Afghanistan the same chance by eradicating the presence of the Taliban. We know we are here for all the right reasons," he said, seeming to come alive at the sound of his own voice.

"Thank-you, general," Alec said, ending the connection. He was tired of the party line. *Democracy was fine, but was it probable for Iraqis?* he asked himself. He no longer was so sure of the answer. *Was it even probable for the Afghanis?* came the follow-up question. To have the Sunnis, Shi'ites, and Kurds peacefully coexist was a tall order, and since the war in Afghanistan had been ginned up a few years ago, the calculus had changed. *But,* he cautioned himself, *one country at a time.*

Turning to the CIA station chief, "Now, I need to see my men. Where are they?" asked Alec, squeezing the communiqués tightly in his left hand, seemingly attempting to strangle the life out of them.

"This way, doctor," Collins said, as he rose from his seat and led Alec out a door at the far end of the room, where a U.S. Marine stood watch. They walked passed a number of offices, most of which were unmanned, save the secondary communications area, where three staffers were working the phones and computers. "Can we get you something to eat?" Collins queried, as they roamed through a dimly lit kitchen that only hours before had been a beehive of activity.

"No thanks."

Alec followed Collins, as he exited through the back door that led to a flower garden and grassy area about the size of a tennis court. Wind chimes, à la Haight-Asbury 1969, sounded the presence of a slight breeze in the warm air.

Alec had not eaten in nearly a day, but he never did when he was in a highly stressful situation. He had often been in surgery for up to fifteen hours, never eating, never even having the need to use the restroom. He had trained himself many years ago as a young intern to self-regulate his bodily functions and desires when it was crunch time.

Alec heard a cacophony of sounds emanating from the building as he approached. "Doctor, this is where the ambassador accommodates large delegations of U.S. officials and the like from time to time."

"You mean members of Congress on their fact-finding missions?" Alec said rhetorically and in a cynical tone.

The CIA station chief confirmed Alec's question, sensing his tone. "The building itself was built on my father's watch as ambassador. And for a few years it had also served as home to various staff members until new facilities were completed for them on Ahmad Shawqi Street about three years ago," he said, as he turned and pointed across the road.

The quarters were nice enough, but Alec wasn't there to assess its interior design qualities, but rather to brief his men and decide how he would deal with Tishermann's *act of treason*.

As the two entered the main area of the quarters, Mackay blurted out, "Doc, will ya no' have a wee dram with us? Come on. Be a good mate."

"Doc, what he's saying is have a drink with us," Bobby offered, as he raised his cold bottle of Bud Light brew and took a long guzzle.

"The pizza is great, too," said Nutworth. "Real pepperoni."

Alec spoke directly. "Men, at 0330 hours we move."

Tishermann asked, "Where to?"

Alec hesitated, searching for an answer that would suffice. He looked at his watch for a beat, then said, "Everyone will know the destination once we're on the road. Make sure that your exos are ready. Do your recalibrations before we leave," he added tersely.

Pratt looked at himself. He had pulled down his exosuit half around his waist, exposing a light gray t-shirt emblazoned with the name Carnegie Mellon University on its front. It was weeks past the need for a strong washing and only a proper burial would do.

"Boss, don't tell me that we're to travel again on those skis," deadpanned Josiah.

"See you at 0330 hours," he said and then disappeared out the door.

Alec's mind raced. He needed time to think, but he knew he had no time. It was now or never.

Collins put him up in the guest room on the second floor of the embassy. It was nice enough…clean linens, plenty of towels, and a Jacuzzi bathtub fit for two. The Panasonic plasma television was even equipped with the latest version of the Sony Blu-Ray DVD player. Not able to sleep, he flipped on the tube and FOX News was reporting Taliban insurgents had hit a unit of the U.S. Army outside of Kandahar, Afghanistan. There were two injuries and one death.

So what's changed? he asked himself.

At 0300 hours, he awoke from a much-needed sleep and was ready to do what had to be done.

By 0331 hours, OS9 was loaded into two non-descript black, bulletproof GMC SUVs driven by U.S. Marines. Two small transporters followed with the team's gear and SandJets. They headed south by southwest toward the Syrian border with Jordan. Alec had determined that the team had two missions yet to accomplish and the separation of the team was the only way to achieve success.

Some thirty minutes into the journey across the hard-packed, parched desert floor that doubled as a road of sorts, OS9 stopped. The dim lights of Damascus flickered in the distance.

With night as their cover, Alec ordered the men out of the SUVs. "Get your gear." As soon as the gear was removed from the SUVs, Alec waived them off. The U.S. Marine drivers sped away without delay as sand spewed from underneath the rear wheels of their SUVs.

With everyone standing about, "Gentlemen, the intel that I received at the embassy has changed our mission." Looking at Josiah, Riemann,

Nutworth, and Mackay, he said, "Once in Irbid you'll board a V-22 Osprey and be flown directly to the Mediterranean coast and onto the Sixth Fleet's Task Force 61 Mediterranean Amphibious Ready Group's (MARG) U.S.S. *Kearsarge*." Pausing for a beat, he continued, "You'll be directly involved in prepping for our move on the Hezbollah camp east of Sûr."

No one saw it coming. The men of OS9 had always thought of themselves as a team, never to be separated, and now Sûr. They had no foreknowledge of the Hezbollah camp.

Alec continued, "Bobby, you, Alvarado, Tishermann and Pratt will join me," pointing to each of them.

Alec decided not to act on the Tishermann issue as of yet, believing that to deal with it now would certainly delay the mission. He had already decided that there was a very quick, clean way to handle it, and it would come once they were in the desert well beyond the city.

Pratt nodded in the affirmative.

"What's this all about, Doc?" Alvarado asked.

"The NSA, in concert with the CIA's humint, tells us that as-Saffah, the Ankabut's first lieutenant, is in Aqabah. So, as I said before, I need the four of you," pointing again to Riemann, Nutworth, Josiah, and Mackay, "to prepare for the big move into southern Lebanon's Hezbollah stronghold. In the meantime, the rest of us will go on a small hunt."

Alec's look turned hard. His mind drifted back to his friend Francis. He knew it was time to avenge his needless death and how better to do it than to capture, if not kill, as-Saffah and to administer justice to a traitor.

"It's time," Alec said.

Once at the starting point for their mission to Amman, adjustments were made to the SandJet skis, backpacks, and exoskeleton suits. They made ready for what was before them. The possibility of a battle royale in southern Lebanon was very real. Bobby was excited by the prospect. Alvarado and Pratt remained typically stoical. Tishermann did not know what to think. Riemann and Nutworth were already planning the specifics of their anticipated submerged insertion into southern Lebanon. After all, they were Navy SEALs and it was what they did best. Alec said nothing and pointed his skis in the direction of Irbid, some 115 kilometers away. He knew that OS9's movements now had to be more secretive, more stealth than ever. The team was compromised, but by how much, it was not known. They had to stay fluid, ready for anything.

The desert kilometers rolled by as Alec's angst continued to build. Soon the Syrian border town of Daraa, *the fortress*, came and went and crossing over into somewhat friendly territory was not too far off.

At 0545 hours, the sun was creeping above the horizon. Alec came to an unexpected stop only kilometers north of Irbid.

The others did the same.

Taking a slow drink of a special liquid that contained an electrolyte replacement with glucose supplement, he began, "Gentlemen, please take a seat."

Unusual to the temper of the desert, the region around them was lush and even pleasant. Alec reached beneath his abaye, relaxed the joint anchors of his exoskeleton suit, and dialed down its Ballistic Electro Reactive Process, also known as BERP, to sleep mode.

BERP was effective in resisting shots from weapons with calibers up to 40mm. It was a precursor to the future of electronic armor plating. Micro-hydraulic actuators could sense an impending impact and cause the exoskeleton suit to harden in an instant, thus protecting the wearer under almost any circumstance.

The newest version of the exoskeleton suit, referred to as the EXO3, was the latest in a wearable robotic fighting system. It turned the soldier into a human version of a futuristic fighting machine capable of feats of strength and athleticism unequalled by anything in the animal kingdom.

These body amplification systems were in constant testing by the U.S. Defense Advanced Research Projects Agency (DARPA), which hinted in occasional news releases that the future of exoskeletons was rich with possibilities. As early as the 1960s General Electric had co-developed an exoskeleton suit nicknamed "Hardiman." It was capable of allowing a ground soldier to lift 120 kilos as if it were a tenth the weight.

As for the version supplied to OS9, it went beyond the norm, even for an exoskeleton suit. It enabled each member to move large objects out of the way, leap high walls with a single bound, and carry 75 kilos while moving at a speed of 16 kilometers per hour. Much of the exosuit's material was a very top-secret, lightweight composite. Each suit was also equipped with electro-burst mechanisms mounted on the soldier's shoulders that could shoot electric charges up to forty meters, immobilizing any enemy in its line of sight. Even the special footwear permitted a soldier to leap forward nearly thirty meters with ease. The global positioning system (GPS) and terrain sensors, added to the exoskeleton's unique characteristics, as did the medical monitoring system that tracked the wearer's psychological and physiological functions.

With a hardened and very serious look, Alec scanned the bearded faces of his men who were seated before him and began, "One of you is a traitor." The idea stunned the team. They looked around at each other incredulously. Tishermann wiped his brow as he sat stone-faced. Alec continued, a growing rage appeared on his face, now heavily bearded and peppered with grains of sands. "One of you has lied. One of you has endangered every other member of this team. Damn it, one of you has decided that the country you swore your allegiance to is no longer worth it."

Everyone stood mentally at attention.

Alec rose up tall, his dark hair framing his strong facial features. "One of you has taken it upon yourself to decide the fate of OS9." Furrowing his brow, his eyes steeled on one man after another. He then continued, "Here me now. I won't let that happen, for you, a traitor to the United States of America and all that it stands for, do not understand the consequences of your actions. You have *b-e-t-r-a-y-e-d* your country. You have betrayed your brothers of OS9."

Alec's stare pierced each man's psyche. He was struggling with his decision. He was about to do something that he knew would haunt him all of his days. Suddenly, a clarity of thought washed across his face. Now he knew what had to be done. He was transformed into an *angel of death*.

Without any warning, he drew his Walther P99 from inside his abaye, turned and walked straight toward Tishermann, who was leaning back against the trunk of a palm tree as its fan-style fronds gently flapped in the breeze above his head. Alec asked flatly, "Bob, why?"

Bobby looked stunned. "It's not me," he said, waving his arms frantically.

"No, it's not you, Bobby," Alec responded.

Blood began to return to Bobby's face.

"Tishermann," Alec said, staring directly into his eyes.

Tishermann said nothing.

"Why?" Alec demanded.

Everyone was silent. Hearts pounded like war drums.

Tishermann jumped up quickly and stood face-to-face with Alec. With eyes opened wide, he said forcefully, "Remember Chatila, Sabra? I did it for them. For them, Alec. I was seventeen. I was in America and I couldn't do anything about it. But I heard the stories, the horrible stories about the massacres. I swore that some day I would avenge my brothers' deaths."

Alec felt Tishermann's breath on his face. He could not believe what he was hearing. Tishermann had sold out the very people and country that gave him opportunity; that gave him freedom. The intensity of his rage continued to grow and was palpable to every member of OS9. Now they too wanted to exact a pound of flesh. They wanted to tear him apart. They wanted to unload a clip or two into his skull.

Tishermann continued, now seething, as visible sprays of saliva shot from his mouth, "Your country and the Jews killed my family. My family Alec," he said with emphasis on "my family." His voice, now audibly trembling, generated the words, "My mother, father, brother, they're all dead." Looking directly into Alec's cold eyes as if what he was about to say would hit home, he added, "My sister, Alec," his voice tightened. "My sister was raped by those animals for three days! She escaped, but I finally found her...." His anger was now burning red-hot.

Alec, his gun held tightly in his left hand, said nothing as Tishermann continued. "The Zionist butchers led by Sharon turned a blind eye as the Lebanese Christian militia slaughtered hundreds of my Palestinian brothers and sisters. I know this, for a fact. Your country just stood by as it happened. Just did nothing." Now staring directly at Alec with greater intensity, "Your America supported the massacre. With guns, knives, and hatchets my people were slaughtered mercilessly. The Zionists were killing young children. It took me time, but I finally discovered who I really was. I am a proud Palestinian who has learned your country's evil ways. You can never win. Remember that my people's cause will be redeemed by the Ankabut and his Khamsin."

Tishermann's diatribe was becoming all too unbearable.

Bobby and the others looked on in disbelief, wondering what would happen next.

In a nanosecond, Alec raised his Walther P99 and said in a cold voice, "This is for Bill. You remember Bill Francis, don't you?" Then he squeezed the trigger. *Pop!* The sound shattered the deep silence as a single 9mm round found the center of Tishermann's skull right between his blank eyes. He fell in a contorted fashion onto the warm sand, limp with death.

An abrupt shock of emotion riveted Bobby and the others. As hardened and well trained for any situation as each man was, not one of them knew how to react to what he had just seen. Bobby whispered above his breath to himself, "Holy fuck. Did you see that? He just fucking blew Tishermann away. Not even a hesitation. He just capped the prick's ass."

Alec, his gun's barrel still hot, dangled at his side as he stared down at a dead Tishermann. Without a hint of emotion, he looked at the small trickle of deoxygenated blood that began to flow from Tishermann's mortal wound.

Everyone remained very quiet, then, "Pratt, call it in," Alec said matter-of-factly.

"Yes, sir," Pratt answered quickly.

No one ever mentioned Tishermann's name again.

CHAPTER TWENTY-NINE

The unconventional Osprey's primary function was as an amphibious assault aircraft to transport troops, equipment, and supplies from assault ships and land bases to combat points along the fields of battle. With a range of anywhere from 200-500 nautical miles, depending on troop requirements, the Osprey cruised at speeds approaching 235 kilometers per hour.

Without notice, scudding sounds raced across the barrenness of the northern Jordanian Desert. As they approached, they became the unmistakable sounds of the Osprey's 12,000 shaft horsepower generated by two turbo-shaft engines, each driving 38-foot diameter, three-bladed props. With the morning sun at their backs, members of OS9 had a clear image of the awkward looking bird as it began to descend vertically about thirty meters away in a hastily marked landing zone. The sands swirled violently. Their loose-fitting abayes wrapped around each of them as they put their forearms up to help deflect the sand from peppering their eyes. As for their ears, they just had to hope for the best.

The mighty Osprey came to a very loud rest facing Alec. All of a sudden, a U.S. Marine pilot, who looked no older than twenty-five years of age, jumped out of the side door and onto the hot sand. His highly polished, black flight boots sank several centimeters into the hot sand. Each step toward Alec required noticeable effort.

Removing his dark aviator glasses, Captain Tommy "Chopper" Goodbottom stated precisely, as he stood rod-straight and saluted Alec, "Captain Goodbottom, here. At your service, sir."

Alec snapped back a salute and waited.

Bobby wanted to say something, but did not.

"Captain," Alec said flatly.

Three U.S. Marines could be seen off-loading supplies for Alec and his men. "We were able to fill your supply order to the last round of ammo, sir."

Alec said without hesitation, "Captain. You'll be flying out four of my men and one dead traitor."

Confused by Alec's comment, the captain asked inquisitively, "Sir. Did you say a dead man?"

"You heard me, captain. You'll be flying back to the fleet Agent Robert Tishermann, now deceased."

Alec glanced back over his shoulder to Tishermann's remains beneath a palm tree. A camouflage-colored tarp covered the dead traitor. *Why did Tishermann have to do it? Why did he turn on his country, on him, on OS9?* Alec fought the thoughts, after all, he was a man trained to give people a second chance, yet now he was putting bullets through the skulls of human beings without hesitating. It continued to pain him inside. It even frightened him at times. He questioned himself, *had he lost sight of who he was or was supposed to be? Whenever he took a life, he felt as if he were a sinner. His only redemption was in the operating room. But he was half a world away from his redemption.*

Alec quickly inventoried the area as his men were boarding the MV-22 Osprey. Off in the distance a wall of coarse sand was growing as it moved toward them. "Move it, boys."

The Khamsin was stalking him again.

Captain Goodbottom did not know what to say. He had never received such a request. Retrieving dead soldiers from the field of battle was one matter, but a *dead traitor....*

The MV-22, the U.S. Marine version of the Osprey, lifted off from the desert floor at 0700 hours and disappeared, flying on a bearing of west by northwest. The magnificent Mediterranean Sea was less than one hundred kilometers away and Task Force 61's Mediterranean Amphibious Ready Group was waiting.

Alec and three of his men remained behind and waited.

CHAPTER THIRTY

IRBID, JORDAN

Situated on the Horan Savanna was the antediluvian city of Irbid, the most fertile area in all of Jordan. It dated back to the Early Bronze Age 7,000 years ago. After having crossed an endless desert the Bedouins called the *Ocean of Fire*, OS9 found it refreshing to learn that Irbid's daily temperature rarely moved above the mid 20s Celsius.

It was now 0730 hours, and the morning haze was rising up from the desert floor. The northern Jordanian Desert, though much cooler than anticipated, was nonetheless a desert. It was feral in a haunting way. It was mysterious in a captivating way. It was dangerous in a palpable way.

"Our Jordanian Intelligence Service operative is to meet us at 0930 hours. We're to stay put until then," Alec said nonchalantly.

Bobby just looked around at much of what he had seen for several days now. It was long expanses of sand followed by still longer expanses of near featureless sand. Its color ran from pale beige to a distinct terra cotta.

Alvarado was predictably quiet. It was just his way. He was always calculating wind speeds and distances or checking the position of the sun, always looking for the next target. He did whatever it took to keep his spotting skills sharp. *If Bobby was to hit the target*, he figured, *he had to have everything just right*, and he always did.

Alec opened up an MRE and appeared to enjoy the unenjoyable. He thought about Karina and Leyla. It had been too long since he had even heard their voices. He hungered for his daughter's hug, his wife's embrace. He missed his life as a lifesaver, but he was convinced that defeating terrorism was for the greater good, and the opportunity to avenge his dear friend's murder was front-and-center.

Bobby just stared, his iPod blaring.

"All right, take what you need from the supply pallets and get ready," Alec said, staring at several piles of supplies left off by the Osprey. "And bury the rest," he added, taking another bite from his MRE.

Pratt interrupted, "Sir, I'm receiving a signal coming from just outside of Irbid."

Alec looked over Pratt's left shoulder at the laptop screen that showed an unidentified land craft crossing one grid after another. "It's our man from Jordan," Alec said, as he walked back to where he was sitting next to a large outcrop of date trees. "What's his distance?" he asked, as he continued pushing around the dismal food that made up his MRE. "It's what?" he said, and then hesitantly pulled off a piece of rubberized egg from his fork.

"About fifteen klicks and closing," Pratt rapped back.

"Good, Jordan's come through for us," Alec stated. He did, however, remind himself that not too many years ago it was a double agent from the JIS who acted as a homicide bomber and killed seven CIA operatives in Afghanistan's Khowst Province.

The Hashemite Kingdom of Jordan reached back to around the year 2000 B.C. It was then that Semitic Amorites made their home around the Jordan River in the land called Canaan. A post World War I Transjordan was born from a jumble of land controlled by the United Kingdom in 1922, with Hashemite Prince Abdullah designated as the leader of the semiautonomous Emirate of Transjordan. In 1950, Transjordan was renamed the Hashemite Kingdom of Jordan.

Today its leader was the young King Abdullah II, the 43rd generation direct descendant of the venerable Prophet Muhammad. King Abdullah sought to be the peacekeeper in a region that had never known peace, while at the same time he has made it known that he resonated with western ways.

0930 hours ticked passed and Alec seemed irritated. "Pratt, now what?" he queried.

Glancing at his Panerai, he said, "They should have been here by now."

Scrutinizing his laptop screen, he said, "The signal stopped, but now it's back again, sir. Can't be more than five or six klicks southeast of our position." The intermittent sand clouds swirled about, making visibility beyond fifty meters nearly impossible.

Alec trained his eyes in a southeastwardly direction. The swirling sand clouds grew larger as they moved closer. A white Mercedes-Benz G550 Gladenwagen roared into view. Emblazoned on its two front doors was the royal symbol of the Hashemite Kingdom of Jordan.

In minutes, the G550's purring V-8 engine could be heard turning the complex four-wheel drive system at high speed. The G550 was one of the world's finest all-terrain SUVs. Its off-road abilities even rivaled those of the legendary Range Rover.

The dusty, sand-covered G550 slid to a stop just meters from OS9's temporary bivouac. Jordan's senior intelligence officer exited the front passenger seat, followed by two rather large, dark-skinned men sporting modified Kalishnikovs. The driver, fiddling with his sunglasses, kept the G550 idling.

Alec walked forward as the senior intel officer's white linen abaye fluttered in the morning breeze. Removing his dark Persol sunglasses with his left hand, the senior intelligence officer said coolly, "Dr. Hakimian." He then offered his right hand, "I'm Dr. Jamal Radhy, senior intelligence officer for the Hashemite Kingdom of Jordan's intelligence service. His Royal Highness King Abdullah II sends his regards."

The two shook hands quickly.

Dr. Radhy was one of the more knowledgeable people in the region on the subject of the Khamsin and the Ankabut.

Alec shook his hand and smiled politely then, "Dr. Radhy, tell his majesty that I appreciate his generosity. His assistance is invaluable to the success of our mission. And remind his royal highness that the next time I see him in St. Tropéz to let me buy dinner."

"*Ana taht amrak, ya hakim.* I will do as you ordered, doctor. Now you are aware that your mission's success does require us to be as surreptitious as possible? The chatter is that as-Saffah and his men were last known to be heading toward Aqabah," Dr. Radhy said in a voice infused with a blend of high English and classical Arabic, having been educated at King's College, the University of Cambridge.

Alec summoned the others. "Gentlemen, Dr. Radhy's intel has confirmed what the NSA and the CIA have also confirmed. The bastard as-Saffah is in Aqabah or arriving any time."

Bobby looked at Alvarado and whispered, "It's showtime, bro."

Alvarado cracked a half smile and gave a thumb's up.

Dr. Radhy motioned to one of his bodyguards to bring his briefcase. He flicked open the gold-plated locks of his pearl-white dyed alligator briefcase. He removed a map and laid it down across the Teutonic looking G550's hood, hot enough to fry an egg. Dr. Radhy ordered the driver to shut off the idling engine. "Dr. Hakimian," he said, pointing to the lower left-hand side of the large map, "Here, this is where they are located." The map revealed the name: Aquamarina II Hotel, Aqabah.

"Dr. Radhy. I am very familiar with the hotel. I was here in my youth, as a college student on vacation. It was not so nice then, but that was a long time ago." Alec's mind began to zero-in on his first true love and their days swimming in the sea near the hotel. Even today, her vivid memory haunted him. Suddenly an image of his wife Leyla pushed the thought aside and he said, "So what's our source?"

"Our source is the sixteen-year-old son of the cell's leader."

"What!" Alec shot back reflexively.

"Yes, doctor. The teenage son of the Hamas cell's leader. He overheard his father talking on the phone about meeting as-Saffah in two days in Aqabah at the hotel."

"Why would he do that? Where is the son now?"

"He told on his father after the father had killed his mother in a fit of rage about a year ago. As for where he is now, well, he is under our protection and will soon leave for southern England where he will assume a new life, with a new family of immigrant Jordanians."

Alec was relieved to hear that the young boy was safe.

Dr. Radhy continued, "Now, once you arrive in Amman, you can prepare in a safe house we have made available for you and your men. It is located just east of the Jordan Intercontinental Hotel. I will have some of my officers escort you there."

Alec looked around for a fleeting moment, then, "Yes, my men need somewhere to rest and refit. The long journey across the sands has taken its toll. But I do need to know more about as-Saffah."

"By all means, doctor. By all means. I am prepared to assist you in this matter," Dr. Radhy remarked without emotion. He again motioned to one of his imposing looking bodyguards to open the front passenger door of the G550. "Dr. Hakimian, any moment," he said, glancing at his Ademars Piquet platinum wristwatch, "your transportation will arrive and take you and your men to the airbase at the edge of the city. We must be very discreet. So for now I must go," he said, shaking Alec's hand vigorously.

The vault-like passenger doors of the G550 all slammed shut simultaneously. In moments, the vehicle disappeared in the direction of Amman, leaving a rooster tail of sand and dust in its wake.

"So now what, Boss?" asked Bobby, somewhat rhetorically.

"Let's pack up, boys," Alec said with a hint of irritability in his tired voice. The time was taking its toll; things were not happening fast enough for him.

Then, all heard the slashing sound. Just above the horizon, Alvarado espied the silhouette of a camouflaged H-92 Sikorsky Superhawk. Its survival design and extended range of more than three hundred nautical miles made the Superhawk a truly twenty-first century fighting helicopter. Its massive rotor blades knifed through the crackling-hot desert air with the ease of a surgeon's scalpel cutting supple flesh. The electronics of the Superhawk were state-of-the-art, and its lift capacity trumped that of its nearest competitor.

The massive helo settled down gently on the carpet of sand before Alec and the others. Alec raised his hand over his eyes to deflect the bright sunlight and blowing sand as he moved to a position that put his back to the sun. A large sliding door opened and two uniformed soldiers jumped out. Alec walked over to greet them.

One officer snapped a salute to Alec and then said, "Lieutenant Omar Kayaleh, sir."

Alec quickly returned the salute. "We're ready."

"Very good, sir. Please," Lieutenant Kayaleh responded quickly, as he turned and motioned for Alec to board the Superhawk. "Your gear needs to be secured before take-off. We will be leaving shortly."

Two airmen methodically loaded the gear into the helo as Alec took his seat. All of OS9 and the chopper's crew boarded, belted in, and put on their protective headgear and noise suppressors. Once all the gear and men we secure inside the mighty H-92 Sikorsky Superhawk, it lifted off from the desert floor and quickly turned and burned its way on a southeast heading. Alec was not comfortable with the fact that it took too long to load the chopper and take-off.

Alvarado, speaking through his headset, said to Bobby, "Damn, this mother moves." He sometimes fancied himself as a special ops chopper pilot. He calculated the chopper's speed and estimated time of arrival in his mind as it scudded across the desert floor.

Bobby kicked back against a bulkhead and seemed to be meditating with his iPod Touch blaring, knowing that the extended play battery had little life left in it. At that moment, he wished that he had some new songs to listen to, but that was not to be and he knew it.

As the Superhawk approached the King Hussein Military Airfield in Amman, Alvarado methodically scanned the seven hills or *jabals* dressed in bleached white stone, three and four-story buildings; most were primitively built. Rome had undoubtedly left its mark in the center of the city. The downtown neighborhoods, peppered with cafés and kabab stalls, had an odor that clung to one's clothing like a cheap dinner over-seasoned with too much garlic.

Alvarado continued to look for something out of the ordinary. It was what he did.

CHAPTER THIRTY-ONE

Amman was certainly a place out of the ordinary. It was almost as old as Damascus and possessed recently excavated buildings that dated back to before 7000 BCE. While under Roman rule, the city was called Philadelphia, named after the third century BCE Ptolemaic ruler Philadelphus.

The Romans built the city with ornately decorated buildings, an amphitheater, and scores of impressive secondary structures. In 635 CE the city, which had been under Byzantine rule by then and had been the seat of a Christian bishop, was renamed Ammon, a Semitic name that today was known as Amman.

The Superhawk hovered effortlessly over King Hussein Military Airfield's massive tarmac, sending several of the ground crewmen's hats flying in all directions. A flagman communicated with the pilot in the language of semaphore, signaling with red flags in each hand as he directed him to set the chopper down near a recently completed series of modern outbuildings that discreetly housed a satellite office of the Jordanian Intelligence Service.

All of a sudden, a crewman gave Alec the sign to deplane from the Superhawk. The winding down of the jet turbine engines pushing the monstrous rotor blades bothered him. His ears had been sensitive for days. *Possibly an infection acquired while crossing the Ocean of Fire*, he thought to himself. He was glad to be on the ground.

As OS9's gear was off-loaded, the team made their way into the Jordanian Intelligence Service's office. Dr. Radhy was waiting patiently.

He was in a pleasant mood; after all, he had just heard that his daughter had given birth to a healthy baby boy named Jamal.

As Alec and his team entered the room, Dr. Radhy quickly stood up and remarked, "*Hakim*, doctor. *Marhaba*, hello. How was your ride? I trust my pilot was kind to you. You know, the Sikorsky can be a rough ride at times, especially when the Khamsin is angry."

"*Naam*, yes, doctor."

"Please, Dr. Hakimian. Can I interest you in a game?" Dr. Radhy said, pointing to an exquisitely carved backgammon set in ebony and ivory.

Alec had been the backgammon champion at the American University of Beirut two years running and thought it better to beg off. He knew it would not be polite to embarrass a man on his own turf. "Thank-you. Perhaps later, but for now my men need to rest."

"By all means, doctor. By all means." Dr. Radhy quickly motioned to two of his aides as he said, "Your transportation is ready. Your equipment is already on its way to the safe house."

"Very good," Alec said.

Bobby heard that and smiled.

Pratt was not feeling well. *Some sort of stomach flu*, he thought. It had never dawned on him to ask Alec. Probably not a good thing though, for Alec never gave advice that involved anything below the base of the skull. In fact, he never gave any medical advice outside his office. After all, his field of medicine required precision at the highest level and just passing out medical advice without a complete examination was not his style.

The two H1 Hummers looked as if they were right out of a Schwarzenegger movie as they sat in repose before the main office entrance. Painted in shadow-black livery, with darkened windows and oversized wheels and tires, they crossed the hot sands with ease. It all served to add to the intimidation factor of the Hummers. Emblazoned on each front door was the Jordanian Intelligence Service's insignia. It sent a message that the king was watching his every citizen.

The Hummers were two of thirty the King of Jordan received as a thank-you from the United States for assisting by way of intelligence in a covert operation in late April 2010 that led to the capture of three al-

Qaeda operatives in Daraa, Syria, and a Taliban operative in Kandahar, Afghanistan.

1200 hours proved to be no different from any other 1200 hours in the Jordanian aspect of the Levant, especially in May. Water could not quench the thirst nor ameliorate the pain from taking in a breath of heat that seared the lungs. On this day, the temperature would surpass 35° Celsius.

The safe house that Jordanian Intelligence had provided was three stories high and painted in a light eggshell color with a crenellated roofline reminiscent of a medieval castle. The architecture of the immense, faux sandstone building looked out-of-place in the middle of the desert. Four castle keeps, each strategically placed at the outside corners of the main structure, jutted out from the skyline and were always a cause of consternation amongst the locals.

The residence was so noticeable that no one would ever suspect that anything covert would be going on inside. One could simply hide in plain sight.

Local history had it that the residence, called *Big Pecos,* was built by a maverick, well-heeled Texas oil baron by the name of Colonel Willis Victory, who came to the sands of the Middle East in the 1930s as one of Aramco's founders. He loved Arabian horses and money but loved even more to show them both off whenever the opportunity presented itself. Colonel Victory had been a close friend of the present king's father, whose stable of Arabian horses was second-to-none.

A Jordanian land developer, who was erecting a new five-star resort along the Dead Sea near Al Mazraah, now owned big Pecos, named after Colonel Victory's prized Texas longhorn stud bull. The developer was sympathetic to the American cause in the Middle East and thus made Big Pecos, with its unique security features, available to Jordanian and U.S. intelligence agencies.

Walking through the gargantuan double front doors fashioned from Texas oak, Bobby gasped, as he looked around the massive foyer, replete with a life-size bronze of Big Pecos himself on the center of the marble floor. "Holy shit! What the hell," he remarked in typical boy-like fashion.

Pratt just shook his head as he did a visual reconnaissance of a Texas oilman's dream house in the Middle East.

Alvarado slowly rubbed the right front hoof of the statue delicately, as if to verify that it was not real.

"Boys, find a bed and catch some shuteye. We'll meet at 1750 hours to go over the intel from JIS," Alec said, scratching the last remnants of the barghash's bite. Other than the slight reddish scar it left behind and the occasional phantom itch, it was thankfully gone for the most.

"Dr. Hakimian," a well-trained guard said, "your gear and hardware are stored in the basement. I have ordered guards placed around the compound for your added safety while you are here."

"*Shoukran*, thank-you," Alec said with a forced smile.

"Over here is a secure phone. It's a direct line to Dr. Radhy's office," the guard added, pointing to a table in the compound's library.

It was a library of considerable presence, filled with myriad classics amassed by Colonel Victory at great cost. Ironically, the colonel had only a fourth-grade education, yet he made it a point to have read the works of Plato, Alcuin of York, Sir Francis Bacon, and Adam Smith, even if he never understood much of what he read.

Once somewhat comfortable inside the confines of Big Pecos, Alec sought the refuge of a bedroom next to the gardens. He paid no mind to the garishness of the décor, but try as he did, he could not sleep. Even the agreeable sound of trickling water outside could not ease his mind. It just would not shut off, not even for a nanosecond. He wondered if Josiah, Mackay, Riemann, and Nutworth had worked out the scenario that would soon ensue in southern Lebanon.

CHAPTER THIRTY-TWO

There it was…1750 hours had arrived before anyone knew it. Alec was the first into the meeting area in the impressive library. He scanned the shelves of rare books, counting how many he had read in his earlier life. Herodotus of Halicarnassus's *Histories*, Niccolò Machiavelli's *The Prince*, Dante Alighieri's *Divine Comedy*, and even Publius's *The Federalist* jumped out at him.

Alvarado was next. He wandered into the library while cleaning the lenses of his high-resolution binoculars. His Mark 23 U.S. Special Operations Command Heckler & Koch .45 caliber sidearm dangled lazily from his right hip. The suppressor and laser sight attachments made it rather cumbersome for some, but he always felt comfortable with a weapon of such accuracy and reliability.

"Alvarado," Alec acknowledged, nodding his head at the same time.

"Sir," Alvarado answered with a salute.

The two were quiet as they looked out a stained-glass window onto the trickling streams that meandered throughout the gardens of Big Pecos. Alec had always respected Alvarado's reticence, knowing that he was a thinking man, the kind that worked out every decision before acting, something he always did as a surgeon.

Bobby was next to enter at 1755 hours. "Sir, what do we need for this op?" was his casual remark, trying to distract from his habitual tardiness that he knew irritated Alec.

"Bobby, this one's going to be very quick and I'm anticipating close quarters." He continued, as his eyes tracked Pratt, who entered the room with his laptop under his arm. "We'll need GH S&F-13s, RGO 78s, and F1s for starters. We need to disorientate and incapacitate them immediately," he finished.

GH S&F-13s, RGO 78s, and F1s were models of hand grenades specially designed to stun, disorientate, temporarily blind, and even maim and sometimes kill the enemy at anywhere from ground zero to a radius of some fifty meters.

"Not knowing what the inside of the Aquamarina Hotel II looks like today, I have to assume that it's close quarters. Long arms won't get it done this time. Expect hotel guests everywhere and the chance of collateral damage is high, very high," Alec emphasized. "I don't want collateral damage," he added insistently. "It's not good for public relations, but it's always a reality." He paused a moment, then continued, "Ali as-Saffah is the man who orchestrated several attacks in Iraq on U.S. soldiers that led to seventeen deaths. He's our target…and yes, if you're thinkin' revenge…damn right it is. This is not a sensitivity test, this is war," he added with emphasis. "This man has to pay for all the killing he's done over the past twenty years. It's no more complicated than that."

The seriousness on Alec's now weathered face was apparent, and the sound of as-Saffah's name seemed to enrage him.

"Remember, we are in a land of *friendlies* for the most part, nevertheless, it harbors those who wish us dead. Pratt, make sure we're linked up to Baghdad. We'll need additional GPS positioning ASAP."

Pratt nodded in the affirmative.

Bobby was fondling his H&K MP5N submachine gun. It was his personal choice of weapon when close combat was the order of the day and he needed real firepower. The MP5N fired 9x19mm NATO ammo at up to one hundred meters. Unlike the standard thirty round clip, Bobby had asked the manufacturer Heckler & Koch to design a sixty round clip reminiscent of the World War II German Navy Luger's snail clip configuration. He also had the MP5N fitted with a suppressor that did not compromise the weapon's effectiveness.

Alec never deviated from his Walther P99 9mm in situations that put him close to the enemy.

"Tune your exosuits for interior terrain," Alec barked.

The exoskeletons could be setup for any number of conditions and scenarios. Where warfare was close combat, each soldier had the ability to adjust the reaction time of his exosuit for short bursts of speed required to move quickly, even in complete darkness.

Alec continued, "Dr. Radhy will arrive soon to brief us on his side of the mission and what to expect." He took a long pause, then finished with, "Men, I want this bastard as-Saffah."

CHAPTER THIRTY-THREE

LOS ANGELES, CALIFORNIA

It was approaching 10:30 in the evening as the Audi A8L slalomed its way south down the 405 Intrastate Freeway on its way to the Los Angeles International Airport. A stiff wind had kicked up, tossing debris about the heavily trafficked freeway. The driver said nothing. Leyla sat mute in the rear-seating compartment with the other man. He had placed his semiautomatic handgun on his right leg and his finger on the trigger. All she could think about was grabbing the weapon and pulling the trigger again and again and again…for this was the man who threatened to kill her daughter.

Once inside the confines of the airport, the driver maneuvered the Audi through a guarded gate and onto the tarmac. The night air was brisk and the moon above cast soft light on the plane that was being refueled as the car approached. The driver brought the car to an abrupt stop some twenty-five yards from the gleaming white Bombardier Global Express XRS private jet.

Leyla looked out the window of the Audi to the plane and knew what was about to happen.

"Please get out of the car, Mrs. Hakimian," the bearded man ordered politely.

Leyla turned to him and just stared.

"Mrs. Hakimian, get out of the car," came out loud and clear, even above the din of the whining jet engines of a Boeing 747 American Airlines jet taking off on a nearby runway. "I will not hesitate to kill you

204

right here if you insist in not getting out," he added, indicating with his eyes that his semiautomatic handgun was at the ready.

Leyla knew intuitively that the bearded man was not about to kill her in the car. There were witnesses around the aircraft. After all, *why would he have kidnapped her and brought her to the airport if he was not ordered by someone else? But, who was that someone else?* she asked herself.

The driver held the door wide open and Leyla unwillingly exited. Standing tall, but feeling very frightened, she clutched her evening purse tightly.

"Please," she said in a pleading tone. "Tell me what this is all about. Why me? What could I possibly mean to you?"

Dismissing her question, he said, "Now, if you'll follow me, we'll board the plane."

The Bombardier Global Express XRS was a rich man's private jet. Two Rolls-Royce Deutschland BR710A2-20 turbofan jet engines made it possible for it to carry upwards of nineteen passengers and a crew of four at a cruising altitude of 45,000 feet. The aircraft was also capable of flying for over 6,000 nautical miles at nearly 600 miles per hour. The interior was nothing short of palatial and the avionics were as good as it got for a private aircraft. However, this all came at a cost of something north of fifty million dollars in U.S. currency.

"Board the plane, now!" he said with fire in his toxic voice.

"Tell me what I want to know first," she demanded, as she stood defiantly.

Suddenly, she felt a piercing pain in her right thigh as her captor reached down and drove a hypodermic needle into it, releasing six milligrams of morphine, a very powerful opiate. In mere moments she was reduced to a catatonic state…all resistance had vanished, as a glaze washed over her dark eyes.

Close-by, a taxiing passenger jet's exhaust sent flying everything that was not nailed down. Holding on to his suit jacket's front panels with his left hand, the bearded man pointed the semiautomatic handgun in Leyla's direction and said very convincingly, "Mrs. Hakimian, now I won't ask you again. I'm not a man of great patience and if it were up to me, I would have already beaten you senseless and had you put aboard the plane like a piece of cheap luggage. Now move."

Compliance was instantaneous.

The plane's crew was immediately made aware of Leyla's circumstance and they acted accordingly. Once onboard the aircraft, she was immediately met by a young male flight attendant, with lifeguard good looks, who gently offered her a flute of Roderer champagne. Leyla refused the offer. She was directed to a large, wide chair that was covered in soft, cream-colored calfskin. Leyla dropped into the chair and wanted to die. This was all too much for her. The fear that she would never see her daughter alive again was fading, as the morphine took more control of her.

Lights on the control panel mounted above her began flashing and the air-conditioning turned on. A very perky female flight attendant by the name of Margie May Morgan rushed up the isle and stopped in front of her. "Mrs. Hakimian, my name is Margie May. I'm to see to it that you are comfortable. Can I offer you something to drink or eat?" Margie May detected that Leyla was having difficulty focusing and said, "Okay then, just call when you need something and I'll be right here."

Speaking to the control tower, the plane's co-pilot confirmed the weather conditions and coordinates that would take the plane to its announced destination. However, its true destination was unknown to air traffic controllers and the Federal Aviation Administration.

The bearded man returned from the cockpit and sat down next to her. He snapped his fingers and Margie May came running. "See to it that Mrs. Hakimian has everything she needs," he said smartly, then got up and walked to the aft cabin.

Asking again, Margie May said, "Mrs. Hakimian, what would you like to drink or eat?" No answer. "Very good then, just push the button on the end of your armrest and I'll be here for you."

In a moment of partial lucidity, she found herself resigned to her fate. Tired of fighting and feeling the powerful effects of morphine, she fell off into a dream world that she had been to before. In times of loneliness, she would travel in her mind to that safe place she told no one about, not even Alec.

It sometimes appeared to her as an isolated island in the South Pacific with palm trees wafting in the equatorial breeze. Other times it was a snow covered chalet high on a mountaintop somewhere in the Bavarian Alps. But since the birth of Karina, her life had centered around her daughter. Alec was always in her thoughts, but much of the time he was at the hospital and when not there, he was traveling the world seeing foreign patients. Then the NSA had come calling. *Hadn't Alec done enough?* she asked herself. However, she knew better. For her, Alec was a man devoted to his country. She often thought, *he cared more for his country than for his family.*

All of a sudden, she was awoken from her meditation by the words, "Ladies and gentlemen, this is your captain speaking. Please fasten your seatbelts and place your seats in the upright position. The attendants will come by and assist you if necessary."

After the attendants made sure that everyone's seat was in the take-off position, the two Rolls-Royce turbofan jet engines spooled up to their maximum revolutions per minute, each spitting out more than 65.6 kilotons of thrust. Lift-off was achieved in a matter of seconds as the high-speed jet wash sent everything that was not bolted down flying into the front of the small terminal building.

Once airborne, the Bombardier Global Express XRS climbed effortlessly to its cruising altitude. The overhead red lights had turned green, indicating all systems in the passenger cabin were functioning properly.

Trying to settle back into the deeply cushioned seat, Leyla again sought refuge in one of her well-used dreams, but before she did so, voices, Arab voices in the background, broke the silence. Even in a sedated state of mind, the words *al-Ankabut* and *Khamsin* jumped out of the men's sentences as they spoke to each other.

As a child, Leyla had always been warned by her parents to stay away from the *ankabut*, for if trifled with, it would inflict a deadly bite. As for the Khamsin, she knew it was the ferocious desert wind of the Middle East that her grandfather used to tell her about at family dinners. He would recite stories of how the vicious wind ravaged desert inhabitants from village to village.

It was their greatest fear.

CHAPTER THIRTY-FOUR

AMMAN, JORDAN

The thought came to Alec out of nowhere. *It had been now too many weeks to count since he had seen his wife. He missed her. And his daughter...how much had she grown?* Then it hit him, again. The ultimate question: *why was he behind enemy lines and not with his family?* He knew the answer and once OS9's mission began, it required that he remain absolutely off the radar screen. There would be no communication with his wife or anyone else outside his team and those in support positions.

By 1235 hours, all were asleep. Outside, members of the Jordanian Intelligence Service surreptitiously made sure that Big Pecos was secure.

1730 hours came in a flash.

Pratt approached Alec's bedroom door and knocked lightly. "Sir," he said in a whisper.

"Yes," came Alec's response.

"CENTCOM-Baghdad has responded. They say that Jordanian Intelligence puts the target in Aqabah itself."

"Give me a minute, Pratt. I'll meet you in the kitchen."

"Will do, sir," Pratt answered.

Moments later Alec appeared in the kitchen. The large Sub-Zero refrigerator stared him in the face. He was hungry. Bobby and Alvarado had already been up and helped themselves to falafel and hummus. It was not what Alec had in mind, but he also was not about to make an issue of it.

"So Pratt, what have you got?" Alec asked, as he leaned his head back to taste the brew.

"Sir. Like I said, CENTCOM-Baghdad confirms that as-Saffah is at the Aquamarina Hotel II in Aqabah and has met with several suspected agents of both al-Qaeda and Hamas."

The Gulf of Aqabah was sandwiched between the antediluvian lands of the Kingdom of Saudi Arabia and the easternmost aspect of Egypt. At its farthest eastern reach lied the thirteenth century Red Sea resort of Aqabah, Jordan's only seaport. The rudiments of communal living in the area dated back to the Caleolithic epoch in the fourth millennium B.C.

Aqabah, known by myriad names since ancient times, most notably Aqabat Aila, was encircled by palm trees, cleansed by pristine waters, and gifted with moderate weather. A recent archaeological discovery in the city proper unearthed the world's oldest church, older than the Holy Sepulcher in Jerusalem.

Alec remembered the Aquamarina II Hotel and the hues of pink paint that caused even the casual passerby to stop and look. The arches that dressed the ground floor of the present hotel gave it a rather stately look. He also recalled many exciting times during his medical school days when he and fellow students would take off on summer break to the Gulf of Aqabah, spending their days in its warm waters and their evenings in the hotel's night club casting about for a fresh catch. The night always yielded a tall beauty or two from one of the Scandinavian countries. Now it had all changed, and forever.

Alec tore off a piece of fresh pita bread and dipped it into a bowl of thick hummus that one of the guards had purchased from a local food stand. Speaking with his mouth half-full, he said, "Has Dr. Radhy gotten back to us?" Before hearing the answer, he took another drink of a Heineken brew and another bite of pita and hummus. He tugged at his cotton-spandex rash guard. It was too warm for him now.

Bobby and Alvarado could not sleep, so they luxuriated in the Jacuzzi and imbibed in one of life's last simple pleasures…cold beer and potato chips.

"CENTCOM-Baghdad, sir, also said that JIS has arranged for a resupply just south of Jabal Ramm. And we're waiting on Dr. Radhy."

"Anything else, Pratt?"

"Yes, sir," Pratt answered with hesitation in his voice.

"What is it?" Alec asked quickly.

"CENTCOM-Baghdad reports that multiple VBIEDs killed twenty-nine just outside the IZ. Fourteen were ours from the 4th Infantry. Their Humvees were taken out in the explosion. Al-Qaeda claimed responsibility. By the way, these bastards have gotten even more creative. Now they're placing small containers of chlorine gas in both VBIEDs and IEDs. The gas is deadly. When exploded, just a few whiffs and you're dead."

Vehicle-borne improvised explosive devices have been the utter bane of both American and Coalition Forces. They appeared out of nowhere and wreaked untold damage to both persons and property. Their cost was low, yet their impact was high. The irony of it all was that more casualties were the result of VBIEDs and IEDs than by enemy fire.

The thought of the fourteen U.S. soldiers killed in a flash, hit Alec like a 50mm round. Every time he heard of a U.S. soldier killed for the cause of freedom, it was as if he wasn't doing enough. He wasn't moving fast enough to end the terror, to stop the Islamofascists who roamed the world fomenting and executing acts of murder and mayhem, all in the name of Allah.

Alec looked back at Pratt, whose face gave away his concern. Alec knew Pratt was not telling all. "Pratt, and what else…," he asked sternly.

"Sir, CENTCOM-Baghdad also reports that Mick Dornan was killed in Afghanistan a few weeks ago."

Alec was nonplussed. He could not speak. Moving over to a chair at the kitchen table, he dropped his body into it. Looking blank-faced, he said very slowly, "Killed? How?"

"Killed in a firefight in the southeastern part of Afghanistan. His Army Ranger patrol was attacked near the village of Sperah."

"Goddamn it. What the hell is going on? A guy decides to give up a dream life to fight for his country, only to lose his life anyway. It just doesn't compute." Trying to shake it off, "Let's get the hell out of here and head for Jamal Ramm," he said, slamming his hand on the large oak table decorated in a southwestern motif of cowboys, cattle, and cuties.

Jabal Ramm was a mountain peak that stuck obtrusively out of the sand and rose to a height of 1754 meters. It looked so bizarre, a towering mountain in the middle of an untamed desert in a most perilous part of the world.

The 350 kilometers from Amman, Jordan, to Aqabah through the southern Jordanian Desert was a trek that caused Alec's most positive side to wince. He and his men had already traveled hundreds upon hundreds of kilometers across burning sands from Iraq to Syria to Jordan and now they were headed to the Gulf of Aqabah. Alec was tired. He was even melancholic at times, but when his mind took him to its nadir, it would inevitably rise to its zenith once more, buoyed by the knowledge that his fight was the only fight worth fighting. It was to rid the world of terrorism, to avenge his friend's murder, to secure freedom, after all…*what else mattered?*

CHAPTER THIRTY-FIVE

By 1800 hours, everyone stood front and center in the library and the chitchat had come and gone, as Alec began to spell out the mission.

Alec began slowly. "It is in the Gulf of Aqabah where Hamas, with the assistance of the Khamsin, had established a position several months before the fall of Iraq to Coalition Forces. They have been patiently waiting for their orders to move WMD into position to launch future terrorist attacks on United States and British interests in the Middle East. Intel has it that the attacks have been in the planning stages ever since additional WMD were shipped from Iraq to Hamas operatives in Jordan. Funding for future attacks came from the sale of opium produced by holy fighters for Islam in Afghanistan and funneled to Hamas by al-Qaeda, both of whom answer to the Khamsin. Additional funds were acquired through secret oil sales by Saudi royals to both France and Germany and brokered by Khamsin operatives working on Wall Street. As-Saffah is in the middle of it all," Alec said, as he took in a large breath.

There was no denying it. *The Ankabut continued to weave his wicked web ever wider.*

"Gentlemen, at 1900 hours JIS officers will meet us here at Big Pecos." Alec did all he could not to chuckle when he said Big Pecos. The monstrous statue of a bull that inspired the residence's name stared straight at him from the grand foyer.

Glancing at his Casio G-Shock chronograph wristwatch, Pratt announced emphatically, "Sir, it's 1850 hours."

"That is all." Alec nodded and walked out of the kitchen area and into the garden. Wandering along, watching the sun that the ancient al-Hazen had so admired, as it made its final descent below the sandy horizon, he tried to make sense of the myriad thoughts caroming inside his mind. He needed to put it all together. He needed to maintain his focus. He needed to get home, but not before he accomplished his mission.

The Humvees rolled up to the heavily guarded entrance. Two JIS guards opened the gates, as the Humvees pulled up to the front door of the compound. The fountain in the center of the motor court displayed a depiction of a cowboy branding a young calf. The sculpture was sculpted out of black marble. A second calf was looking on, all the while urinating into the pond. It was a sight only a Texan could appreciate. Anyway, it was Big Pecos.

A guard opened the front door, as Dr. Radhy, followed by two bodyguards, walked hastily through and into the library where he found Alec starring impassively out the bay window. Looking at Alec through his aviator glasses, he said, "Doctor."

Alec rose up and extended his hand in a gesture of respect. Without preamble, he said, "We are ready, Dr. Radhy."

"Very good, Dr. Hakimian. My men will take you first to Jamal Ramm, as the plan dictates. There we will have your supplies and munitions. Your Op-Loc Baghdad has already made the delivery. I must say that your pilotless aircraft is truly impressive."

Op-Loc was shorthand for operating location.

Alec nodded in agreement.

Dr. Radhy continued, but there was a clicking sound in the background that caught his attention. Bobby was adjusting the trigger pressure on his H&K MP5N submachine gun. If he could not use his sniper rifle, then the H&K was what he relied on, especially in close combat. Dr. Radhy gave Bobby a look, smiled, and continued. "Once in Aqabah, from there you will be, how do you say?" Pausing for a beat, he finished, "On your own."

Alec knew what it meant. Jordan walked a very high tightrope in the Arab world. Every time it exhibited any degree of sympathy for the Western world, the noose tightened around its neck, yet it owed the United States. Secretly, King Abdullah still harbored great regret for having released the butcher al-Khalayleh under a questionable amnesty ruling a few years before.

Alec also understood that when it came down to crunch time, the U.S. was on its own. Even the JIS had to maintain a safe distance, for fear it would look too much like a lackey for the United States.

The nation of Jordan has historically made furtive overtures in the direction of the West, but it has always done so with great discretion, fearing reprisals from within the Arab world, a world controlled by Islamic fundamentalists. These religious radicals, bent on worldwide domination through violent jihad, were fueled by money from the Ankabut, Saudi Arabia, and other aspects of the Muslim world.

It was a world that the Khamsin was determined to make its own at all costs.

CHAPTER THIRTY-SIX

The Humvees were loaded and OS9 set out for the military airport, where the chopper was waiting. As the Humvees entered the off-limits area, Alec cast about, searching for any sign of reality. His world had become all too surreal now. He knew it had changed to a fight to the finish.

As the team exited the Humvees, a camouflaged H-92 Sikorsky Superhawk was being towed by an aviator tractor out of an immense hangar. The Superhawk in particular was one of twenty wise purchases from the U.S. Government and it gave the Jordanian Intelligence Service capabilities that were the envy of the region.

Military helicopters were extremely complicated machines that required a great deal of maintenance and a great deal of magic to keep them flying. A pilot deftly guided the awkward bird off the ground and through the air using a cyclic stick, a lever situated between his knees and controlled by his right hand. He used the cyclic stick to tilt the main rotor to set the direction of the aircraft. He also used his left hand to control the collective, which had a throttle at its end. It increased or decreased the pitch of the main rotor, which was in effect the torque and lift, giving the aircraft motion in any direction. To stabilize the aircraft, the pilot used two pedals at his feet. These pedals controlled the small rotor on the tail that prevented the body of the helicopter from spinning out of control at the mercy of the main rotor.

Once Alec and his men were onboard, Dr. Radhy leaned into the passenger compartment and said, "Gentlemen, I have men waiting for you at Jabal Ramm. After you are refitted, they will accompany you to Aqabah about forty kilometers southwest of Jabal Ramm." He finished with a smart salute to Alec and his men.

The Superhawk helo left the ground like a Saturn V rocket reaching for the moon. The main rotor blade whipped up the air, creating a curtain of hurricane force wind that blew up and across the tarmac, as it angled-off toward one of the Middle East's tallest mountain peaks.

The flight to Jabal Ramm was as expected, uneventful.

The pilot set down the Superhawk like a mother laying her infant down to rest.

Alec and Pratt exited first. Bobby and Alvarado followed close behind. Their abayes blew wildly until the main rotor of the helicopter came to a full stop. Bobby showed his annoyance by tearing at the garment, as if trying to rip it off.

The refitting at Jabal Ramm went accordingly, and there was even a pleasant surprise. CENTCOM-Baghdad had sent a new, advanced version of the experimental exoskeleton suit. DARPA had developed the latest version in concert with the Army Research Laboratory and the University of Delaware.

The newest version employed a highly secret form of Kevlar-type fabric dipped in an amalgamation of superfine silica glass and a unique polymer liquid. Once the fabric was saturated in the special liquid, it maintained its flexibility, but when hit by an object such as a bullet, the particles in the liquid joined together and formed an impenetrable shield. This *liquid armor* component enhanced the quality of the new EXO4 by giving it greater mobility, less weight, and a faster response time.

As the men settled themselves in for the ride to Aqabah, Alec stared up at the top of Jabal Ramm, and in a fleeting moment of luscious insanity, he imagined himself on a clear and crisp December morning skiing down Bald Mountain in Sun Valley, Idaho, with his wife next to him.

In time, the Humvees rumbled into Aqabah, entering from its northernmost point. The men adjusted their new V.4 exosuits, checked their weapons, and readied themselves for what was to come.

At times, Alec thought that with the introduction of each new version of the exoskeleton suit, OS9 was the ultimate test laboratory for the engineers at DARPA. However, he was not complaining, for it was surely the advantage that OS9 needed to get the job done.

Bobby could not help but make a comment. "Well, at least this new bionic clothing fits better," he said, as he looked himself over. "And the air-conditioning system is cool, really cool. Get it?" he added laughingly.

Alvarado continued to scan the streets as Pratt sat silent, checking his computer's readouts.

Nighttime made the odd-looking Humvees less obvious, yet caution was the order of the night. As they traveled south down Prince Hassan Street, Alec's mind began to wander again from thoughts of his family at home to the recent death of the patriot Mick Dornan. Turning left down Ash Sharif al-Hussein bin Ali Street, Alec's Humvee hit a pothole that jarred him back to the moment and what had to be done.

Speaking to the driver, Alec commanded tersely, "*Ya Sahibi*, my friend. Take us to the back entrance of the hotel." Pointing to several tall shade trees near the hotel's rear entrance, he said, "There. Park there."

"Yes, sir," the driver said obediently.

The Aquamarina II Hotel, where the mustard gas, a favorite of Hussein's, was believed to be hidden, was situated on al-Nahdah Street, just a few streets southwest of Princess Hala Circle and a few hundred meters from the Gulf itself. It seemed an unlikely place for mustard gas to be hidden, but in the terror trade nothing was off limits and nothing made sense.

The Humvees came to a halt several hundred meters behind the rear entrance to the hotel. "Boys," Alec said, commanding their attention. Exiting the Humvee, he continued, "Let's do it. Pratt, get us linked to Sat 5 and give me a view of the interior grounds of the hotel." Standing at the front of the Humvee, he continued, "Bobby, get me a fix on all the entrances. Alvarado, give me radiuses of cover."

An unmarked, dark green Lexus approached the two JIS drivers. Men in both vehicles exchanged words and then the Lexus disappeared into the deep night.

"Sir," Pratt said pointing to his laptop screen. "Here's the pool area inside the grounds. And over here's an entrance that leads to a subterranean storage area that is heavily fortified."

"So what's our best play?" Alec asked.

"The back entrance," Pratt said with confidence.

"Sir," Alvarado interjected. "We've got clear distances surrounding the grounds between twenty-five to thirty-five meters, but not much room to move."

Alec was computing all the possibilities, all the scenarios. OS9 had to consider the several hundred hotel guests and day-trippers that were certainly in the hotel and surrounding area. He ran through the scenarios as if he were prepping for a delicate brain surgery. Everything had to be accounted for. Arousing suspicion would only increase the chances of innocent lives being put in danger. Alec knew they had to move with stealth and steel. "Pratt, find your position. Bobby, you and Alvarado, do the same. I'll recon the interior."

Alec adjusted his communications gear and activated his exosuit's full compliment of capabilities hidden beneath his well-worn abaye.

Entering the rear entrance, he was immediately met by a hotel security guard. "Sir, may I help you?"

"*Minfadlak*, please. *Abhath al saed Mahabi*. I'm looking for Mr. Mahabi." Alec knew that as-Saffah had used the name Mr. Mahabi in the past and thought it was as good as any way to find out if the intelligence on him had been right.

Given Alec's look in a Bedouin's tunic, his impeccable, classical Arab diction caught the unsuspecting security guard off balance. "Sir," nodding to Alec. "Are you a friend of Mr. Mahabi?"

"Yes. Yes, he is my first cousin on my mother's side," Alec fired back with a smile.

Holding his breath for the guard's response, Alec quickly scanned the immediate area as three tourists strolled by jabbering in some Scandinavian language.

"He told me that he'd be here this week. Perhaps you can check."

"But your cousin left here early this morning," the guard said. "I helped load his car."

Alec just held his breath for a beat and then said, "Do you know where my cousin went? We were supposed to go boating today."

"No. He left with three men. That is all I remember. I didn't look at which direction they went. Sorry. Perhaps the front desk can give you more information. Would you like me to take you up front and you can ask?"

"*Shoukran*, thank-you. But I'll try to call him on his cell phone." Alec certainly could not risk arousing any suspicion. "You've been most helpful. I think I'll just go into the restaurant and relax with a tea."

"All right. I hope I was of some help. I must go now. I'm late for my rounds." The security guard's innocence was only exceeded by his general lack of any real formal education beyond a few years of grammar school.

Alec excused himself and made his way to the restaurant. "Pratt, I'm in the main restaurant," he said, speaking into his lip mike. With frustration in his voice, he continued. "I just learned from the security guard that the motherfucker beat it out of here early this morning. He didn't have a clue where he went."

A sense of frustration inhabited Pratt's voice. "Goddamn it. We were so close."

Pratt's comment did not make Alec feel any better. *Sure, weapons of mass destruction were better than nothing, if in fact there were WMD in the hotel as reported,* Alec reasoned. *But getting as-Saffah was worth much more personally to him.*

"So what do you have for me?" Alec demanded.

"Sir, the subterranean storage area is accessed on the other side of the pool area," Pratt said. "That's where the WMD should be."

Alec adjusted his earpiece. "I'm going to take a look. Have Bobby and Alvarado standby."

Alec made his way out to the pool area. Earlier in the day, it was carpeted in pale sun lovers, mostly from Scandinavia, and mostly women. The young ones were as one would expect, healthy and hot. Alec now looked disinterested as he walked to the opposite side of the pool area, passing couples exchanging looks of love and sipping red wine. There he opened a door that led to a stairwell that pointed down two flights. Scanning the area for watching eyes, he closed the door behind himself and quietly stepped down the stairway. Reaching to open the door at the bottom, he found it locked. "Pratt, I'm at the door under the pool area, but it's locked. I'll pop it with some Gel-X."

Gel-X was an explosive with unique characteristics. It had the explosive power of the plastic explosive C-4, yet made no sound, released no smoke, left no chemical signature, and was undetectable by X-ray. It was in essence, *a stealth explosive.*

Alec carefully applied less than fifteen grams of Gel-X to the lock. Detonation was by remote control. *Boom...open says me.* The now opened door, twisted by the explosion, concealed behind it a long hallway that had the smell of a recent paint job. He said in a hollow tone, "Pratt, I'm in. There's a long hallway. Give me two minutes. If you don't hear from me, send Alvarado."

Alec sensed the long hallway, with fresh paint, was a recent construction, possibly in the past couple of months. Five meters down the hallway, it turned left. He pointed his exosuit's visual finder to see around the corner. There he saw two men dressed in typical Arab garb. They sat in front of a large door drinking tea, puffing seriously on cheap-smelling cigarettes, and playing backgammon at a card table held together with meters of duct tape. "Pratt, I'm just steps from two guards seated in front of a door that obviously holds what we're looking for. Their AKs are in plain view."

"Sir," Pratt responded. "There's someone entering the staircase."

"What timing," Alec said, as he watched the intruder in his viewfinder screen embedded in the left forearm of his new exosuit.

Alec turned around and moved back several steps. Looking back to where he entered, he saw the hotel security guard walking quickly toward the turn in the hallway. As the security guard made the turn, Alec surprised him with a sentry takeout, deliberately forcing his Ka-Bar combat knife into his left carotid artery, and then completely severing it with one powerful pull of his arm. Blood shot against the wall as the guard dropped lifeless to the ground.

"Sir," Pratt said with urgency in his muffled voice.

"What?" Alec questioned, as he turned the corner and lobbed a GH S&F-13 flash grenade on the card table. The two men looked at it, as it rolled across the table and then.... The percussion of the grenade killed both of them and blew the backgammon board and chairs in every direction. The sound was muffled by the fact that it was about six meters under ground.

"Pratt, what did you say?" Alec asked, as he applied about forty-five grams of Gel-X to the three-inch thick steel door. The detonation was instant and complete. Alec stepped over the mangled door and into a large room. It was empty, but his instincts told him that it had not been for too long. He activated his exosuit's SniffEx-2, a biomagnetic sensor capable of detecting even the minutest residues of chemicals. Immediately, the sensor picked up latent chemical signatures that revealed the presence of mustard gas.

Mustard gas was a very strong vesicant that blistered the skin, caused blindness, and has been known to produce various cancers. The military use of the gas dated back to 1917, when the Germans, who referred to it as Kampfstoff LOST gas, subjected Canadian soldiers to its deleterious effects. In 1989, thousands upon thousands of Kurds were murdered in northern Iraq by the then *Butcher of Baghdad*, Saddam Hussein.

In its purest form, the gas was colorless, odorless, and was a viscous liquid at room temperature. Its name derived from the impure form that has an odor similar to mustard or garlic.

"Sir," Pratt said.

"Yeah," he answered.

"CENTCOM-Baghdad says that there could be a possibility that a suitcase dirty bomb is in the room where you are."

Alec then set the exosuit's SniffEx-2 to detect radioactive materials. It immediately registered the residue of a radioactive material, possibly Plutonium-239.

Now it started to make sense to Alec. *As-Saffah had come for the dirty bomb*, he reasoned. He continued to scan the room back and forth. He found no bomb, just the residues of chemical and nuclear agents. "I don't see it. I don't see the suitcase dirty bomb. Wait! Now I'm registering some Fusion B. Ever heard of Fusion B?"

"No, sir. Never heard of it," Pratt replied.

"Well, I have. I also know that the friggin' French had something to do with it being here," he added with great disgust. "They didn't support our asses when we forced Saddam's hand years ago. In fact, they were selling both technology and weapons to him for years, so why should I expect anything else from them?"

During the First Gulf War, a consortium of United States and British military contractors developed Fusion B in great secrecy. Much like the Manhattan Project during World War II that developed the A-Bomb, Fusion B was created under the codename Black Magic.

The principle of Fusion B was quite simply the fusing together of several deadly biological agents, for which there was no antidote. Fusion B's effects were devastating at every level, from physical to psychological. When dispersed, it brought about the destruction of all living organisms within a large kill zone.

Alec searched farther into the room and then he saw it. It was a door no higher than two meters, most of it covered by two large, empty pine crates. His SniffEx-2 detector picked up chemical signatures again. He adjusted the airtight mask of his exosuit then cautiously slid the crates aside. "Pratt. I've got something here."

"What's that, sir?" Pratt fired back.

"There's another room inside this room and I'm about to open the door."

"Sir, do you detect any C-4?" Pratt questioned.

"The sensor says no."

"Good, but go slowly," Pratt cautioned.

With the small door half opened, he shined his Surefire LED flashlight into the room. "Pratt. There's canisters in here. A dozen at least. Looks like mustard and probably *sarin* gas and there's one canister of Fusion B. We've got to get this crap out of here. Get Alvarado and have the Humvees backed up to the rear entrance next to that small outbuilding that we saw coming in and wait until I give the order," he said, cold and precise.

"Will do, sir," answered Pratt.

"Pratt. Have Bobby cover the backdoor. Get a hold of CENTCOM-Baghdad. Tell them the canisters will be in the Humvees and that we will rendezvous along the coast at Aqabah Fort outside the city. Have the choppers there at 2100 hours."

"Roger that, sir," Pratt fired back.

Bobby had cleverly embosked himself within a cluster of shrub-like trees just off the parking area. Suddenly, he spotted two unidentified men moving quickly toward the rear entrance as a group of late-nighters pulled up in a faded purple-colored tour bus. The two men hid behind a transport truck and waited until the cackling group disappeared through the back entrance near the pool area, then they moved in. It was Bobby's choice. He set his machine gun to semiautomatic, attached a silencer pod and then calmly squeezed off two shots...just two precise shots. *Thud. Thud.* The two men proved Sir Isaac Newton right as they hit the ground, thus obeying the irrefutable law of gravity.

Alvarado had one of the Humvees waiting near the back entrance. "Pratt, get Alvarado to come down and help me out with this shit," Alec commanded.

Speaking quickly into his lip mike, Pratt said forcefully, "Alvarado. The Doc says to get down the stairs and help him remove the WMD canisters."

"I'm on my way," Alvarado said reflexively.

Bobby dragged the two dead men out of the way and stuffed them in a shed that probably once served as a small dwelling for the ground's keeper.

Hauling the canisters up the stairs proved somewhat problematic, despite the exosuit's ability to increase hand strength by several hundred percent. Each canister's awkwardness was multiplied by its slick, cold steel exterior. They were not designed to be moved by human hands.

Alec struggled to complete the removal of the last canister, the fourteenth in all, from the basement room. "Alvarado, make sure that the Fusion B is set to the right side in the back of the Humvee across from the mustard and sarin gases. Strap everything down in both Humvees. Although they are not known to be particularly volatile when left alone, let's take no chances, these canisters are the real shit."

Bobby and Pratt ran up next to the loaded Humvees. With a nod from Alec, the convoy started out from the Aquamarina II Hotel and headed out. Aqabah Fort was just a few klicks north of town. Hopefully, the chopper would be on time.

As the Humvees neared the fort, a faint image of what could have been a medieval castle somewhere in the Scottish Highlands appeared between great gusts of sand.

The Khamsin was at work again, blowing walls of nearly molten sand one hundred meters high across the land.

Aqabah Fort, a classic medieval example of the stonemason's art, struggled to maintain some sort of permanence. The carcass of a small goat next to a wall served as carrion for vultures that circled above. A few treadless tires were scattered about, with spent pop cans signaling a certain sign-of-the-times. In a land of antiquity, modernity had now insinuated itself into the severe landscape.

As the convoy of Humvees continued to the rendezvous point, Alec's thoughts began to roam the vast convolutions of his complex and troubled mind. Tucked in a far corner was the thought of the rest of his team. *Were Mackay, Josiah, Riemann, and Nutworth ready for the final push into Lebanon?*

To have the entire OS9 team together again put a wide smile on his face, and seeing them again was now only hours away.

The driver of Alec's Humvee pulled to a stop just a few meters short of the fort. Turning to Alec, "*Hakim*, doctor. We are here."

Alec searched the vicinity. He remembered that during World War I Lawrence of Arabia once visited the fort, originally built by the Crusaders. *Where was the helo now?* he asked himself. *Why was it not on time?* "Pratt, what was your last communiqué with CENTCOM?"

"Sir, they said the helo would arrive at 2100 hours. It's now 2050 hours," he said, looking at his Casio chronograph.

"Did you tell them that we missed the bastard as-Saffah? Did you tell them that he left with three men and no one knows to where? Tell them he had to have taken the dirty bomb with him." Alec's calm voice belied his true thoughts.

"Sir, they were informed," Pratt responded flatly, knowing that Alec was infuriated.

"Boys, secure the area and then prepare to board the helo when it arrives," Alec said as he exited the Humvee. One of the JIS officers made a call to his headquarters in Amman. He called to inquire if they had any sighting of the U.S. Navy helo. The answer came back a confirmed *no.*

2100 hours came and went…no helo. Not a sound. Yet the star lit sky, with the moon hung high, was a remarkable sight.

Alec paced around the Humvees, counting the mustard and sarin gases, as well as the Fusion B canisters tied down inside the rear compartments. Each circumnavigation of the parked Humvees caused his level of concern to rise.

"*Hakim*, doctor," the Jordanian Intel officer said to Alec, "we cannot leave ourselves open."

The fort was essentially on the beach and was necklaced by the ubiquitous Middle Eastern palm tree. The sight of two military Humvees and oddly dressed men would undoubtedly draw unneeded attention.

The officer's admonition fell on deaf ears. Alec was not about to be deterred. He would wait all night if need be. "Pratt, call CENTCOM-Baghdad and find out what the hell is up."

Pratt tried his best, but his communication batteries were now spent to the point of deep discharge. No signal, no response.

"Sir," Pratt said, looking at Alec with a forlorn face. "The batteries are gone. We have no communications ability. It'll take three to four hours to have the solar-cells recharge in good sunlight, if at all. They're completely discharged. I can't explain it and the extra sets weren't in the drop shipment. Maybe the heat destroyed some of the cells."

Suddenly, everyone heard the sounds of massive rotors slashing through the hot, thick night air of the southern Jordanian Desert. In the far off distance, a silhouette of a monstrous helicopter was sighted. Pointing to the figure, Bobby blurted out, "Helo at 9 o'clock, sir."

There it was in all its glory. The sound and prop wash of the intimidating Boeing CH-46 Sea Knight helicopter forced most of the desert nocturnal creatures to scurry for cover like a mischievous child disturbing a beehive.

The medium lift Sea Knight helicopter had been a mainstay of the Marines and amphibious assault vessels for decades. Its two GE-T58-16 engines drove fifty-one foot fiberglass blades that carved gapping holes out of the air, one after another, as it pushed forward at 145 knots.

In combat trim, the Sea Knight carried a pilot, copilot, crew chief, two aerial gunners, and the ability to ferry twenty-five troops into enemy territory. Its tandem-rotor configuration gave it special handling abilities in windy conditions, and now it was to carry WMD canisters across Israel to the U.S.S. *Kearsarge* anchored off the coast of southern Israel. The ship was a unit of the Amphibious Squadron, Six Amphibious Group Two, U.S. Atlantic Fleet.

The Sea Knight began its short descent onto the light-colored sand that was now in chaos, blowing in every direction. The Humvees gave no protection, with sand beginning to fill the seats and floorboards. By the time the pilot set the big bird down, there was a blanket of coarse sand that had settled inside the Humvees.

The pilot was obviously one of the best, as evidenced by the manner in which he brought the chopper effortlessly to a full stop, like a great Monarch butterfly lighting on a rose petal.

The payload door was pushed open and an unusually tall crew chief exited, his ear protectors hung loosely about his albatross-long neck. The pilot followed seconds later.

Alec stepped up and said, "We were beginning to…."

"Sorry, sir, but the goddamn winds of the Khamsin forced us into Egyptian territory for a bit. They must've been blowing at over 110 knots. We almost lost it," Captain David Willy said sharply.

"Glad you're here," Alec said, thankfully.

"Got to load up now, sir. Fuel's low," the crew chief said, as he pointed toward the Humvees. "The winds were costly. How many canisters do we have?"

"Fourteen, chief," Alec said immediately.

"Very good, sir," he remarked, marching deliberately toward the trucks.

"Bobby, Alvarado, Pratt, give 'em a hand," Alec barked out. The JIS officers joined in.

The mustard and sarin gas canisters and the Fusion B were loaded aboard the Sea Knight in short order. Turning to the Jordanian Intel officers, Alec said, "*Shoukran,* thank-you. Tell Dr. Radhy that he was a great help, and tell your great king that the United States appreciates his assistance. *Leyle saideh, ya sahibi.* Good night, my friend," Alec said, as he shook the hands of both men. The officers saluted, did an about face, then returned to their vehicles.

"Sir, it's time," the crew chief yelled out to Alec, as the pilot started the two massive General Electric turbo engines that spooled up until they were each spitting out nearly two thousand shaft horsepower.

Once the big bird lifted off, Alec felt an immediate sense of relief. Looking back at the find stored in a specially secured compartment, he thought it was a good day. The 240 kilometers along the Egyptian-Israel border passed without incident. Alec spent the time gazing out the window into the darkness of night, trying desperately to rest his tired mind.

As they approached the Mediterranean Sea, the pilot radioed the Wasp Class Amphibious Assault Ship U.S.S. *Kearsarge.*

"There's that big, bad-ass bitch. Hot showers here we come," Bobby shouted out. He followed it with a *hooooray* to emphasize his excitement.

The enormous U.S.S. *Kearsarge* was the namesake of the *Mohican*-class sloop-of-war from the Civil War era. It was easy enough to spot in the deep blue, ancient Mediterranean, a sea that from 264 B.C. to 146 B.C. caused Rome and Carthage to battle for the control of Spain, Corsica, and Sicily, and to have the right to call the Mediterranean Sea *Mare nostrum*, "Our Sea."

Nearly three football fields in length, the U.S.S. *Kearsarge* made a tempting target, sure enough, but it was usually protected by faster, more heavily armed vessels that were all part of the U.S. Navy's Atlantic Sixth Fleet.

"The stick is not responding. Something's wrong. It's fighting me. Can't get enough pitch," the pilot, whose call sign was Wicked Willy, said in a calm voice to the ship's landing crew chief as the Sea Knight approached.

"Do you think you'll be able to put her down?" the landing crew chief asked.

"Looks too close to call," Wicked Willy said again with great calmness.

"We're readying the super trap for you. As you approach, let us know. The wind's at forty knots, blowing south-southeast. It's your call," the landing crew chief said emphatically, shouting into his head mike, trying to make himself heard over the background noises of choppers taking off and landing.

The super trap was rarely used, but in dire circumstances, a chopper could set down in a great steel net hung off the blunt stern of the ship. Using the super trap made it easier to land the chopper in gale force winds or if there was a mechanical failure. It also served to preserve the landing deck. A damaged landing deck caused an interruption in daily flight activities, something that was always on the captain's mind. He was charged with keeping the flight deck fully operational at all times.

"Gents," Captain Wicked Willy said in his Texan accent. "Hold on to your asses, this is gonna be a bitch." He began his first and only approach to the ship.

It has often been said that landing an aircraft on a ship at night was like standing in a dark room and falling forward, all the while having just one chance to hit a postage stamp with your tongue.

"Wicked Willy, this is Wild One again," the landing crew chief said. "What's it to be? The trap?"

"We're goin' for it," he answered confidently.

"Roger that," he said.

It was not the WMD that troubled Alec the most. He knew that the case-hardened steel canisters were designed to withstand both high impact and intense heat. Alec was concerned about his men. He wanted every one of them to stay healthy. He was determined to return all of them to their families alive.

Wicked Willy maneuvered the Sea Knight near the fantail of the pitching ship. Red lights flashing everywhere on the instrument panel told the tale…fuel was critically low and the chopper's mechanicals were malfunctioning. As he lowered the mighty chopper to within just meters of the deck, it lost complete power and dropped onto the deck, missing the super trap and snapping off both front landing gear. The main rotor blade came to an immediate stop after slashing the side of the first floor of the multi-storied "island," which housed the flight control and bridge on the starboard side of the vessel. Emergency crewmen raced to the helo with fire hoses and medical gear. A crewman opened the main hatch and, "Gentlemen, welcome to the U.S.S. *Kearsarge*. Everybody okay? Oh, and you missed dinner," he added in a distinctly Cajun accent, signing the comment with a big smile. "But I'm sure Pop can fix something up."

The landing was not what they had expected, but they were alive and well.

Bobby's eyes lit up at the thought of it. Yelling over the deafening sound of aircraft taking-off and landing, he asked, "How about a hot shower first?"

Adjusting his communication headgear, the crewman answered kindly, "You betcha."

Captain J.B. Ruger called down from the command deck to inquire about Alec and his men. "Sir," looking straight at Alec, "Captain Ruger asked if you were okay, and if you'd meet him in the situation room ASAP," a young junior grade officer said. "Permit me to show you the way, sir."

Alec looked up at the command deck several stories above the main deck. He espied Mackay, Riemann, Nutworth, and Josiah looking down with wide smiles painted across their faces. Removing his abaye, he did his best to steady himself in the buffeting winds on the ship's enormous flattop. He then snatched a momentary look back over his right shoulder at the southern Israeli coastline and the faint lights of the embattled Gaza Strip.

"Sir, please, this way," the junior officer said, as he tapped Alec on the shoulder, motioning for him to follow. "The captain and your men are waiting for you."

Alec disappeared with his men through a hatch of the U.S.S. *Kearsarge's* gargantuan stack.

CHAPTER THIRTY-SEVEN

The situation room on the command deck of the U.S.S. *Kearsarge's* "island" was set high above the mammoth landing deck. An expanse of large, cantilevered bulletproof windows gave the captain and his officers an unobstructed view of the ship and the Mediterranean Sea it lived on.

Opening the hatch to the situation room revealed the cheering sounds of those of OS9 who had spent their time at sea, while Alec and the others found caches of the vanquished Saddam Hussein's WMD that most of the world were convinced or wanted to believe never existed. Alec thought, *the president's now in the catbird seat, for he would soon reveal to the naysayers that WMD had indeed existed inside Iraq while Hussein was in power.*

"Doc," Mackay shouted out. "How about a wee dram of the peat water?"

"Mackie, good to see you," Alec said, summoning up a half smile and embracing his comrade.

Pratt, Bobby, and Alvarado shook hands and bear-hugged their brothers-in-arms. They were all glad to be together again as OS9. Josiah, Mackay, Riemann, and Nutworth had felt cooped up in the U.S.S. *Kearsarge*, where they had been preparing for the assault on the Hezbollah encampment east of Sûr, Lebanon.

Captain Ruger stood back out of the way for a beat and just observed what soldiers in battle were all about. Their love and respect for each other knew no bounds. They would give their lives willingly for their fellow soldiers…a selfless act rarely if ever encountered in civilian society, and rarely if ever understood by the very same.

Alec was the first to speak. Nodding to the ship's captain, he said, "Captain Ruger, I and my men thank-you and your crew for your assistance and hospitality. It's been a very tough time, yet a great deal has been accomplished. As you probably now by know, as-Saffah escaped our grasp, taking with him a dirty bomb most likely made with Plutonium-239." A tight smile grew on Alec's tanned face as he added resolutely, "As-Saffah has managed to stay a step ahead, but not for long."

A hearty clapping of hands and whistles erupted at the thought. Alec continued, "And now there's one more operation for which your ship's services will be required."

"Dr. Hakimian," Captain Ruger responded, in his relaxed Midwestern style. "We of the U.S.S. *Kearsarge* are prepared to assist you in every way possible."

In the background, aircraft were heard taking-off and landing, for military maneuvers were 24/7, because the tyrants of terror never took a day off.

CHAPTER THIRTY-EIGHT

Tyre, Lebanon, today called Sûr, situated just 83 kilometers south of Beirut, was the insertion point for OS9's final mission.

Tyre was ancient Phoenicia's most important city. The Queen of the Seas was once an island paradise the envy of the known world. Its great wealth attracted traders from far-off lands. The Greek Herodotus of Halicarnassus, the Father of History, dated Tyre back to the twenty-eighth century B.C. By the twelfth century A.D., it had come under the control of the Crusaders until 1291 and the end of the Crusades.

The mighty U.S.S. *Kearsarge* moved in stately fashion atop the ancient sea some thirty-one kilometers west off the coast of southern Lebanon. The flickering lights of Sûr were visible in the distance, as were those of Beirut to its north.

Deep into the night many of the ship's one thousand-man crew were fast asleep, having gotten used to the constant screaming of jet-turbine engines lifting helicopters off the massive landing deck or the sounds of sea craft scudding the deep blue waters in search of intelligence and enemies.

Alec waved his right hand, commanding everyone's attention. "Gentlemen. As you know, we have been charged with one last mission. Tomorrow before dawn, we will leave on an ASDS. Intel from CENTCOM confirms that a massive quantity of VX gas is located in a large Hezbollah camp southeast of Sûr near Qānā. My guess is that as-Saffah is there. He's the link to the Ankabut himself, and I can't wait to shake his hand," Alec said sarcastically.

VX gas was an extremely deadly and toxic nerve agent that entered the skin and lungs to upset the nervous system and ultimately stop respiration. In the 1950s a British consortium developed the deadly gas. The "V" stood for venom; it was said to be far too dangerous to be used; it was considered the deadliest nerve agent ever invented. The VX gas attack on the Kurds in 1988 by the deposed and now dead despot of Iraq was testimony enough to its deadly efficacy as a WMD.

Hezbollah, a Shi'ite militant organization stationed in Lebanon, has over the years exerted great influence on the politics and society of the country. Hezbollah, or *party of God*, detested the West and sought to establish a Muslim state fashioned in the mold of Iran. They hated with a violent passion every Israeli and anyone who sympathized with the West. Hezbollah was sponsored by both Syria and Iran since the early 1980s, and its global reach deemed it a major concern on every continent.

"Doctor," Captain Ruger interjected with a soft, yet distinct Midwestern accent that bordered on a Canadian inflection. "This just came in for you," handing Alec a sheet of paper.

Alec took the communiqué and quickly read it. It indicated that several HVTs from al-Qaeda were in the camp as well as several members of the al-Aqsa Martyrs' Brigades. No less than three hundred non-military enemy combatants were also training in the camp.

Alec thought, *could any of these High Value Targets be the elusive Ankabut or possibly Fadeel al-Khalayleh or al-Zawahiri or even Usama bin Laden?* It was counterintuitive given that Hezbollah was Shi'ite, but he did not discount the possibility. Both fundamentalist Shi'ite and Sunni interests were at stake if the West prevailed.

"Captain, when will the ASDS be ready?" Alec asked straight away.

"The U.S.S. *Virginia* is due at about 0300 hours," Captain Ruger answered, looking at his TAG Heuer Aquaracer chronograph. "That will give you and your team about three hours to prepare."

"Captain, I hope that includes a little shuteye," Bobby chimed in.

Alec just looked at him.

Shrugging his shoulders, Bobby said, "What? Just thought I'd ask."

"Men," Alec said, gazing up at the large clock on the opposite wall that was somewhat askew. "Let's get it done."

There was was an annoying beeping sound that popped up in the immediate background. A junior officer quickly grabbed for the phone and listened intently. Turning to the captain, he said, "Sir, the weather operator reports that there's a storm heading our way and will arrive at 0300 hours."

"What storm?" the captain asked incredulously. "This is late spring. There were no reports indicating a storm."

"Captain, USCENTCOM weather communications out of Florida said the storm was unexpected, but that it was caused by a strong Sirocco coming off the northeastern coast of Africa," the junior officer on watch answered.

"But it's almost summer. What the hell's going on? In my twenty years on the Med, I've only seen it once before. This is some kind of freak storm," the captain fired back. "Remember that global-warming goofball Gore? Maybe he caused it," he said, ending with a chuckle to himself.

The Sirocco flowed into the southeastern Med from Tunisia, Libya, and Egypt. Though very rare, it was always a sailor's nightmare.

"Captain Ruger. The Sirocco's still in its winter season that runs from the beginning of October to the end of May."

Captain Ruger shot him a look but said nothing. All the captain could think about at the moment was the USS *Virginia*. It was due to rendezvous with his ship at that very same hour. Getting men and equipment aboard the ASDS could be challenging enough in calm seas, but the motion of ships with just thirty meters separating them definitely upped the degree of difficulty.

At 110 meters, the U.S.S. *Virginia,* commissioned in 2004, was the lead ship of the Virginia class of nuclear attack submarines that were fast and aggressive. At a cost of nearly three billion dollars, it was also world-class in every way. Heavily armed with 12 VLS tubes for Tomahawk cruise missiles and four 21-inch torpedo tubes for MK-48 torpedoes, it was a deadly adversary when confronted.

Driven by a single nuclear reactor, and arcing across the globe from sea to sea at surface speeds exceeding 32 knots, the killer-designed, whale-like U.S.S. *Virginia* was on a mission of its own. Alec and Captain

Ruger knew that the success of OS9's mission to infiltrate and eliminate the Hezbollah camp, hinged on the ASDS, and the ASDS had to arrive a few hours before dawn. OS9 needed enough time to make the southern Lebanese coast before the sun rose again.

CHAPTER THIRTY-NINE

MEDITERRANEAN SEA, SOUTHERN COAST OF LEBANON

The pre-dawn canopy overhead was dotted with twinkling stars, some of them of the pulsar variety. Newton's *orb* showed brightly.

The radio operator aboard the U.S.S. *Kearsarge* received a vital transmission and relayed it to the watch officer. "I've got the *Virginia* at twenty kilometers out, sir."

"Very good, Madsen."

The officer on watch turned and called the captain. "Captain, sir. The *Virginia's* some twenty klicks and closing."

"Good, Moore. Captain Thomson always comes through," the captain replied, as he sighed in relief.

Captains Ruger and Thomson had been classmates at the United States Naval Academy, and both had received their commands the same year. Their paths had crossed again during Gulf War I, and now they were comrades-in-arms again in the war on terror.

The captain knew that OS9 was on a mission-critical timeline and every minute counted.

Placing a call to Alec's quarters, Captain Ruger apologized when Alec answered. "Sorry to wake you, sir. But I thought you'd like to know that the ASDS will be arriving in less than an hour."

Alec had a brief moment of elation. He imagined the end was near, that it was the last mission, but he knew otherwise. Thoughts shot through his psyche like a series of Tomahawk cruise missiles that had rained down on Baghdad during the early days of "shock and awe." He questioned himself, *would this really be his last mission?*

He had remembered that during his years with the CIA there were a few times when it was to be the last time, but the last time never came...until that fateful day in 1989. Now he was facing some of the same thoughts, knowing that OS9's last mission would only mark a point in time, for the war on terror would never end. He knew it in his bones. He also knew that he was no longer the same man. Yes, he was in the abstract still the surgeon who loved to save lives. Yet, he also knew that the reality of it all was quite different now. The question that now haunted him was...*could he ever return to his first love...saving lives?* He did not know.

While the men and women of the next shift aboard the U.S.S. *Kearsarge* were still asleep at 0310 hours, the attack submarine carrying the Navy's most modern submersible had arrived only minutes behind schedule. It sidled up next to the leviathan U.S.S. *Kearsarge* with Swiss watch-like precision. As it floated alongside, attached by thick steel tethers, it gulped thousands of gallons of fuel and took on munitions, military hardware, and other matériel OS9 required.

The sixty-five foot Advance SEAL Delivery System vehicle was the Navy's newest submersible designed specifically for covert operations and assigned to SEAL Delivery Vehicle Team #1 stationed at Norfolk, Virginia.

The ASDS *Miraculous* minisub was transported to a theater of operations on the back of the U.S.S. *Virginia* attack submarine. The sixty-ton ASDS carried up to sixteen SEALs plus two operators, none of whom needed to don scuba gear until they were ready to begin their designated covert mission.

Fourteen silver-zinc batteries shielded in titanium bottles provided the ASDS's power. Although classified, the capabilities and power of the submersible were said to be remarkable in every aspect.

The hull of the ASDS was fabricated from a variation of the very same, highly classified materials that were used to construct both the F-117 *Nighthawk* stealth fighter and the B-2 stealth bomber. Its design also allowed it to take a major hit from enemy ordnances and keep on moving. Its range was a comfortable 200 kilometers, with a diving depth of some one hundred meters. As would be expected from such a technological marvel, most of its operations were computer driven. For obvious reasons, the exact specifications were *top-secret*.

Several radar and sonar devices kept the ASDS in the know at all times. What looked like a conventional periscope jutting out of its deck was instead a very sophisticated communication's mast, while the periscope itself was actually an extremely high-definition video camera.

Advanced Weapons Systems, DARPA, and SARA had specifically outfitted the ASDS *Miraculous* for OS9's top-secret, black ops mission.

The cost of the ASDS program didn't come cheap, since Defense Department records indicated that more than two billion dollars had already been spent developing the unique submersible delivery system.

Presently, the Expeditionary Strike Force 1 in the Persian Gulf was home to the *Miraculous* minisub.

◆ ◆ ◆

The early morning dawn flirted with the dying dark of night. The predicted but highly unusual winds and high seas had continued in full force, as the two ships began to pitch back and forth. The U.S.S. *Virginia* had to work deliberately to stay in position as the U.S.S. *Kearsarge* lost little energy doing the same.

As the waves grew in height, white caps broke on a regular schedule, every ten to fifteen seconds. To the untrained eye, the black, stealth Macañudo-shaped minisub looked to be precariously perched atop the U.S.S. *Virginia*, yet it was able to traverse the great seas of the world easily.

It was apparent that time and weather would soon prove to be additional obstacles to OS9's final mission, for time was running out and the weather continued to deteriorate. The sea grunted and groaned, as if it were trying to expel a foreign object from its belly.

The trip to the Lebanese coast would take some doing, but thankfully, much of the journey would be beneath the sea's surface, where one felt very little of the angry sea above.

Two cooks from the mess had prepared a before dawn breakfast for the OS9. It comprised scrambled eggs, thick-cut, western-style bacon, hash brown potatoes cooked very crispy, Florida orange juice from concentrate, with blueberry muffins completing the menu.

Bobby's eyes bugged out as he said, "Damn. It's good to have an

American meal for once." Turning to the others, "How long has it been guys? Too long. That embassy food in Damascus wasn't exactly what I'm used to where I come from. By the way, where's the Starbucks?" he said with his typical juvenile-like smile intact. Pratt and Alvarado nodded in agreement and delved into the feast with their usual gusto.

"Riemann," Alec ordered. "I want you and Nutworth to head down to the ASDS and do a once over after we're finished. Check the new weaponry using acoustic and electromagnetic waves, and even heat. You are probably familiar with most of it. Also, they supplied us with the latest version of the *Starlight* nighttime vision system that utilizes a single contact lens with a computer chip that turns night into day."

Not only did this technology permit the wearer to see in the dark, but it did so without any of the obvious limitations of shadowing and peripheral boundaries inherent in infrared night-vision goggles.

Alec continued, "And aside from the 'wonder weapons,' make sure there's plenty of Gel-X, flash grenades, GH S&F-13s, RGO 78s, and F1s. Satellite intel tells us that there are multiple buildings in the Hezbollah complex near Qānā with about 300 operatives inside. We believe the VX is stored in one building in the center. Pratt, once we're there, I'll need nuts-on coordinates. Have the unattended ground sensors placed where you want them. Oh yeah, and calibrate your electro-burst units for long range."

"Yes, sir. I can do that," Pratt said. "I'll pull off the satellite both heat and spectrograph readouts. That'll give us the exact location of the VX."

Turning to Nutworth and Riemann, he said, "Now. You two will secure our *six* after we've entered the compound. Then I'll need you to set charges. I want the whole friggin' area leveled when we leave. Nothing's to be left behind but sand. Understand?" Alec said with calm resolve.

Nutworth and Riemann, members of DEVGRU, had trained extensively in the ASDS. It would be their charge to bring the others up-to-speed ASAP.

Alec continued, "Mackay, Josiah, I'll need the two of you to set up points near the building that holds the VX. Pratt, keep us shaking hands with USCENTCOM at McDill and in Baghdad. Pratt, make sure Captain Ruger and Commander Vulekovič are in the loop at all times. We'll need a ride home," he said with a chuckle.

"Yes, sir," Pratt replied.

"Men," Alec said, his facial expression turning serious. "I'm not going to shit you here. This won't be easy. Truthfully, I don't expect all of us to make it back alive." Somber expressions covered the faces of every member of OS9. He continued, "We'll be surrounded at all times with hostiles. One misstep and…," Alec stopped in mid-sentence. Holding his thought for a pregnant pause, then taking a deep breath, he continued again. "Finish up here, download the latest updates for your exos…you'll need them. And…I want as-Saffah. I want that son-of-a-bitch. He's going to give me the direct line to the Ankabut or…," his voice trailed off as he began to stare out the window of the situation room. The sea was roiling as never before.

DARPA was constantly adding to and refining the exoskeleton suit's abilities. The latest version of the suit included enhanced motion and reflex healing abilities. The exosuit was even capable of synchronizing with the latest in field medical care, the *trauma pod*.

The trauma pod, controlled either by a rear-field medical support team or stateside from USCENTCOM's McDill Air Force Base, robotically attended to an injured soldier in the field, applying onsite medical care that included both the stitching of lacerations and bullet wounds to the setting of broken bones and the stemming of bleeding. It was also capable of diagnosing most injuries and sending the data back to a rear field medical doctor. The trauma pod would then retrieve the wounded solider and return him to a rear field hospital for additional care.

Turning to leave the room, Alec gazed for a moment out the large-paned window again, pondered the moment, and then said calmly, "If any of you pray, pray now."

Everyone looked solemnly at each other as Alec left. They quietly ate the remainder of their breakfasts and then left the situation room without speaking.

One of the ship's junior officers escorted Riemann and Nutworth to the area where two large, steel cables acted as tethers from the U.S.S. *Kearsarge* to the U.S.S. *Virginia*. Hanging from one cable was a simple, high-impact carbon-fiber cage about two, by two, by two and a half meters. Inside was a blue-polyurethane bench that accommodated up to six men. The men entered the cage and sat down. Looking below their feet, the angry sea was trying to reach up and swallow them.

"Men," the officer said loudly, as the sea tried its best to drown out his voice, "hold on tightly, this could be a rough ride." Nutworth acknowledged the officer's admonition with a nod. The officer gave the order and shut the cage door.

The cage that dangled from the thickly woven steel cable swayed back and forth, as it slid down toward the submarine in zip-line fashion. The ride across took no time at all. Suddenly, it hit the other side with a thud. Two large, neoprene bumpers on the sub's conning tower took the impact.

After the cage was secured to the side of the U.S.S. *Virginia*, Riemann and Nutworth stepped out carefully and were met by a junior officer and several deckhand specialists. Even though it was late spring in the southeastern Mediterranean, where daytime temperatures on shore could reach 40 degrees Celsius, standing on the deck of the attack submarine in the pre-dawn mist proved a bone chilling experience.

Saluting the commanding officer, Riemann and Nutworth were escorted directly to the ASDS. They entered the special-operations minisub from a hatch on its underbelly. Inside the accommodations were not exactly five-star, but for a minisub it was better than the twenty-two foot submersible rides that most SEAL teams were accustomed to.

Looking around, Nutworth said to Riemann, while pointing to several wall racks loaded down with exotic AWS weaponry, "When we trained in this sub the first time most of this was not here." The bizarre-looking thermal gun developed by Oak Ridge National Laboratory used radio-wave technology to heat the human body to 41.6° Celsius, the temperature at which the human body overheats and dies. It excited Nutworth. The emotion seemed pedestrian for a man of Nutworth's background.

He was the third of five boys in a military family. His father rose to the enlisted men's rank of chief petty officer in the U.S. Navy and served in Vietnam. His mother was from a family of U.S. Army officers. Two of his older brothers served in the Granada and Gulf War I conflicts and have since retired to run the family maple syrup business in Vermont.

"Nutty, look at this bitch," Riemann said, pulling an acoustic rifle, also referred to as a sonic rifle, off the uppermost weapons rack.

Scientific Applications and Research Associates, in concert with the U.S. Pentagon, developed the acoustic rifle that shot a lethal audio frequency at an enemy combatant, liquefying the bowels and causing a complete, involuntary excretion of the intestines. A variant of the acoustic deterrent principle utilized several small devices placed around a friendly or enemy perimeter as an *acoustic fence,* deadly to any trespasser.

Nutworth knew what it was at first glance. "Viking, this is mine. A squeeze of the trigger and the dude is dead. Not a drop of blood. Don't you just love it?" he said rhetorically, with a hint of glee in his deep voice.

"Try this," Riemann suggested, handing Nutworth a Star Wars looking weapon that used electromagnetic waves. When pointed at the enemy it would cause him to lapse into an uncontrollable epileptic seizure that would eventually lead to a very painful and certain death.

"Bitchin'. I used one of these at Oak Ridge about two years ago. I and a couple of Delta guys were asked to test them. This," he said, fondling the frightening looking weapon called the *Buzzer,* "will waste a guy in a nanosecond."

Riemann reached for another of what the Pentagon referred to as "wonder weapons." Only some military officers and select members of Congress had knowledge of this weaponry, and then, only in the most nonspecific terms. Security around the development of such futuristic weapons was at the highest level. The most interesting of the antipersonnel weapons onboard the ASDS was the much-ballyhooed "Pulse Wave Myotron II." About the size of a pack of cigarettes, the Myotron II jumbled the signals from the motor cortex area of the human brain. When tuned to its greatest capability, the effects were ugly and always lethal.

Then Riemann saw it. It was the H&K MP5N "S" machine gun. The MP5N "S" was very conventional in appearance, but it shot the FCS *"smartshot"* projectile that had embedded in it a minute, heat-seeking sensor chip. Once fired, just like a Cruise missile, it found its target, no matter where. In essence, it was a precision-guided munition, where every shot fired hit every target, every time.

Riemann and Nutworth felt as if it were Christmas in May. They knew that the others would be jazzed to know that the success of the mission to the Hezbollah camp in southern Lebanon was of the highest priority to the president and the Pentagon. The wonder weapons would give OS9 the edge it needed.

Then Riemann hurriedly reached for one last weapon that caught his discerning eye. It was the Pentagon's "Dazzler," a particle-beam energy gun that at first stunned the enemy, then caused irreversible blindness. The Dazzler would easily add to OS9's firepower.

The remaining handguns, grenade launchers, landmines, and communication devices were also more like Star Wars paraphernalia than conventional pieces of military hardware. They were all products of Advanced Weapons Systems and Future Combat Systems. Both systems pushed United States military weaponry and communications beyond known limits.

Future Combat Systems in particular was a joint program involving all branches of the military. The branches were connected via a complex network of advanced communications. There were eighteen systems in all, plus the soldier himself, linked together. The objective of FCS was to provide an individual soldier, connected to units of manned and unmanned platforms and sensors, with continuously streaming data that allowed the soldier to know exactly what was around him and therefore, execute the best course of action.

"Gentlemen," Commander John Vulekovič said, as he entered the area. "Welcome to the Navy's *Miraculous*," he said proudly. After years of barking out orders to his subordinates, his voice had been honed to a razor's edge.

Riemann liked the sound of the name...the *Miraculous*. He believed in miracles. After all, his father had been diagnosed with inoperable lung cancer...and that was nine years ago. He was convinced it was a miracle...so were the doctors.

"I see that you are enjoying yourselves. When I heard about these weapons, I didn't believe it. This stuff is otherworldly. By the way, I don't mean to take you away from your toys, but you are wanted on the main deck."

Chapter Forty

0330 hours marked for Alec a time he had waited years for, a time to even up the score for what had happened in 1989.

The thought of three hundred fanatical Hezbollah non-military enemy combatants hold up in an encampment east of Sûr focused his thoughts. He imagined the jihadists training in the camp, readying themselves to commit yet more unspeakable acts of terror on the innocent. He had no illusions. He knew instinctively that the Ankabut would be nowhere near the terrorists' encampment. He was too smart for that, because he was never in the fight. He just directed it from afar.

By 0335 hours, the entirety of OS9 was front and center before Alec in the ship's situation room. A few of the ship's crewmen who were present in the room thought the exosuits were great curiosities. Their basic Navy issue clothing seemed insignificant when compared to the Spiderman-like exosuits of OS9.

Alec's eyes zoomed in on a large map and several recon photos placed in the center of the conference table. He brushed up behind the captain's dark-blue leather chair positioned at one end of the table. With both hands placed on the chair's tall back, he began, "Intel from USCENTCOM gives us this view of the encampment." Pointing to the map, he said with focused eyes, "The valley just east of Qānā, here," moving his finger from Sûr to indicate a point just east-northeast of Qānā "shows the main area of the encampment some one-thousand by two-thousand meters in area. This outbuilding here is where the VX is thought to be, probably underground."

The recon photo showed that the building was not much more than a large structure of stacked cinder blocks covered by a galvanized steel, corrugated roof.

Without warning, a screaming AV-8B Harrier aircraft lifted-off in vertical fashion from the flight deck. Its high-decibel sound broke Alec's concentration for a brief moment. He glanced out the window, as the Harrier disappeared from view over the far side of the ship.

Turning back to the map, "There are two sets of barracks. One here in the northeast quadrant of the main compound, as you can see," pointing to the recon photo and then the map. "The main compound sits in the center of a series of low, featureless hills that form a natural barrier to uninvited eyes." Tracing with his index finger in a straight line, he continued, "Two dirt roads here that run along the north and south sides allow Hezbollah to move vehicles and contraband in and out of the area. Another, smaller barracks is over here," he added, pointing again to a specific area on the map. "It's next to what looks like some sort of par-course." The map showed a series of jumps, water hazards, climbing ropes, and the like that the fighters for Allah trained on for months before they were released out into the world to murder the unsuspecting, all in the name of their god.

Satellite photos also indicated dozens of individuals moving about from building to building. Nearby hillsides were dotted with large, earthen holes and gutted automobiles, the result of Hezbollah's testing of extreme explosives. Southeast of the smaller barracks was a much-used firing range. Most of the structures in the main compound were constructed of cinder blocks and flat-steel rooftops. Situated right in the middle of the compound was the commander's office.

The encampment needed no concertina wire or high walls. The amount of firepower inside its natural perimeter was enough to keep intruders at bay. Local herdsmen would occasionally pass by as if they had seen nothing unusual. They had to. Their lives depended on it.

Alec went on without pause, "Roving guards work the perimeter 24/7. They use the Russian-made UAZ 469B 1970s variant of the American Jeep given to them by the Syrians to patrol the hillsides while training is going on. On this hilltop," Alec indicated with his left index finger, "the communication tower here needs to be taken out from the get-go. Riemann and Nutworth will set unmanned sensors and explosives across the entrance to the valley where the main area of the compound is located. Any questions so far?"

"And Josiah and I'll reconnoiter the area and give you a better idea of what we are dealing with once we get closer," Pratt added.

Josiah nodded in the affirmative.

"Mackay," Alec said staring straight at him, "you'll also need to be with Pratt. Everyone pay attention to the readouts on your exos. They'll tell us much of what we need to know in real time." Still looking at Mackay, he continued, "Any outside intel will give us the edge. Once we're in position, you then fall back to a vantage point where you can watch our backs."

"Yes, sirrr," Mackay said straightaway. "Will do, sirrr," he added, saluting Alec with a wink of his eye and a tilt of his head.

"Now, hopefully we can get in and out before dawn. AWS has been kind enough to let us use *Eagle Eye*."

The UCAV, or unmanned combat aerial vehicle, was cutting edge technology by anyone's measure. *Eagle Eye* looked like an aircraft reminiscent of the *Jetson's* animated television series of the early 1960s. It was capable of lifting-off vertically in the worst weather conditions imaginable from an amphibious ship and fly by remote control at 400 knots. It possessed eight mini-Cruise missiles, each with a two hundred kilometer range. Its functional lift capacity was some four hundred kilograms.

"We'll use the transporter and the UAV to get the WMD out. This will shorten our travel time and increase the chances that we'll all make it home," Alec said with a most serious look.

"Where's the UAV coming from?" Josiah asked inquisitively.

"It's onboard ship," Alec said.

One could sense a slight rocking motion aboard the U.S.S. *Kearsarge* as the Mediterranean would not relent. Winds at thirty-nine knots buffeted the deck hands and made take-offs less frequent. The U.S.S. *Virginia* was rocking and rolling, as the waves pounded her sides. The ASDS *Miraculous* stood firm, as two sailors continued the prep sequence.

"By the way, Pratt. FCS sent you a toy as well," Alec said, somewhat cryptically.

Pratt's interest was piqued. "What, sir?" he asked.

"Along with *Eagle Eye* they sent the latest version of *Golden Eye*."

Pratt was aware of *Golden Eye*. The special operations community talked about its capabilities in hushed tones.

Golden Eye accomplished wide area surveillance on several levels. Its special ducted fan design permitted it to change direction, and even speed, instantly by adjusting different sets of control vanes. Since the rotor blades were enclosed, they were not exposed, thus it had the much looked-for ability of flying in close proximity to people, buildings, and landscaping. As a wide area surveillance projectile, it was perfectly suited to street-level warfare operations by sending back to home base streams of valuable data, including the identification of both chemical and biological agents.

Pratt knew *Golden Eye* would give OS9 the advantage they needed in terms of surveillance. He needed to be able to keep everyone informed of what was happening around them. After all, as a before dawn mission, OS9 needed every possible advantage, for the compound was flush with hundreds of Islamic fundamentalists bent on *the destruction of ordered society*.

A knock on the steel hatch of the U.S.S. *Kearsarge's* sitroom immediately got Alec's attention. Riemann and Nutworth entered, both wet from the high seas frothing up over the USS *Virginia's* deck. Saluting the captain and Alec, Nutworth began, "Boss, the ASDS is in order. We've got some really trick arms and we're ready to go."

"We leave in about thirty." Alec left the sitroom without further comment.

After Alec had left, the men sat down at the conference table and scrutinized the updated surveillance map courtesy of *Golden Eye*. Captain Ruger just stood staring out the window onto the flight deck. A Harrier was on approach and two ASW helicopters were about to do the same. The air boss moved slowly in the heavy wind that sprayed chilled saltwater in his face, pissing him off.

Early morning on the southeastern Mediterranean Sea always put one in a state of mute awe. The sun this day was still hours from rising over the horizon to complete its quotidian duty of illuminating the ancient waters, as it had for myriad eons. It was one of nature's greatest performances.

Looking contemplatively out of the command window, Captain Ruger had made his decision about the communiqué he had received via USCENTCOM only thirty minutes ago. He would tell Alec before the mission. He would have wanted it that way had he been in Alec's position.

Chapter Forty-One

The mighty Mediterranean Sea continued to roil as never before. Long, foamy white-capped waves continued to batter the U.S.S. *Kearsarge* still situated twenty-five kilometers off the southern coast of Lebanon. A briny sea mist coated the exterior of every aspect of the gargantuan amphibious assault ship. While still tethered to the U.S.S. *Kearsarge*, the U.S.S. *Virginia* did its best to keep its distance, for a collision could be catastrophic.

The dark of night was a prelude to another day of vigilance and continued operations for the ship's crew.

"Captain," the junior communication's officer said. "There's a problem with the ASDS."

Turning on his heels, he asked, "What?"

"The navigation systems are malfunctioning, sir. Commander Vulekovič is asking for a delay."

"How long, Smitty? How long?"

The officer called back to the *Miraculous*. "Sir, I've got Commander Vulekovič," he said, handing the phone to Captain Ruger.

Captain Ruger reached for the phone as the ship's superstructure was violently broadsided. Ordnances were instantly detonated and an immense fire broke out. Flames reached nearly up to the very window that the captain had looked out of only seconds before. Startled, he said to those in the room, "What the shit was that?"

An officer jumped up and rushed over to the window. Looking

out, he saw a chopper, mangled on the flight deck. "Sir, one of the Sea Knights hit us," the officer said, with mild alarm evident in his voice.

Alarms were set off in every direction. Rescue teams rushed to help the injured and put out the fires. Aside from the safety of the men, the *on deck* operations had to continue. Flights had to be made, for training and reconnaissance were paramount to the success of any military operation.

A bit irritated, Captain Ruger nonetheless continued with Commander Vulekovič. "Commander, how long is the delay? OS9's timeline requires it to reach shore before dawn."

"I'd like to say, to be safe, three, four hours."

"That forces OS9 to wait until about 0700 hours. Too late." Captain Ruger knew it probably would not work, and Alec would be thoroughly pissed off, because the operation was synced to this day at this time. *Golden Eye* and *Eagle Eye*, the unmanned aerial vehicles, were set to fly.

"Wish I had better news, but the navigation systems must be one-hundred percent or it's a no-go."

"Yes, yes. One-hundred percent," the captain agreed. "I'll inform them."

Captain Ruger turned to the duty officer and barked the order, "Get me Dr. Hakimian."

"Yes, sir," the duty officer responded and immediately rang Alec's quarters.

The odd sounding phone rang and Alec answered. "Yes," the dryness in his tired voice apparent. "What is it?"

"Doctor, please hold for Captain Ruger."

"Doctor, this is Captain Ruger. Commander Vulekovič of the ASDS informed me just minutes ago that the nav systems are down. And the communications mast was also giving the tech officer problems. We're looking at about three hours or more to remedy the situation."

"Three hours," Alec echoed. "We don't have that kind of time. We're set to go now. I need to have my men on land before sunrise. It's imperative," he said with insistence.

"I understand Dr. Hakimian, but the nav systems have to be right. It's dangerous enough when everything's perfect."

"Notify USCENTCOM. They need to know that it's off." The captain's face hardened, as he heard Alec.

"Reschedule the UAVs for tomorrow," Alec ordered, with disappointment in his voice.

Taking a deep breath, Alec said as he ended the call, "Then tomorrow it is."

Alec was concerned about the change of plans. He never liked not being in control of the situation. During every lifesaving brain operation he had ever performed, he demanded to be in control. He had always planned it that way. And now, things were different and that troubled him terribly. OS9's contact on shore had to be told of the delay. He knew that there was a very small window of opportunity. The success of the mission, his last mission, was paramount to locating and eliminating from the Middle East yet more of Saddam's WMD. But more importantly, and more personally, he wanted as-Saffah and the Ankabut. It was now or never, but he would have to wait until tomorrow.

CHAPTER FORTY-TWO

Alec and OS9 spent the first part of the *lost* day relaxing as best they could. It was a low moment. They were geared to go; they were psyched. Much like an NFL team on Super Bowl Sunday, they were ready to take their pound of flesh. As it was, they had no choice but to sit back and wait. Josiah and Mackay played game after game of chess. Josiah bested Mackay at will, but Mackay was committed to learning how to beat him. Bobby was lost in his music, his iPod's headphones blaring loud enough to cause ears to bleed and possible long-term brain damage. He loved the Beatles and Mark Knopfler's latest release. Cat Stevens's unique music had also been a favorite until he learned the Cat had become Yussef Islam.

Toward evening, the team met in the sitroom to visualize the mission that was before them. As Alec reminded everyone again, it was not expected that every member of Operation Star 9 would return to the U.S.S. *Kearsarge* without being injured or killed. It was that kind of engagement...fast, furious, and bloody.

Seated in a far corner were Riemann and Nutworth. They had spread out maps on a large mess-like, aluminum table that had more than its share of cuts and dents from years of constant use. They talked strategy about their demolition plans; how they would set their unattended explosives; and how they would contain the perimeter of the compound with sonic devices.

The weather had not improved and tomorrow's prediction was

not encouraging. Alec would have preferred a moonless night for the insertion and assault on the Hezbollah camp, but it was a now or never situation. The re-scheduling did force Alec and OS9 to re-think certain aspects of the mission.

"Listen up, boys," came out loud and clear. "The ASDS will place us within about a kilometer of land. At that point, we will board the Mark VIII SDVs for the final move to the insertion point."

The SEALs utilized Special Delivery Systems to get to targets that required far more equipment and firepower than they could haul on their backs while swimming. These highly specialized vehicles were powered by electric motors. Carrying from two to six men each, they could travel at six knots per hour for up to one hundred kilometers.

While approaching the insertion point underwater in the Mark VIIIs, the onboard air-support system would keep OS9 alive. Armed with two MK37 torpedoes used to fend off water-bound attackers, they were a formidable addition to the special operations' bag of tricks. The SDVs had proven to be the perfect compliment to the larger ASDS that had become the backbone of SEAL special operations.

"Men, once we hit land at our insertion point, we'll travel the twenty klicks southeast of Sûr to Qānā by SOVs. As you know, the encampment is northeast of the city in a very remote area that's been off-limits to the Lebanese for years. No one dared get near the hornet's nest of Hezbollah operatives until now." Alec paused to look out the window, hoping that the weather would turn his way.

The design of the Special Operations Vehicles meant that they required very little support. Titanium framed, they were extremely lightweight and provided superb off-road capabilities in a small package. The four-wheel drive version, coupled with the SOV's long-travel suspension setup, was able to trace over the surface of virtually insurmountable topographical obstacles. Its shades-of-biege over sandy-brown camouflage paint scheme made it difficult to identify from a distance. Because many of the components were essentially off-the-shelf items, repairs proved relatively simple in most cases.

The SOVs for OS9's final mission carried specially designed configurable weapons suites with M2, Milan, and Hellfire missiles. The massive storage compartments permitted OS9 to carry substantial payloads of ordnances, MREs, and additional supplies.

"Who's positioning the SOVs," the characteristically quiet Navy SEAL Riemann asked.

Alec answered while he scrutinized the now serious faces of the team. "We'll be met by forces sympathetic to the West's cause in Lebanon and historically pro-U.S. They are remnants of the Lebanese civil war back in the '70s and '80s. At the end of the war, the Syrians were able to establish a strong toehold in Lebanon and today they are exerting even greater control there." Alec looked up from the men now seated at the long table and took a couple of breaths. "Shi'ite Muslims hold sway in Sûr, so the risk to the Christian militia that's assisting us is very high," he emphasized in a clear voice. "You've got to know that the Syrians are in close communication with Hezbollah, and the man who's in the center of the mix is none other than a savage of a man that you know to be Ali as-Saffah, the *Shedder of Blood*. As-Saffah's reputation precedes him on several levels. To begin with, he's personally slaughtered somewhere in the vicinity of five hundred Christians and pro-U.S. sympathizers. So needless to say, the men helping us would love nothing better than to get their hands on this asshole. Oh, did I mention that as-Saffah enjoys killing his victims by slitting their throats and watching them bleed out?"

That focused everyone's attention.

Alec's eyes narrowed, as he continued with great emphasis. "He sold out his own mother and sister, both devout Christians, to Muslim extremists, just to prove his mettle with these bastards. He himself was a Christian until he went over the edge. And now he leads Hezbollah extremists and takes his marching orders from the Khamsin's Ankabut. This is one bad motherfucker." He ended his history lesson and diatribe with a closing admonition. "Boys, we've traveled over some of the hottest, most unfriendly places on the planet, found caches of WMD when many said there were none, and now we are only hours away from the big show, so let's get it done…this one's for all the marbles. I believe we'll hit the mother lode, so we need to bring our 'A' game. There's over three hundred of them and eight of us," he said solemnly, scanning the faces of each man.

"Sounds like a fairrr fight if you ask me," Mackay, the career Marine recon expert and medic said with his Scottish Highland brogue embellishing his every word.

"No. It's not," Riemann said, with a big grin peering out from under his bearded face.

Deliberately circling the table, Alec rolled on, "USCENTCOM requested updated satellite shots that show the overall area of about twenty hectares. It appears that there's at least a dozen outbuildings that we can confirm. As we've discussed before, the main storage facility for what we believe is a cache of VX and mustard gases lies in the center of the compound. There's also an unconfirmed report that they may be processing *sarin gas* as well. Here is a cluster of cinder block shacks not clear in our earlier photos," he said emphatically, pointing to a specific area on the center of the map. He continued, "Possibly underground. And here," as he pointed to another area on the map, "is one of the two communication towers. The other's over here," he said, almost poking his finger through the map. "These need to go at the outset."

First developed in Germany in 1938, sarin gas was similar in molecular structure to toxic pesticides known as organophosphates. In its purest form, it was clear, tasteless, and possessed no odor. As the most lethal of nerve agents, it can spread easily as a vapor into the environment. It worked by interrupting the nervous system's normal functions, which leads to over stimulation of muscles and vital organs. Just one drop can kill instantly. Last used during the Iran-Iraq War of the 1980s, the gas was subsequently employed again with lethal results in two terrorist attacks in Japan in 1994 and 1995. The thought of its use today caused terror in those familiar with its deadly capabilities.

"How many of the crazies did you say there are?" Bobby asked, somewhat astonished that so many would be in one location.

"At least three hundred," Alec fired back, perturbed by the interruption.

"Holy crap," Bobby said, "three hundred assholes."

"That's right, Bobby. Three hundred, and if I can help it, when we leave they'll all be dead. It's my very own *scorched earth* policy that I want to impose on these fucking animals."

"Scorched earrrth," Mackay said aloud. "Sounds like a big barbeque and beers on a Sunday afternoon," he said laughingly.

"Kind of, but it's more like General Ulysses S. Grant's march on Richmond or General William Tecumseh Sherman's destruction of numerous Confederate cities during the American Civil War. We are going to scorch their earth so that nothing, I mean nothing survives. Total destruction," Alec said firmly, with fire in his voice.

Bobby intoned with a Southern smile, "We'll get 'em, sir."

The face of as-Saffah was front-and-center in Alec's mind and his capture would make it all worth the risk. In truth, what Alec wanted was to kill him with his bare hands. He wanted to wrench the life out of him, to see him die, to feel him die, to hear him take his last, pathetic breath.

"I know we will prevail. We must prevail. You are twenty-first century RECONDO men. You are soldiers who can smell an enemy one hundred meters away and know what he had for dinner the night before. You can hear a round chambered in his weapon and know instantly the make and model. You can steal away the element of surprise from your enemy. Stealth is your best weapon. Boys, all of your abilities will be required to complete this mission. We're on our own. No one knows we're alive once we make our way inland. I can't stress it enough. This is the blackest of black ops," he said with a voice that lowered half an octave. Taking a breath, he continued, "We hold nothing back. The Commander in Chief, through USCENTCOM, has given us carte blanche here. They don't want to know the specifics. Just get it done. The president is watching this one."

Bobby's ears were piqued, since his father had been an alumnus of the RECONDO School, aka *long-range reconnaissance tactics and commando operations.*

The school began in 1966, when the need arose to train special operations soldiers to perform at a level never realized before. It was the ultimate finishing school for special operations units that performed tasks ranging from field analysis and reconnaissance to the elimination of high-level Vietcong operatives. They were known by their moniker MACV-SOG, which stood for Military Assistance Command, Vietnam–Studies and Observation Group. These highly trained and motivated soldiers were the precursors of the ubiquitous Task Force groups that identify special operations units today. The RECONDO School was terminated in the early 1970s, as the war in Vietnam was winding down, but the legacy of the school and its unique purpose lives on in the men of Operation Star 9.

Looking up at the clock on the opposite wall above a wide window, Alec marked the time. "All right then, any questions?"

"...and the wonder weapons, sir," Bobby said, wanting to be assured.

Alec gave Bobby one of those looks again and continued. "We leave at 0300 hours. The ASDS is now ready and the SDVs have been loaded with everything, including the wonder weapons. Riemann will operate one and Nutworth will take the other. And the LCAC will bring us home."

The Landing Craft Air Cushion, referred to by its acronym *LCAC*, was an ominous if not downright intimidating machine. It was designed to transport assault essentials, weapons systems, cargo, and equipment of the U.S. Marine Air/Ground Task Force from ship-to-shore and back.

The LCAC, "*Ell-Cack*," was also a high-speed, military amphibious hovercraft capable of traveling from the water to an over-the-beach theater of operations while carrying a 33-kiloton payload at speeds surpassing 40 knots per hour. It was not uncommon to see enormous M-1 tanks onboard an LCAC as it made a rapid, pre-dawn, over-the-horizon attack on an enemy's position without exposing ships to enemy fire.

At some 25 meters in length, it floated on a cushion of air as it scudded along virtually any surface. Because of this capability, it was accessible to more than eighty percent of the world's beaches.

Four centrifugal fans powered by four Avco-Lycoming TF40B gas turbines rated at 3955 shaft horsepower each drove the LCAC. It also carried its own protection in the form of two 12.7mm machine guns and an Mk-19 Mod3 40mm grenade launcher. An M-60 machine gun rounded out the firepower. With five Special Warfare Combatant-Craft Crewmen to assist, the LCAC moved its heavy payloads, including 24 troops, from over a distance of 80 kilometers off shore.

Everyone's attention was at a febrile pitch as Alec gave the last admonition to his team. "You've got a few hours before we go. Use them wisely."

Alec left the sitroom first, while the others tried to break the chill of what they had just heard by chatting about their families and friends waiting for them back home. Bobby traced an image of a far off rain cloud on the window that had condensation on it from the bitter cold outside. He had hoped the weather would break by the time everyone hit the shore. *It would sure help*, he thought, as the Beatles' *Eleanor Rigby* blasted in his stereo earbuds.

CHAPTER FORTY-THREE

The intrepid *Los Angeles Times* crime reporter George H. Smith, a Pulitzer Prize winner, was the first to break the story in the morning edition. His lead was *Los Angeles Socialite Disappears. FBI Won't Discuss Details.* The east coast *New York Times* headline read: *Renowned Brain Surgeon's Wife Is Missing, Kidnapping Suspected.* By noon Eastern Standard Time, the wire services had promulgated the story across the globe.

Newspapers, radio, and television reported that Mrs. Leyla Hakimian, the wife of eminent Dr. Alexander Hakimian of Bel-Air, California, was returning to her home from a night at the Beverly Hills Hotel where several hundred people celebrated the philanthropic work of Dr. Raymond Raissi. Police said that what they learned at the Hakimian residence from one of the staff indicated that a kidnapping had occurred.

The police were unable to locate Leyla Hakimian's husband for comment.

CHAPTER FORTY-FOUR

Captain Ruger was in the command tower watching his charges execute the daily, deadly ballet of aircraft coming and going. He strained at the thought of what he was about to do.

"Sir," the lieutenant junior grade said, interrupting the captain's thought.

"What's up, Smitty?" he asked, still inexplicably trying to hold on to the thought that pained him.

"Captain Thomson and Commander Vulekovič, sir, say that the ASDS is a go."

"Fine," Captain Ruger said reflexively. "I'll notify OS9."

The phone in Alec's quarters rang. He raised his head and just looked at it. It rang again. He looked at it again, willing it to stop, but it did not. Reluctantly, he reached for it. There was no voice on the other end. Slamming the phone down, his mind turned to the thought of the impending battle and that it would be an outright bloodbath. Hezbollah operatives were not about to give any quarter, nor would he. Yet something kept nagging him. He worried about his men, but he also worried about himself, what he had become...a killing machine once again. Yes, he had rationalized the killing some time ago, but a single thought kept circling back. He could not shake it. *How matter-of-factly he would raise his gun and pull the trigger...then pull it again and again and again without hesitation. Was he really Dr. Alexander Hakimian?* he asked himself. He was not sure anymore. The thought of who he had become was now an all too familiar refrain.

The knock on the hatch came out of nowhere. "Doctor, Captain Ruger here."

Alec did not want or need to talk to anyone at that very moment. He just wanted to be.

"Doctor, are you there?" the voice queried through the hatch.

Alec answered incuriously. "Yes, captain."

"I need to speak to you," Captain Ruger requested. "May I come in?"

Alec walked deliberately over to the steel hatch and opened it. Captain Ruger stood rod-straight before him. His graying hair belied a man several years Alec's junior. His was a demanding job.

"What is it, captain?"

"Can we sit?" the captain asked.

Alec thought the request odd but nevertheless agreed. They sat down at the small table in his quarters.

Facing each other, the captain began, "Dr. Hakimian," looking straight into Alec's now observant eyes. "Firstly, I was just told that you and your men are good-to-go."

Alec was pleased.

"But, doctor. There's something else. I just received a call from CENTCOM-Baghdad. When I heard it, I was stupefied. I told them it didn't make any sense. I asked General Meade if he would please re-confirm what he had just told me. He did."

"In all deference to you captain, what the hell are you talking about? I'm about to head into Hell and now's not the time to play 'I've Got a Secret' with me," Alec said sternly. He had no tolerance for anyone who spoke obliquely.

"Doctor, your wife has disappeared."

Alec went blank. He could not comprehend the words *your wife has disappeared*. Trying desperately to speak, to find his voice, he snapped back, "What the hell are you saying?" Grabbing the captain's right sleeve and staring into his face, he said emphatically, "What's this all about? Where's my daughter Karina? Where's my wife? Captain, what happened?"

"I was told your daughter is with family. As for your wife, all we know at this point is that she was returning home from an evening out. Reports have it that she was abducted at home."

It hit him like buckshot from a twelve-gauge pump shotgun… everywhere. His body instantly became immobile. His mind froze. He became dislocated from reality. He was not in control, *again*.

The thought of *his Karina safe with family* gave him a scintilla of momentary relief.

"Would you like the chaplain to see you?"

Dismissing the question, Alec stood up, walked over to the window that looked out onto the flight deck and just stared for a long count. Turning around, his face seemed to morph into a robotic humanoid from a low-budget, sci-fi movie. "Captain. Are you sure?" *It didn't compute.* "What do you mean, she was kidnapped?" Alec waited for the captain's response.

"She was kidnapped. At this point, not much is known. I wish I had more for you."

"Who did it?" he questioned.

"Doctor, all I know or CENTCOM-Baghdad knows comes from USCENTCOM. They say the FBI's Hostage Rescue Team is on it and *POTUS* has been briefed."

POTUS was the acronym used by the Secret Service as a shorthand reference for President of the United States.

Staring directly into the captain's concerned looking face, Alec drew a deep breath then continued, "Do you know if the kidnappers identified themselves?"

Captain Ruger's face grew pallid. "No. Not that I know."

Alec sat back down, placed his head between his hands, and was silent. While struggling to raise his head, his fingers poking into his scalp, he said, with his heart nearly in a state of tachycardia, "You mean to tell me that's all you know? That's all anyone knows? Goddamn it. It's my wife we're talking about here." His rage bordered on the incandescent. Nothing was registering.

Captain Ruger's blue eyes squinted a bit, as he tried to stay calm himself.

Alec paced the floor in his room. He immediately thought back, *Leyla was supposed to have attended a celebration in Raissi's honor.* "Captain, I need to get home to my daughter. I need to find my wife."

The captain broke the silence with, "Doctor, I don't have any answers. And I sympathize with you, but I was also told to inform you that as the leader of OS9, it's impossible to just step out of your command right now."

"Are you telling me that if I wanted to return home right now to find my wife I couldn't? Is that what you're telling me, captain?" Alec asked, with a purple rage rising.

"Sir, it's not my call. General Meade himself is doing his best to find out more, but he said that the mission is far too critical for any change to happen now. The mission needs you. It can't come off without you. Those were his orders," the captain said, with cautious optimism, trying to be diplomatic at the same time.

Alec was not convinced. In fact, he thought, *what was he doing? His wife was kidnapped.* Thoughts continued to race about his beleaguered mind. *His daughter was without her mother,* he said to himself, *but at least she was safe with family.* Now the questions and doubts became an avalanche that was crushing his psyche. *Hadn't he done enough? Would he have a family to come back to? And now, what was being done for him? How could his wife possibly have been K-I-D-N-A-P-P-E-D? What he was about to do had to be done, for who else would do it? Yes, he knew that it was his country first. He was ashamed that it wasn't his family first, but that's how it was for now,* he convinced himself. In truth, he had reconciled it long ago.

Dr. Alexander Hakimian could not explain it, other than to say that he owed his adopted country for the opportunity to pursue his dreams. After having fled his homeland of Lebanon, he lived with the self-imposed moral responsibility that protecting America was his duty. After all, the unavoidable clash of cultures had now arrived at his doorstep in all its unchecked fury. And now, he was about to return to his homeland, but this time to eliminate an entire Hezbollah compound of Islamic terrorists.

Captain Ruger just stood there as Alec held on to a blank stare. "Doctor, what can I do for you?" he asked cautiously.

Alec continued to stand motionless, staring into space. An image of his young daughter Karina appeared before him. She smiled and reached out her hand. He withheld the urge to cry, but his eyes misted over anyway. As he reached out to touch her, the ephemeral image faded as quickly as it appeared. His mind fought to stay inside the boundaries of sanity. One more step and he would….

"Doctor," the captain asked again.

Alec took three deliberate, deep breaths and turned around. His dark eyes focused on Captain Ruger's ruddy face. "Captain, tell me that my wife will be okay."

The captain knew he could not give Alec a guarantee. He did not know what the real story was. He sensed that the normally stoic, cool, and calm Dr. Alexander Hakimian was beginning to unravel at the seams. "Doctor, I believe our agencies stateside and the White House will find her."

Alec knew that what he had asked the captain was bullshit, and that the captain's response was equally bullshit. He knew there were no guarantees. *Ever.* Then, reaching deep inside, he pulled himself up rod-straight and said resolutely, "Captain Ruger, my men and I will be ready by 0300 hours. Have Captain Thomson prepare to leave. Notify Commander Vulekovič we need the ASDS loaded." He then left the room without another word and walked out onto a nearby deck.

Captain Ruger stood silently in Alec's cabin. In his long and distinguished naval career, he had been in the presence of outstanding officers from all five branches of the U.S. military. During that time, he had witnessed several instances when an officer under great pressure either crumbled and faded away or rose to the occasion and answered the call. But, he had never seen anyone under the stress of learning that his wife had been kidnapped and his baby daughter was thousands of miles away, without either her mother or father, exhibit such steely resolve. Alec had displayed a level of certitude and determination in the face of such great personal crisis that he was in awe of him. He had just seen a man, a husband, a father, a talented surgeon make the willing choice to soldier on and finish what he came to do…eliminate an encampment of religious terrorists bent on destroying everything he and every American held sacred. The truth was that the captain was not sure he would have responded the same way.

CHAPTER FORTY-FIVE

The unruly Mediterranean Sea was not about to give any quarter. Even though the southern Lebanese coastline was just over the horizon, getting there would not be easy for OS9.

At 0210 hours, members of the team began to congregate early in the situation room. Bobby was the first in, with Alvarado next, and Josiah after that. Riemann, Nutworth, and Mackay trailed in minutes later.

"Where the fuck is Pratt?" Bobby asked aloud.

Mackay responded, "He's probably in the loo."

"The loo?" Bobby remarked jokingly. "What? Whacking the willy?"

Alec, with heavy black stubble marking his face, marched toward the situation room just steps behind Pratt. Pratt quickly stepped aside and permitted Alec to enter first. Everyone snapped to attention at the sight of an exosuited Dr. Alexander Hakimian.

Borrowing from the U.S. Military's *Future Combat Systems*, OS9 was equipped for the southern Lebanon mission with futuristic weapons' technology never before seen by any of its enemies, let alone most of the U.S. military. Some thought the latest exoskeleton suit and all of its accoutrements were still far too experimental for the mission at hand.

Activity aboard the U.S.S. *Virginia* was ratcheted up. Multi-million candlepower xenon lights flooded its wet flight deck and spilled over onto the sea below. Deckhands scurried about in foul-weather gear, answering to the orders of officers trained to be ready when it counted. Additional gear was being loaded aboard the *Miraculous* Advanced SEAL Delivery System. Its matte-black, cigar-shaped hull was difficult to see in the early morning, despite the lights, and that was the idea.

Operation Extreme Prejudice was about to get underway.

"Gentlemen, this is the big one. It's Operation Extreme Prejudice, our last mission together, then we go home." Cheers rose up instantly out of nowhere. The thought of home excited the men. It had been a long time. "We've succeeded in Syria and in Jordan, and this will be no exception," he said with detachment. "You know what you must do. We want as-Saffah and the WMD and we want to leave nothing behind. I mean leave no...thing behind!" he said in a raised voice to punctuate the importance of the statement.

Staring at his Panerai chronograph, Alec scrutinized the minute hand, as it moved to number thirty, indicating that it was approaching 0230 hours.

The men sat silently at the conference table, staring at each other, some with blank looks, a few with big smiles. Moments later three shipmates from the galley broke the silence as they arrived with bowls of fresh fruit, eggs, toast, both wheat and white, assorted jams and jellies, and hot coffee, both caffeinated and de-caffeinated in hand. "Eat up," Alec said, as he sat down and began to fill his plate with scrambled eggs. "Josiah, please pass the toast."

"Doc," Bobby said, "Cappuccinos? Better yet, where's the beef? No. How about a Bud?"

Alec knew that if anyone would ask such inane questions at such an inappropriate time, it would be Bobby.

Not answering Bobby directly, Alec said, "Fill up. It's our last meal before our return."

For a fleeting moment, the men acted more like boys at a summer camp dining table than men who were about to enter the Viper's Pit.

When men of special ops prepared for battle, they often chose food that was easy on the stomach, but high in lean protein and complex carbohydrates. It was necessary that what they ate did not cause gastrointestinal problems. They had to be one-hundred percent. Their lives depended on it.

Josiah looked at Nutworth, as Pratt looked at Riemann, while the others kept eating. They did not like the words *last meal*. None of them did. Trained as they were, as prepared as they were, and as seasoned as they were, they made it a point to avoid any words of negativity or finality. It was not lost on them that when they signed on to OS9 they knew they might not return unharmed or even alive. Denying the obvious helped them get from one day to the next. Admittedly, each one knew that he was a psychiatrist's dream patient.

Alec finished first and stood up with a half cup of java in his left hand. Raising it to his mouth, he took a last sip, savored its taste, and said, "Finish up, take a piss, and meet me at the cage."

The flight deck of the U.S.S. *Kearsarge* was a challenging place in a pounding sea as it reconnected with the USS *Virginia* after tearing loose a support cable an hour before. Alec was the first to climb into the transfer cage as Pratt, Josiah, and Bobby joined him.

The exosuit's radiant heating system proved invaluable, as the winds hammered the deck of the attack submarine unremittingly. One of the ship's mates on duty spoke into his headset to one of the deckhands on the U.S.S. *Virginia*. A junior officer pressed a green button next to the cage and it started its shaky descent down the zip-line, or flying fox, and across to the attack submarine. The angry sea thrashing below drowned out the whirring of the cage's pulley wheels rolling across the thick cable. The cage rocked and rolled, buffeted by the winds. It came to an abrupt stop with a jarring thud against the rubber bumpers.

After the men exited the cage, it returned to the U.S.S. *Kearsarge* by a small, yet powerful, polyphase electric motor attached to a large wheel onto which the cable was wound.

Next up was Riemann, who had already taken the ride the day before, as had Nutworth. The two stepped into the cage, followed by Mackay and Alvarado. The door closed and the cage raced down the taught zip-line to the attack submarine again. Its sudden stop against the rubber bumpers caused the door to unlatch itself and fly open. A ship's mate quickly reached out and grabbed the cage, steadying it as it finally settled to a stop.

The ship's Captain Thomson and the ASDS's Commander Vulekovič, both salty dogs from an earlier generation, met the entirety of OS9 on the pitching deck of the U.S.S. *Virginia* in the frigid darkness of the early morning.

"Dr. Hakimian," Captain Thomson said. "Welcome to the U.S.S. *Virginia*. All is ready for you and your men."

Alec returned the cordialities and introduced the members of OS9. Momentarily, he fixed his eyes on the menacing sea. It had transformed itself into a most foreboding, anthracite black-colored liquid; he hoped it was not a harbinger of things to come.

Commander Vulekovič stepped forward and reassured Alec that the ASDS was at the ready. "Dr. Hakimian, I'm Commander Vulekovič. The *Miraculous*," he said, gesturing with his hands covered in rubber coated gloves to the ASDS, "stands ready to move your men at your command."

Alec nodded a confirmation, as the wind raced through his ears, stinging briefly, and then causing momentary ringing. Without warning, an AV-8B Harrier jet aircraft screamed off the pitching deck of the U.S.S. *Kearsarge* and out over the sea into the darkness punctuated by a glorious spray of twinkling stars peeking through the cloud cover.

Fierce waves pounded the U.S.S. *Virginia* in a constant cycle of every twenty seconds. Periodically, a rogue wave would come out of nowhere and crash over the top of the deck. The ASDS just stood silent, in eerie repose, awaiting its charges.

"Gentlemen," Commander Vulekovič bellowed out above the howling din of the sea, "it is time we get to it." Motioning toward the ASDS, he added, "You'll enter from under its belly. Officer Mackintosh will assist you."

Alec and his team began the thirty-meter walk to the ASDS. Each held tightly to the woven steel cable that ran nearly the length of the attack submarine and served as a support to hold on to in turbulent seas.

The Advanced SEAL Delivery System was state-of-the-art when it came to underwater military delivery systems. No nation had anything like it and soon Hezbollah was about to come face-to-face with OS9, courtesy of the *Miraculous*.

The ASDS's internals were very complicated, with digital gauges flickering everywhere, pipes running back and forth like medieval serpents on the loose, and racks loaded with hi-tech weaponry. It also carried the two modified SEAL Delivery Vehicles that gave OS9 the ability to move on shore without being noticed.

By the time Alec had boarded the ASDS, he still did not have confirmation that the U.S. Special Ops Vehicles were at the rendezvous site. He knew that once OS9 hit the beachhead, the SOVs were paramount to the success of the operation. It had to move quickly out of sight and on to the area of operations. The SOVs would need to traverse a foreign countryside composed of primordial hills and valleys that served as hiding places for any manner of unscrupulous individuals since the time of the ancient Romans.

Stealth was OS9's *modus operandi.*

Once secure inside the Advanced SEAL Delivery System, Commander Vulekovič ordered the hatch sealed. He then radioed to Captain Thomson, informing him that he was good-to-go. It was not but another few ticks of the clock and everyone felt their bodies become temporarily lighter as the U.S.S. *Virginia* began to submerge. It was as if they were sliding down a greased tube at about a thirty-five degree angle.

In a few more ticks of the clock, they were at a depth of twenty fathoms, a depth that was sufficient for the mission at hand. The U.S.S. *Virginia* increased its speed to thirty-two knots and then decreased its depth to some twelve fathoms as the sea floor rose beneath it. Although counterintuitive, it was twice as fast under water than on the surface.

Alec checked his Panerai again. Although the darkness of night was holding on, he knew every minute counted. His anxious thoughts were drowned out by the prospect of finding large caches of WMD and purging the area of some three hundred evildoers.

The *Miraculous*, still piggybacked to the mighty U.S.S. *Virginia*, began to emit a low-level but powerful humming sound. The fourteen silver-zinc batteries encased in titanium bottles sent a high-voltage electric charge through the drive system that began to spin the propeller shaft at extremely high revolutions.

It was time for Operation Extreme Prejudice to begin.

"Gentlemen," Commander Vulekovič said above the annoying hum of the massive electric motor, "in about fifteen we are a go."

Everyone looked solemnly at each other, their faces painted in black-and-green camouflage. They said nothing. Tension was palpable. After adjusting their exosuits, they began the laborious process of donning their scuba gear over them.

Crewmen moved about in a carefully orchestrated manner, for space was at a very high premium inside the ASDS. The second in command contacted Captain Thomson. They spoke for a few seconds and then the captain turned to Alec and said, "Dr. Hakimian, you're good-to-go."

Alec was checking his gear, especially the breathing system, as were the others. "And the gear —" he was cut-off in mid-sentence by a jolt. The ASDS was about to leave the mother ship.

Anticipating the end of Alec's question, the commander said directly, "Your gear's attached to the tow hooks on your SDVs. Your weapons and ordnances are sealed in polymer, waterproof cases." Commander Vulekovič's voice was conditioned to the loud ambience of the ASDS. He was a well-seasoned submariner, whose grit and go-get 'em attitude were inspiring.

The *Miraculous* was on her own. Torpedo-like, she glided effortlessly through the briny liquid, whose density was 800 times that of air.

Alec was still troubled, for he had not heard from the Lebanese Forces. He knew that the SOVs' four-wheel-drive systems ate up kilometers of sand like a Cuisinart liquefying bananas, but time was crucial to mission.

The Lebanese Forces were remnants of the Phalangist militia that had held sway during Lebanon's civil war of 1975-1990. They received their imprimatur in 1982 by Israeli officials to slaughter hundreds of Palestinians in the Sabra and Chatila refugee camps in Beirut. For thirty-six hours, the attacks raged on, assisted by Israeli military forces led by Ariel Sharon. The political and social fallout from the massacre had consequences still felt today.

The marriage of OS9 and the Lebanese Forces demonstrated the hard reality of war…*it was inherently violent and alliances often made no sense. The irony of it all was that in any war, on any given day, your enemy could become your ally.* Witness the war between Iraq and Iran during the 1970s. The United States armed Saddam Hussein, the very tyrant they deposed in 2004.

Alec reminded himself that he and OS9 had just a few precious hours to pull-off a successful, surprise attack. They had to verify and remove the WMD, and eliminate as-Saffah and hundreds of Hezbollah operatives.

CHAPTER FORTY-SIX

Alec gave his last instructions before OS9 departed for the ancient coastal city of Tyre, today known as Sûr.

"Men, this is it. Once we hit the beach, Pratt will give us the latest data from *Golden Eye*. It's been surveying the area for the past several hours. *Golden Eye* is our eyes for the duration. *Eagle Eye* is also available to us should we find the need to transport any additional, highly volatile materials to the *Kearsarge*. It's also loaded with serious firepower. And the trauma pod is at our disposal." The thought of the trauma pod's use caused a slight concern amongst the men, for it meant that someone was injured or worse.

"Sir," Josiah said, scratching his unkempt beard, a beard accented with a small shock of dark red on its left side. His involuntary facial twitches were the result of his now hirsute appearance; an appearance certainly not up to the military's dress code, but then again, nothing OS9 did observed military code. They operated under the radar. "How far are the SOVs from our insertion point?" he asked.

Pratt jumped in and said, "Boss," looking to Alec. "CENTCOM-Baghdad just confirmed that the SOVs are in position."

Alec answered, "Hopefully, less than fifty meters away. As planned, they are squirreled away in a deserted commercial storage facility. We'll have to bring them to our gear. Pratt, once we arrive in Sûr, you'll link up with *Golden Eye*. Riemann, Nutworth, you'll keep watch on the gear as the rest of us retrieve the SOVs." Alec added one more comment, "God's speed, boys."

Every member of OS9 clasped hands together and held a thought for a three count.

Commander Vulekovič interrupted the moment. "Men, it's time. There's light fog cover that extends about two hundred meters from shore. Now's the time. You've got plenty of air." The coarseness of his voice gave added meaning to his words.

While locked in the airtight chamber at the rear of the ASDS, the men of OS9 climbed onto the Special Delivery Systems that were equipped with GPS navigation, infrared night vision lights, oxygen tanks, and two MK37 torpedoes for protection from marauding vessels. Each man had had considerable training in underwater operations, so operating in a submersed environment was of little concern.

Once released from the ASDS, OS9 moved in the SDVs at six knots. It took just minutes to reach shore. The choppy sea threw one-meter high waves at the beach every twenty or so seconds in sets of three. The SDVs were tossed about like flotsam upon the sea, but Riemann and Nutworth handled the situation without serious incident. The gear attached to each SDV kept pulling it back into the waves, so a light throttle had to be applied until it was all off-loaded onto the beach.

Alec immediately surveyed the area. Adjusting his Starlight night-vision system from the keypad on his exosuit, he was able to make out several structures some distance away without difficulty. A car passed across his field of vision about four hundred meters out. "Let's move." After removing and stowing their scuba equipment, they set their exosuits to *pursuit mode*, thus enabling each man to kangaroo leap several meters at a time.

"Sir, there it is," Mackay said, pointing to the beige and brown building set back near a cluster of shade trees and scrub brush thirty meters away.

As they cautiously approached the building, an armed guard appeared from around the corner. Alec called out in a low voice, "*Marhaba. Ana sahbak Al-Hakim*. Hello. I am your friend, The Doctor."

The guard, flashlight in hand, wheeled in the direction of Alec. He crept forward cautiously, one step at a time, machine gun in hand, squinting his eyes in an effort to focus through the soupy, low fog. Alec stepped forward. "*Ya Sahibi*. My friend."

The guard was not exactly sure where the voice was coming from. He called out to those inside the building. "*Ya shabab, taalou barra.* Guys, come on out!" he shouted in a panic.

Alec and the others moved closer.

An unusually tall man for an Arab emerged from the backside of the building and walked fearlessly toward Alec. By his manner, Alec sensed the man to be the de facto leader of the troop, yet Bobby kept a bead on him just in case. "*Ya zaiim. Ana Al-Hakim.* Commander. I'm The Doctor."

A wave of relief rolled over the man's face, as he gawked at Alec's camouflaged exosuit. "*Nahnou kina biintizarkon, hakim.* We've been waiting for you and your men, doctor," he announced, as he continued to stare curiously at Alec's exosuit.

Alec showed himself to the commander. "*Marhaba.*" He stepped forward and shook the commander's hand, a hand that years ago was the unexpected target of a Syrian's rocket propelled grenade that blew his right index finger off.

The RPG was *de rigueur* for the modern-day terrorist. It was easily obtainable, inexpensive, simple to use, alarmingly accurate, and capable of bringing down a commercial jet airliner with the pull of the trigger.

"I am Commander Karim Aziz," he said with great pride, as he snapped Alec a salute. "Your vehicles are here. Come see. Please, there is little time." The commander hurriedly directed Alec toward the building, motioning with his right hand, all the while brandishing an automatic handgun with confidence.

Alec signaled to the others to follow him. The building's busted-out windows had permitted a thick layer of light-colored sand and dust to cover nearly everything in it. Once inside, they saw the SOVs draped in camouflage material.

"*Shilou alghata. Bisiraa. Bisiraa.* Remove the covers. Hurry. Hurry," the commander ordered. Looking to Alec, "Doctor, our sources tell us several transport trucks were seen at the entrance to the Hezbollah camp. We believe that additional weapons were brought in from Syria."

Alec paused and then said, "Our intel tells us that the compound is

full of VX and mustard gases. Maybe even sarin gas. And what about
Ali as-Saffah?"

"I do not know, Dr. Hakimian. He's an illusive one, but we do know
they are planning something big, very big. They must be stopped." His
urgency was patently apparent. "So, please. You must be on your way.
You and your men must go now. Hurry now. Please." His tone of voice
punctuated the urgency.

Josiah was already in the second SOV and fired up its engine. It
came to life, muffled by special noise suppressors that allowed it to keep
its sound level below thirty-five decibels.

The fully tricked out SOVs were serious machines equipped to deal
with anything that came their way. Their camo paint schemes gave them
a very low level of visibility. Unlike much of the Middle East carpeted in
desert sand, southern Lebanon was very verdant. Attached to the SOVs
were pup trailers designed to carry heavy loads of weapons, munitions,
and foodstuffs,

"*Zabet, shoukran.* Commander, thank-you," Alec said, with gratitude
in his voice. Turning to his men now in the SOVs, he said, "Let's
move!"

The cover of fog was unfortunately lifting too soon for Alec's liking,
and he knew that OS9 had to make their way around the outside of Sûr
before its denizens came to life for another day of struggle and strife. He
figured that they had only five, maybe six hours to get the job done.

On the beach, the rolling waves were still sizable, causing the SDVs
to flounder. The men quickly off-loaded the gear and supplies and
placed them into the pup trailers.

When the loading was complete, Riemann and Nutworth turned
the SDVs around and drove them out just beyond the breaking waves.
There they activated the SDVs' submersion modes and turned on their
homing devices.

The submersion process was accomplished by releasing the
compressed air that each SDV held in its side pods, then filling them
with seawater. The homing devices transmitted a continual signal to
Pratt's computer. Suddenly, they quickly dropped to the bottom of
the sea, out of sight. As a precaution, a spot was marked by sighting a
tall shade tree on the shore that was directly opposite the submersed
SDVs.

With everyone seated, and the gear and weapons secured, Alec and Josiah set the SOVs in the direction of east-northeast. They nodded a good-bye to Commander Aziz and his troops, then hit the throttles hard, and moved most riki-tik, as they maneuvered the two SOVs out of the dilapidated building and onto the damp sand.

Some twenty kilometers away was the Hezbollah compound, home to hundreds of highly motivated, Islamic fundamentalists.

All hell was about to break loose and Alec relished the thought. As far as he was concerned, *it was winner take all.*

CHAPTER FORTY-SEVEN

THE VIPER'S PIT, SOUTHERN LEBANON

It was early morning, with darkness still in control. Alec felt uncharacteristically uneasy. Plans had to be changed. He did not like that. He remembered the admonition that *once the first shot of war was fired, all plans changed.* The admonition did not comfort him, for this was the blackest of black ops missions. Everything had to be perfect, or else....

A southern Lebanese wind tried in vain to fracture the threatening cloud formations that hung overhead as dark specters that foreshadowed events to come.

The two highly modified Special Operations Vehicles pushed on, as the sand turned to a soft, variegated grassy-topped earth beneath their knobby tires. The city of Sûr faded into the distance as Alec and Josiah found the handling of the SOVs very precise and quick. The four-wheel drive mechanisms performed as expected. The pup trailers in tow bounced and bobbed at will.

Most of the men thought it odd that unlike in the United States, highways in the early hours before dawn in Lebanon were fairly deserted. However, they did expect to see the occasional ratty Nissan pickup truck stuffed with aluminum soda cans and scraps of metal or the ubiquitous Toyota automobile swollen with people about to fall out of opened windows. Since the fifteen-year civil war ended in 1990, the once treacherous highways were now reasonably safe to travel. Despite the reality, Alec and Josiah made it a point to keep their distance from public roads.

"Sir," Pratt said to Alec in the lead SOV, "I just received from *Golden Eye* the latest view of the compound. It's about five klicks northeast of the outskirts of Qānā.

Alec asked, "Repeat that." The constant drone of the SOV's engine and churning wheels masked Pratt's words.

Leaning into Alec's right ear Pratt shouted with his right hand directing his voice, "Sir, *Golden Eye*'s latest look has the compound northeast of Qānā about five or six kilometers. There's a great deal of activity. Looks like a truck is refueling a storage tank. Then there's the Mi-24 K/Hind G-2 Russian helo that just landed since our last map download."

The Mi-24 Hind was an impressive assault gunship helicopter that had the capability of carrying eight troops and a significant payload. Driven by twin 2,200 shp Isotov TV-3-117 turbines capable of moving the helo at speeds in excess of 300 kilometers per hour, the Hind was the Russian answer to U.S. AH-64 Apache. It was most lethal.

The words *Russian helo* caught Alec's attention. The heavily armed helo was not what concerned him, but rather what it might have taken into or out of the compound. It was no surprise to Alec that the Hind was being used, for it was an aircraft to be reckoned with, after all, the Russian Igor Sikorsky had invented the helicopter, yet it was the Armenian Mikoyan who gave the then Soviet Union its deadliest air weapon.

Alec slowed down the SOV to a near idle. He finally came to a stop below a rise. "Pratt," Alec asked, "let me see the map."

Pratt handed Alec the Dell military-spec notebook computer. The organic light emitting diode display was extremely easy to read, even in the glare of the brightest sun. "There it is," Alec said, pointing to the image of the daunting Russian chopper. Its insect looking front-end with bug-eyed air intakes over the cockpit and droopy wings weighed down by multiple, menacing rocket pods served to give it an ominous, otherworldly presence.

Moments later Josiah's SOV came to a sliding stop on the grassy ground. He stepped out to stretch his legs, as did Alvarado and Bobby. Nutworth and Riemann followed suit. Mackay stayed put and casually scanned the area, tuning his Starlight night-vision system for optimum resolution and deep penetration.

Alec and Pratt sat in the SOV intently scrutinizing the map on the computer screen. Switching to a streaming image mode, they saw a man dressed in military fatigues with a long *keffiyeh* wrapped around his neck emerging from the chopper. Floppy epaulets on his khaki-colored officer's jacket, reminiscent of Yasser Arafat, signified a man of high rank, followed by five heavily-armed individuals in typical modern terrorist garb, balaclavas and all. Alec had hoped it was Ali as-Saffah, the *Shedder of Blood.* He wanted him for his own selfish reasons. He wanted to stand mano-a-mano with him, the man responsible for the horrific torture and death of his friend William Francis and hundreds of others.

With financing from the Khamsin, Alec was all too aware that as-Saffah had setup the Hezbollah compound some fifteen years ago to train rebels, homicide bombers, as well as al-Qaeda operatives. The camp was called *Gohr al-Afaa,* "the Viper's Pit," and it lived up to its moniker, for several of the 9/11 terrorists had spent time training there. Those who trained in the camp were recruited by the Khamsin from every Islamic fundamentalist organization in the world, including Abu Sayyaf in the Philippines.

Alec looked up for a brief glimpse of what was ahead and then closed the notebook computer and handed it to Pratt. "Men, this is it. You are about to come face-to-face with men devoted to a cause that they are willing to die for. Many of these men are smart...I mean they are not just zealots, but intelligent zealots. Many have college degrees. As-Saffah holds a degree in chemical engineering from the Massachusetts Institute of Technology. So don't assume anything other than they will fight and fight hard and smart. You know the attack sequence." Pausing for affect, he then repeated Todd Beamer's immortal words uttered aboard United flight 93 that fateful day of 9/11/2001, "Let's roll."

Even in the fading darkness, the region around Qānā reminded Alec of La Jolla, California, with its undulating hills blanketed in verdant grass and the occasional conifer tree.

Bobby was about five meters away taking a piss when he heard the call. Quickly finishing his business, he rushed to get into the SOV as it pulled away.

The two camouflaged rigs continued their race across one hill and valley after another as they churned up miles of sand beneath their nobby tires. The flickering lights of Qānā slowly faded in the distance.

CHAPTER FORTY-EIGHT

0500 hours came and went. The dark sky was slowly turning to light as Alec and Josiah's SOVs came to a stop on a rise peppered with rocks and small outgrowths of greenery. A few pine trees accented the stark surroundings. "Sir," Pratt said, looking at his computer's GPS, "the compound is just over this hill and set in a valley about a hundred meters below." Off in the distance a shepherd staggered along with a single Christ burro and a dozen well-aged goats and sheep in tow. His faint handlight dimmed as he turned away from Alec's view.

The Christ burro, or donkey, earned its name centuries ago because of its distinctive white cross marking on its back. It has been the choice of herders and farmers for centuries because of its tenacity, endurance, and longevity.

A strong wind began to whip around them, spitting up fleck-sized bits of sand and dirt. "Motherfuckerrr," Mackay yelled out, grabbing his neck and contorting in pain.

Everyone turned toward Mackay. "What's up laddie?" Bobby asked jokingly.

"Goddamn it. Something bit me. The bugger," he yelled, as he furiously rubbed a spot behind his left ear.

"Let me take a look," Bobby said. Lifting up Mackay's bushy hair, he saw the bite. "You'll live," he said. "But I'll bet a shot of the good stuff would help right about now," he chuckled.

Probably a barghash, Alec thought.

Mackay knew what Bobby meant. An old Scottish Highland legend said that three drams of a good single malt Scotch whiskey would ease the pain considerably, and if it did not, three more drams would guarantee it.

Alec and Pratt walked to the far aspect of the rise and stopped near a meticulously stacked pile of stones that probably served as an ancient survey marker. There they continued to converse, as the others adjusted their new exosuits made of newly refined E-textiles and upgraded software.

Embedded in the fabric of the latest version of the exosuit were highly responsive sensors that allowed the soldier or Marine to detect biological and chemical toxins within nanoseconds. The exosuit also had Hazmat protection qualities that would prove useful.

Bobby fiddled with his special order H&K MP5N machine gun that the military's Future Combat Systems had modified with infrared scoping, a ninety-round magazine loaded with hypervelocity smartshot armor-piercing 9x19mm NATO ammo, and a composite chassis. Riemann pulled out his combat knife made of 1095 carbon steel from its Cordura Nylon sheath and gently cut a piece of an apple he had taken from the U.S.S. *Kearsarge*.

The wind slowed somewhat, but was nonetheless an annoyance, for OS9 needed all the advantages it could get. Crosscurrents of air, when firearm accuracy was critical, were not an ideal situation.

Alec turned to the team and said flatly, "This is it, boys. It's time to get it done. It's combat mind-set time. See the elephant and take the shot. This is no police action. This is war. Never forget that." Looking at his Panerai, he said without emotion, "We move at 0550 hours." Each man glanced at his watch. "Pratt, find your position and don't move, no matter what. We'll need continuous intel."

Pratt, OS9's Army Ranger communications specialist, reveled in such situations. He was prepared.

Alec went on, "Bobby, Alvarado, you need to neutralize bodies moving on the perimeter." Bobby, fondling his machine gun, smiled a "roger that." Alvarado remained stoic.

"Viking and Nutty, I want the communication towers taken out from the get go. We must sever all communications they have with the outside world. Make sure to activate the cell phone jammer. Then move on to the other structures on the perimeter. Gel-X is your best bet, so let's light 'em up."

Riemann and Nutworth had spent their entire careers as Navy SEALs demolishing all kinds of shit, so they just looked at Alec and smiled, for they had already choreographed every move they were about to make. To them it was all one big, beautifully orchestrated dance.

"Josiah, you'll stay with me," Alec said flatly.

Josiah knew that his linguistic abilities were now a moot point, but his familiarity with small to medium arms would serve him well in the hours to come.

"As you know, the building that we believe contains WMD is dead center in the compound and probably in a subterranean room. Assume it's heavily guarded. We also need to know that once they realize we're here, the plans will become very fluid. Pratt will feed you intel, but you'll need to assess it on the fly. No time to hesitate. No second chances. No redos," Alec said starkly.

"Sirrr," Mackay interrupted.

"Mackie, you watch our backs as we move in."

"Right, sirrr," Mackay responded, waving his composite, modified LMG M60E3 "S" gleefully. The M60E3 "S" light machine gun also fired "smartshot" rounds of the 7.62x51mm NATO caliber variety that ensured anyone hit by one would no longer be a threat. Mackay was a human arsenal, with two additional FWS handguns strapped to his thighs, and an added acoustic rifle tethered to his medic backpack. His exosuit assisted in his moving rapidly with nearly forty kilos of firepower and medical supplies.

"All right, make sure that your exos are set for *external terrain mode*. We'll need to move quickly. Remember, there's at least three hundred of these assholes who won't be fond of us crashing their party. Everyone activate your electro-bursts and *chameleonix*," said Alec. "Pratt'll get the *Eagle Eye* to lob a few party favors into the compound when we need them."

Chameleonix mimicked the chameleon's ability to disappear in plain view by changing, ever so delicately, the angles of it scales to lower the refraction rate of light and to pick up the ambient colors. It was an example of nanotechnology.

The nanotechnology found in the latest exoskeleton combat suit multiplied exponentially each team member's capacity to move at super-human speed, detect and eliminate enemies, both human and biochemical, survive most enemy fire, and become nearly undetectable to the human eye.

The essence of nanotechnology was built upon the concept of arranging atoms to produce a desired product, whether it was lighter, stronger, faster, etc. It utilized at least one dimension measured in nanometers, with a nanometer equal to one billionth of a meter.

The nanotechnology that made the exoskeleton *sui generis* to the world of military combat gear was still in its nascent stages, and future, even more innovative variants were in the pipeline. Moreover, the newest version of the exosuit easily controlled the wearer's body temperature. Each exosuit incorporated NASA spacesuit cooling technology. Hair-thin polymer capillaries populated the exosuit's skin and larger arteries fed a self-replicating refrigerant to each capillary throughout the entirety of the exosuit's fabric. All the wearer had to do was input the desired temperature and humidity levels on the control panel located on the left side of the chest and it would be maintained, no matter the outside ambient temperature.

On a hill directly above the Viper's Pit, OS9 made its final preparations. At least a dozen campfires peppered the compound. Dim lights that illuminated most of the buildings made them readily identifiable.

Riemann and Nutworth moved out first, carrying a dozen acoustic sentinels to be placed strategically around the compound. Once activated, no living thing could cross the acoustic fence and survive, although when necessary, each member of OS9 had the ability to deactivate the acoustic sentinels with a preset digital deactivation code, after which the system would automatically rearm itself in five seconds.

Bobby sat silent about two hundred meters from the compound's main entrance as Alvarado took a sighting point just about a meter to his left. Riemann and Nutworth had already set two of the acoustic sentinels in place as Alec and Josiah worked their way closer to an area just south of the main entrance. Mackay watched, while Pratt had embosked himself within a stand of heavy foliage.

CHAPTER FORTY-NINE

Most inside the Viper's Pit were still asleep. The quarter moon tried in vain to break through the gray clouds, but it ultimately faded from view again. A few men walked about preparing for the next shift of non-military enemy combatant trainees. They stoked smoky campfires with damp, freshly cut cedar and pine. The occasional sentry lazily marched from one point to another, rarely looking beyond the smoke that floated from his American cigarette.

Fajr, the early morning Muslim call to prayer, echoed across the compound, as the two sets of barracks at opposing corners of the main compound began to spit out brace after brace of Hezbollah true believers marching to an exercise area similar to a parcourse. After the call to prayer, the war games began in earnest. These religious fanatics were readying themselves to meet Allah sooner than they had realized.

"Sir," Bobby said. "I count about a hundred of 'em, just in the one area."

"It looks like some sort of regular exercises. They haven't made us," Pratt added.

In the far-off region of the compound shots rang out. Bobby placed his weapon's composite stock cheek piece to the right side of his face and took aim. Alvarado quickly did his calculations and relayed the coordinates and other data to him. They waited. Alec and Josiah positioned themselves behind an outcropping of rocks only a few meters from a small shack on the perimeter of the compound.

"Bobby, what was that?" Alec asked.

"Sir, it looks like a shooting range of some sort. Guys firing AKs and…." Pausing, then, "I can't make out what else," he said, as he tried to get a closer look through a handheld scope. Bobby set his H&K to single-shot sniper mode and engaged the Camoflex technology with the flick of a switch, thus making it nearly invisible to the human eye. Bobby knew that with the smartshot round he could not miss, not that he ever did.

"Sir," Riemann said, speaking into his mouthpiece. "We've setup six of the acoustic sentinels. Six more to go."

Each acoustic sentinel stood sixteen centimeters high and emitted a specific, high frequency sonic wave that first debilitated a trespasser then caused agonizing death. It was the biological effects of beamed energy utilized most effectively for military anti-personnel purposes.

"Give us the word when it's ready. The moment you're done, we'll cross over before you activate," Alec said, while scrutinizing the area within the compound. He could see a number of operatives entering and exiting a building situated near the central building where WMD were located.

Mackay was scanning the area back and forth with his high-resolution binoculars, ever vigilant. He knew that the first sighting of any member of OS9 by the enemy would eliminate their element of surprise, setting off a powder keg.

"Josiah," Alec said, motioning to him to move east of where they were. "I'll move closer to the building nearest the barracks. Riemann and Nutworth will follow. Once in, they'll set the charges for the com towers. Then Bobby and Alvarado will follow." Moving his lip mike closer, he continued, "Mackay, where are you now?"

"On your six, sirrr."

"When I give you the word, move in."

"Rogerrr that, sirrr," rolled off Mackay's tongue.

"Bobby, next to the building about two hundred meters out there's two tangos looking this way." Bobby and Alvarado sat silent like deer hunters in a dense forest. A call from someone out of sight summoned the two men away.

"Sir, the fence is ready," Nutworth said. "Now we're —"

Pratt cut-in, "I have a sighting. Two large personnel trucks moving toward you, sir. Must be about ten men in the back of each."

"How far out?"

"Probably two klicks."

Alec paused for a moment, then said, "Before they get anywhere near the entrance take them out."

Eagle Eye and *Golden Eye* circled high above like hungry vultures looking for quarry.

"*Hounak!* Over there!" the guard called out. "*Wara al-sakhra!* Behind the rocks!"

The guard *made* Bobby and Alvarado. They needed to act fast. "Two hundred and twenty-five meters," Alvarado said to Bobby. Bobby sighted the two of them. Alvarado gave the wind speed and direction. Bobby made his micro-adjustments and pop, pop. The smartshots from his custom H&K found their marks. Two Hezbollah operatives fell dead.

Alvarado raised his thermal gun as three more moved closer. A gentle squeeze of the trigger and intestines were turned to Jell-O and excreted from their mouths, nostrils, and anuses.

Riemann said quickly, "The fence is ready. Everyone in?"

Mackay was the last to answer. "I'm in," he said flatly, as he crossed over the fence's laser line.

Pratt stayed behind to monitor the situation via encrypted Iridium satellite phone communiqués from USCENTCOM and computer feeds from UCAVs and UAVs. "Sir, the trucks are almost at the turn into the valley."

"Now. Fire now!" Alec said.

Pratt sent the signal to *Eagle Eye* to fire the heat-seeking mini-Cruise missiles that utilized a depleted uranium warhead. The first hit was direct. The second, the same. Both trucks and occupants were instantly transformed into half-dollar sized shards of metal and flesh. Numerous explosions were suddenly heard within the compound. Men rushed across the open area in peripatetic fashion waving their AKs wildly. The barracks were cleared of all occupants. Upwards of three hundred non-military enemy combatants were now visible and armed.

"Sir, the towers are ready," Riemann said.

"Take them down," Alec ordered.

Two distinct, primary flashes were seen before the communication towers exploded. The explosions showered the area with flaming billets of wood and skeins of sparkling, contorted wires. Clouds of dust smothered an area that extended for a radius of some hundred meters in every direction.

Without warning, Alec saw him. A small figure silhouetted in the dusty air. Anger was the first feeling to reach the surface and then came disgust, but it was a laser-focused determination that took front-and-center in his mind. A bearded as-Saffah walked hurriedly out of a building in the center of the compound in a most deliberate manner. He then moved briskly across the ground toward another building near the Russian helo. Shots rattled off pell-mell from every AK-47 and AK-74 held by a non-military enemy combatant. Errant shots hit the grassy areas and ricocheted off rock formations outside the compound with no results.

Alec took measured steps closer.

Josiah set the range of his electromagnetic gun's wave distance to two hundred meters, its maximum setting. He held the trigger down on the Buzzer. Within a few ticks of the clock, more than two dozen men fell to the ground, as Grand Mal seizures wrenched the life out of their bodies. Others looked on in horror, as their comrades died without bleeding. Still others dropped to the ground and began praying, while many stood mute, astonished at what they had just witnessed.

As Alec ran across their field of vision, his leaps of five to seven meters at a time appeared to the enemy as something otherworldly. Josiah did the same. Firing his Buzzer again, more fell in fits, as if Saint Vitas had taken hold of them.

By now, Alec had moved closer to the center of the compound, eyeing the building where as-Saffah had entered. Alec was not about to let him leave without saying *hello.*

Another explosion leveled a food storage depot in a thunderous way, attracting the attention of still others in the Viper's Pit. Additional explosions sent two former Soviet UAZ troop carriers airborne, and then crashing spectacularly to the ground. A burning body was ejected from one of them and landed atop two other dead non-military enemy combatants.

"Sir, the *Golden Eye* sensors picked up residue signatures of both VX and sarin gases in the vicinity," Pratt said.

"Hold tight, Pratt," Alec said, as he crossed behind one of the barracks.

Josiah took a position atop the roof of another barracks, his Buzzer at the ready.

"Sir," Bobby said, "I'm repositioning to the left of the buildings on your right. Alvarado will be sighting to my left."

The sound was more like a burst of air from a paintball gun. Alvarado's aim was spot on. His thermal gun hit one, two, three, and then a fourth man. At first, the reaction was undetectable, aside from the heat wave that emanated from the thermal gun. Seconds later the four men grabbed their heads and screamed in excruciating pain. Extreme anguish covered their faces. By the time they hit the ground their brains were fried and blood began leeching from their ears, nostrils, and mouths.

Simultaneously, Bobby fired off no less than fifteen smartshot rounds, each one hitting its target. The impact of a smartshot was difficult to look at. When a limb was hit, it was blown clean-off the body. When a torso was hit, the body was violently split in two. And when a body was merely grazed, the smartshot would rip fist-sized chunks of flesh from it. Even seasoned military veterans hesitated to look at a tango hit by such a deadly round.

Alec reached to make sure that the Pulse Wave Myotron II was still attached to his exosuit. Suddenly, several rounds from an AK-74, the Chinese model of the Russian AK-47, hit the corner of the building next to Alec. One errant shot ricocheted, hitting him on the back of the left shoulder. Other than causing him to flinch, the exosuit's reflexive armor worked its magic, even though there would be a good-sized bruise to contend with later.

Alec fired back with his Walther P99, hitting the attacker in the breastbone, killing him instantly. He felt confident with the P99; it was his go-to weapon of choice, especially with the new smartshot technology employed in its 9mm rounds.

Caught by surprise, a number of Hezbollah operatives ran from the area, each one hitting the acoustic fence barrier. Death was slow and painful. Each man screamed as if he were having his back molars extracted with a pair of mechanic's pliers by a Medieval dentist.

Bobby's H&K MP5's barrel was white hot, as one smartshot after another roared out, each seeking, and then hitting its mark.

Nutworth and Riemann had finished setting explosives around

three other buildings in the farthest reach of the compound. "Josiah, stay where you are," Riemann said emphatically. "Those buildings are about to disappear."

Riemann, a smile covering his tanned face, pressed the hand-held detonator and…gone. The only remnants of three cinder block structures were small piles of pulverized bricks and mortar enmeshed with twisted steel rebar and human body parts. Alec saw another non-military enemy combatant with a bright red keffiyeh wrapped tightly around his neck moving toward him with bald-faced impunity. Alec tried to get a fix on him, but plumes of black and white smoke obscured his view. He could not make the face out. As the man moved closer, he drew from his hip a large handgun and pointed it in Alec's direction. Alec was nonplussed by the bold action. The man shrieked the Islamic war cry of *Allahu Akbar*. Alec fired two rounds. Round one hit his throat. Before the first spurt of blood splattered on the ground, the second round went clean through the center of his forehead.

Strategically placed Gel-X raised several smaller buildings. There was no flash of light from the explosive; no sound, save the rancorous racket of debris crashing to the ground. It was total destruction. The men inside suffered the same fate.

Chaos within the confines of the Viper's Pit was just what Alec had planned for from the beginning. Men frantically yelled out orders while moving from one area to another in a state of absolute pandemonium. Riemann and Nutworth had set additional charges near structures that caused one explosion to trigger another, further increasing the level of chaotic movement amongst the enemy. They tossed a half dozen GH S&F-13s and RGO 78s grenades into several other smaller structures for good measure.

"Riemann, do you see the fuel depot?"

"Roger that, sir. We've got it wired. You want to blow it now?"

"Yes, blow the son of a bitch!" Alec said loudly.

The explosion of the fuel depot was spectacular, spreading flaming diesel fuel over a wide area, burning to death at least twenty-five to thirty additional non-military enemy combatants. The screams of agony echoed throughout the valley. Fires raged in several places as others ran for cover, wildly firing machine guns in every direction. Clouds of dark smoke blanketed much of the compound.

Just then, out of the corner of Alec's left eye he saw a man walking deliberately toward him, speaking words that he could not hear above the din of gunfire and explosions. As the man's face came into focus, he recognized it. He had remembered the photo that Seddons had shown him of a radical named Habib Hassim, the Khamsin's cell leader in Damascus. He was certain it was the same man.

Now only twenty meters away, Alec aimed his Walther P99 at Hassim. He would not stop; his eyes glazed over. Without warning, a gust of wind blew sand in Alec's eyes as Hassim fired two shots in succession. The first one hit the side of Alec's left leg, knocking him to the ground, but no penetration. Grabbing his leg, Alec turned and fired at Hassim, now crouched at the corner of a small, wooden shack about ten meters away. Alec's 9mm smartshot round raced clean through the man's torso. Alec then turned back and shot another non-military enemy combatant approaching from behind. As he fell to the coarse ground, blood gushed from his wide-opened mouth. Then without hesitation, Alec continued along a path between two outbuildings. The exosuit's ability to protect from small to medium arms fire made its uncomfortable aspects inconsequential, for the rounds could not penetrate the exosuit's reflexive armor.

Two Hezbollah training officers spotted Mackay as he stepped closer to the center of the compound. They both took aim, but before they could get off a shot, Mackay squeezed off several smartshot rounds. One man's leg was severed at the knee. The follow up round found its mark in the abdomen, eviscerating him instantly. Some would say the second man was luckier. His head was cleanly blown off when a smartshot round hit his skull. "What a wonderful thing," Mackay said, looking at his machine gun.

Alec heard a call from Pratt but was unable to respond in real-time. He was bent on taking out Ali as-Saffah. He knew he was still in the building that housed WMD. "Bobby, Alvarado, I'm closing in on the building. There's a pilot in the chopper. Can you see him?"

"Roger that. You want him gone?" Bobby said gladly.

"Yes." After he said *yes*, the pilot suddenly slumped over in the seat. The main rotor continued to turn slowly.

Just then, a brace of men exited the building's entrance with Ali as-Saffah, who hurriedly followed the bodyguards. Each man clutched an AK-74 in one hand and a cell phone in the other. Their eyes darted back-and-forth. As they approached the Russian chopper, Alec made his move. He traveled the nearly ten meters in just two leaps. Leveling his Walther P99 at the first man, the shot was clean through the middle of his throat. Blood spattered against the chopper's Lexan canopy door, as he fell onto its landing gear. Out of nowhere, Mackay squeezed the trigger of his machine and let loose several kill-shot rounds that bifurcated the other man's chest like a butcher splitting a chicken's breastbone. As-Saffah looked back in shock, as Alec approached him in mid air. As-Saffah desperately reached for his sidearm, but not in time. Alec tackled him at the waist. The two rolled over and over until they came to a stop next to one of the dead bodyguards.

As-Saffah grabbed a twisted piece of galvanized steel pipe that was laying against the building and struck Alec on the left shoulder. Wincing a moment, Alec put an elbow to as-Saffah's head. As-Saffah responded with impudence. "*Ya khanzir*, you pig. I am Ali as-Saffah."

As Alec placed his hands on as-Saffah's neck and began to strangle the life out of him, he said with great emphasis, enunciating every word, "*Ana Al-Hakim*, I am The Doctor."

Nervously fluttering his eyelids in a futile attempt to clear the dirt and debris kicked up by the chopper's idling rotor, as-Saffah looked directly at Alec. Disbelief rolled over his heavily creased, dark-skinned face. He fought to break free of Alec's grip. *It couldn't be*, he thought. *The Doctor was dead...years ago. He had to be dead. This was not The Doctor*, he said to himself. He had heard several times over the past twenty years that the most feared man in the intelligence community was dead, although there was never any confirmation. Today Ali as-Saffah learned otherwise.

One story had The Doctor shot to death in a failed CIA operation in Syria in late 1989. Another placed his death in Cairo in 1991. Since that time, The Doctor had become a legend in the Middle East. The Syrians and Iranians insisted he was dead or that he never existed. The Khamsin, al-Qaeda, Taliban, Hamas, and Hezbollah shuttered at the thought of his name. They all tried to deny his existence, but The Doctor had come to settle accounts.

CHAPTER FIFTY

Riemann and Nutworth had destroyed the last two structures on the perimeter of the compound. The remainder of non-military enemy combatants numbered no more than a dozen men, most of whom wanted to escape, but the acoustic fence was their gatekeeper. Trapped, they now found their hopeless situation reason enough to charge Bobby, Alvarado, and Mackay, all of whom stood at the ready. They unleashed the awesome killing power of their electromagnetic and acoustic guns, felling every non-military enemy combatant in sight.

At the same time, Riemann and Nutworth proceeded to the entrance of the building that held the WMD. Opening the two steel doors revealed wide steps that descended into the darkness. They entered cautiously, their xenon 25W Metal Halide HID tactical flashlights attached to their weapons. At the bottom of the steps, a massive steel door confronted them. Riemann reached for it.

"No!" Nutworth shouted. "No."

It was too late.

The booby-trapped steel door blew outward. Riemann was instantly pinned under its immense weight. Blood began leaking from under the door. Nutworth turned up his exosuit's lifting capacity to maximum. Raising the door that weighed at least one-hundred and seventy-five kilograms was done quickly. He looked down at Riemann, his breaths short and weak. His face, painted in spent blood, was the result of numerous head lacerations. Flash burns on his exosuit gave Nutworth cause for great concern. His comrade, his partner, was seriously injured. The exosuit's reflexive armor had done its job, but at such close range, a direct hit sometimes had catastrophic results because of the shear percussive nature of the blast. Needing to get Mackay's attention, Nutworth shouted into his background-noise-canceling lip mike, "Riemann's been hit. Mackie, do you read me? Viking's been hit. Call the pod. I said, call the pod and get over here!"

CHAPTER FIFTY-ONE

Alec and as-Saffah were still entangled in a fight to the death just meters away. Bobby's first instinct was to take aim and kill off as-Saffah. It would not be difficult, but something told him that Alec wanted to do it himself.

Alec now had as-Saffah pinned against the side of the chopper. Its main rotor's prop wash caused constant dust clouds that made seeing difficult. With both hands wrapped around as-Saffah's neck, Alec squeezed tightly, choking the life out of him, then he stopped. Staring at him, eye-to-eye, he loosened his grasp somewhat. With a close-by campfire's flickering light illuminating as-Saffah's Semitic facial features, Alec now thought he had seen him before.

As-Saffah gasped for breath after breath, his face flush with blood, his arms flailing, yet Alec was still in control. With saliva dripping from the corner of his mouth, as-Saffah was flummoxed by Alec's hesitation to finish him off. *"Anta msh al-Hakim.* You are not The Doctor," as-Saffah said with great arrogance and distain, still gasping for breath. "The Doctor would not hesitate to kill me. You are an impostor," he said arrogantly, and then spit in his face. "You don't have the nerve to kill me. I am as-Saffah. You are a coward. I killed many of your people and I will kill you, infidel!"

In a last-gasp effort, as-Saffah managed to push Alec off and lunge for him, but Alec's physical conditioning, shear speed, and training proved too much. He sidestepped as-Saffah, causing him to fall clumsily to the ground. Like a matador playing with a bull, Alec's expression challenged as-Saffah to charge him again. As as-Saffah rose to his feet, he retrieved a handgun from one of his dead bodyguards. Pointing it at Alec, he pulled the trigger, but sand had fouled the firing mechanism. He pulled the trigger again…nothing.

Alec said with a hint of glee, "Your time has run out."

"You want to kill me. Do it, you coward. Do it," as-Saffah said in full voice, his corpulent hands gesturing madly.

As-Saffah charged Alec again. Alec stood his ground, as he approached. The moment he was within Alec's grasp, a SOG Duo Desert Dagger appeared, as if by magic, in Alec's hand. He quickly grabbed as-Saffah, pulling him into the serrated stainless steel blade. He forced the knife's long blade deeper into as-Saffah's gut. A slow, gurgling sound emanated from his throat, as involuntary spasms forced blood to pour from his mouth.

Alec felt as-Saffah's breath begin to fade away. He lifted up on the dagger, splitting his bulbous gut. He pulled up even more tightly on the knife and heard a breastbone snap. Entrails gushed out of his dying body. Alec stepped back, as his prey fell to the ground for the last time. As-Saffah's body deflated, much like the air suddenly let out of a large children's balloon. Looking deeply into his dying eyes, Alec said in a cool voice, "Mr. William Francis sends his regards." Alec whispered to himself, *the Shedder of Blood is dead.*

As-Saffah's eyes showed a blank stare. His mortal gut wounds, a certain sign that death was imminent.

CHAPTER FIFTY-TWO

"Riemann's been hurt. A bomb. The door was booby-trapped." Bobby's face said it all.

"What?" Alec fired back reflexively.

"The door to the WMD was rigged."

"Sir," Bobby said, looking down at Alec. "We need to get going. We've got to get Riemann help. Mackay's bandaging him up, but he looks bad. Real bad, sir."

Alec paused for a moment over the body of as-Saffah. He looked closer at his face. He wanted him to feel more pain, but it no longer mattered anymore.

Wiping as-Saffah's blood from his hands and right cheekbone, Alec turned to Bobby. Suddenly, in a last moment of desperation, as-Saffah managed to summon up a burst of nervous strength and pull a small handgun from inside his jacket. In the final throes of death, but fighting like the immortal hydra, he raised the weapon toward Alec and struggled to squeeze the trigger.

"Sir!" Bobby warned. He quickly pointed his H&K machine gun in as-Saffah's direction, but before he could squeeze off a shot, Alec wheeled around on his heels and cleared his Walther P99 from its holster clip. Two rounds, one on top of the other, shot clean through as-Saffah's mouth. The entry wounds began leaking rivulets of spent blood.

Looking blank-faced and as if nothing serious had just happened,

Alec turned to Bobby and said, "Did anyone call the trauma pod?" Alec knew that it probably did not matter now, but it was a reflexive comment, hoping that Riemann's wounds were not mortal.

"Yes, sir. Mackay says it's on the way," answered Bobby.

Alec added, "Pratt will contact the U.S.S. *Kearsarge* and inform them that you'll be coming in early and that we have a casualty. We'll remain here to remove the WMD," he said, as he held tight to his emotions.

Pratt came down from his position atop a rise and approached the group. Somewhat exhausted from hauling forty kilograms of communication's gear, he said, "Sir, shall I call in *Eagle Eye?*"

"No. He goes in the helo." Alec then walked back toward the mortally wounded Riemann. He was being held by Nutworth and Mackay. Alec reached for Riemann's right hand, but it was too late. He saw him draw his final breath. His exosuit was soaked in blood and his bandaging revealed one closed eye. He was dead from his wounds.

"Sirrr," Mackay said in a forlorn manner, looking to a saddened Alec. "He's gone, sirrr."

Trying desperately to hold back tears, each of the men walked over to the now dead Riemann, their comrade-in-arms, and looked at him for a long moment. They prayed for his soul.

There was now no longer an urgency.

"Sirrr," Mackay said softly. "Just before we shipped out his wife Rita called him with the news that she was four months pregnant with twin boys and now…."

Nutworth took a deep breath, his throat tight from the visual of his partner lying dead before him. He had no words.

"Call off the pod," Alec ordered quietly, as he looked across the eerie sweep of the Viper's Pit, now reduced to specks of sand, flecks of metal, and fragments of human flesh.

A palpable depression hung over the men.

Alec turned and stared down at Riemann's body again. He felt helpless. Riemann's death brought into sharp focus the thought that his wife Leyla was in great danger and his daughter Karina was crying for him. His heart was torn asunder. His mind was enraged.

CHAPTER FIFTY-THREE

Josiah and Mackay had retrieved the SOVs and were wailing flat out across an arid ground. As they approached, Alec scanned the area. Fires and smoke disturbed the still of the early morning. It was now 0635 hours. Buildings were gone, leaving behind only a few visible foundations and endless mounds of debris. *It was total destruction*, he thought, *and General Grant would have been proud*.

Over Alec's shoulder Pratt espied something moving in the distance between two smoky fires. There was someone still alive. Then he saw another silhouette of a man running past a pile of rubble with a weapon in his hand. Alec saw him, too.

"All right, Bobby, Alvarado, that way," Alec said, gesturing to the east.

"Josiah," Pratt warned. "Go wide. Two men at your two o'clock."

Josiah swerved the SOV abruptly to the left and maneuvered it behind an outcropping of rocks. Shots hit the rocks nearest the front of the SOVs. They pinged and ricocheted wildly. One dinged the front of the frame. Another blew out a headlight.

Alec closed in on the spot where he had sighted the second man. Bobby and Alvarado positioned themselves about fifteen meters ahead and to the right of Alec. Bobby was the first to spot one of the men. He was peering through the wreckage of an UAZ's shattered window.

"I'll take the shot, sir," Bobby said, speaking to Alec. The H&K

MP5N submachine gun rattled, sending several smartshots hurling toward the man. The impact blew him back ten meters.

As shots were fired, the second man crossed in front of Alec's line-of-sight some twenty-five meters away. He ducked into what was left of one of the barracks. Alec moved closer. He was stalking the last of the Hezbollah hostiles that lived and trained in the *Viper's Pit*.

Bobby and Alvarado held their positions.

All of a sudden, the man came running out of the bombed-out barracks, wildly firing a weapon. He continued charging straight toward Alec, as he shrieked, *"Al-mout aala al-kouffar.* Death to the infidels. *Allahu Akbar, Allahu Akbar.* God is great, God is great." Through the billows of dust, Alec made out a belt of explosives strapped to the man's waist. He was a homicide bomber.

The madman kept coming. Alec reached for his Myotron II, but instantly realized it had been knocked loose from its leg strap in the battle with as-Saffah. Calmly raising his Walther P99, he took aim and pulled the trigger, but it jammed. He tried to clear the slide. He pulled the trigger again...no report. The madman was now closing in on him, all the while firing his AK-74 wildly, seeming to be in some sort of self-induced frenzy.

Before Alec could find a weapon that worked, a shot from an AK-47 zoomed within millimeters of his head. Stepping back, he tripped over a dead non-military enemy combatant. Regaining his balance, his only option was to fire his electro-burst mechanism. Pressing the activation button, two short bursts, one from each shoulder of his exosuit found their marks, surging through the madman's body, inducing a fatal heart attack.

Unexpectedly, the homicide bomber was able to detonate his waist bomb. The result was body parts flying in every direction. Minuscule bits of flesh and bone splattered on Alec's exosuit and face. Wiping his face, he could feel the flesh was still warm, and the blood had a viscous touch and smell of instant death.

Without losing a beat, Alec ordered, "Bobby, Alvarado, secure the area. Pratt, where are the choppers?" Alec continued to walk toward the WMD storage area.

"Sir, they left the *Kearsarge* about thirty minutes ago. They should arrive soon. By the way, sir. How'd you manage to get the Sea Knights?"

Alec answered, "It was all preset. Our president called President Affoud of Lebanon before we left and informed him that we found WMD in his country. At first, President Affoud balked, but was reminded that the U.S. Marines had a history of flying into Lebanon to give aide and assistance. They were there on peace missions in the 1950s and even in the 1980s. By the way, an ultimatum was also given, informing Affoud that he had to give his approval or the Marines would proceed anyway and were told to fire on sight should anyone have the idea of stopping them, for it was our national security that was at stake," Alec said with force.

A big smile rolled over Pratt's face. Bobby and Alvarado gave a thumbs up.

"Now, let's take a look," Alec said, as he moved toward the opening to the underground storage area.

Alec and Pratt proceeded cautiously down the steps to the place where the door blew open and killed their comrade.

Bobby and Alvarado kept watch.

Mackay, Josiah, and Nutworth moved through the compound, scanning the aftermath of the battle that had just taken place. They were looking for any sign of life, but OS9's work was very thorough.

Alec and Pratt could still smell the residue of some sort of C-4 or Semtex type explosive in the cavernous room. The humidity in the air held a putrid mustiness that irritated their nasal passages. Standing before the entrance to the large, tomblike room, Alec saw where Riemann's body took the direct hit. Looking deeper into the room, he spotted a second steel door. Stepping forward, Alec and Pratt activated their exosuits' chemical sniffers. The readout on their panels registered a range of chemical signatures. Alec thought, *why hadn't Riemann done the same before he opened the first door?* Nevertheless, he carefully opened the second door. Once inside, each man activated his Starlight vision. Then, they saw them…canisters lined up in neat rows. The two smiled. There they were, VX gas canisters, red-tipped Katyusha missile warheads, and smaller containers designated mustard and sarin gases. There was even a container of the deadly *ricin* poison amongst the chemical WMD.

Ricin was a by-product of the benign castor bean. Known as a toxalbumin or highly toxic protein molecule, ricin has been feared as one of the world's most toxic substances for decades.

Alec thought, *he personally would have been satisfied with as-Saffah's death, but the finding of additional WMD made it that much* sweeter. After all, it was the mother lode of Weapons of Mass Destruction.

"So what do you think?" Alec asked Pratt rhetorically. "I'd like to get the VX and mustard out first. The warheads are too heavy and too many. The choppers can handle them. Let's get *Eagle Eye* to fly the ricin and sarin out now."

"Yes. I'll call *Eagle Eye* in now, but I've got to return to the top to get a signal," Pratt answered.

Once he turned to return to the surface, he saw as-Saffah. Dark, coagulated blood surrounded his lifeless body. Contusions encircled his short neck. He was all but disemboweled. He was entering the early stage of rigor mortis. Pratt then linked up with the circling UCAV. One command and it began its descent like a trained bird of prey. He skillfully soft-landed it just meters from where he was standing.

Small fires burned throughout the compound and devastation was everywhere. OS9 had reduced the Viper's Pit to a heap of pulverized cinder blocks, splintered wood, twisted metal, and dead and decaying bodies. Now the complicated and arduous task of removing the WMD was before them.

Bobby heard them first, the whirling, slashing sounds of two Boeing CH-46 Sea Knight helicopters approaching from a westerly direction. They pushed through the thick air at 145 knots per hour. Two GE-T58-16 engines spun the massive main rotor of each chopper as if it were a child's hula-hoop.

"Did USCENTCOM acknowledge our casualty? Where's the LCAC now? And has Captain Ruger been notified of Riemann's death?"

"Sir, I just finished talking to Smitty aboard the *Kearsarge*, and the captain's been told. The LCAC will be in place to meet us when we arrive. All's set. Commander Aziz will be there to back us up," Pratt said.

Transportation of the dangerous VX and mustard gases required that they be transported with extreme care. The *Eagle Eye*'s payload capacity would be strained to its limit, but Pratt had assured Alec that it would be able to get the cargo to the U.S.S. *Kearsarge* safely.

"All right, so let's do it. First, make sure that Riemann is secure before we load." The men of OS9 moved into action. Alec continued, "Once done, we're out of here."

Then in an instant there they were. The occasional flash of refracted light off the choppers' fuselages could be seen in the growing light. They began their slow descent, as Pratt directed them to set down as near as was possible to the underground storage building.

Sand and dirt started to swirl about violently. Alec and Pratt stepped back. As the choppers set down, two AV-8B Harrier aircraft passed overhead. They were running cover for the return mission. It felt good to Alec that he had backup...the WMD had to be safeguarded...they had to be seen by the world.

The first pilot to step out of a Sea Knight was Captain William "Chubby" Wright. He walked briskly toward Alec, who was again wiping sand from his eyes. "Sir, Captain Wright at your service," came out precisely, as he snapped a salute.

Alec stared at the word "Chubby," set off in quotation marks, emblazoned across the front of Captain Wright's flight helmet. "Glad you're here," came out directly.

"I know, sir. Everyone looks at my call sign and wonders how I got it."

Alec nodded, not knowing exactly what the captain had said over the sounds of rotating rotor blades and jet engines winding down.

"Well, sir, as you can see, I'm anything but chubby. In fact, I barely made the weight minimum at Annapolis. It's kind of a joke, my name, that is. It's a long story," the captain said politely.

"I understand Chubby, that is, Captain Wright," Alec said with a grin, as he padded him on the shoulder.

Just then, the second chopper set down. The pilot jumped out of the cockpit and marched straight toward Alec and Captain Wright. The "Rock" removed his flight helmet and turned for a moment, motioning to his crewmen to move faster. Alec and Captain Wright moved in Captain Artunian's direction. Turning back toward Alec and Captain Wright, he said straightaway, "Captain Artunian, sir." He quickly saluted Alec, who did the same. "We're ready to move them, sir" he said assuredly.

Captain Artunian's call sign the "Rock" was inspired by the country where he was born thirty-three years ago. His father, Commander of the British naval base on the very narrow peninsula of Gibraltar, was the offspring of Armenian parents who moved to Great Britain after the partitioning of the Middle East post World War I. Later the family moved to the United States where his father became the British liaison to the United Nations.

Alec always appreciated those who demonstrated confidence. Looking first at Captain Artunian and then to Captain Wright, he said, "Gentlemen, before we start the loading of the WMD, I need to apprise you of what you probably have already been told."

Both pilots looked at each other, not knowing what to say.

Alec continued without expression. "We will be traveling with a casualty, Navy SEAL Sergeant Bernard Riemann. He was a warrior who gave his full measure. I want him properly secured before anything else gets loaded. After that, you'll need to have your crews bring the warheads up from down in the storage facility of this building," he added, pointing to his right. It looked odd to be the only building still standing in a compound that once had held upwards of two dozen buildings and three hundred non-military enemy combatants, but OS9 knew it was one of the spoils of war.

Fighting the rank smell with rags tied across their faces, the first crewmen to enter the storage room were astounded by the number of canisters and warheads. One mumbled aloud, "Holy shit." The WMD were not only heavy, but were also very hard to handle. The VX and mustard gases were encased in high-tensile strength, steel canisters twenty centimeters in height and ten centimeters in diameter. The one canister of ricin was double encased, as was the sarin gas.

"Gentlemen," Alec said affirmatively, "time is of the essence. What we did here is now known to others and you've got to believe that they're headed this way."

"Not a problem, sir," Captain Artunian said, while the crew members continued to move the warheads with a portable pneumatic lift designed to crawl up and down steps and other surfaces.

Although Alec appreciated the captain's resolve, he knew what could happen.

The massive Sea Knights were now nearly full of their precious, dangerous cargoes. The hazardous work moved at a syncopated pace. The crewmen were Hazmat specialists. They were very aware of the loading and transportation requirements of such cargo.

CHAPTER FIFTY-FOUR

The rising sun continued to expose Operation Star 9's work in the Viper's Pit.

By 0735 hours, it was no more. The Hezbollah organization had been castrated, as-Saffah eliminated, and the WMD were headed to the U.S.S. *Kearsarge*. OS9's job was complete, or so they thought.

With a bottle of water in his hand, Captain Artunian, standing at the entrance to the storage building, took a long sip. Speaking to Alec, Captain Artunian said blithely, "Who's that pathetic looking motherfucker?" pointing to the very dead as-Saffah on the ground a few steps away.

Alec looked at as-Saffah without emotion and said, "He's the man who killed my friend Bill."

"...and you did him?"

"Yes," Alec said flatly.

"Well," staring down at as-Saffah's now lifeless body, "the United States Marine Corps sends its regards, you piece of shit." Captain Artunian signed his comment by removing the U.S. flag Velcroed to his shoulder and slapped it on as-Saffah's bloodied forehead. Without pause, he adjusted his sunglasses and said, "Sir, looks as if we're about ready to head back."

Alec saluted Captains Artunian and Wright, then said, "Thanks, boys," as the two Harrier jets passed over the compound again. The pilots dipped their wings, indicating that all was well.

In a matter of moments, the mighty Sea Knights roared to life and grabbed for the sky as they simultaneously lifted themselves airborne, followed by *Eagle Eye*. The men on the ground tried to shield their eyes as sand and debris blew in every direction.

It was now 0750 hours, and southern Lebanon was beginning to come alive, as the sun's bright rays peered through the dark clouds and crept across the primordial landscape, one ray of light at a time.

CHAPTER FIFTY-FIVE

It was the surreal mental image of his kidnapped wife and frightened daughter before his eyes that told Alec what he must now do.

With the Sea Knights and *Eagle Eye* aloft, one carrying OS9's fallen comrade, Alec pondered the irony of the loss of Riemann and the finding of WMD. *Was the trade worth it?* he asked himself. He knew the answer.

Alec gave the order for his men to get into their Special Operations Vehicles. The team took one last, long look at what was the infamous Viper's Pit, once a major breeding ground for Islamic terrorists.

Alec hoped the LCAC would be on time. He had also hoped Riemann's body would be returned to his wife and family with all due dispatch. He knew that families who had lost loved ones in battle would start the healing process sooner if the remains of their loved ones were at home.

Chapter Fifty-Six

The SOVs were crossing the landscape at a comfortable rate of speed when Pratt interrupted Alec's thoughts. Speaking directly into his right ear, he said, "The LCAC is on its way. The SWCC team has approached the OTH, so it's on time."

SWCC or "swick" was the Navy's Special Warfare Combat-craft Crewmen. They were special operations units designed to function in maritime situations, in specialized, fast moving naval landing craft, where large naval vessels could not maneuver.

Alec adroitly maneuvered the SOV around a deep rut a meter wide and about one-half meter deep. As the limits of the suspension were tested, Bobby nearly fell out of the vehicle, holding on as best he could.

It was not the first time Bobby almost fell out of a special ops vehicle. After all, he had never given much thought to seatbelts, but then he quickly buckled up, but not before pulling the top of his exosuit down around his waist. He simply wanted to feel the warm morning air pass over his tired body.

The time was now nearing 0900 hours, and the sun began to break through the *cumulonimbus calvus* cloud formations behind them. They appeared at about five kilometers up as great splashes of God's glorious paint cast upon the morning sky.

The SOVs approached the sands of Sûr cautiously, for the city had already started its day, and the sight of Special Operations Vehicles was sure to attract attention.

Alec and Josiah brought the SOVs to a sliding stop not too far from the building where only hours before OS9 had picked up their rides to the Viper's Pit. Alec jumped out and stretched his long legs for a moment, then quickly dusted himself off. The others did the same, all the while scanning the area for possible unfriendlies.

The foggy, dull morning and the coastal treeline obscured the view from the road to the beach.

Alec glanced down at his Panerai chronograph. It indicated 0915 hours. He thought, *the end was near for Operation Extreme Prejudice; the mission to destroy the Viper's Pit and find WMD had succeeded; but finding the Ankabut was yet to come. And what about his wife? Was she still alive? And how was his darling daughter Karina?* The questions continued, but he needed to shut them off.

The mammoth LCAC was now less than a thousand meters from shore and the noise began to draw unwanted attention. Its whirling, monstrous fans produced a near deafening cacophony of sounds. Centrifugal fans pushed the air, leaving behind a turbulence that looked as if a category five hurricane were coming ashore.

Commander Aziz's men kept onlookers at a distance, while the operations were underway.

The LCAC moved effortlessly onto the beach. Its look gave the commander and his men great pause. They all moved back a few meters as it came to a sudden stop, digging into the wet sand about thirty meters onshore. The loading would begin in earnest, the moment crewmen secured the LCAC.

Alec pulled Commander Aziz next to a clump of bushes, placed his hand on his shoulder and said, "Commander. I am thankful and my country is thankful for your cooperation. Your efforts were mission critical, and I will never forget your willingness to help my country." The two continued to talk for several minutes, then Alec said, "*Shoukran,* thank-you again. *Mael salama,* good-bye."

Before Alec turned toward the LCAC, Commander Aziz said in a clear voice, "I believe in your country and what you are doing. I hope to return someday to your beautiful land. My years as a foreign relations student at Boston University were good to me. Very good, indeed." With a strong handshake and a pat on the shoulder, the commander said proudly, "*Mael salama.*"

"We would like to have you again in America," Alec said, with a smile on his now heavily bearded face. He nodded to the commander then turned on his heels and headed toward the awaiting LCAC.

The front loading platform was lowered, revealing Lieutenant Junior Grade Billy Rogers in all his splendor as he walked forward. In truth, his walk was more of a swagger, for he hailed from Dallas, Texas, and his family was in oil. Billy Rogers did not have to be on a beach in southern Lebanon. He could have easily afforded to buy the whole damn country out of petty cash, but he liked the action. He was an adrenaline junkie. The red, white, and blue bandana under his government-issue sea cap said all there was to say about Billy Rogers.

Lieutenant Rogers jumped off the front of the LCAC and approached Alec. With a snappy salute, he said, "Sorry about the casualty, sir. I only spoke to him once when you all were onboard the *Kearsarge*. He seemed like a nice guy."

"Yes, he was, lieutenant," Alec said, as he gritted his teeth in an effort to withhold emotion. "He was more than a nice guy. He was a great warrior."

A trained team of *swicks* quickly loaded the men, matériel, and SOVs onboard the LCAC.

Alec stood silent next to the loading platform. Once all the members of OS9 were accounted, along with their weapons and gear, he snapped a sharp salute to Commander Aziz, who looked on from the beachhead.

"Lieutenant, we're ready," Alec said flatly.

"Very good, sir," Lt. Rodgers said. He then immediately turned to those behind him and shouted, "Then let's do it."

Alec looked to his men. "It's time, boys."

Bobby yelled out, "Thank God for the good ol' U.S. of A." With the realization of it all, he added, "Son of a bitch. We're going home."

Alec scanned the area one last time. With everyone accounted for, he looked to the open sea. Suddenly, the loading platform began to rise as the massive turbines spooled up, and the giant fans whirled wildly.

As the monstrous LCAC turned-and-burned, Nutworth removed from a side zipper pocket a small electronic device. He pushed a sequence of alphanumeric buttons and instantly, both SDVs' that laid on the sea floor activated their homing devices and automatically returned to the mother ship.

By 0955 hours, the LCAC was on its way back to the U.S.S. _Kearsarge_, while the two Harriers made one last pass overhead.

The sun was now completely unclothed, as the clouds moved south toward the Israeli border, most likely to settle over Nahr Al-Urdun, the Jordan River, the lowest river in the world.

In no time at all the LCAC was closing in on the mother ship. Alec stood off to the front side of the vessel as it raced across the Mediterranean Sea at 40 knots. In the distance, two small fishing boats bobbed in the rough water. Enormous waves of blue water and white-sea foam shot up from the front of the LCAC. Off to the right Alec saw a picturesque rainbow form over the top of one of the local fishing boats, as he contemplated the obvious..._this was not the end. His wife and daughter were in danger. He needed to save them...it was his job._

CHAPTER FIFTY-SEVEN

THE PENTAGON, WASHINGTON, D.C.

At the daily Pentagon briefing, a journalist for the *London Times* asked the spokesman if he would confirm or deny reports out of the Middle East that a Hezbollah encampment in southern Lebanon was raided and destroyed by American *Special Forces* in a nighttime attack that left 301 enemy dead and one American casualty.

The spokesman denied any such reports and added that there was no Hezbollah encampment in southern Lebanon. Another journalist managed to get in a follow-up question, a question that was much more probative and proved disturbing to everyone in the room.

"Sir," a journalist from the *Washington Times* asked forcefully, "if there was no such raid, do you then also deny the existence of a deep *black ops* unit called *Operation Star 9*, led by a man known only as *The Doctor?*"

There was complete silence in the briefing room for a very long moment. People stared at each other with looks of incredulity painted on their faces. Then the spokesman, with irritation in his voice, answered. "The existence of any such unit and the existence of this man you call The Doctor have always been nothing more than rumors, fueled by journalists with very active imaginations."

CHAPTER FIFTY-EIGHT

The National Security Agency was not pleased with having to keep tabs on Dr. Raymond Raissi at the behest of numerous agencies of the Federal Government, but higher-ups in Washington, D.C., were convinced that doing so was very necessary, given his public persona. Moreover, the recent situation in Nottingham, England, gave it great pause. MI5 and the FBI found numerous photos and name-specific data regarding Raissi amongst the belongings of two Arab students linked to a terrorist cell in Chicago. It was actionable intelligence. He was deemed a *prime target* of the Khamsin. DSS agents, through the State Department, notified Raissi in London of the situation and offered protection, which he flatly refused.

The NSA was not permitted to spy directly on American citizens, especially within the confines of the United States, so they sought to do so surreptitiously by employing the British under the UK/USA Agreement. It was an alliance of Anglosphere countries led by the United States. Using the *signals intelligence* system known as *Echelon*, the British kept a constant eye on Raissi from afar.

Echelon was a highly secretive surveillance system used to intercept and process international communications passing via U.S. communication satellites that began more than sixty years ago during World War II.

With the invention of the radio by Nikola Tesla in the late 1890s, governments and other agencies gained the ability to pass communiqués to receivers across continents. However, given the nature of telecommunications, the capacity to eavesdrop on virtually any such communication was omnipresent. Enter cryptography, the science and art of creating secret codes and the business of signals intelligence.

The Echelon signals intelligence system intercepted messages from telephone and radio transmissions, the Internet, undersea cables, and also from eavesdropping equipment installed inside embassies, as well as orbiting satellites that monitored signals anywhere on the earth's surface.

The primary computer system at the very center of Echelon's signals intelligence processing operations utilized the *Dictionary.* In mobile operations, it utilized a briefcase-sized version referred to as the *Oratory.*

The Dictionary computers scanned communications inputted to them and then they ran them through a series of filters that culled data for the purpose of generating a report to be forwarded to analysts studying profiles of interest.

Every day millions upon millions of communications were captured, resulting in less than one in a thousand ever seeing human eyes. The essence of the Dictionary was to reject the greatest percentage of intercepted information.

The very secret Project P-415, at the heart of today's system, resulted from Echelon's constant effort to update its capabilities. Although the present operation of the NSA's intelligence gathering system, called Echelon 2, was still located at Menwith Hill, in central England, it did maintain numerous stations worldwide.

The NSA learned that during Raissi's most recent stay in London, he rarely went to his company's local offices located in the Bank of England, in the city proper, but desired to spend most of his time escorting a scintillatingly attractive woman to the city's most posh restaurants and nightclubs. On occasion, he would play tennis or squash at one of the many private clubs he was a member of over the past twenty-some years. Although he was not the most physically attractive of men, he was nonetheless, a very capable athlete who enjoyed engaging others in games of physical skill.

It was only last year that the Prince of Wales had invited him to the ancestral home of the royal family at Balmoral, Scotland, for a shoot. Red deer were the preferred game, with a brace or two taken every morning by the hunting party. The day's efforts always ended with an evening of fine dining followed by the obligatory dram or two of Laphroaig thirty-year-old single malt Scotch whiskey and a fine Opus X Havana cigar. Occasionally, when not inebriated to the point of falling down, the two would engage in a game of billiards.

It was all in a day's work for Raissi, a man who prided himself on being liked, on being trusted, and on being respected, and even feared. He gloried in it.

CHAPTER FIFTY-NINE

During the late afternoon of a reasonably quiet and uneventful May day in London, Dr. Raissi's Rolls-Royce was sighted by an Echelon satellite. The ostentatious vehicle was making its way toward London's Hyde Park from its home in Lowndes Square. As the car rolled down Kensington Road, all appeared to be normal. The Rolls turned onto the Ring's West Carriage Drive as expected, but then it stopped unexpectedly where the cycle path intersected the Ring, the main thoroughfare that bifurcated the park. The satellite detected that the car's engine was still running. One photo after another, followed by streaming video, poured onto the NSA computer screens. The car remained stationary. Everything seemed routine, for it was not unusual to find Raissi passing through the historic park on his way across town.

Analysts assigned to Raissi's case did not consider the first high-definition satellite photos and streaming video that came through on this day of any consequence. But, unexpectedly a cyclist towing a small, enclosed two-wheeled children's carriage came to a stop no more than a couple of meters from the car. That heightened an analyst's curiosity, if only to see what would happen next.

The immense size of the Rolls-Royce forced passersby to maneuver their vehicles around it, as it straddled the crown of the road. A tall, statuesque, dark-haired woman exited the Rolls-Royce as the chauffer held the door. She was exquisitely attired in a deep cobalt blue, bespoke gabardine suit. Her Borselino hat was a bright, scarlet red with an equally bright red and blue moiré taffeta band. She moved toward the cyclist in a sashaying style, as people in every direction just stared. She was stunning, captivating.

The cyclist, swarthy in appearance and dressed in typical cycling clothes, sans helmet, opened the carriage's clear-plastic door as the woman approached. There was a short verbal exchange, and then the woman in blue peered into the carriage. A few moments passed, then the cyclist, with great effort, removed about a meter long, black-anodized hard-shell aluminum suitcase and placed it on the ground. He pulled a long handle from the top of the suitcase and showed the woman the roller wheels on the bottom. She took the handle, turned on her heels, and walked deliberately, albeit somewhat labored, back to the idling Rolls.

The chauffeur immediately jumped out of his driver's seat and opened the immense boot. He politely took the aluminum case from the woman and lifted it into the cavernous boot, his natural strength very evident. Shutting the boot, he hurriedly closed the door on the woman's side and proceeded to take his seat. The Rolls slowly started out again and moved farther into the park. It passed the Serpentine and eventually motored out of the park and turned right on Bayswater Road.

The cyclist continued down the path and eventually disappeared in traffic south of Kensington Gore.

A lone analyst viewing the goings on was convinced that the situation was anything but routine. He knew immediately that what he saw on the screen needed to be brought to the attention of the senior analyst on duty. He summoned the senior analyst, who immediately gathered a review team in one of the many secure conference rooms at the Menwith Hill facility.

A discussion ensued for nearly an hour. People scrutinized the data, particularly the still photos. Flat-panel computer screens sat before each person seated in the large, windowless room bathed in a soft blue, indirect fluorescent lighting.

"Garrett," senior operations analyst Blake Tollbridge said emphatically, "get me a close-up of the cyclist," pointing to the seventh photo on the screen. The twenty-two year-old Garrett, eager to please his superior, zoomed in. "Closer please," Tollbridge insisted in his rather affected British tone. Garrett zoomed in again, this time close enough to count the clusters of black hair on the man's bearded face.

Others in the room focused on their individual computer screens. One barked out, "Reza. That's Reza Farkhani. We lost him over two years ago."

"The bastard's in London. Good god!" Chester Withmoore, a recently minted analyst by way of the London School of Economics and Political Science, said. "He's the Khamsin operative involved in the kidnapping of the two Americans in Indonesia a few years ago."

"Chester is right, sir," Ms. Broadstreet said.

Ms. Meredith Broadstreet's comely look had always been of interest to the fifty-something Tollbridge, thrice divorced. "Farkhani is an Iranian. In fact, at one point he was the head of the secret police. He all but sleeps with the Khomeini. We believe he was a player with al-Qaeda in the massacre at Fort Hood, Texas, a few years ago. Somehow, he's able to keep below the radar much of the time. Langley never confirmed it, but it all adds up. He's very high in the Khamsin hierarchy, even though he's a Shi'ite."

"Let me see the video," Tollbridge asked.

Garrett punched up the video. "Here's when she takes the suitcase," he said excitedly, pointing to the computer screen before him. The hand-off was obvious.

"Do we know what's in it?"

"Sir," Garrett said with a solemn face. "The preliminary spectrograph analysis from the Cal Tech satellite indicates that it's hot. A radioactive signature. No doubt."

"Goddamn. What we're witnessing here, in essence, is a transfer of some sort of nuclear device from Iran to this woman who could be linked to Dr. Raissi in some way. Ms. Broadstreet," he asked, subtly staring at her breasts, "Where is Dr. Raissi now?"

"The last data on Dr. Raissi has him in Liverpool for a luncheon with civic leaders. Seems he donated a considerable sum of money recently to finance a new hospital wing. He's there to be honored."

"And to think that he might be dirty," Tollbridge interjected, looking down over his reading spectacles. A look and feeling of incredulity took hold.

The thought reverberated throughout the room. *The famous Dr. Raissi, dirty. Not possible!* The man had done so much for London. For people everywhere. A philanthropist held in very high esteem.

Tollbridge thought, *it just couldn't be.* "Garrett, are you sure about the suitcase?"

"Sir, it's a dirty bomb," he said levelly.

"Is that Dr. Raissi's Rolls?" Tollbridge asked.

"It's the only one like it, sir. The plate reads *RR 1.*"

Tollbridge pondered the enormity of the situation, if in fact it was what he saw before him. "Pull up on the woman. Close," he commanded.

Garrett immediately zoomed in on the image of the woman.

"Please give me a freeze frame of her face. There," he said, indicating a frontal view. "There. Stop," he demanded rather excitedly.

There was no doubt about it. *She was one ravishingly beautiful woman*, Tollbridge thought to himself. Her exact age was difficult to ascertain, but she was very well preserved. The stylish suit's skirt clung to her well-defined, firm buttocks like Saran wrap; her jacket served to accentuate her generous breasts. Tollbridge just stared at the photo with a perverted smile on his face. Her beauty nonplused every woman in the room. Scratching his head, he said, "I've seen her before."

Cigarette smoke floated in the stale air and permeated the clothing of every person in the room. It was a very tense time for Toolbridge.

Ms. Broadstreet, wanting to impress Tollbridge, offered some unsolicited advice. "Mr. Tollbridge, perhaps we should search the photo databases. Let's say," pausing slightly, "over the past twenty years. Europe and the Middle East to start."

Tollbridge looked at her, feigning surprise. "Very good, Ms. Broadstreet. Order it," he said in a commanding voice.

Ms. Broadstreet had been with Echelon only two years, but her London School of Economics education had served her well…and so did her sylph figure and movie star smile. She was what they called *a looker.* Some said that she was a member of the highly sought after group of women in London known as *Sloane Rangers*…very attractive, well-educated, and high-borne. Admittedly, Tollbridge had often dreamed of shagging her on a Caribbean island.

"Let us meet back here in," Tollbridge said, glancing at his watch, "shall we say two hours. That'll give the boys downstairs time to answer our request. Very well then, it's set, two hours."

Chapter Sixty

The NSA's Menwith Hill facility was coming up on a three-day holiday for most of the lower and middle level employees, so there were those who scurried about peripatetically, making ready their exit from the mammoth, heavily guarded facility. Many were going south to London, others just wanted to stay home. The harsh weather made the decision for most particularly easy.

Tollbridge was the first to enter the conference room at 1055 hours. He was always early, just to take a mental note of everyone who followed after him. He had a deep disdain for even a hint of tardiness. He understood that the signals intelligence business had no room for such an irresponsible action. His was a business of life or death and national security. In moments, the room was full again. Computer screens showed photo after photo, and some streaming video, of the woman in question. Each photo was the product of filtered searches of Echelon's work over the past twenty years in Europe and the Middle East.

Garrett punched up the first photos on the huge OLED wall monitor of persons of interest from London to Lebanon and even India. The Echelon satellite high-resolution cameras never missed a thing. The photos were grouped according to numerous criteria that Echelon kept very close to the vest. The photos on the monitor and individual computer screens showed the woman's likeness in various surroundings over the past two decades.

"So Garrett, what have we got?" Tollbridge said without preamble. He was nothing, if not to the point.

"Sir," Ms. Broadstreet interrupted.

"Yes, Ms. Broadstreet," he said in a slightly lascivious tone.

"Excuse me, sir. But photo number two. Please look at photo number two."

Tollbridge and the others immediately zeroed in on the second photo on the screen. There she was, as breathtaking as ever, but she could not have been more than twenty. "Who's the man?" Tollbridge demanded to know.

Speaking up again, Ms. Broadstreet had the answer. "He is. I mean he was her boyfriend."

"...and so —"

"Well," hesitating for a beat, "the MI6 file on him says that he was a student at the American University of Beirut in the 1980s. After that, he immigrated to the U.S. and became a medical doctor."

"Very good, Ms. Broadstreet. But what's his name?" he said with a certain serration in his voice.

"Alexander Hakimian. Dr. Alexander Hakimian. He has a medical practice in Los Angeles. He's married, with one young daughter named Karina. His wife Leyla is the daughter of Federal Judge Robert H. Vanley. We recently learned that she was kidnapped."

"What do you mean kidnapped? You mean she disappeared?" Tollbridge fired back.

"No, sir. Kidnapped. It seems that several days ago she was taken from her home in Los Angeles. At the moment the FBI has no solid leads."

"So, where is this doctor, this Dr. Hakimian fellow now?"

"Well," she said, raising her nicely groomed eyebrows, "that's the problem. He vanished. He's a ghost."

Tollbridge slowly processed her words and said, "Contact Director Caccavale's office at NSA headquarters, and I want to know who this woman is yesterday, and not one minute more," Tollbridge said with an edge of sarcasm, as he gawked at the photos of the woman. One in particular caught his eye. She was exiting a fiery-red Ferrari 599 GTB Fiorano in front of Cartier on Bond Street. He noticed instantly that she wasn't wearing an under garment of any sort." He removed his reading glasses and blinked his eyes several times. He then smiled, turned quickly and marched out of the conference room, but not before taking one last look at the woman exiting the Ferrari.

CHAPTER SIXTY-ONE

MEDITERRANEAN SEA, COAST OF ISRAEL

Once again the Mediterranean Sea gave no quarter…it never did. Since the ancient Greeks plied its waters millennia ago, it has swallowed vessels of every size without warning.

Just outside of Israeli waters the Wasp Class U.S.S. *Kearsarge* amphibious assault ship fought to keep its top deck level in the turbulent sea. At the same time, the USS *Virginia* nuclear attack submarine was on its return journey to its temporary base in the Persian Gulf.

The remaining members of OS9 tried to get beyond their teammate's death just for one fleeting moment, if only to mentally and physically replenish themselves. The President of the United States had been notified of Riemann's death and the mission's overall success. The body of OS9's team member was already on a military transport bound for Cody, Wyoming, where a full military funeral service was waiting.

Alec and Captain Ruger met in the officers' wardroom. Two presidents had dined there, as had the Duke of Edinburgh, and even a former Speaker of the United States House of Representatives. The room was wood-paneled and tastefully decorated. The two men experienced food that was certainly better than what the enlisted men were used to, and the service was first rate, as was the view, despite the midday's thick draping of storm clouds in the distance.

"Captain," Alec said levelly. "Is there any word on my wife?"

The captain looked straight at Alec and spoke slowly, "Dr. Hakimian, your wife has not been heard from since her disappearance, but the FBI says that they have several leads. And there's been no ransom demand as of yet."

Alec began to question in his mind what he was doing at that moment. *Had he lost his mind? Had he risked it all, and in the end, maybe even his marriage?* Trying to gain control, he said to Captain Ruger, "What does USCENTCOM say? What does the FBI know?" Now with fury and frustration in his tired voice, he exclaimed, "What the hell does anyone know?"

"Dr. Hakimian," the captain paused. He was searching for the right words. "I don't mean to be insensitive, but the NSA just sent over photographs that they need you to look at. It seems that they need you to identify someone in a photo."

A ship's mess attendant entered the room and asked the captain and Alec if they wanted coffee and freshly baked berry napoleons for dessert. Alec begged off, but the captain answered in the affirmative. Alec was annoyed by the triviality of the moment.

"Let's see the photos," he asked.

The captain turned to the waiter standing in the corner and said, "Andy, have Lieutenant Ricard come in."

Lieutenant Ricard, a freshly minted Annapolis graduate, aimed to please. His athletic good looks and Midwestern style were infectious. "Captain Ruger, Lieutenant Ricard reporting," he said, snapping a salute to the captain.

"Lieutenant Ricard, this is Dr. Alexander Hakimian," he said, gesturing to Alec seated to his right at the executive dining table.

"My pleasure, sir," the lieutenant said respectfully.

"Lieutenant, please show the Dr. Hakimian the photographs we received. By the way doctor, Ricard here is with naval intel."

"Yes, sir," the lieutenant said quickly. "Dr. Hakimian," he said, while slowly removing the photos from a large, gray manila envelope marked with two red stripes and a "top-secret" classification. Handing Alec the photos, he continued, "These photographs were received from NSA within the last few days and the others cover the past twenty years. Echelon ran thousands of photos through a sequence of filters and they came up with what we have here." Taking a long breath, he continued, "NSA believes that the woman in each photo is the same. The men are different. As you can see in the first one," pointing to a specific area of the photograph, "the woman is with Dr. Raissi in London. These photos were obtained during routine surveillance of the doctor. NSA believes that he is either in danger of being assassinated by the Khamsin or part of the organization. At this point, it's very unclear."

Alec instantly knew the woman. He stopped momentarily. *Sahar alive? What was Raissi doing with Sahar? It did not compute.*

"What the NSA would like you to do is to confirm that the woman in the second photo," he said, handing Alec the photo, "seated next to you at what appears to be a resort, maybe somewhere in the Middle East, is one and the same. Anyway, sir. Is she the same woman pictured in the other photos as well?"

The captain looked to Alec for a response and an explanation.

Alec listened, as he stared at the photo. His head began spinning out of control. It was Sahar. His Sahar. *Could she really be alive? Had Raissi lied? What was she doing? Why was the NSA interested in her? What was going on?* He was overwhelmed with shock and disbelief. He thought, *it couldn't be her. No. Not Sahar. With Raissi?* He remembered her silhouette. How his hands used to roam the contours of her voluptuous body, tracing every nuance; her silken, raven-colored hair entwined in his fingers. Her dark eyes would reach into his soul and he would become transfixed, entranced. *But she was supposed to be dead. How could this be?* he questioned. And now…there she was…it was Sahar! Feelings began to well up inside of him, as if it were yesterday that he was with her as young university students on vacation in Palmyra. Oh, the times they had. Stabs of savage, petrifying, twisted emotions ripped through his mind.

"Doctor," the captain exclaimed.

Alec was mute and motionless.

"Sir," the lieutenant said, looking directly at Alec.

Alec passed the photo from one hand to the other. Appearing to scrutinize it, he said without prelude, "Yes, lieutenant. It is definitely the same woman."

"Who is she, sir? What is her name? Do you remember her name, sir?" the lieutenant questioned enthusiastically, as if he were about to break open a difficult case of mysterious identity.

Alec thought to himself, *remember her name. He remembered everything about her. He remembered how her sweet breath filled him with euphoria when they kissed. He remembered when they made love liquid joy would connect their bodies for what seemed like eternity, and he remembered the day she died, at least according to Raissi,* he reminded himself.

"Why do you need to know her name?"

"Sir, please take a look at these photos that Echelon captured today in Hyde Park," he said emphatically, and handed Alec two more.

Alec took the photos reluctantly.

"You see her there?" The lieutenant pointed to the photo directly before Alec. "She's the supposed girlfriend of Dr. Raissi. NSA believes that she could also be a go-between for him. The man she's taking the suitcase from in the photo," he said, pointing to Sahar in the photo taken in Hyde Park, "is Reza Farkhani, a lieutenant for the Khamsin."

Every time Alec heard the name Raissi and the connection with Sahar, he was dismayed, incredulous, and incensed. He struggled to maintain a semblance of decorum. "There must be another explanation lieutenant. It's just not possible."

"How's that, sir?"

"She's dead."

"With all deference to you, Dr. Hakimian," the lieutenant said. "As you can see, she's very much alive."

At first blush, he thought that *it was quite obvious. The suitcase exchange between a ravishing woman and a cyclist did not appear to show that she was retrieving a suitcase of clothing after a sleepover.* Something had gone down that he did not want to hear about, but he still believed that Sahar was not part of it, no matter what the photos showed.

"What's the suitcase about?" Alec questioned.

"The suitcase you see her taking has a signature that leads us to believe it is *hot.* That's right, sir. It's a dirty bomb. Probably with a timed detonation. Who knows, maybe it's been set. There are any manner of possibilities."

A dirty bomb was a radiological dispersal device that utilized a conventional explosive such as dynamite and a radioactive material such as Plutonium-239, Cesium-137, or Uranium-239. When detonated, the bomb first kills and injures by virtue of the initial concussion of the blast, after which thousands of more deaths would result from airborne radioactive particles and contamination, hence, the name "dirty bomb."

Depending on the radioactive materials used, the immediate population density, and wind speed at the time of detonation, the effects of a dirty bomb were always frighteningly lethal. Exposure to over 600 rads, *radiation absorbed doses*, would cause individuals to experience nausea, violent vomiting, and uncontrollable diarrhea within the first hours. Rapid emaciation would lead to certain death by the second week. In time, those who lived beyond the initial high dosage of radiation would develop any number of cancers, many of them terminal in nature, due to low-level ionizing radiation.

The construction of such a bomb required little sophistication other than the basic knowledge of conventional bomb building. As for the access to radioactive materials, the United States alone had 21,000 organizations licensed to use such materials, with some sort of nuclear material stolen every day!

One thing was for certain, although the dirty bomb was capable of causing death and destruction, its real threat was more as a *weapon of mass disruption*.

A dirty bomb set off in a city such as New York, Los Angeles, or even Chicago would create a state of instant chaos. People would scatter pell-mell, the financial district would shutdown, and there would be a massive and chaotic exodus of people. The domino effect would travel across the country, as it did when the airline and financial industries were brought to their knees post the 9/11 attack.

Alec wanted to push aside what he had just heard. "Her name is *Sahar Tayyim*," he said reluctantly, as his voice trailed off. He threw the photo down on the table. He rose and walked around, stopping at the porthole that looked out over the flight deck and to the deep, green-blue sea. He continued, "Yes, her name is Sahar Tayyim, or at least it was when I knew her. I haven't seen her for many years. We were together for two. I was told she died in a car crash."

Alec saw the profound irony in it all. *Think of it*, he said to himself. *A Christian Armenian, born in Lebanon, in love with a Muslim Palestinian, who now looks to be involved in some way with Dr. Raissi, who in turn, appears to have some connection to the Khamsin. It just couldn't be. The very same Raissi who flew him out of Lebanon to safety on his own private jet appears to be a terrorist himself!*

Alec continued, "Since we parted, I have not seen her nor heard from her. I thought she was dead, in fact, Dr. Raissi told me personally that she died in a car accident on her way to warn me that my CIA cover was blown. As for what she might be doing in this photo, I can't give you an answer. I can't explain it other than to say that it looks as if she's a messenger for Dr. Raissi, if that's his car." Alec wanted to believe that Sahar was caught in a terrible situation, not of her own making. *He could not have misjudged he; after all, he almost married her.*

Alec simply could not get his arms around the thought: *his first love Sahar in collusion with his friend Raissi and for what reason? It just couldn't be true. Raissi was his friend.* It was irrational to him, counter-intuitive. He had always held a warm thought for her, but now, *if it's true,* he reasoned, *she had defrauded him out of every wonderful memory he had kept deep inside himself for so many years.*

Alec excused himself and shuffled off to his quarters. He needed to escape the moment, and he had hoped sleep would soothe his wounded soul and refuel his exhausted body. He was bled dry by the thought of Sahar and the sobering fact that Raissi, the man whom the world respected, might be involved in terrorism. *He never saw it coming.*

Alec could no longer endure the thought.

CHAPTER SIXTY-TWO

Alec's wish for sleep went unanswered. He tossed about in the narrow bed, sweat seeping from his clothed body. Robbed of wonderful memories by Sahar and tortured by his present state of affairs, he needed to get to his wife, to his daughter. He needed to get home. Suddenly the thought hit him dead center in his psyche. *What if Leyla's kidnapping was not the result of her being in the wrong place at the wrong time? What if she was the target?* Alec was not a man given to rationalizing such happenings by way of coincidences. *What if she was the target to get to him?* he questioned. *But why?* he challenged himself.

At 1150 hours, Alec had finally fallen off into a sleep of sorts, when unexpectedly there was a light, but crisp knock on the hatch to his quarters. "Dr. Hakimian. Dr. Hakimian," whispered Captain Ruger.

Denying the obvious, Alec did nothing.

The knock came again. "Dr. Hakimian. Captain Ruger, here."

"Coming, coming," Alec said, stumbling out of bed, his wet clothes clinging tenaciously to his skin. He stood up slowly, glanced out of the porthole, only to see a day of stormy seas and no sun. He reflexively brushed back his tousled hair with his hands as he walked to the door. He pulled on the latch, but it was stuck. The constant exposure to a briny sea air that reached deep into the bowels of a ship, even the size of the U.S.S. *Kearsarge*, corroded most everything at some point. A second attempt and he yanked it open.

Captain Ruger removed his cap and said, "May I come in, doctor?"

Alec replied by stepping aside and waving him in. He immediately zeroed in on the red-striped manila folder with the appropriate "top-secret" classification emblazoned across the top. Captain Ruger set it down on the small table. Alec thought that *it looked just like the one he had seen earlier.* They both took a seat and the captain got right to it.

"Doctor, permit me to be frank and quick about this. I just received this from Washington," he said, as he opened the folder to reveal the contents. "NSA picked up a phone conversation between Dr. Raissi, who is in Washington at an event, and Sahar Tayyim. Although their Arabic conversation was scrambled, Echelon's system was able to decipher it. It was immediately sent to NSA headquarters where analysts refined the initial translation." Handing Alec the transcript, he continued, "They said, you needed to see this."

Alec immediately realized, *the nightmare would never end.* Picking up the transcript, he began to peruse it and then said, "Did they send the original Arabic transcript?"

"No, sir. They did not."

"I would have preferred to read the original," he said, his voice trailing off as he began to read.

Start of transmission.

Sahar: "Dear, it's me. I miss you. When do you return? Don't forget tonight."

Raissi: "What about the package?"

Sahar: "There's something you must know."

Raissi: "What is it?"

Sahar: "There was an attack on the camp in southern Lebanon. Hundreds of our Hezbollah comrades were killed. They were slaughtered. Every one of them, dead, including as-Saffah. Our spy in the Lebanese forces informs us that The Doctor and his team of mercenaries were responsible for the massacre."

Raissi: "I should have killed him in '89."

Sahar: "Yes, but I stopped you. I believed that his love for me would have weakened him, that he would have become one of us. He would have been a great warrior for the cause of jihad against the infidels. It would have pleased Allah. My darling, my powers of persuasion have failed you."

Raissi: "Remember. I possess what The Doctor is willing to die for, and he will. I have his wife. She will be there when it is time. What about the package? Is it —"

Sahar: "Don't worry. When can I expect your return?"

Raissi: "Soon. Everything is in place. I will slay the *infidels* by driving a *holy saber* through their dark hearts. I will avenge those whom the infidels have killed. Allah will be glorified in the highest. What I have planned will surpass all that has been accomplished before. I will end their precious way of life. The evil Americans will bow before Allah! The sinful Westerners will fall to His will. It will be greater than our 9/11 lesson to the Western devils."

End of transmission.

The revelation was overwhelming. It all coalesced. Alec was now convinced of it. *Raissi was the "true leader" of the Khamsin. He was the Ankabut. He had kidnapped Leyla to get to him. And now, with a dirty bomb in his possession, Alec knew that the Ankabut planned something truly horrifying.* Alec's expression, his mindset, had changed forever in that moment. *It was not over yet. There was one last mission.*

The captain continued, "Dr. Hakimian, NSA has sent the *Aurora XP* to meet you and your team in Nicosia, Cyprus, which is about 150 kilometers from here. The helo is ready, and your gear has been loaded. It is imperative that you get underway by 1530 hours. Once there, you and your men will be flown back to Washington for further briefing and to receive your orders," the captain said calmly.

Alec understood the urgency of it all.

"Dr. Hakimian, what you and your men have done for our country can never be repaid. You have eliminated as-Saffah and found WMD. You have seriously damaged the inner-workings of the Khamsin. Every citizen of the United States thanks you."

Alec nodded politely. The captain then walked out of the room and straight to his quarters one deck above.

Alec took a moment to splash some cold water on his face at the bathroom sink, and then left for the sitroom room to talk to his men.

CHAPTER SIXTY-THREE

Bobby was his usual, happy self, munching on a bag of potato chips while his head rocked to the beat of Eric Clapton pounding in his ears. Josiah and Nutworth were consuming vast amounts of roasted beef tenderloin, courtesy of the captain. Pratt, Alvarado, and Mackay played cards and munched on tortilla chips and salsa.

"Gentlemen," Alec barked. "One more time."

They stared at Alec with a look of blatant incredulity on their faces.

"One more time," Bobby repeated flatly. "What does that mean, sir?"

"It means that there's one last job to do. We now know that Dr. Raymond Raissi is the Ankabut, the leader of the Khamsin." The words Dr. Raymond Raissi and the Ankabut in the same sentence proved hard for Alec to fathom…it just did not make sense. To him it defied logic, but he continued, "Intel and the local chatter have it that he has plans to detonate a dirty bomb somewhere in the United States within the next few days. And," taking a deep breath, he finished, "he has kidnapped my wife."

The looks of mild curiosity turned to astonishment. "What the hell, sir," Pratt said. "What do you mean kidnapped? Your wife was kidnapped by the Khamsin?"

Painted on every face in the room was a feeling of utter shock.

"When did you find this out?" Bobby questioned.

"Just before we hit the Viper's Pit."

Josiah took a calm stance and asked, "Why your wife?"

"It's his way of getting to me," Alec fired back.

Bobby piped in, "Wow. Let's find the piss ants and finish this bullshit once and for all."

"I'm with Bobby, sirrr," Mackay added dryly.

"Boss, we need to do whatever it takes to catch this Ankabut and end the reign of terror that America's been living under for far too long. So let's get it on," Nutworth pronounced forcefully.

"You heard us, sir. We are with you all the way," Bobby said with a smile while he pumped his right arm defiantly.

The sentiment was universal.

"I knew you boys would want to finish this. The chopper's waiting."

Chapter Sixty-Four

In 1989, an oil-exploration engineer sighted a bizarre-looking plane in the shape of a triangle in hypersonic flight over the North Sea. Since that time, journalists and conspiracy theorists alike have dubbed the plane the *Aurora*. U.S. Government officials have routinely denied the name or even the existence of such an aircraft.

The name *Aurora* came about when a censor's slip-up permitted the name to appear in the 1985 Pentagon budget request. Projects such as the *Aurora* were referred to as *Special Access Programs*, yet they were more often called *black programs*. As for its real name, it was ultra top-secret. The famed Lockheed Skunk Works in Southern California, home to the U-2, the SR-71 *Blackbird*, the F-117A *Nighthawk* stealth fighter, and the mighty F-35 *Lightning II*, was reputed to have been the defense contractor for the *Aurora* program.

The *Aurora* XP, or *extreme performance*, was the latest version of the program, designed to achieve *super hypersonic speed*s of Mach 10 or greater.

The definition of hypersonic speed was any aircraft capable of traveling at no less than Mach 5.4, or 8,687 kilometers per hour. More specifically, when the air in front of an aircraft's leading edges became motionless, thus not able to flow around the aircraft, it caused high temperatures and pressures, indicators of super hypersonic travel.

The *Aurora* XP presumably derived its power from either *pulse detonation wave engines, pulsejet engines,* or *advanced ramjets.* The truth of the matter was inevitably still very hush-hush.

On rare instances, the extremely low-drag coefficient, triangular-shaped supersonic *Aurora* XP was pressed into service. This was one of those instances.

"Sir," the flight deck chief said to Alec, trying to be heard over the Sea Knight's main rotor's chopping sound and the wind racing off the surface of the rolling sea. "We're ready."

In moments, OS9 was onboard and the pilot ordered a final check. Seconds later the helo lifted off the flight deck. The massive ship faded away in the distance as the afternoon was about to do the same.

It was now 1550 hours, and OS9 was on its way to Cyprus aboard the Sea Knight. Although its 145 knots per hour speed was sufficient to traverse the distance on the open sea in about one hour, it was bucking a considerable headwind. OS9's eventual arrival would be about fifteen minutes behind schedule.

CHAPTER SIXTY-FIVE

The formerly Greek-Turkish-British island of Cyprus, the third largest of the Mediterranean islands, was situated only sixty-four kilometers off the southern coast of Turkey. It became the Republic of Cyprus in 1960, and subsequently joined both the United Nations and the British Commonwealth the next year. The island's capital city of Nicosia dated back to the seventh century B.C.

"Gentlemen, Nicosia coming up on your right," shouted Captain Artunian. "We'll put down southeast of the city, some twenty klicks from the airport. There your ride back to the U.S. is waiting."

Although early versions of the *Aurora* required staggering amounts of runway length to take-off or land, the XP had conquered the problem, requiring a runway similar in length to what was encountered at most commercial airports.

As the Sea Knight began its descent, a large camouflaged hangar was sighted, nestled between two hills covered in sparse clumps of grass and scrub brush. A very long, paved runway drew a gray line that ended at the hangar. Several U.S. Military Humvees rolled along the runway. As the enormous chopper set down on the tarmac near the hangar, two men with officers' markings on their camouflage fatigues exited a small office.

Neither Alec nor any of the team thought it odd that there was no communication between their chopper and the landing crew. After all, the airfield was top-secret. The United States had made a special arrangement with the Cypriot Government some years ago, that permitted the maintenance of a special U.S. military airbase on their island in exchange for monetary and trade considerations.

The hangar's imposing doors gave little hint as to what was on the other side. The *Aurora* XP was not the type of aircraft that could ever be exposed to the outside elements other than when in flight. Just like the B-2 stealth bomber, its unique near zero-drag skin and avionics needed to be maintained in near surgically clean, hermetically sealed conditions.

Alec was the first to exit the chopper, followed by two crewmen, and then the rest of OS9. The gear was already being off-loaded when a tall, thin man walked up to Alec. "Dr. Hakimian, I'm Colonel William Britan, U.S. Air Force," he said, saluting Alec. "Welcome to Camp Phantom."

Alec answered his salute and remarked, "Thank-you, colonel." Looking around, his thoughts lingered for a long moment on the first time he had been in Cyprus. His father had taken him, his sister, and mother to the island in 1974 for a vacation.

Bobby popped up, "So colonel, sir. Where's the *Aurora?*" As a young boy, Bobby loved building model planes, and he remembered building one similar to the *Aurora.*

Colonel Britan answered, "She's hiding, sergeant. It was a long trip. Well, in truth, time wise it was very short."

The answer piqued his interest. "From where, sir," Bobby shot back.

"From Diego Garcia. It arrived at 1400 hours. The ground crew has been prepping her since then. At 0010 hours you're scheduled to leave for the States."

The British Indian Colonial Territory of Diego Garcia, an island of the Seychelles in the Indian Ocean, was the result of the formation of defense and communications facilities by the governments of both the United States and Britain in response to the menacing threat of the Soviet Union's presence in the area.

Alec thought, *because of President Ronald Reagan, the Soviet threat was no more.*

"Dr. Hakimian, permit me to introduce you to your pilot for the flight home." The colonel held up his right hand and pointed to a man exiting from the building's office door.

In a deliberate, syncopated manner, Air Force Captain Johnny "Ghost" Oddy marched out of an office from a far corner of the massive hangar. Although not tall in stature, the man held more air speed and distance records than any other living being. His knowledge of the *Aurora* XP's abilities was unchallenged. His call sign, the Ghost, was the result of his having flown more top-secret missions than any other pilot.

"Captain," Colonel Britan said. "This is Dr. Hakimian." The captain offered his hand, not knowing that Dr. Alexander Hakimian's position required all military personnel to salute him. Alec, who was not one to stand on ceremony, extended his hand as well.

Without pause, Captain Oddy said rather pedantically, "Dr. Hakimian, we will be taking off at 0010 hours. Please have you and your men in the prep room by 2300 hours. They'll need to get into G-suits. As for the flight time, the *hop* is about ninety minutes to Andrews."

The G-suit, or more accurately, the anti G-suit, was designed to prevent a blackout under extreme acceleration when the body's blood pooled at the lower extremities, thus depriving the brain of blood.

Alvarado did a quick calculation. *It had to be flying at around Mach 10*, he thought. *That's nearly fifteen times faster than a commercial jet aircraft in order to make Andrews in ninety minutes.*

Bobby said, "That's movin'."

The others just nodded their heads.

Everyone in OS9 felt relieved to be out of the exosuit, but while U.S. Government issue fatigues were a welcomed change, they now had to put on cumbersome G-suits for the flight back home.

"Doctor," Captain Oddy requested, "let me have you and your men come into the facility. There you can clean up and have a special meal."

The men were enticed by the words *special meal*.

Alvarado, a man of few words but with a big appetite, was the first to comment. "Captain, sir. You said 'special meal'."

"Yes, I did sergeant. I did say that," the captain answered with a wry smile.

"Does that mean steak, sir?" Nutworth asked.

Every one of OS9 relished the thought of a good American steak.

"No, sorry sergeant. No steak. It's egg whites, dry toast, no butter, and orange juice," the captain answered.

"Why?" several of the men asked in unison.

Bobby followed with, "Why not a big, fat steak and baked potato and all the fixin's?"

"That's because flying aboard the *Aurora* XP does not permit anything but the simplest of meals. We can't have any gastrointestinal problems at thirty-two kilometers up in the air and at over 11,000 klicks per hour, and with the staggering gravitational forces you'll be exposed to, we simply can't take any chances. Other than that, it's a nice ride," he said with an impish smile. "By the way, any tear or hole in your flight suit and your blood will boil instantly. So be careful, be very careful. Enjoy your meal, boys."

Everyone's jaw dropped.

CHAPTER SIXTY-SIX

2300 hours came all too soon for the men of OS9. It seemed as if they just had time enough to pack their gear. They had gone nearly two full days without any sleep and adrenaline was flowing fast and furious. They wanted to get home, yet they knew they had one last job to do.

Colonel Britan met OS9 at the personnel entrance to the hangar.

Even though each member of OS9 was accustomed to the latest in battlefield technology and even though the tools-of-their-trade were exoskeleton suits and wonder weapons, nothing could prepare them for the site of the *Aurora* XP. It exceeded anyone's expectations. It seemed truly from some sci-fi movie.

A member of the ground crew opened the door leading into the windowless hangar. Each man entered, one at a time. One look and they became nonplussed. Dumbstruck. The *Aurora* XP stood before them, its triangular fuselage onyx-black in color. On its belly, a massive air intake. At some forty meters in length, the *Aurora* XP carried eleven passengers, including a crew of two, for special missions that required unconventional, strategic global positioning.

The *Aurora* XP's skin said *stealth* all the way. Its armament was simply its speed…nothing on earth could catch it. Absolutely nothing!

"Men," remarked the colonel, as he raised himself up to his full height. "I know you understand the *Aurora* XP does not exist to the outside world. The hop you are about to take *never* happened. Remember. Never happened. So let's do it."

Once onboard the aircraft, Alec and his men sat silent. They were mesmerized by the level of technology before their eyes. Even the passenger compartments had computer screens that permitted them to monitor *nearly* all aspects of the flight. Pratt was particularly impressed with the aircraft's communication systems.

The pilot directed the co-pilot to see to it that each member of OS9 was secure in his individual compartment and ready for take-off. Once finished with his lengthy checklist, the pilot gave the order. "This is A271XP. We are set for take-off."

The gargantuan, camouflage-colored hangar doors opened wide. There was a slight lurching forward as the pilot released the brakes. A large tractor hooked up to the aircraft and began to tow it out of the hangar. By the time the *Aurora* XP was completely out of the hangar, the pulse-detonation engines had ignited. It then moved under its own power to the center of the runway. A short pause, a bit of chatter between the pilot and co-pilot, and then…the brutal acceleration was instantaneous. Within 3,000 meters the *Aurora* XP was airborne. The climb rate was classified, but any experienced flyer of jet aircraft would easily conclude that its climb rate was rocketlike.

In a matter of seconds, it leveled off at an altitude of thirty-two kilometers and held a speed of Mach 10. Depending on altitude, Mach 10 translated to approximately 11,200 kilometers per hour.

"Gentlemen, this is the 'Ghost.' Are you comfortable?"

Pratt and Alvarado would have appreciated more legroom.

"Captain, when can I give my drink order?" Bobby said facetiously.

The captain replied with a noticeable chuckle, "Sonny, we'll land before your ice melts."

Alec sat silent, contemplating what was about to take place in a matter of hours. But where, that was still the question for which he had no answer. He hoped that when he found Raissi, he would find his wife. *How she must be frightened. How she must be worried for their daughter. Was she thinking of him?* He knew the answers would come soon.

As the minutes ticked by, sea and land passed beneath the *Aurora* XP in a blur.

"Dr. Hakimian, there's a change of plans," the pilot announced. "I just received word from Washington. Seems this Raissi guy you're after is in Chicago and not Washington, so we'll be setting down at Scott Air Force Base. It's a bit out of the way, but the Feds will have a G100 waiting to take you to Chicago."

Scott AFB, home to the 375th Airlift Wing, was located about fifty miles east of St. Louis, Missouri. There, a Gulfstream G100/C-38A Special Missions jet aircraft awaited OS9.

The G100/C-38A hailed from the 201st Airlift Squadron, Andrews Air Force Base, Maryland. Designed to perform special missions, the aircraft flew farther and faster, with greater efficiency, than any aircraft in its class. At Mach 0.85 cruising speed, getting to Chicago would be a short hop for OS9.

Alec knew that *the clock was ticking*.

Landing the *Aurora* XP required a deftness of hand rarely seen amongst most pilots. The deceleration from Mach 10 was no easy task and necessitated unique braking abilities far beyond those of conventional jet aircraft.

Alec's one-time experience flying in the two-seater version of the SR-71 had given him an idea of what it would be like to experience the dramatic, bone-crushing deceleration needed to land a hypersonic aircraft. *But the others, well,* Alec thought, *they were about to find out.*

"Gentlemen, it's showtime!" Captain Oddy said flatly. "We're preparing for deceleration."

The comment startled Bobby, whose iPod Touch was playing the music track entitled "Sunny Side of Heaven" from Fleetwood Mac's *Bare Trees* album. He was a classic rock aficionado to-the-bone.

It was showtime, indeed. The pilot set in motion the *Aurora* XP's air inversion, deceleration process. Just as in the acceleration mode, deceleration caused continuous *skyquakes* of the magnitude that seemed to shake the very solar system itself. Windows in town after town it passed over exploded; car alarms were set-off; fish and fowl thrown into a state of panic; horses and cattle stampeded; and the general population thoroughly angered. The landing of the *Aurora* XP so close to a high population area was considered highly unusual, but then again, it was a highly unusual circumstance.

The landing at Scott AFB would be in a slight wind from the west. The airbase was equipped with the ILS or instrument landing system that facilitated landings in inclement weather or at night.

The *Aurora* XP slowed dramatically from Mach 10 to below Mach 1 as it entered local airspace. The air traffic supervisor on duty wanted this one.

"A271XP, we have you on final approach. Runway 14 Left is yours, captain," the supervisor said, with pride in his voice. *The opportunity to call the landing of the Aurora XP was something that he would tell his grandchildren about, and it would certainly look good on his résumé,* he thought to himself.

By now, the city of St. Louis and its environs were aware that something unusual was taking place. Aside from broken windows and pissed off residents, anyone who was awake in the middle of the night and looked out their window to the sky above, was going to have a grand time spinning tales of how they saw an *unidentified flying object* landing at Scott Air Force Base near their city.

A moment of recollection and regret began to fill Alec's troubled mind. *Why hadn't he stayed with his wife and daughter, after all, he'd done his duty? He'd fought the good fight for so long. He'd lost his best friend. But he also knew that it would never end, that freedom needed an army, and he was not about to desert the cause of freedom. More importantly, his best friend's murder had to be avenged. As-Saffah was dead, but there was one other that had to pay. Revenge to Alec was a very simple emotion that few ever acted on, but he would, again.*

CHAPTER SIXTY-SEVEN

For security reasons, the *Aurora* XP always landed in the United States in darkness…no landing lights. The pilot utilized an advanced version of Starlight technology to see the runway in the dark of night.

Two Humvees and a transporter approached the *Aurora* XP as it taxied toward the special hangar designed to receive such top-secret aircraft. Having served the needs of the *Aurora* XP once before, the protocol was in place to handle the special circumstance. Security was at the highest level, and all personnel assigned to the *Aurora* XP's landing team underwent a special re-evaluation and background check. The officer in charge of the aircraft while it was at the base was Air Force Lieutenant General Mitchell "Shotgun" Trainer.

Lt. General Trainer, a Congressional Medal of Honor recipient from the First Gulf War conflict and a former SR-71 pilot, was a by-the-book commander. His no-nonsense style made Scott AFB the logical place to land the *Aurora* XP.

Finally, OS9 had arrived back in the United States after a lengthy period in the middle of the Ocean of Fire. While the *Aurora* XP was taxiing to a stop, Alvarado thought to himself that *a conventional jet airliner on the same course would barely be crossing into Eastern Europe while the Aurora XP had already landed 11,200 kilometers away from its flight of origin in Cyprus.*

Lt. General Trainer walked into the hangar, followed by a dozen heavily armed Air Police. A member of the ground crew directed the aircraft into the hangar, as two Humvees followed. Once inside, the *Aurora* XP stopped in the middle, flanked by two F-22 stealth fighters that had recently returned from a security mission over the U.S. Capitol.

"Gentlemen, we're back on good ol' U.S. of A. terra firma. I hope you enjoyed the ride in our little plane," Captain Oddy said, with a sense of fatherly pride.

"Wow. Wow," Bobby remarked with childlike enthusiasm, as he removed his flight helmet.

Each man deplaned from the hypersonic aircraft, their senses bludgeoned by the flight from Cyprus.

"I could sure use a wee dram," Mackay said, feeling somewhat lightheaded.

"It was an 'E' ticket ride for sure," uttered Nutworth.

"Yeah. An 'E' ticket for sure," Bobby confirmed happily.

Lt. General Trainer met Alec straightaway. After exchanging perfunctory cordialities, the general said, "Dr. Hakimian, Washington has your ride to O'Hare waiting. You and your men will be briefed onboard the aircraft by the FBI's Hostage Rescue Team leader. You're scheduled to leave at 0340 hours. In the meantime, can I offer you and your men something to drink and eat?"

"General," Alec said, "we all would certainly like to get out of these funny space suits."

"By all means, Dr. Hakimian. I'll have Captain Ribald here assist you."

After changing their clothes, the men of OS9 followed in lockstep to the mess hall, lead by an Air Force sergeant.

CHAPTER SIXTY-EIGHT

"Sir, you've got to try the steak. It's awesome. Goddamn New York prime," said Bobby, waving his fork with a bite on it, as Alec stood at the mess hall doorway.

"Not hungry, just something to drink," Alec responded, as he entered the room with a sense of emptiness in the pit of his stomach. Food was the last thing on his mind. The only thing on his mind was the safety of his wife and daughter. He wanted them back and he was prepared to do whatever it took.

"Sir," Captain Ribald exclaimed, "we leave in twenty. The plane is ready and your gear's been loaded."

Everyone wolfed down the last bites of food, with Alvarado taking one more mouthful of crème brulé. He quickly wiped his mouth and followed the others out of the mess hall.

The Gulfstream G100/C-38A sat quietly on the tarmac about thirty-five meters from the hangar. Its color scheme resembled that of Air Force One, the famous presidential aircraft. The forward entry door was open and the staircase extended. Two MPs stood at the ready, flanking the entrance to the aircraft. Alec was the first to climb aboard, followed by Mackay, Alvarado, Nutworth, and Josiah. Pratt came next just steps behind.

"Alvarado, where the hell's Bobby?" Alec asked, with a tone of detectable irritation. Alec took his seat across a table from a man in his early fifties, with thinning hair that was nearly snow-white in color.

The man held out his heavy hand to greet Alec. "Dr. Hakimian, I am Special Agent Rick Douglas. We'll be working together," he said with a professional smile.

Bobby finally arrived, with his iPod now seemingly fused to his body. He had always defended his use of the MP3 player by saying that it helped him get through difficult moments. It served as a momentary distraction.

"Gentlemen, please fasten your seatbelts," came the pilot's call.

The G100/C-38A was the transcontinental special mission version of the Gulfstream private jet aircraft. It had been configured to allow a dozen or so passengers to travel in a relaxed atmosphere, but the atmosphere on this day was anything but relaxed.

With everyone seated and properly secured, the aircraft began to roll out and onto the lit runway. The whirring sound of the two Honeywell TFE 731-40R jet engines served to mask Alec's thoughts for a brief moment. He gazed out the window into a clear, dark sky.

It was 0340 hours. Night would soon give way to day.

Alec knew *the clock was ticking*.

Once airborne, the G100/C-38A reached its Mach 0.850 cruising speed at an altitude of 41,000 feet in short order. It was a quick hop to O'Hare, so Special Agent Douglas wasted no time. He needed to bring Alec and the rest of OS9 up-to-speed, for he knew that in a hostage situation time was never on their side, and with what he was about to tell them, he also knew the *calculus* had changed dramatically.

Leaning into the table, Special Agent Douglas of the FBI's Chicago unit of the Hostage Rescue Team said, "Dr. Hakimian, about four hours ago we learned that Dr. Raissi's plane landed at O'Hare."

In the background, Alec could hear Bobby asking for the restroom. The others sat quietly listening to Special Agent Douglas, as he continued. "We swept Dr. Raissi's private jet. We had reason to believe that he was transporting an illegal explosive device, but the plane was clean! He and his entourage passed through customs without incident."

Alec thought that uncharacteristic of Raissi. He was convinced that Raissi would not have let the dirty bomb out of his sight. He was anal about control.

"Dr. Hakimian, we also learned that Prince Faisal bin Hillah, the Saudi Arabian Ambassador to the United Nations, landed thirty minutes after Dr. Raissi. He gained entrance into the country under the legal protection of *diplomatic immunity*, thus giving him the ability to transport contraband without concern by way of the *diplomatic pouch*. His entourage numbered forty-three, including Abdel Hmimssa, a diplomatic aide linked to a number of Islamists. There were also more than one hundred pieces of luggage, all of which passed customs unchecked," the special agent said, staring Alec in the face.

Everyone was listening intently.

Alec grasped the implication instantly...the *dirty bomb* was in the country!

"Doctor, we now know that the pouch contained what we had expected all along. Echelon's intel relayed to us via NSA Maryland has confirmed it. The Saudis brought into the country a '*dirty bomb*,' and the detonation device has been activated. There's also no doubt that the Khamsin is in the middle of this."

"Goddamn Saudis," Bobby remarked. "They talk in public like they love us, and then they stab us in the back. I'm no political scientist, but it doesn't take one to know that they've duped us for decades. If it weren't for us they'd be sucking sand. We defend their oil and their very way of life. You'd think that they'd feel that they owed us some sort of loyalty. Instead, they finance bin Laden and his crazies. There, I've said my piece, so let's get this Raissi motherfucker and find your wife."

Turning to Bobby, Special Agent Douglas replied, "Very well done."

"So, where do you think it is?" Alec asked.

"Like I said, Saudi Ambassador bin Hillah and his entourage landed a half hour after Dr. Raissi. There must be a set hand-off place and time. We also know that Dr. Raissi maintains a penthouse in the John Hancock Center. In addition, he has a suite of offices at the Willis Tower. As for what his plans are regarding the device, we can only surmise. We must be there when the hand-off happens. Obviously, he has plans on using the bomb, but where, is anyone's guess right now."

Alec paused for a long trice, then asked flatly, "Where is my wife? I want to know what you are doing about finding my wife." Alec decided not to hold anything back anymore.

"Sir, we've had our team working on it since we learned of her kidnapping. When we land in Chicago, handpicked members of our team will meet with you and your men. They've mapped out several strategies based upon scenarios that we believe are possible, including Raissi using her as a shield."

"Special Agent Douglas, I'll tell you what's possible."

"But, sir," the special agent replied. "We have certain protocols that we must follow. We've done this before." The agent sat back in his seat, as Alec moved closer to the small, oval table that divided them.

A quick sideways motion was felt in the cabin, as turbulence buffeted the aircraft.

"You've never, and I mean *never* dealt with a man of Raissi's intellect and ruthlessness. As you should know by now Special Agent Douglas, Raissi is the leader of the world's most sinister and powerful terrorist organization, the *Khamsin*. For the greatest impact, I'm betting that he's probably planning to blow-up the Hancock Building or the Willis Tower, two of the world's tallest structures. They both stand as beacons of everything that Islamic fundamentalists revile...*freedom, capitalism, democracy*, and *love of life*. That my friend is not only what might happen, that's what's going to happen if we don't stop him now!" Alec said in an agitated voice. "What's more, the son of a bitch has my wife. My wife is everything to me, and if I have to slit his fat gut from *his balls to his brains* to save her, that's what I'll do and damn the protocol... Special Agent Douglas." His rage was now incandescent.

Special Agent Douglas listened reluctantly. The others wore a subtle smile. Alec was their leader taking charge, as he always did.

Special Agent Douglas steamed inside. He thought, *who the fuck does this guy think he is?*

Alec continued, "Over two months ago OS9 received *Presidential Executive Order 331*. That means the President of the United States gave us explicit authority over every mission we undertake, including this one. OS9 appreciates your assistance and welcomes it, but to be frank, that executive order gives us the imprimatur to do anything that we deem necessary for the preservation of America's sovereignty and safety," Alec said, with a cold formality and finality in his voice.

Alec was in full-frontal attack mode.

CHAPTER SIXTY-NINE

At approximately 0500 hours, the G100/C-38A landed at O'Hare International Airport's National Guard facility. The air traffic never seemed to wane at what many called the world's busiest airport, even during the slumber hours. Chicago was a forest of skyscrapers, museums, fine restaurants, and home to the celebrated John Hancock Center, once the tallest structure on the face of the earth, towering 344 meters or 1,127 feet. Affectionately referred to as "Big John," it even had its own weather system.

On this day in May, Chicago, a city governed by its weather more than most, was milder than most. A few clouds dotted the see-through sky and the temperature would eventually make its way to a pleasant 65 degrees Fahrenheit. Denizens of the *windy city* were often prey to the vicious wind they called *The Hawk* that blew regularly off Lake Michigan. The winters were defined by daily travel from one's residence to either a store or workplace and then back home. Stepping outside into the inclement weather for any extended period was generally not smart. Residents faired no better in summers that were a mixture of heat and The Hawk. Despite the risky weather on any day, Chicago was one of the great cosmopolitan centers of the world.

The FBI escorted Alec and the rest of OS9 into a security area that they maintained at all major airports. The conference room was nothing out of the ordinary, other than to say it had an unobstructed view of the central runways. Every time a jumbo jet took off, it seemed to defy the laws of flight, much like the common bumblebee, whose wings were far too small to lift its oversized body into the air, yet, it flew.

A probational special agent offered the men hot coffee and pastries. Alec took the cheap java, refused the pastries, while the others took both. Each man assumed a seated position on rather finely upholstered chairs, not what one would expect from the FBI.

"Any cappuccinos?" Bobby asked. "Just joking," came back quickly after Alec looked over his shoulder at him.

Special Agent Douglas spoke first. "Dr. Hakimian, permit me to introduce to you and your men members of the Hostage Rescue Team that'll be working with you. Mattingly, " motioning to Special Agent Rupert Mattingly. "Call them in."

From a side door, he ordered five members of the FBI's famed Chicago HRT unit to enter.

The FBI's Hostage Rescue Team, part of the Tactical Support Branch of CIRG, the Critical Incident Response Group, was the *first call* unit responsible for counterterrorism operations within the confines of the United States. The HRT took its marching orders out of the Strategic Information Operations Center, located in the J. Edgar Hoover Building in Washington, D.C. When needed, it was assisted by the local FBI division's Special Operations Group, and on occasion, by the Investigative Support Units that employed behavioral scientists.

Each team member was highly practiced in hostage rescue, close-quarters combat, long-range sniping, and even rappelling from buildings. Although negotiation was HRT's public image, its unspoken primary purpose was to rescue hostages taken by terrorists. Their philosophy was *to shoot first and ask questions later*. They understood that a quick thinking offensive kept its team members alive and saved hostages.

Bobby was the first to comment. Leaning into Alvarado, he remarked in a whisper tone, "Look at that. Must be double-D." Bobby was talking about Special Agent Salma Hajj, a six-year veteran of the agency.

Special Agent Douglas made the first introduction. "This is Special Agent Bill Runyon, our unit's profiler. And here is Special Agent Salma Hajj, our best sharp shooter," he said, pointing to Special Agent Hajj. "We always hope that she does as little work as possible."

Special Agent Hajj nodded politely.

Most men found it difficult to get past Salma Hajj's stunning looks and, well, her breasts were just…. During her training to become a sniper, her instructor was always flummoxed by her uncanny ability to shoot straight when so much was in the way. With eight commendations, and yet only thirty-two years of age, Hajj was the agency's top sharp shooter. She always managed to keep her head about her, a quality most desirable in her line of work. Moreover, as an added bonus, she was fluent in both Arabic and Farsi.

Bobby and Alvarado could not take their eyes off her. Pratt, Josiah, and Nutworth were also impressed with Hajj's obvious attributes. As for Mackay, yes, he agreed, but still complained about not getting his wee dram of the good stuff that Alec had promised once they reached the United States.

"Gentlemen," Special Agent Douglas said loudly, in an effort to get everyone's attention. "Here's Special Agent Karim Hannan, our close combat specialist. Oh, and he's also fluent in Arabic."

Mackay said to Bobby and Alvarado quietly, "Where's the fucking firepowerrr? It seems these people figure we're just gonna talk those shitheads into giving us the bomb and the Doc's wife."

"And here," looking to his left, "is Special Agent Cooper Daniels. He doubles as our resident explosives specialist and small arms expert. And our negotiation's expert will be here in about ten." He glanced at his wristwatch and then out the window.

Alec was not thinking about negotiations, he was thinking about *saving his wife and revenge.*

Special Agent Douglas went on. "This is Special Agent Harris Talbot," turning to recognize him. "He is the Critical Incident Response Group unit leader. He's our liaison with Washington. Even though you, sir, are the mission's leader and executor of the final plan, CIRG will assist with additional intel from headquarters. And Special Agent Talbot will also deal with all media issues."

Alec stated emphatically, "Special Agent Douglas, you and your team are imminently aware, are you not, that *OS9 does not exist?*"

Special Agent Douglas looked at Alec and nodded a simple *yes.* The others of the HRT did the same.

Suddenly, a very comely woman, in a finely tailored, deep-red pinstriped suit, entered the room. All eyes turned and focused on her. She tossed her long, wavy brunette hair ever so slightly, causing the men to refocus and Special Agent Hajj to frown a bit. Mica Seddons came to Alec's mind. Both women were about the same age and had curiously enough the same comportment. As the woman stepped into the room, her movements said *look at me.*

Special Agent Douglas immediately stood up and said, with a detectable nervousness in his now somewhat high-pitched voice, "Gentlemen, allow me to introduce to you Special Agent Jolie Olufsson. She is our unit's chief analyst and a former field agent. She spends most of her time in D.C., now keeping the suits off our backs as much as possible."

"Hello," the men in the room said rather lasciviously. After innumerable weeks in the middle of the Ocean of Fire, the sight of a woman such as Jolie Olufsson or Salma Hajj rested easy on the eyes.

Special Agent Jolie Olufsson stood confidently before everyone in the room and began. "Gentlemen, and Special Agent Hajj." Special Agents Olufsson and Hajj knew of each other by reputation and that was as far as it went. "Permit me to get right to it. I just returned from D.C., and met with DHS and the FBI. They confirm, via NSA, that Dr. Raymond Raissi and the woman called Sahar Tayyim are presently in his Hancock Center Penthouse. Tonight they have reservations for dinner at the center's Signature Room on the 95th."

The restaurant's extraordinary culinary offerings were only surpassed by the building's spectacular view of Chicago's skyline and Lake Michigan, the only Great Lake that was entirely within the United States. Altitude sickness, and even vertigo, could prove to be a real possibility if one looked over the edge of the building for too long.

Special Agent Olufsson continued, "They also have confirmed that Dr. Raissi's brother Raja arrived in town two days ago with an entourage that included a well-dressed woman in her mid-thirties, believed to be Leyla Hakimian. They entered the Marriott on Michigan Avenue at around noon that day. Amud al-Jalili, just released from Gitmo three months ago, was among them, as was Salama al-Quar, aka the Indonesian Danny Rong."

Alec knew it. *Leyla's alive. Leyla's close,* he said to himself. His level of intensity raised itself exponentially. Every member of OS9 looked over to him.

"Any questions? Dr. Hakimian, any questions, sir?" Special Agent Olufsson asked softly but directly, in a breathy voice.

Alec answered slowly and succinctly, "No questions." All he was thinking about was getting Leyla back and stopping Raissi from carrying out his diabolical scheme to detonate a dirty bomb. *One thing was for sure*, he thought. *Raissi couldn't have picked a better place to set-off a radiological dispersal device than in the city famous for its severe winds and tall buildings.*

It was now 8:00 A.M., and the day was coming alive. A strong wind blew outside the conference room, as shade trees in the adjacent parking lot leaned southward some ten degrees. More than a few men's jackets and women's coats bellowed, as they walked across the parking lot to the opposite building's rear entrance.

"Oh yes, and the agency has made choppers available. The Chicago Police Department stands at the ready with whatever assistance you need. They'll handle crowd control," she concluded.

"Why don't these guys just leave and let us handle it on our own?" Bobby asked Alvarado quietly.

Alvarado agreed.

"Thank-you, Special Agent Olufsson," Special Agent Douglas said in a somewhat suggestive tone. Two years ago, he had been written up for what was deemed a sexual harassment incident to which he pleaded *nolo contendre* and was sentenced to forty hours of sensitivity training.

"Gentlemen," Special Agent Olufsson said in an official tone, "if there are no further questions, I must return to D.C. I'm behind on paperwork, but I have to admit, there are times when I envy you. I miss the field work."

Special Agent Olufsson turned about and strutted out of the conference room. She knew eyes were watching every wiggle in her walk. In two beats, she spun on her heels and peeked back into the room. "By the way, boys. What you're wearing. What are they?"

Bobby jumped in, "Exosuits, miss. Exoskeleton suits to be exact," he added happily.

"Okay, your e-x-o-suits then. They'll draw too much attention. We want to maintain the lowest profile possible, so I'll arrange to have our standard black NOMEX suits with the name 'ACC Services' on the back delivered here in about...." Looking at her watch, she continued,

"In twenty minutes. They're one-size-fits-all. Sorry about that, but you know, government issue. Oh, one last thing. The boss at *1600* wants this over ASAP."

"Ma'am, what's ACC Services?" Bobby asked loudly. Several others were thinking the same thing and wanted to know.

"Well," she began, brushing her hair back behind her left ear in a seductive manner. "It's a company that cleans up messes. Let's just say you gentlemen are taking out the trash."

NOMEX was a DuPont patented magic fiber that possessed unique flame-resistant and heat properties as well as special textile qualities. When it came to protective apparel, NOMEX has been the choice of police departments, special tactics teams, and the military for decades.

Special Agent Douglas looked at her and said, "Thank-you again." With a twinkle in her eye, she sashayed out the door without another word, leaving the men saying to themselves....

Alec had had enough of it. If he had to choose, he did not need the FBI. He did not need anyone but his team. There was a part of him that was feeling fractious. It was time that he took over.

The clock was ticking.

Alec stood up and walked about the room. He gazed out onto the tarmac as an Air France Airbus A380 touched down, its lumbering body almost crushing the pavement below its wheels as it strained to come to a stop. The wind had picked up slightly, and he could feel the bright sunlight warm his nearly spent body. He thought, *it had been too long, but OS9 had succeeded in ways that the public will never know. He was pleased, yet he knew it had come at great personal expense, but when it was all over and his Leyla was at his side and his Karina was in his arms, he'd never leave home again.*

"We need the HRT to confirm that Raja and his thugs are still at the Marriott with my wife." *That's right, my wife,* he thought. "A 24/7 surveillance can tell us a lot. Pratt, you need to get your *com lines* up." Scanning the room, he continued, "Bobby, Alvarado, once we know for sure where they've taken the bomb, you'll set up. I want you airborne."

"Like ducks in a pond, sir," Bobby said emphatically with a tone of confidence.

"Special Agent Hajj, you'll be in the second chopper. Josiah, I want you with Mackie and Nutworth. Oh yeah, Special Agent Hannan will also cover our six o'clock." He eyed special Agent Hannan. "And Special Agent Talbot, keep the media off my back. I mean I don't want to see them within a thousand meters of this operation. Now, nothing can happen until we know where they're taking the dirty bomb. Make no mistake about it, they have every intention of *detonating the bomb*. Special Agent Douglas and his men will monitor the Marriott. So, until we know where we're going, we need to get ready. That means your weapons and exosuits have to be calibrated and programmed for what we're about to deal with. Just to be clear, you'll wear NOMEX over your exos. As far as weapons are concerned, I want this as bloodless as possible. We must assume that we'll encounter innocents, therefore, stay with laser-sighted handguns and thermal guns. Low-burst grenades are a last resort."

"Doctor," Special Agent Douglas said. "We'll use unmarked helos."

Alec furrowed his brow at the obvious and then said, "Just keep the Hajj's helo at a distance until Bobby gives the word. I don't want to give them cause to go underground. I want them to come out to play," Alec said, with a flat grin. "I want my wife alive, the bomb recovered, and Raissi dead…preferably in that order."

He did not need to elaborate.

CHAPTER SEVENTY

The forty-six floor Marriott Hotel on Chicago's *One Mag Mile* was blessed with unobstructed views of what Chicago had to offer, architectural eye candy. From two of the world's tallest buildings to the Navy Pier and the Great Lake Michigan coastline, the windy city had it all. Culinary vagabonds were treated to fine dining, while the arts and croissant crowd could indulge their fantasies at some of America's finest museums and galleries.

Two FBI Special Agents sat patiently in an unmarked car parked across the street from the hotel. They chatted about whether the Cubs would ever make it to the World Series again or was it a *fait accompli* that they were destined to remain in the cellar forevermore.

"Hardy," the driver said quickly, tapping Hardy Happer on his left shoulder. Special Agent Happer was a middle-aged father of six just trying to get through one day at a time. Only a few years from a fishing boat in the Florida Keys, he was not about to rock the FBI's boat.

"Yeah," he replied, half asleep.

"Looks like that guy," holding a mug shot up to examine it. "Danny Rong is coming out front."

"That's him, all right," FBI Special Agent Happer said reflexively. "What's he doing? How tall is that guy? Five two." He stuffed another cheap donut down his gullet.

"Looks to me like he's lighting a cigarette," replied Special Agent Treant Jefferson.

The two sat, staring at the subject through the obligatory dark sunglasses. Danny Rong walked a few steps out in front of the hotel's main entrance. He stood in his black Hong Kong tailored silk suit just under the hunter green canopy and took a puff. Another puff and he took another step. He gazed up from the street and appeared to be looking in the direction of Big John, the John Hancock Center. He stared intently at the monstrous building, raising his head, as he seemed to count every one of its one-hundred floors. With forty-nine floors dedicated to luxurious condominiums, each with an awe-inspiring vista, Big John proved to be *the address.*

"What the hell's he doing now?" Special Agent Happer asked.

The Khamsin recruited Danny Rong in Indonesia seven years ago. Because of his unquestioned devotion to radical Islam and his bloodthirsty ways, the Khamsin selected him to recruit other Asians in the Malaya Archipelago and subsequently he established an arm of the Khamsin known as the Jemaah Islamiyah. Rong was the principal operative in the 2002 hotel bombing in Kuta, Bali, that killed 202, mostly Australians. It was Indonesia's deadliest terrorist attack.

"Looks like he's smoking the same cigarette he lit just a minute ago, you asshole," Special Agent Treant Jefferson said laughingly. Special Agent Jefferson, an all CIF basketball player from Compton, California, was new to the HRT detail and was still very anxious.

Danny Rong averted his gaze for a moment and looked south down Michigan Avenue.

CHAPTER SEVENTY-ONE

From the 91st floor of the John Hancock Center, Dr. Raymond Raissi looked down upon Michigan Avenue in the direction of the Marriott Hotel. His eyes fixed on a spot moving on the sidewalk. It was Danny Rong, who at the same time looked up in the direction of Raissi's penthouse perch.

"Why does he keep looking up?" Special Agent Happer asked.

"Doesn't that Raissi dude live there in the Hancock?" Special Agent Jefferson said, as he flipped through a briefing book and located the intel on Raissi. "Yep, here it is. Dr. Raymond Raissi maintains a residence in the Hancock Center and it looks like about," he counted, "ten other places throughout the world. He even has offices at the Willis. Now that's money, honey," he remarked with a smile full of Arctic-white teeth.

"What's he doing then, giving him some kind of sign?" Special Agent Happer asked laughingly, looking at Danny Rong. "Maybe some kind of secret code,"

Slapping Special Agent Happer on the back of his right shoulder, Special Agent Jefferson said, "Look," as he pointed to the stretch limousine that just rolled to a stop in front of the Marriott Hotel.

"Run the plate," Special Agent Happer said.

Special Agent Jefferson ran the plate and it came up as belonging to the Kingdom of Saudi Arabia consulate. "It's a Saudi Arabian consular car."

The two special agents eyed the car and Danny Rong at the same time. All at once, two men exited the hotel and walked arm-in-arm with Leyla Hakimian, who tried unsuccessfully to resist their grasps, to the waiting limousine. A frantic looking Leyla strained her neck, scanning the sidewalk in both directions, trying to get someone's attention. The two men quickly forced her into the limousine and shut the door.

"Hey, isn't that her? Isn't that the doctor's wife?"

"Sure as shit it is," answered Special Agent Jefferson, as he flipped through the briefing book again. "The woman's a looker."

Dialing his cellular phone, "This is Special Agent Happer," he said. "Danny Rong and two others left in a limousine licensed to the Saudi consulate. They had Leyla Hakimian with them. I'm sure of it."

"Was Raja Raissi with them?" the voice on the other end asked.

"Negative," Special Agent Happer said, as he stared at a recent photograph of Raja Raissi.

CHAPTER SEVENTY-TWO

Raja Raissi, the Khamsin's stateside first lieutenant, was still in his suite on the phone to his brother. "*Amrak*, it will be done," he said.

Dr. Raissi ended the call, as Sahar began to massage his shoulders, easing the tension he was feeling. The two watched, as a large tanker ship bearing the name Global Petroleum Resources slowly pushed through the rough waters of Lake Michigan off Lake Shore Drive on a south by southeast heading.

"It is a delicious irony, my dear," Raissi said *sotto voce*. But then, his voice began to amplify with excitement as he said, "*Habibti Sahar*, my darling Sahar. The first phase is nearing its end. The infidels buy my ship full of the black liquid that runs their country. They are paying for their demise."

Sahar embraced Raissi and whispered softly, "It is our destiny. *Inshallah*, God willing."

"*Inshallah*. The mighty Khamsin will blow the American infidels out to sea," Raissi said, with a maniacal smile growing on his broad, dark-skinned face.

Sahar's mysterious eyes reached deep into his being and tugged at his soul, for she was in control. She was the temptress whose perfidy knew no bounds.

CHAPTER SEVENTY-THREE

The long, black-as-oil Saudi Arabian consular limousine snaked its way along the One Mag Mile that was Michigan Avenue. It moved quickly toward the Chicago River, as an unmarked Ford Crown Victoria followed at a safe distance.

The limousine continued toward the Chicago River and then turned right onto Wacker Drive and followed it with the river on its right.

"They're headed toward the Willis Tower. It's got to be. I'll bet two tickets to the Bulls," Special Agent Happer said emphatically to Special Agent Douglas. "It's the Willis Tower! Do you want us to move in?"

"Hold your position for now. Since we can't be sure that they have the dirty bomb, we can't just go in," Special Agent Douglas said.

"All right."

The limousine stopped before the mighty 110-story Willis Tower, formerly the Sears Tower, located at 233 South Wacker Drive at Adams Street, opposite the south branch of the Chicago River. A valet at curbside reached for the door. Danny Rong, one of the Khamsin's most loyal foot soldiers, was the first to exit. Another man exited on the street side. Leyla Hakimian, dressed in a black dress and multi-colored Burberry shawl, was the last to exit the limousine. She looked very alone and frightened.

In a nanosecond, HRT unit leader Special Agent Douglas received the information. He immediately moved to notify Alec.

Alec was in the conference room as Special Agent Douglas entered.

"Doctor, we've just received intel from our surveillance team that your wife left the Marriott Hotel with the Khamsin's Danny Rong and an unidentified man in a Saudi consular limousine. They drove to the Willis Tower, and entered the building. It seems that Raissi has offices there as well."

"Did they enter with the dirty bomb?" Alec queried.

"No. No Dr. Raissi or his brother. And like I said, no suitcase."

Alec's mind instantaneously shifted into overdrive. He turned to his men. He was now in battle mode and began, "Gentlemen, we now know that my wife is at the Willis Tower, so that's where the bomb will be. They're using my wife as a human shield. But the bomb's not there yet."

"Sir, what's the play?" Pratt asked.

"The hand-off hasn't happened yet. Raissi's brother Raja is going to deliver the bomb to the tower himself. I just know it."

Alec knew of Raja's ego. He was possessed by the need to beat his famous brother at something, and delivering the bomb was that something. Word would spread that he was the one who blew the dirty bomb at the top of the Willis Tower.

"Where's Dr. Raissi?" Josiah asked.

"Raissi will direct the plan from afar, possibly from his penthouse at the Hancock. That's his style. He doesn't like getting his *dirty hands* dirty." Alec flinched inside when he thought of Sahar with Raissi. He wished *he could have stopped it there*. He wished *he could have erased her name from his mental database, but he couldn't, not even after he had realized that she was involved with Raissi*.

While FBI agents were monitoring Leyla Hakimian, Raja Raissi was about to meet with an emissary of the Saudi Arabian consulate in his suite. It was agreed that the exchange would take place then and there, after which he would join his men who held Leyla captive at the Willis Tower.

An entourage of Saudis entered the Marriott with several identical steamer trunks in tow. After their check-in, three bellhops escorted them to a suite two floors above Raja's suite. Moments later two Saudi aides took one of the trunks to Raja's suite.

Once in the suite, a Saudi aide opened the steamer trunk. Inside was the special black-anodized, aluminum case that held the dirty bomb.

The destructive power of the device was frightening, and Raja relished the thought.

The clock was ticking.

"This will do great things," Raja said to the Saudi who had come down to his suite. "Dr. Raissi is grateful for your cooperation. When will you and your people be leaving the city?" Raja asked.

"We will be flying out by 2 P.M. The ambassador has already left Washington."

"Very good then," Raja said.

As the men turned to leave the suite, Raja declared, "*Ittafakna*, it is agreed. *Allahu Akbar.*"

The men, all but one dressed in the traditional Arab white *disdasha*, responded in kind.

Another of Raja's aides shut the large, solid oak double-door. Raissi began circling the suitcase, tempted to open it. He knew better. The liquid crystal display had a small green light that was on. Also visible was a ruby-red light that flashed continuously. A beeping sound was barely audible. The digital countdown clock read *4 hours, 01 minutes, 45 seconds*, 04:01:44, 04:01:43.

Raja caressed the suitcase, moving his hands over the black-anodized, aluminum protective shell. It felt cold. He looked at his watch. He knew the hour was near...04:01:23, 04:01:22, 04:01:21. Everything was in motion.

Speaking to his aide Amir al-Shami, Raja ordered, "Take this to the car. Yussef should go with you. I will follow."

It was now lunchtime in Chicago. The business district was flush with tens of thousands of people crossing the common areas between buildings, many on their way to eat, others just stretching their legs, and the rare few having a smoke. Within less than an hour, they would be back in their offices in the forest of skyscrapers that was Chicago.

04:00:29, 04:00:28, 04:00:27.

CHAPTER SEVENTY-FOUR

Leaning into the table in the middle of the FBI's sitroom, Alec laid out maps of central Chicago, the Hancock Center, and the Willis Tower. "Boys, here's where we are," pointing to an area on the map that indicated O'Hare's location. "We'll be leaving here and heading to the Willis Tower in about 20 minutes. Once at the tower we'll position ourselves as follows." Everyone in the room was waiting for what came next.

"Bobby, you and Alvarado will be in the first chopper, and to confirm, Special Agent Hajj will follow your lead in the second. The ideal situation would be to get to my wife and the bomb before they can get to the top. They won't blow it inside the building because that would reduce its effectiveness. My guess is that they will blow it on the *Skydeck* at the top. Since the bomb's a deadly, radiological dispersion device, they would want to take advantage of the wind at the top. Remember, these guys are *homicide bombers*," Alec said with a stern look. "If the bomb goes off, they know they're gone, so they won't stop on their own. We'll have to get to them before —"

"Doctor, I can have Special Agents Hannan and Daniels position themselves at the observation deck and relay intel to you."

"For now it's better if they remain on the perimeter of the building. Innocent people will be everywhere. They will be more useful there."

"Understood," Special Agent Douglas responded.

Alec looked at his Panerai and then said, "Any questions? Okay, let's roll."

Every member of OS9 fell into line. They were ready to do it, one more time.

Two black Chevrolet Suburbans pulled out from O'Hare International Airport just before noon. The wind had picked up, as did the traffic. Red lights atop the vehicles helped pave the way into town along the crowded Interstate 290, officially called the Dwight D. Eisenhower Expressway. Everyone aboard was silent, just waiting. Some were reaching under their NOMEX suits to adjust their exosuits for close-combat-mode and to activate the SniffEx-2 detectors. Others looked out the window, thinking about what was to go down. No one knew when the dirty bomb was set to go off or where it was. They all followed Alec's instinct.

The clock was ticking.

CHAPTER SEVENTY-FIVE

A rented Ford Econoline van stopped before the Jackson Boulevard entrance to the Willis Tower. The entrance was designed to provide direct access to the Skydeck observation level of the building. With visibility that reached out some fifty miles and the ability to see four states, the Skydeck was always flush with sightseers from the world over.

Raja, dressed in a black, bespoke silk suit, looked as if he were attending a dinner party at the Museum of Modern Art or a funeral. He exited the passenger side and ordered Amud al-Jalili, Amir al-Shami, and Yussef Hanifa to remove the large, black-anodized, aluminum suitcase from the rear of the van. "Now take it to the elevator. Wait for me at the door."

Suddenly, a black Sikorsky S-76 helicopter came out of nowhere and whirred across the sky above Raja. He looked up for an instant, but thought nothing of it. He then continued on into the building. Adjusting his suit's jacket, making sure it covered his twenty-five extra pounds, he then proceeded to the kiosk that was just steps from the elevator. "*Keef halak,* how are you doing?" he said to Omar Radhi, the security guard, who was also a Raja operative. He had worked at the tower for the past two years in preparation for this moment. He was able to pass the security background check because the individual who oversaw the process was another of Raja's very well-paid foot soldiers who had also been preparing for this day ever since he joined the Khamsin brotherhood.

"*Kelshi hader*, all is ready," Raja said, and then walked to the awaiting elevator. Two visitors sought admittance to the same elevator, but Raja closed the doors in their faces. They looked to the guard, who held up his hands as if to say that he was helpless to do anything.

Moments later, the elevator doors opened on the main floor that held the Global Petroleum Resources suite of offices. Raja and his men were met by Danny Rong. He and his confederate had been guarding Leyla and awaiting their orders.

Raja immediately grabbed Leyla tightly by the left arm, as he ordered Rong to push the buttons for both the 66th floor and the Skydeck on the 103rd. With everything in place, Raja looked over to Amud al-Jalili. He held the handle to the suitcase containing the dirty bomb in his right hand. Raja felt good, very good. *Allah would be vindicated*, he thought to himself, as the elevator, one of the building's 104 such lift cars, suddenly came to a stop at the 66th floor. He nudged Leyla to move forward toward the entrance to the Metropolitan Club's dining area. It was Raja's intention to keep Leyla away from the Skydeck until the dirty bomb was in its pre-determined location.

Raja quickly turned back and said to his devoted hirelings, Hanifa and al-Shami, "You know what to do. When you are there, call me."

Hanifa and al-Shami were told to backup Rong and al-Jalili once everyone was in place on the Skydeck.

Once seated at a table for four, Raja leaned close to a frightened Leyla and said in a sinister tone, "Any outburst, any attempt to cause a problem, Mrs. Hakimian, and your precious, little daughter will be killed." His foul breath made her nearly vomit. She winced and recoiled in her chair.

Suddenly, panic washed over her face as the words *your precious little daughter* came out of his mouth. Leyla had no idea that Karina was with her family. She hated Raja with all the venom she could summon. She wanted terrible things to happen to all of them. She wanted to be home with her daughter and she wanted Alec back. *Where was Alec?* She had asked that question a thousand times before. *And why hadn't Alec contacted her? Did he even know?*

Raja faced Leyla directly and said more pointedly, "Do you understand? I will kill her without a thought."

Leyla cautiously nodded her head, indicating she understood. Dark images of her darling daughter in danger stabbed her repeatedly in the heart. The feeling would not leave her. Her anger grew.

"Now," he said with feigned politeness. Adjusting his jacket, he added, "What is your desire for lunch? The crusted tuna looks good." He waited for Leyla's answer, as he continued to peruse the menu.

She could not believe just how calm he was, while at the same time prepared to kill thousands of Chicagoans in just a few hours. She thought, *there was no reasoning with a man of such idiotic ideology. How could one of the world's great religions, a religion of peace, be so corrupted and convoluted in such men's minds?*

The FBI sent notification to the authorities at the Willis Tower indicating that OS9 and the HRT were heading there and that a dirty bomb might be in the building. Moreover, *do not evacuate* was the present standing order; trying to evacuate the thousands of people who worked in the building would cause untold chaos, thus jeopardizing the operation. So, they were instructed to observe and contain the situation until OS9 and HRT arrived, and to be prepared to execute their evacuation plan when given the command.

02:30:10, 02:30:09, 02:30:08.

CHAPTER SEVENTY-SIX

The Wacker Drive lobby entrance to the Willis Tower welcomed some 13,000 visitors every workday. Most entered through its three-story main entrance that displayed Alexander Calder's *Universe* sculpture, a sculpture that critics have said depicted the endless possibilities of the human imagination.

It was decided, OS9 and HRT would access the building from the east entrance on Franklin Street, in hopes of not attracting too much attention. However, the sight of men in black NOMEX suits carrying exotic weapons could not help but turn heads. They needed to be as unobtrusive as possible.

As soon as Alec and his team entered the service elevator and the doors closed, the security guard Omar Radhi made a call to Raja.

"*Sidi*, sir. Several armed men are going up now," he said with great urgency.

"Where were they going?" Raja asked immediately.

"I do not know, *sidi*."

"What did they look like?" he queried.

"Some looked like FBI and others like SWAT in black tactical suits," he replied.

Raja's face showed concern after he ended the call. He had no real idea what Omar was talking about, but it could not be good. Leyla sensed that Raja had just heard distressing news, and that it would bollix his plans.

CHAPTER SEVENTY-SEVEN

Alec stopped the service elevator some fifty floors up. "Bobby, are you there yet?" he asked, speaking into his lip mike.

"Yes, sir. We're about 700 meters up and over the river," Bobby answered in a rat-a-tat-tat, barely audible voice. "I also see a chopper sitting on top of the rooftop just below the building's main module where you are."

"Bobby, switch to your exo's communications. I can't hear you well enough. And what about Hajj?"

Bobby immediately switched to his exosuit's satellite communications ability. "She's hovering off the Franklin entrance, sir," came out crystal clear.

"Now that's better," Alec replied.

Hajj would have to rely on HRT's less capable communication hardware.

Looking to Special Agent Douglas, Alec ordered, "Make sure that you keep in contact with Hajj. Bobby will take the long shot if necessary. Also, find out who in the hell has a chopper on the top of the module next to us. I don't want any of these bastards getting away." Refocusing on Special Agent Douglas, he continued with a detectable sharpness to his voice. "That chopper better not be media. Have your people keep the media out of my sight," he commanded. "I don't need that problem now."

Special Agent Douglas knew that kind of comment was coming. He had had his people do a background check on Alec that came up craps. *He wasn't military, yet he was leading a special black ops military unit. He wasn't CIA. The NSA said they never heard of him. The FBI denied any knowledge. So who the hell was he?* he asked himself.

Special Agent Douglas realized it was going to be an OS9 operation all the way, and that his jurisdiction held no water. The situation angered him. What he sensed was that Alec did not give a damn what he thought at this point. As much as HRT was a viable and effective tool of law enforcement, Alec's wife was the hostage and he was going to rescue her. That was all there was to it and he knew it.

"Will do," came the reply from Special Agent Douglas. He clenched his teeth every time he had to answer to this mystery man. He was going to find out everything about Dr. Alexander Hakimian.

Special Agent Douglas answered a ringing cell call. Ending the call a few sentences later, he said, "Dr. Hakimian. That was Police Chief Starbird asking what we need. He'll be here as soon as he can. He's detained with DHS."

"Tell him to keep the perimeter clear. It's only a matter of time before we make our move and when we do, people will panic. He and his men must contain it. Get people out of the building ASAP without too much confusion. Don't let anyone in from this point on."

"Okay," replied Special Agent Douglas. He then placed a call back to Chief Starbird and relayed Alec's orders.

Turning to his team, Alec said, "All right men, we have to assume the dirty bomb's already in the building. When we find Raja and his goons, we'll find the bomb and my wife. We must also assume that the bomb has a timed detonator and that it's activated. What time is left, we do not know. But we have no other option."

01:59:27, 01:59:26, 01:59:25.

"Bobby, you and Alvarado maintain your position. Keep behind the river until I call you in," Alec proclaimed. Facing Special Agent Douglas, he continued, "Have Hajj stay on the backside of the tower. She needs to watch the Franklin entrance. Keep your men just outside the perimeter on the Skydeck until I call."

"Yes, sir." At the same time, Bobby was pointing the laser sight on the suspected target area as Alvarado began computing distances, wind speed, drift, and direction. Even humidity was a factor under such a circumstance. He knew that Bobby needed all the information he could give him. Shooting a moving target from a moving helicopter added greatly to the difficulty of the shot.

OS9 and HRT made their way up and stopped on the 102nd floor, just below the Skydeck. At the same time, in the Metropolitan Club thirty-six floors below Leyla Hakimian was using her fork to push around a piece of crusted salmon and capers on her plate. Raja stared periodically at her while he methodically sipped his iced tea. As a devout Wahhabist, alcohol was forbidden, at least in public.

Plucking his ringing cell phone from his coat pocket, he said, "*Salamat*, hello."

Immediately the voice on the other end asked, "Is everything ready? Remember, *do not spare her life. She must die with the others.* For Allah, the most merciful, will be pleased," came out loud and clear.

"*Naam*, yes. I understand, I understand my brother," he responded.

CHAPTER SEVENTY-EIGHT

Dr. Raissi ended the call and gazed back out on to Lake Michigan. It was as if he were in a state of meditation. Sahar, wearing a black, shear silk blouse and nothing else, walked into the cavernous living room where he was seated in a stately red leather, reading chair. She stopped directly in front of him and said in a sultry, alluring voice, "You must prepare yourself, my love."

Looking up at her half-naked body, her raven-colored hair flowing over her left shoulder, he gently slipped his hand between her long legs and slid it up to where they joined. A soft caress, a long sigh from her, and then, as if nothing had just happened, he exclaimed, "In less than two hours we will be on our way, my dear Sahar. We will leave the infidels' cesspool of life behind us and return to the land of Allah."

With the backdrop of the Chicago skyline framing her sensuous body, Sahar took his right hand and pressed it firmly against her essence. Raissi smiled, then withdrew his hand. "You must go now *habibti*, my darling. I will meet you at the airport soon, but I must finish this first," he said with urgency. "I have the helicopter awaiting me at the tower. When I have made certain everything is in place, I will meet you and then we will be on our way home. I want to tell his wife that her husband, the man who owes me his life, and whose life I am about to take, can't save her or the thousands of infidels that are about to die with her." Raissi was convinced of the outcome of what was about to take place.

Sahar turned and disappeared into her dressing room. Her scent still lingered.

Raissi scrutinized his platinum Rolex wristwatch, a birthday gift from Sahar. She had the unique timepiece especially designed in Switzerland at considerable cost. It possessed a special mechanism to communicate with certain designated electronic devices. Rolex executives had asked questions at the time as to why such a timepiece was required. The response was to generously pass around stacks of Euros, then there were no more questions.

The wristwatch had activated the dirty bomb, and it was the only means by which the dirty bomb could be deactivated and defused.

Dr. Raymond Raissi wore on his wrist the future of Chicago.

01:35:17, 01:35:16, 01:35:15.

CHAPTER SEVENTY-NINE

Dr. Raymond Raissi was shadowed from his suite to his private elevator in the John Hancock Center by Kamil, his chauffeur.

At the same time, Raja casually answered his ringing cellular phone in the Metropolitan Club. While looking at a frightened and frustrated Leyla, emotions overloading her psyche, he said, "*Marhaba*, hello. Very well then, wait until we are on the deck, then I will call you." He ended the call and took another sip of his iced tea. He then made a call back to Rong, informing them that he and Leyla were about to leave the Metropolitan Club. He ordered him to position Hanifa and al-Shami at the elevators that exited onto the Skydeck. Once the bomb was on the Skydeck, they were to make sure that no one would enter or leave the area.

With the suitcase dirty bomb secreted away in a janitor's storage room on the 102nd floor, Rong and al-Jalili awaited their next instruction from Raja.

"Sir, would there be anything else?" the waiter asked Raja.

"No," came out cold and dismissive, as he fingered his cell phone on the table.

"Very well, sir," the waiter said courteously. He placed the check before Raja, said thank-you, and backed away.

After signing the check, Raja stood and said, "Good then. Let us go, Mrs. Hakimian." He attempted to pull her chair back but she recoiled. She slid the chair back herself and stood defiantly. He motioned for her to walk in front of him to the elevator.

CHAPTER EIGHTY

OS9 and HRT were ready to begin their well-orchestrated assault on the Skydeck. The killing or injuring of innocent civilians was always a possibility, but their safety was the charge of the HRT and Special Agent Douglas knew it. He had his men prepared to evacuate as many people as possible from the immediate area.

Speaking into his lip mike, Alec said, "Bobby, we're ready to move. Are you in position yet?"

Because of the Sikorsky S-76's advanced rotor design and high engine output, it was a helicopter capable of hovering in place for long periods of time, even in intense crosswinds, and could move sideways at 40 knots per hour to evade direct enemy fire. "Sir, got it," Bobby answered as quickly as the question was asked.

"Bobby," Alvarado said, "we're now about 750 meters out. Keep it tight on the front windows of the deck. I count forty-one people in my line of sight."

Bobby kept his camo-colored .50 BMG caliber Barrett long-range sniper rifle he called "Big Dawg," trained on the Skydeck. It was his weapon of choice when the shot was long and difficult. One of the qualities of a great sniper was his ability to keep his weapon aimed at the target with the precision of a gyroscope, and Bobby's hands did just that. The pilot, combat trained, followed Alvarado's every word, maneuvering the S-76 helo with great precision. Alvarado was ever vigilant, knowing that at such an altitude and in winds beyond the norm for a kill-shot, adjusting for wind drift became mission critical.

Bobby scanned each window, looking for the kill-shot.

Speaking to Special Agent Douglas, Alec said, "Tell Hajj to hold tight. Tell her that Bobby will cover the front and right sides and she should cover the left and backside of the Skydeck. Keep your men here until we've ascertained who and what is up there," he said, as he began to climb the stairway to the floor above.

Special Agent Douglas, who had returned to the FBI command center, responded immediately.

Leyla exited the elevator first. She saw several dozen men, women, and children walking about, commenting on what an amazing view it was from so high up. People were gawking, pointing, and taking pictures of the skyline and themselves. Raja was just a step away. He tapped her left shoulder and indicated that he wanted her to move over to the far corner where no one was at the moment.

Leyla complied reluctantly. Inside she was thinking, *rage had replaced fright. She knew that she needed to be ready to make her move... Alec had taught her that.*

Raja, his black suit and thinning, slicked-back, dyed-black hair instantly cast him as a movie villain. He picked up his cell phone and made a call. "Danny, we are here," he said with a smile. He knew what was next and relished the moment. "Bring it now," he ordered. Hanifa and al-Shami, watching the elevators, were to make sure that once the bomb was on the Skydeck, they would not allow anyone else to enter, nor exit.

CHAPTER EIGHTY-ONE

"Sir," a loud voice in Alec's earphone said.

"What is it, Bobby?"

As the wind buffeted the helicopter, he answered with calm, "She's there, on the deck." Sighting Leyla through his US Optics SN3 T-Pal 3.2-17x44mm sniper scope, he emphasized, "I can see your wife and Raja Raissi." Alec became frozen in time. His mind stalled, then he heard it again, "Sir, your wife's standing in a black dress in the right corner of the Skydeck. Raja is also in black and is next to her. He's got an arm around her waist and a gun in his hand."

The thought of Raja's arm around his wife's waist enraged Alec.

"Sir," Bobby pleaded, expecting to hear Alec's response.

"Yes, Bobby. Hold on Raja." Turning to Pratt, "What do the sensors say? Is the bomb there?"

"Yes, sir. The signature is certain, but I still can't tell how close," Pratt exclaimed, reading the remote sensors he had placed near the Skydeck level. They would give him the freedom to move about while he kept tabs on the dirty bomb's whereabouts.

"Stay on it and let me know when you have a fix. Nutworth, Mackay, you two follow me to the Skydeck. Josiah, you cover the elevators and stairway."

Josiah nodded in the affirmative, as he clenched his weapon tightly. He had opted for the Myotron II, knowing that its ability to fry human nerves, causing instant and lethal paralysis, would do the trick, with no collateral damage, and he liked that. Nutworth and Mackay held firmly onto their thermal guns. They had conventional semiautomatic handguns at the ready, but in such close quarters and with so many people on the Skydeck, flying lead would surely be a major risk.

CHAPTER EIGHTY-TWO

Dr. Raymond Raissi's traditional, ebony-black Cadillac limousine looked like many others, apart from its full armor-plated body, and one-inch thick, bulletproof tinted glass. It motored south down Michigan Avenue toward the Willis Tower relatively unnoticed, save the Illinois license plate that read "RR 1 USA." Raissi sat quietly in the far backseat, mentally preparing himself for what was to come. He saw himself as a modern-day Saladin, the twelfth century Muslim leader and the faith's greatest hero, who had vanquished the Christians during the Third Crusade. Looking at his Rolex wristwatch, his plans were now in motion and like the great Saladin himself, he would see to it that his Muslim brothers would once more defeat the Christian infidels in *his Crusade* and rule the world again.

01:01:02, 01:01:01, 01:01:00.

CHAPTER EIGHTY-THREE

As Alec opened the stairwell door into the large crowd circulating around the Skydeck, a young boy yelled out "Daddy, look! It's a ninja!"

The young boy's father turned around to see Alec standing at the stairwell door. Alec quickly gestured to him to take his boy, move over to the far corner of the Skydeck, and not say a word. Others began to notice Alec, who put his index finger to his lips indicating that they say nothing and then pointed for them to move off to the side.

Moving slowly out of the doorway, followed by Mackay and Nutworth, Alec could see the confusion, as people's faces indicated that something was not right. Pratt stayed in the stairwell trying to identify the exact location of the dirty bomb by utilizing the technology provided by his exosuit's SniffEx-2 biomagnetic sensor, often used to locate antitank mines, other explosive devices, and munitions.

Raja and Leyla remained in the corner on the opposite end of the large Skydeck, partly obscured by tourists milling about. He had no idea that Alec was near.

"Bring it up. It is time," Raja said. While closing his cellular phone, he took his eye off of Leyla for a nanosecond, but that was all she needed. She bolted toward a door just a few steps away, only to find it locked. She struggled with the doorknob, but to no avail. Raja chased after her. People began pointing at Leyla. She frantically looked about for an escape route, but Raja pulled her toward him.

Two men, one in his early thirties with two children and a wife looking on and the second, a man about fifty, rushed to a screaming Leyla's aid.

Raja drew a small caliber semiautomatic handgun from his inside jacket pocket and pointed it at the older man, who stopped in his tracks. Those on the Skydeck were now in a state of panic, as they rushed for cover, some pushing the elevator button endlessly, while still others hid behind building supports. A cacophony of screams summoned Alec's heightened attention.

Alec cautiously took another step out of the doorway, followed by Mackay and Nutworth. Then her saw her. Leyla, *his Leyla*. In a flash, all the months away from her had vanished in an instant. It now seemed as if he had only earlier this morning left her for the hospital, and he was now returning home for the night.

Then Leyla saw his face, tired and unshaven, but resolute. "Alec," she shouted. "Aleccccccc," came her cry.

Raja grabbed her, put his handgun to her head, and said, "Shut up, you bitch." His eyes, manic as ever, looked around for Alec.

Alec wanted to make his move toward Raja, but he knew that he would certainly kill his wife in an instant because he was a coward.

Mackay stood just off the doorway. He spoke into his exosuit's lip mike to Bobby. "Bobby, do you have him sighted?" came the question.

"Mac, in my sights. In my sights, my boy," he answered.

"You see Alec?" asked Mackay.

"Yes, to my left," Bobby said flatly.

"Do you have a clear shot?" asked Mackay.

"Not yet."

With the chopper now hovering about 600 meters out, Alvarado told the pilot to move in closer and to the left.

"Now I do," Bobby said with a chuckle.

"Bobby, dial it in now," Alec broke in, his eyes steeled on Raja and Leyla.

Raja glanced over his shoulder only to see the S-76 Sikorsky helicopter hovering 300 meters directly in front of him. He immediately stepped back behind a building support with Leyla still in his strong grasp. Shouting frantically and pointing his handgun at whomever made eye contact with him, he said, "Everyone. I said everyone." Everyone froze where he or she stood. "All of you. Move to the windows. I want each of you to stand next to each other along the windows and face out." He glanced back at the black, unmarked helicopter. It was now about 200 meters out. Raja's eyes darted back-and-forth from the helicopter to Alec. He knew those inside of it were not sightseers.

Alec weighed his options, as Leyla begged for him with pain in her eyes. Then a voice came into his head, "Sir," Pratt uttered, "the bomb's near. Very near." Alec took another step closer.

"Bobby, how about now?" came the question from Mackay.

Josiah stood watch over the elevators, as well as the fire escape entrance. Rong and al-Jalili began to roll the dirty bomb out of the fire escape door when they saw him. Before they could react, Josiah hit Rong with the Myotron II. Rong instantly fell to the ground, wrenching with uncontrollable convulsions and howling in pain. With some effort, al-Jalili pulled the suitcase dirty bomb in front of him. Josiah knew he could not take the shot, too many people too close and the dirty bomb was probably *hot*. Pointing an H&K P30L 9mm semiautomatic handgun at Josiah's head, al-Jalili motioned for him to back away. Josiah tracked him with his eyes, as al-Jalili rolled the twenty-kilogram, dirty bomb out to the center of the Skydeck. Everyone looked at the dirty bomb and then to the digital clock readout.

With his nerves on edge and crazily waving his handgun back and forth, Raja shouted, "Everyone stay where you are. Listen to me. I said stay where you are. The next person who moves is dead."

"Looks like we're dead anyway, asshole," came out of someone's mouth from across the Skydeck.

"Who said that?" Raja demanded to know, as he scanned the area, his handgun tracking with his eyes.

"I did, fuck head," said a young man with tattooed forearms wrapped tightly around his frightened girlfriend. "You worthless piece of shit, if I had —"

Bang! The young man fell facedown on the floor, a bullet lodged in his upper torso.

His girlfriend screamed in horror. "You killed him," she yelled. "You bastard."

"I am not kidding here," he said, his Middle Eastern accent now more apparent than ever. Leyla struggled to free herself from his grip, but it was too strong. "Stay back," he cautioned the dead man's girlfriend, "or you will join him."

Children began crying as mothers sought to comfort them. Fathers and other men stared at Raja with the look of determination on their faces. Alec sensed their rage, but hoped that none of them would do anything. It would only lead to more needless deaths.

Raja looked back to Alec and trained his handgun on him. "Ah, Dr. Hakimian," he said smoothly. "I knew you would come. I had anticipated our meeting like this. You should know that the bomb will kill us all. It will kill thousands and your wife will be one of them. There is little time left," he added with a bizarre expression of glee.

Alec focused for a beat on the bright, digital clock readout. The remaining time was less than an hour. He thought, *did Raja have a way of detonating the dirty bomb earlier than the time indicated on the readout? Could he get to Raja before he killed his wife or could Bobby get the shot off? And what about the dirty bomb? Could it be deactivated and how?*

Alec, Mackay, and Nutworth began to separate themselves so that it would force Raja to take his eyes off one to see another. Mackay and Nutworth held their thermal guns at their sides. Raja paid no attention to them for the moment; he knew he was holding the trump card, Alec's wife.

Alec looked over at the ominous black-anodized, aluminum suitcase that contained the dirty bomb. By now, al-Jalili had attached it to one of the building's support columns with a heavily-woven steel cable that wrapped around the column and was secured in place by a massive combination lock. The lock was capable of surviving a direct shot from a large caliber gun.

"Over here," Raja ordered Hanifa and al-Shami. The two raised their guns as Raja continued, "Watch these people. Make sure that no one moves. If they do, shoot them," he said with nervous anger. Sweat was now visible on his flat forehead. The scar on the right side of his neck bulged, straining under the pressure.

Chapter Eighty-Four

00:39:43, 00:39:42, 00:39:41.

Police black and whites necklaced the entirety of the several acres that comprised the immense Willis Tower footprint. The Wacker Drive entrance was carpeted with at least two hundred Chicago Police officers, as was the Franklin Street access. Emergency vehicles of every stripe had their light bars flashing. Crowd control was proving difficult; a wave of panic had washed over the immediate area. Loved ones of those inside the building demanded answers. The governor's representative wanted answers as well. *What was going on at the top of the tower and who was OS9?*

Raissi's limousine slowly came to a stop before the main entrance on Wacker Drive. A police sergeant approached the car. "Kamil, I will talk to him," Raissi said with confidence. The officer tapped on the driver's window, as Raissi lowered his. "Officer," his face framed by the opened window, "I am Dr. Raissi, and it is imperative that I get inside the building."

"Dr. Raissi, that won't be possible at this time. We have reason to believe that there is a bomb in the building," the officer said in an official tone.

By now journalists, local television and radio stations, and even the gossip rags had reporters crowding the area in front of the tower. Networks already had correspondents on planes flying to Chicago. No one had any idea how big the news story at the Willis Tower was about to become.

Raissi was having none of it. "Officer, I would like to talk to your superior."

The officer gave Raissi, and then his limousine, a long look. He realized that he might be a very important person, and that he should defer to his superior. "Yes, Dr. Raissi. I will contact him." Taking a step back, he began to speak into his communication device clipped to his left shoulder. "Captain Moody, this is Sergeant Borderbund. I have a Dr. Raissi here. He has asked to speak to you. He's at the Wacker Drive entrance to the tower. Very good, sir."

Raissi gave the officer a feigned smile of thanks.

Looking to Raissi, he said, "Dr. Raissi, he will be with you in a few minutes."

The wind was now blowing at about 35 miles per hour, with gusts to 50, even 60 at times. Raissi thought, *the day was just right for a radiological dispersion device.*

Moments later Captain Phineas Moody approached. "Officer Borderbund, is that the gentleman?" he asked, pointing to the black limousine now sandwiched between a fire truck and one of the police department's mobile command units.

"Yes, sir. He's waiting for you."

Captain Moody walked over to Raissi's car. As he looked into the opened rear window, Raissi looked out. "Pardon me," Raissi said, startling the captain.

"Dr. Raissi, Captain Phineas Moody," he said, reaching out to shake his hand. "I am told that you insist on entering the building."

"Yes, Captain Moody," Raissi said flatly.

"I can't let you do that for your safety and the safety of others," he said, as he shaped his moustache with his right hand.

"Captain, many people in the building are my employees."

"I understand your concern, but I can't take any chances."

Raissi saw that he was getting nowhere with the captain. Thinking a moment, he decided to exit his limousine. Standing rod straight and almost eye-to-eye with the captain, he said quietly, as several police officers and firefighters looked on, "Captain Moody, I understand your concern, but I can tell you that both Police Chief Starbird and Governor

Richards would reward your efforts to assist me." The captain's expression immediately changed to one of apprehension. Raissi added, leaning close enough to smell his breath. "I can guarantee it Captain Moody. Guarantee it," he repeated, patting the captain on his shoulder.

Captain Moody felt put upon, but knew that he had no choice. Assessing the situation, he saw in front of him an extremely well-dressed man driven about in his stretch limousine, who dropped the names of his boss, and even the governor. Only two years from retirement, he decided to take no chances. Summoning Sergeant Mick McDougal, a middle-aged man who would understand the circumstance and not ask questions, he said, "Mick, Dr. Raissi here needs to be let into the building. Please assist him." Sergeant McDougal nodded in the affirmative.

"Dr. Raissi," Sergeant McDougal said, "please follow me, sir."

"Thank-you captain, for your understanding. I will notify your superiors of your willingness to be helpful," Raissi remarked. Turning to Kamil, "Kamil, please stay with the car while I am gone."

Kamil responded with reverence, "As you wish." Kamil sat in the driver's seat and waited pensively while emergency vehicles moved about helter-skelter.

Raissi, holding down his thinning hair with his left hand as the wind attempted to lift what he had left from the crown of his head, followed Sergeant McDougal up to the main doors that led to the immense entry of the Willis Tower.

The Willis Tower, built of nine framed tubes or megamodules, and once called the Sears Tower, soared to a pinnacle height of 1,730 feet above the west side of Chicago's downtown Loop. Its 16,100 bronze-tinted glass windows reflected and refracted light, day or night. It was the greatest directional reference point in the city.

Since the 9/11 attacks, the Willis Tower, whose naming rights were now owned by a London-based insurance company, has always been an obvious target for terrorists, and although the management has taken precautions, the tower's size and location have made it truly impossible to protect with any real certainty. As such, many high-profile tenants had since left.

As Raissi began to walk up the steps leading to the wide, canopied entrance, a female reporter in her early thirties from CBS local news jumped in front of him and asked, "Sir, can you tell us what's going on?"

Sergeant McDougal asked the reporter to step aside as the door opened.

"But sir, what is —?"

Two young police officers stood by the entrance as the reporter insisted on pursuing Sergeant McDougal for answers. Suddenly, another police officer grabbed her by the sleeve and escorted her out of the building.

"Dr. Raissi, where is it that you wish to go?" Sergeant McDougal asked in a very submissive tone. "We have an emergency on the Skydeck, so we must stay clear,"

"My offices are near the top."

"What floor?"

"The 92nd."

Security guards and police officers did their best to calm those caught in the foyer when the incident began, but it was proving all too difficult to maintain some sort of order in the face of sirens, flashing lights, and law enforcement personnel scurrying about in peripatetic fashion. The decision was made to escort the employees out of the building in small groups, in an effort to hopefully control a situation that could very quickly become out-of-control.

"Officer Williams," Sergeant McDougal said to the security guard closest to the elevators. "Does this go to the 92nd floor?"

"It does, but —"

"We have to go up. I have orders," Sergeant McDougal said flatly.

The officer reluctantly pushed the *up* button. In just a few seconds, the doors opened and Raissi and Sergeant McDougal entered the elevator. Sergeant McDougal scanned the panel containing the floor numbers as Raissi watched. He pushed the button that read 92nd floor. The doors closed silently and the elevator shot up like a Saturn Five Rocket. With the sergeant marveling at the speed of the elevator and commenting to Raissi how amazing it was, Raissi suddenly reached over with his right hand and pushed the *stop* button. He then shoved the sergeant to the back of the elevator and pointed a snub-nose Smith & Wesson model 340 .357 magnum hammerless revolver at him. The

.357 magnum caliber round was capable of blowing through just about any object that it hit. Its lethalness was never in doubt.

When it came to handguns, Raissi was very conservative. He favored the classic revolver-style handgun over the semiautomatic, if only for the reason that it never jammed.

"What the hell is this, sir?" Sergeant McDougal questioned, startled by the sight of a gun in the hand of a man whom he thought was a very important person, a man who was friends with the chief and other influential people. "Do you realize what you are doing, Dr. Raissi?" he questioned in a shaky voice.

Looking smugly at the officer, he said, "Shut up."

"What do you mean, Dr. Raissi?" he fired back loudly, his tenor voice infused with fear.

"I said shut up. Now push the button for the 103rd floor. I want to go to the Skydeck. I hear the view is wonderful, especially on a day such as this," he said with a villainous smile.

"No, I won't. Are you crazy? You'll never get away with whatever you have in mind."

"Whatever I have in mind, as you say, is already taking place, officer. And now I must leave you."

Sergeant McDougal slid slowly down the elevator's back wall and slumped in the corner. The .357 magnum caliber hollow-point shell had ripped his aorta in half. He was no more.

Raissi pushed the button on the elevator panel that read 103rd, Skydeck. The elevator shot up the remaining floors and stopped at the 103rd. The doors opened onto the Skydeck.

CHAPTER EIGHTY-FIVE

"This is Kelly McNeel with your CBS local news at 4:30," the thirty-something broadcaster said in a solemn voice, flashing her da Vinci dental veneers.

"Just moments ago, we received a report that the Willis Tower's Skydeck, full of visitors, was taken over by several unidentified men. We don't know how many people have been taken hostage or why, but we have our CBS Copter One flying near the tower's top." Speaking to the reporter in the helicopter, she asked, "Jay, this is Kelly McNeel. What can you tell us about what's going on at the Skydeck of the Willis Tower from your vantage point aboard the CBS Copter One?"

"Well, Kelly. I wish I did have something to say, but honestly, officials won't let us near the tower. Right now we're told to stay at least 2,000 meters away. That's over a mile, which makes it difficult to see anything. Sorry, Kelly," Jay said apologetically.

Feeling somewhat embarrassed, Kelly tried to shrug it off by saying, "Well, that's live television, folks. I know that our trusty Jay Chin will get back to us as soon as he has more information. In the meantime, it was reported by the BBC that five English women walked naked in front of Parliament protesting the —"

Special Agent Olufsson sat in her office Washington, D.C., watching the circus on television. Thoroughly disgusted, she shut it off in anger and reached for the phone. Dialing a number, she stated with fury, "Harry, call Bob Zorn at CBS in New York. We can't have reporters in helicopters flying around the Willis Tower, goddamn it. It's going to become a public relations disaster for the FBI if we don't contain this. Then call every other goddamn television station and tell them to stay away. I'll have their asses in court if I see anything else on television."

"Right away," Special Agent Harry Mims pronounced. "Right away."

CHAPTER EIGHTY-SIX

The situation on the Skydeck had deteriorated into a state of mass hysteria for those who were there simply for the view. Children were crying and cowering around their mothers and fathers; young lovers quivered together with uncontrollable fear; and men stood, some enraged, others motionless. Everything seemed to be moving at warp speed. In a far corner, Raja held Leyla close with one arm still wrapped around her mid-section like a boa constrictor strangling its prey. The other hand clenched the powerful magnum-caliber revolver. He was waving it wildly back and forth, pointing it first at an elderly couple near him, then desperately pointing it at a tour group of young children about ten feet away. Leyla could smell the panic and fear on his breath.

Looking straight at Alec, he commanded, "Get the helicopter out of here now, or I'll kill her. You hear me? I'll kill the pretty little thing."

Alec hesitated, then said coolly, "Bobby, back-off. He wants you to move away."

"Sir, how far?"

"Just back off one hundred meters."

The S-76 Sikorsky helicopter, buffeted by rising winds, moved slowly back to the 500 meters mark. On the backside of the tower, Special Agent Hajj of the HRT hovered in another S-76 helicopter, waiting for her chance to take a shot. Threatening clouds loomed in the distance.

Suddenly, Raissi appeared on the Skydeck. What he saw pleased him, although he was mildly surprised. It was Alec. At first, he imagined he was mistaken. *It couldn't be,* he thought. *Not Dr. Alexander Hakimian. Not the man he'd saved in '89. But it was! It was him.*

"Alexander, I had hoped you would come. After all, I have your wife," he said maniacally, looking to Leyla in the grip of his brother. "A man must always protect his wife. Is that not the case?"

Alec did not answer. He quickly managed to put himself between Raissi and Raja. He was book-ended by two powerful forces of evil. From the time had he heard of his wife's kidnapping prior to leaving for southern Lebanon, he had made the decision. He would find and kill her kidnapper, regardless of the consequences.

A now very anxious Raja fought to contain Leyla's reptilian movements, as she squirmed to escape his grasp. With the handgun pointed at her head, Mackay whispered to Bobby at the ready in the helicopter. "Bobby, do you have the shot?" Mackay knew that Alec counld not communicate with Bobby without giving away his plans.

Alvarado, the spotter, ordered the pilot to ease his helicopter closer again. The wind at nearly 500 meters up had settled down somewhat.

"Bobby. What about now?" Mackay asked.

"Almost there," Bobby replied, coolly looking through the precision gun sight. "I'd like you to get a little closer. There it is, the bastard's dead center in the crosshairs. Big Dawg has him now. He's gonna bite!"

Then without warning, Alec commanded, "Take it. Take it now."

Bobby waited for a two count until everything was perfect.

Raja whipped his head around to see the helicopter now closer than before.

Alvarado leaned into Bobby and said calmly, "Bobby. It's your shot. Take it, brother. The wind's running at ten knots from left to right and it's 400 meters out."

Bobby took a deep breath, and with an almost surgical detachment, he dialed in his US Optics SN3 T-Pal 3.2-17x44mm sniper scope. He knew he had the shot. With a slow, Zen-like squeezing of the specially shaped trigger, custom-made for his right index finger, the .50 BMG caliber projectile was released from its long, brass casing and rocketed down the spiral bore of the long-range sniper rifle's barrel. The lethal projectile was on its way. Before Raja could blink his eyes, the rocketing bullet, whose muzzle velocity was supersonic, penetrated one of the Skydeck's triple-thick glass observation window-ledge panes with barely a puff sound. It smashed into the left side of Raja's head just above the ear. His head twisted violently to the right, as the round continued to bore threw the skull bone, traveling across the convoluted gray matter of his brain, and exiting out the right side in a very violent way.

It was a *supreme kill-shot*.

Death was instantaneous.

Fresh, warm blood spattered the left side of Leyla's face, hair, and dress. She recoiled from the horror of it all, as Raja released his grip and fell to the floor, landing in a supinated position, with his head contorted from the bullet's lethal inertia. Blood oozed from the clean, one-centimeter entrance wound, while the back of his skull was gone.

Leyla was now motionless, psychologically paralyzed, stunned by what had just happened.

"Got the son of a bitch," Bobby said, as Alvarado and the pilot cheered. "Clean through, boys. Clean through. *Like ducks in a pond.* Right through the front observation ledge window." Bobby refocused, reloaded. He was ready for the next target. *What a bitchin' shot*, he thought to himself.

Then, "Boss, step back," Bobby said to Alec.

Alec stepped back to clear the way for Bobby's next target, leaving him out of reach of Leyla.

Alvarado quickly gave Bobby the updated coordinates and the constantly changing wind speed out of the west. He quickly computed the bullet's potential drift. Then, the second shot from Big Dawg found its mark, as it slammed into the building's tinted glass like a laser and ripped through the center of al-Jalili's neck, all but decapitating him, his body falling onto an elderly woman. The two hit the ground simultaneously with a noticeable thud. A female college student quickly helped the blood-spattered elderly woman, now hysterical, to her feet. Everyone was horrified by the sight of al-Jalili's body sprawled on the Skydeck's floor, his spinal column visible from the near decapitation.

With the sight of his brother and al-Jalili lying lifeless on the floor, Raissi said, as if hot steam were passing through his clenched teeth, "Allah will avenge the deaths of my brothers." Veins bulged on both sides of his forehead, while a sinister smile grew on his round face. "And you my friend," he said with great intensity, aiming his gun at Alec. "You will die with the rest of them. *Iradat Allah*, it is Allah's will."

Every person on the Skydeck stared at the dirty bomb's digital clock. The tension was palpable. The fear was ever-present. The future was very uncertain.

00:24:44, 00:24:43, 00:24:42.

Leyla's nerves were riddled by the horror of it all. She stumbled over Raja's body and rushed to Alec's arms. Words failed the both of them, but their eyes spoke volumes. Shielding her from Raissi's line of sight with his body, Alec faced him. "Why?" was his first thought. "Why you?"

Mackay and Nutworth took new positions along the perimeter of the Skydeck, thermal guns in hand, waiting to unleash the deadly power of thermal offensive technology if necessary. Josiah remained on the perimeter as well, his Myotron II at the ready. Pratt had returned to street level to coordinate communication with OS9, HRT, FBI, and local authorities.

The platinum Rolex dominated Raissi's left wrist below the cuff of his suit jacket. The revolver was still present in his right hand.

"Only I hold the power," Raissi said, with the tone of a diabolical martinet. "For you see, the suitcase you are looking at contains a dirty bomb. Yes, a bomb that will spread radioactive particles throughout this city of non-believers and kill them all. You hear me? Kill them all!"

The words *dirty bomb* caused further panic to reverberate through the minds of those in earshot.

Raissi, aware of the helicopter still hovering a few hundred meters off his right shoulder, stayed behind a support column. Surveying the situation, he knew that if he did not act quickly, his plans would fail. He knew he *must prevail for the Khamsin, for his Muslim brothers, for Allah.*

Alec spoke aloud. "This is not the way. You will kill thousands of innocent people."

"*Ya sahibi*, my good friend. You were once my friend and there are no innocent people. I am saddened that our friendship has come to this. We thought in time you would become one of us. Americans, their European allies, and the Zionist dogs kill my Muslim brothers without cause…in Afghanistan, Iraq, and Palestine. For centuries, the innocent people you speak of have slaughtered my brothers. They have given us no peace, no life, only war and death. And now you say that I should not do this. That innocent people will die. Let them." He finished, first glancing at his watch. "It is now their turn to die, and now," taking a quick gulp of air, "it is your turn to die for my brother's death and for the deaths of Allah's children."

Alec saw it. He saw the watch. It all made sense. There it was. He saw the unusual bezel that had two extra push buttons on its side. Now only some ten feet away, his exosuit's electronic sensors picked up signals emanating from Raissi's watch. Alec reasoned that the watch had an electronic connection to the ticking time bomb just feet away.

It was a gut instinct.

He had to get the watch.

Now! *Move now*! With the élan of a hungry tiger, Alec lunged forward, pushing Leyla out of the way. Raissi hesitated for a split second, shocked by the unexpected action. The lunge was directly at Raissi's gun hand. Before he could respond, Alec's forward motion took Raissi to the ground much like an alligator takes his prey down in a death roll. They rolled toward the elevator doors. Raissi broke loose and stood up. He took aim at Alec. The first shot hit on his left side, spinning him around. Thankfully, under the NOMEX, the exosuit's reflexive armor worked again. Although the close-range shot knocked the wind out of him, he was able to get up. In that moment, Raissi, rushing to the elevator, accidentally dropped his gun. He watched in disbelief, as it slid across the floor, just out-of-reach. He knew that he had no time to retrieve it, so he ran for the nearest elevator and pushed the button that would take him down twelve floors to the rooftop entrance of one of the building's modules where a Hughes 369 Cayuse helicopter waited for him.

Alec rushed for the elevator, but he was too late. The doors had closed. As he darted for a second elevator, he yelled back to Mackay, "Mackie, let me know which floor he stops at. And get everyone out of here!" Alec disappeared behind the closed doors of the elevator. He waited.

"Sirrr," Mackay said, speaking into his lip mike.

"What floor Mackie? What floor?" he begged to know.

"The 91st, sirrr. The 91st," came the answer.

Alec pushed the number 91 and down it went. The doors opened seconds later. He scanned the corridor in both directions. Eying a rooftop access door ajar, he rushed toward it and saw Raissi running for the helicopter. The pilot waited anxiously, as Raissi, out of breath, took his last steps closer. The wind atop the module's roof had slowed him down. Then a swift gust knocked his feet out from under him. Alec lunged, grabbing Raissi's left leg. As the two struggled, rolling over and over, the helicopter's downward thrusts of wind from the main rotor's wash blew small bits of dirt into their eyes. Blinded for a moment, Alec tried to clear his eyes with his finger. It was then that Raissi picked up a two-foot piece of steel scaffolding pole left behind by the building's maintenance crew. With his eyes now blurred by the dust, he swung it wildly at Alec. Alec managed to deflect the steel pole with his right forearm. Raissi swung again, missing him. He tried yet again, but this time Alec caught the steel pole and thrust it back at him. Raissi stumbled backward, but regained his balance. Alec charged him. He hit Raissi with an elbow to the left cheekbone, stunning him, drawing blood. Alec then reached for the wristwatch, yet Raissi managed to resist the attempt. He turned away and ran the final few steps to the helicopter.

Within just a foot of the helicopter, he ordered the pilot, "Go now."

The command confused the pilot.

"Go now!" Raissi repeated in desperation.

The pilot began to rev up the jet engine and pull back on the cyclic stick. As the helicopter started to lift off, Raissi leaped for the right door. Grabbing for Raissi's left arm, Alec tore the Rolex wristwatch from his wrist. Holding the watch in his hand, Alec held his breath a moment and looked at Raissi. He had one foot on the landing skid and one hand on the door latch, as the helicopter lifted off. Some 1,200 feet above Wacker Drive, he struggled to hold on, but it proved futile.

The evening news would report that the world-renowned industrialist and philanthropist Dr. Raymond Raissi fell to his death today from the Willis Tower. *The exact reason for his death was under investigation.*

00:11:59, 00:11:58, 00:11:57.

CHAPTER EIGHTY-SEVEN

Alec watched as Raissi plummeted to his death below. The police had already cordoned off the area around the base of the tower for a radius of some three hundred feet and had dispersed many of the locals, gawkers, and reporters before the body met the pavement. Even from 1,200 feet up, Alec had a very clear sense of the impact of Raissi's body. For the moment, he relished the thought that on the way down Raissi had enough time to realize his impending death in such a humiliating manner. With mild curiosity, he continued to watch, as Raissi's body, his arms flailing desperately, finally exploded on the pavement below. Alec heard no sound. It was a silent death.

With the Rolex in hand, its broken band dangling from the sides of the case, Alec raced back to the elevator. By then Josiah had appeared and said, "Sir, Mackie and Nutworth have evacuated your wife and the others from the Skydeck."

Alec breathed a sigh of relief. He had no time to think beyond the moment now that his wife was safe. He then moved quickly toward the elevator, as he said, "Come with me, now!"

Alec and Josiah rode the service elevator to the Skydeck. Once inside, Alec hurried over to the dirty bomb. "Josiah," he said, staring first at the dirty bomb and then at him. Alec looked closely at the digital clock. The countdown was getting closer to the detonation time. He looked intently at the watch. "Something on this watch is connected to the bomb detonator. I just know it."

Josiah leaned in next to Alec and scrutinized the face of the Rolex.

"Get Pratt up here ASAP!" Alec ordered loudly. He then pushed the first button on the side. *Nothing.*

00:04:25, 00:04:24, 00:04:23.

He pushed the second button and waited. *Still nothing.*

00:04:14, 00:04:13, 00:04:12.

Security team members were now present and sensed the immediacy of the moment. There was little time left and they knew it.

Josiah cautioned, "Please don't contaminate the crime scene. Make sure that only those who can present the proper credentials be allowed anywhere near this area."

Other members of the building's security force and police officers continued to scour every floor to make sure that everyone had been evacuated to safety and that there were no other assailants in the building.

Alec tried endless combinations of the buttons. His mind narrowed in on the task at hand, as if he were in the most delicate phase of a skull-base surgery to remove a massive, life-threatening tumor.

00:01:16, 00:01:15, 00:01:14.

Thinking for a tense moment, Alec pushed twice on both buttons simultaneously. Everyone stood mute, looking at the dirty bomb's digital screen.

*The clock stopped ticking...*00:00:55.

Enter Code: _____ appeared above the frozen digital time readout.

"It's deactivated," Alec uttered, his sense of relief obvious. Everyone else took a deep breath and just stared at the digital clock frozen on the time 00:00:55.

"It's not active now, but we need the code to defuse it."

Josiah said, "Sir, what do you mean?"

"I mean that we've stopped the bomb from exploding, but it could still be deadly. They've probably built into it a motion detector, and the slightest movement sets it off. It most likely contains dynamite or some other explosive substance to initiate dispersal of the radioactive substance. The wind does the rest. It would be catastrophic. I mean catastrophic with a capital 'C.' It has to be defused. There's a code. A code that we don't know. If the code is not entered within a specific period, I'm betting the triggering mechanism probably reactivates the detonator. It's kind of like a computer's reboot," Alec said with disquiet in his voice.

Alec circled the *dirty bomb* still strapped to the support column on the Skydeck. He stopped and leaned down. His discerning eyes scanned the dirty bomb.

The digital readout still read...*Enter Code*: _____

CHAPTER EIGHTY-EIGHT

Pratt arrived on the Skydeck, half out of breath, but with computer in hand.

"Pratt, we need the bomb squad. Get them in here. The bomb's been deactivated, but it has to be defused. It may have a mercury device, or some other type of motion detector that prevents it from being moved without setting it off."

Fire Chief Bill Monarch, three other safety officers, and the police department's bomb experts were now on the Skydeck level with Alec.

A plump-sized man in his early fifties approached Alec. "Mist—," Fire Chief Monarch said.

Alec interrupted. "The bomb's been deactivated for now, but as you can see, it requires a code to defuse it." He pointed to the bomb and said, "I interrupted the countdown sequence at precisely *fifty-five seconds before detonation.*"

Scratching the back of his neck, Fire Chief Monarch studied the situation and replied, "Well, sir. I'm thankful you managed to stop the process with only seconds to spare, but who are you? Why are you here?"

"I am with a special governmental unit," he answered with reserve in his voice. "My name is Dr. Hakimian. Dr. Alexander Hakimian."

"What does that mean, *a special governmental unit?* And what does *ACC Services* on the back of your suit stand for?" he threw back at Alec.

"I wish I could tell you more, but I am not at liberty to do so. And if I did, then I'd have to kill you," he said, half jokingly, breaking the tension of the moment. "As for the name on the back of my suit, let's just say that we take out the trash. How's that for an answer?" he added rather sarcastically.

Several police officers exited the service elevator. Among them was the city's assistant police chief, Lew Risk, a man with more than thirty years experience in protecting a city the size of Chicago.

"Bill, what do we have here?" questioned Assistant Police Chief Risk.

"This man here, Dr. Hakimian," motioning to Alec next to him, "has stopped the bomb from going off."

"Excuse me, doctor. Is that correct? You are a doctor?" he said, with doubt as to Alec's credibility and authority.

"That's correct, I am a medical doctor," Alec answered with mild disdain in his voice.

"So...you are here because...?" the assistant police chief asked. He eyed the large letters on the back of his black NOMEX suit: ACC Services. "What's ACC?"

"As I explained to Chief Monarch, I am not able to be more specific other than to say that I and my men are part of a special governmental unit that was in search of this RDD. More than that, I can't say, other than if you need more information you can contact Special Agent Olufsson at FBI headquarters in Washington."

Just then, Special Agent Douglas of the FBI's Chicago HRT unit arrived. Looking at Assistant Police Chief Risk, he said, "Chief, I am Special Agent Douglas of the FBI's HRT unit here in Chicago. Dr. Hakimian is here because my unit has been working with him and his team to find this bomb."

"I understand," he said, in a condescending tone.

"I'd like to have your men and my HRT expert neutralize this dirty bomb. We've got to get it out of here," remarked Special Agent Douglas.

"Chief," a police officer said to Assistant Police Chief Risk, "it's your office," handing him a cellular phone.

"Unless it's very important, take a message," he barked back.

The chaos below the Shydeck was ginning up.

Turning around to Alec, he continued, "Doctor, do you have any idea what the code might be? I mean, who put this son of a bitch here? Do you know? Some fuckin' psycho I'll bet," he said, scanning the area. "You know, I love it every time I come up here. What a view. I can see the river runnin' way out. Goddamn beautiful, I'd say."

Alec thought briefly, as to how much he should say. "I'm not at liberty to reveal much, but what I can tell you is that the bomb was placed here by a group whose capabilities are very sophisticated."

The assistant police chief looked at Alec and wondered what he meant. "Sir, we need to defuse this bomb and we need your help," he said.

With everyone now standing around the dirty bomb, Josiah said to Alec, "The code's got to be something that makes sense to the Khamsin. After all, Raissi did orchestrate this whole thing. He probably set it up with a code that meant something to him or his cause."

Josiah and Alec were feeling crowded by those standing above them. "Gentlemen, would you please step back so that we can get this done?" Josiah said in a perturbed tone.

Assistant Police Chief Risk, Fire Chief Monarch, and the others looked at Josiah with incredulity, but obeyed.

Just then, several more police officers and firemen entered the Skydeck. "Please keep the men back," Fire Chief Monarch said to one of his captains.

Alec and Josiah knew that they had to bring the bomb squad in to assist, but that they had to be careful as to how much information they should reveal regarding why they were there and what the mission was about.

Sergeant John Bronte, the police department's top bomb expert, interrupted. In a loud voice, he said, "I've seen this type of setup for a radiological dispersion device before in a tech manual. The actual detonation device is somewhat complicated. It sends a wireless electronic signal to the dirty bomb's countdown device. The signal is a specific, high-frequency one that only the detonator can identify. By the way, this mother probably has a mercury device, so if we try to freeze it, it'll blow. Whoever built this was no idiot. Probably a degree in engineering I'd say." Looking at the watch Alec was holding, he added, "That watch must have a special electronic oscillator that generates a certain frequency which, like I said, communicates directly with the dirty bomb's digital detonation device. But I'll tell you what worries me. Remember about three months ago that the Fermi Lab, west of the city, reported to the IAEA that three kilograms of Plutonium-239 had disappeared? It never made the papers. Wonder why? In fact, of the 20,000 plus companies, agencies, and organizations that have and use nuclear materials, the security at many of these places is often minimal at best. Actually, there's a theft of nuclear material on average, once a day. That's right, you heard me, once a day," he said explosively. "Anyway, what if that's what's in this suitcase or something like it? That shit'll kill a whole lot of people. I mean, the city'd be gone," he said pedantically.

"Thanks John, now I feel much better," the assistant police chief said, furrowing his deep brow, and chuckling under his breath.

Alec was unimpressed by the short course on nuclear nonsense. Turning to Josiah, he said, as he looked intently at the dirty bomb's ominous black exterior, "I agree with you. Raissi was a megalomaniac of the first magnitude. He would do something that one, he'd remember, and two, that made sense to him. Something that would demonstrate his control. Something that had his signature."

Bronte questioned, "This Racy guy. Who was he?"

Alec turned to the now apprehensive Bronte and said, "He's the man responsible for what we're looking at."

"The arrogant asshole," Josiah chimed in.

"Well, maybe the guy set the code based on something that showed who he was. Like what the doctor said. You know, computer hackers sometimes break into systems by first trying names and or numbers that have meaning to the owner of the computer. For example, I'll bet that the password for my neighbor's computer is probably the name of his dog, child, or favorite baseball team. You get what I mean?" Sergeant Bronte said.

Alec was already there. He had been searching his mental database for the answer. He questioned aloud, *could Raissi have created a code based upon the Arabic language? Was the code something like Mecca or Medina?* Then he questioned, *what about Khamsin?*

The irony of it all, Alec had no idea that Sahar had given the wristwatch to Raissi as a gift. Staring at the Rolex, he still held in his left hand, he examined it more closely. He noticed that next to each of the two additional buttons on the right side of the watch's case there was a number. When he pushed the first button, the number changed, very much like the *date* feature on watches of such quality. Pushing the second button did the same.

There must be a sequence of numbers that defused the dirty bomb, he thought aloud. *If so, possibly the numbers have some value beyond simply their numerical value.* He remembered as a young boy in Beirut, he and his friends had a secret club that met on the second floor of a deserted apartment building in the neighborhood. The password for admittance to the club's meeting place was a word translated into a sequence of numbers that corresponded to each letter's numerical value in the Arabic alphabet and each boy had to figure it out. *Could it be that he constructed the code the very same way? That the code was a series of numbers translated from a word or words?*

"Josiah," Alec said. "I have an idea. What do you think about the code being a series of numbers that correspond to a word in Arabic? That word could be rendered as a sequence of numbers that designate the numbered position of each letter in the Arabic alphabet. What do you think? I know it sounds crazy, maybe even too simplistic, but it's certainly worth a try."

"What are you guys talking about?" Sergeant Bronte asked.

"Just follow me," Alec said point-blank.

Holding the watch out for Josiah and Sergeant Bronte to see, Alec began. "Let's try the word *Khamsin*. The 'Kh' is represented by one letter in the Arabic alphabet and its numerical equivalent is '7.' Since the 'a' in Khamsin is silent, there is no numerical equivalent. The next letter is 'm,' whose numerical equivalent is '24.' The 's' is the 12th letter. The 'I' is the 28th letter of the alphabet, and 'n' is the 25th letter." Alec pushed the first button until the watch's special dial read "7." He decided to push the second button until it read "24." He alternated buttons until he had entered the five numbers corresponding to the five Arabic letters in the word Khamsin, but nothing happened on the digital clock. "Well, either Khamsin is not the word or the buttons have to be pushed in another sequence, or I'm all wet. The permutations are endless."

Alec now fingered the watch in his right hand, thinking of his next move. He took another close look at its face, hoping to divine the answer to the code. He rubbed his thumb over the watch's protective crystal, then around its bezel. Then, for some inexplicable reason, he looked where he had not looked before, on the back of the watch. He saw the marks and numbers that Rolex stamped onto the back plate of every watch it made in Switzerland. It was part of the identification and authentication process. Running his fingers over the stampings, he saw that everything was as it should be, except for a string of numbers that were obviously engraved on the watch after it had left the factory. They read 18, 25, 22, 2, 27, and 3.

Thinking about the Arabic alphabet equivalent for each number, Alec began, "The the number '18' represents 'A.' Next, the number '25' represents 'N.' Then comes 'K' and the number '22'." He did not need to say anymore, he did not need to compute anything else. There it was, in cipher, *A N K A B U T, the spider.* It was Raissi being himself. It was Raissi, the spider. "Yes, the Ankabut!" he said aloud.

Everyone on the Skydeck was stunned.

Alec said nothing for a moment. Then, "It all makes sense now. It's very simple. It was right before our eyes, the perfect place to hide it. But now, what button in what sequence?"

Turning to Pratt, he said, "Pratt, I want you to run an algorithm that can tell me in what sequence I need to punch these two buttons using the numbers *18, 25, 22, 2, 27, 3.* And give me probabilities, percentages. We don't have all day. I'm convinced that these two buttons are what Raissi used to activate the dirty bomb. He wouldn't have come here if he didn't have the ability to deactivate and defuse it if plans changed," he said, with certainty.

Special Agent Douglas, who had just returned to the Skydeck moments before, asked, "Dr. Hakimian, do you think it'll work?"

Looking at Special Agent Douglas, he said, "Do we have any other choice? Do you want to take the chance that this son of a bitch doesn't have a motion detector inside?"

Pratt inputted the numbers and hit enter. The military notebook computer's hard drive light was flashing, while row after row of data came spewing forth onto the Organic LED screen from a software program designed to ferret out the percentages and probabilities that Alec had requested.

"So, what have you got?" Alec queried, with the others waiting at a distance in rapt anticipation.

"Just about there, sir," Pratt said judiciously.

They all watched intently, as the permutations of numbers scrolled down the screen, sequence after sequence, percentage after percentage, page after page. Then, "Sir," Pratt proclaimed, "here's the sequences and percentages you asked for."

Alec leaned in closer to the computer screen. He started to analyze and dissect the numbers.

"So what is it?" an anxious Sergeant Bronte asked.

"Here's what we have," Alec began. "The probability that the numerical sequence 18, 25, 22, 2, 27, 3 represents the word *Ankabut* is 97.3%. Also, according to the Thomson Permutation Sequence Formula, the numbers here indicate that the buttons should be pushed as follows...."

Alec started to push each button as Josiah spoke. "Push the first button until the number '18' appears, then push both simultaneously. Next, push the first button again until the number '25' appears and do the same. Then push the second button until the number '22' appears. Now push both buttons at the same time again. Now back to the first button. Push it until the '2' appears. By the way, '2' is a prime number. Now repeat by pushing the two buttons at the same time again. That leaves the numbers '27' and '3' to deal with."

Alec had many of those in the room wondering what he was doing. Numbers intimidated most people, many of whom had trouble reconciling their checkbooks. The bomb experts did things differently, but since they had no answers, they were glad that Alec took the lead. Working with numbers to deactivate an explosive device was certainly not their bailiwick.

After Alec entered the final numbers and was about to push the two buttons simultaneously for the last time, Sergeant Bronte, cringing a bit, asked with uncertainty in his deep voice, "Are we sure that we want to do this? What if it blows?"

With a wry smile, Alec responded somewhat flippantly, "It won't matter, will it?"

"Wait a minute, doctor," Assistant Police Chief Risk said in his best police officer's voice, all the while waving his arms back and forth. "This doesn't seem right."

"Then what does?" Alec said.

His answer was unspoken…. He did not know.

All eyes were locked on the dirty bomb's digital clock. The time *00:00:55* was still frozen in straight, red lines. Above it, the words *Enter Code* were still visible. Then Alec just did it, pushing both buttons at the same time.

Beep…beep…beep could be heard. Every heart in the room was almost in a state of tachycardia. They saw the countdown clock start again. The beeping was now as loud to each person watching as the pounding of Thor's hammer on an anvil.

00:00:04, 00:00:03, 00:00:02, 00:00:01, 00:00:00, and then the digital clock flat-lined as it showed a series of dashes and then the words *"Deactivation Complete"* appeared.

Alec smiled.

It was over.

The sweat on brows began to evaporate.

Alec had won the race to deactivate and defuse the dirty bomb.

CHAPTER EIGHTY-NINE

Hordes of employees continued to pour out of the Willis Tower. Police officers and firefighters kept delivery trucks, taxicabs, and the like at bay.

Special Agent Douglas spoke to Special Agent Rupert, who informed him that Special Agents Happer and Jefferson arrested both Hanifa and al-Shami at the Marriott Hotel. He learned that Omar Radhi, another of Raja's hirelings, disappeared into the crowd at O'Hare International Airport. Agents were unable to apprehend him but were now combing the area.

It was nearing 5:00 P.M., as Alec, Josiah, Assistant Police Chief Risk, and Fire Chief Monarch stepped out of the tower's first floor foyer. Sergeant Bronte, the bomb squad expert, followed with the suitcase dirty bomb in tow. Several police officers stayed behind on the Skydeck to assist forensics in the criminal investigation.

The FBI still insisted that news helicopters keep their distance, while the ground media resisted demands at every turn to stay behind the police lines setup to control the curious and unnecessary.

Alec saw both FBI and local police officials questioning people that were on the Skydeck during the crisis. He searched about for Leyla. "Where's my wife?" he demanded to know, asking one of the police officers. "Where's my wife Leyla Hakimian?" he repeated.

As the police officer was about to answer, Special Agent Douglas approached Alec. He placed a hand on his shoulder and said politely, "Dr. Hakimian, your wife was taken to the triage center for observation."

Alec's heart dropped. "What do you mean for observation?"

"Sir, an emergency medical technician attending to evacuees said that she was complaining of light headedness and blurred vision."

"Where's the triage center?" Alec fired back.

"There," he said, pointing to a group of large, white medical trucks bivouacked across the street and marked with the ubiquitous Red Cross insignia.

Alec scrambled across the street to the trucks. Speaking to a police officer standing at the entrance to the portable triage center, he asked quickly, "Where is Leyla Hakimian, Mrs. Leyla Hakimian?"

"I don't know, sir. You'll have to ask one of the EMTs."

Alec spotted an emergency medical technician crossing behind the officer. Waving his hand, he said, "Excuse me. Excuse me, but where are you keeping Leyla Hakimian? Thirty-two, dark hair, very attractive."

The *very attractive* part of the description caught the man's attention. "Oh! She's over there in that unit," he said, pointing to a very large, white eighteen-wheel semi truck directly behind him.

"Thank-you," Alec said, his heart beginning to pound, almost leaping out of his chest. He was a man whose work constantly put him on the edge, and he dealt with it with equanimity of emotion…grace under pressure. But now it was his wife, the wife that he had not seen for months, with the exception of a few short moments on the Skydeck. He knew the time apart had tested their relationship, once again. It had tested him in ways that he had no control over. His life had always been about control, but not now. *Once the trauma had passed*, he thought, *would she ever again embrace him with the same love and desire she had for him before? Would his daughter ever say daddy again?* He knew that he had pushed his marriage beyond the limits of normality, but in spite of everything, he hoped that it was reconcilable.

Alec stepped up into the van's entry. Introducing himself to one of the nurses walking about, he said, "I'm Dr. Hakimian, and I'm looking for my wife Leyla. Leyla Hakimian."

The female nurse stared at Alec's NOMEX suit for a moment, thinking that he had just dropped in from the latest Ninja movie.

With his impatience growing, Alec persisted, "Where's my wife, Leyla Hakimian?"

"Follow me, doctor," the nurse offered, looking Alec over with the inquisitiveness of a grammar school student.

Alec walked back to a room in the rear of the large triage unit. There she was, attended to by a physician taking her vitals while a nurse adjusted an intravenous saline drip.

He stopped and stared. She was the most beautiful woman in the world to him. Her face, pale. Her eyelids, shut. Stepping closer, Alec spoke to the doctor attending his wife. "Doctor, I am Alexander Hakimian, Dr. Alexander Hakimian. I am her husband." Concern was visible on his bearded face.

"Dr. Hakimian, I am Dr. Burchfield," the lanky, rather befuddled looking doctor said, in a voice laden with an annoying nasal quality. Extending his hand to Alec, he continued, "Your wife's blood pressure was 72/57; she felt faint; and her vision was blurred. Does she have any medical conditions?"

"No. None," Alec said flatly.

"Fine, but she still needs to rest here for a while and we need to get more fluids in her before we can release her."

Alec said nothing. He just focused on Leyla lying in the bed, the intravenous drip in her arm, her body weighed down by the events of the day. "Thank-you, doctor," he said with exasperation in his voice.

Suddenly, Leyla's big, dark eyes fluttered open. She looked at Alec. A smile grew across her porcelain-skinned face. She tried to speak, but the energy just was not there yet.

"Don't speak, *hamov*," he said. "I am with you now." She smiled again, trying to lift her hand. Alec held it softly, kissing it several times. She drifted off again.

"We gave her a mild sedative," Dr. Burchfield said in a whisper.

Suddenly, "I must see Dr. Hakimian," came a voice from behind.

"Sorry sir, but —"

"I said, I have to speak with Dr. Hakimian," Special Agent Douglas said sternly, showing his FBI credentials.

Alec turned around and walked toward him. "What is it?"

"Two of my agents at O'Hare just received word that Dr. Raissi's airplane is scheduled to take off within an hour. The pilot filed a flight plan for London."

"Do you know who's on the plane?" Alec asked instantly.

"Seems that this woman Sahar Tayyim was thought to be aboard, but we can't confirm it."

"Can you hold the plane?"

"We need probable cause," he answered.

"What do you mean *probable cause*?" Alec said, with both restraint and disbelief in his voice, as he stood tall next to Leyla's bed.

"I mean that DHS in Washington has said that if we don't have a damn good reason to stop the pla—"

Alec interrupted him in mid-sentence. "That's Raissi's plane, damn it. He was the man who tried to set off a dirty bomb that would have killed thousands of people in this city. He was the leader of the world's deadliest terrorist organization, and she was his girlfriend. If that's not probable cause…," he ended.

Special Agent Douglas went silent.

Still standing in the doorway of the triage unit, Alec waited for his response.

"My hands are tied, Dr. Hakimian. There are rules," Special Agent Douglas said categorically.

With fury in his voice, Alec fired back, "Break the *effing* rules Douglas. That plane's got to be stopped. It can't take off! You hear me?"

"Let me make some calls," he said reluctantly, and promptly disappeared.

Alec returned to Leyla's bedside. "Dr. Burchfield," he said. "What's her B.P. now?"

"It's now 101/65. She's looking better. We won't know about the dizziness and blurred vision until we get her up in about two hours."

"I can tell you that her B.P. is normally low," Alec informed the doctor.

Seeing the concern on Alec's face, he said, "Doctor, we'll take care of her. You needn't worry. Now why don't you get some coffee and something to eat, and I'll let you know when she can be released."

Alec stepped aside for a moment and called Assistant Police Chief Risk. "Chief Risk, I'm here in the triage unit. My wife's asleep now and won't be released for about two hours. I need a favor from you. Can you arrange to have her taken to the Palmer House. I need to get to O'Hare before Raissi's plane takes-off. Please make her comfortable, and tell her that I'll be there ASAP, but don't tell her where I'm going."

"Dr. Hakimian, I will gladly take care of her for you," the assistant police chief answered.

Alec took one last look at his sleeping Leyla. He leaned over and gave her a gentle kiss on the forehead, then turned on his heels and walked out of the triage unit. Once outside, he ran across the street cluttered with law enforcement and emergency vehicles. Bobby, Alvarado, and Josiah were there waiting next to the police operations truck. Nutworth, Pratt, and Mackay appeared moments later.

"What's up, Doc," Bobby said laughingly.

Alec tried to find humor in the comment, but he just could not. He sighted Special Agent Douglas in his dark blue FBI windbreaker at the end of the block talking to three police officers. Alec began to move in his direction when Special Agent Douglas noticed him a second time. He excused himself from the men he was conversing with and walked briskly toward Alec. In a somewhat loud voice, Alec beckoned to special Agent Douglas. "I need this Suburban," he demanded.

Special Agent Douglas could not quite hear Alec. He continued to walk closer.

Alec repeated his request. "I need this vehicle," pointing to the big Suburban parked across the street.

"What for?" came back instantly.

"I'm going to O'Hare and I need your ride," came the response.

"Doctor, you can't. Washington said no! And besides, it's government property," he added emphatically, finally feeling a sense of power over Alec.

Alec did not acknowledge the response and said curtly, "I'm going to the airport. What about a chopper?"

"But doctor, we do not have probable cause. And a chopper is absolutely out of the question. It can't be cleared, even if I wanted to. As I said, 'there's no probable cause here.' We can't just stop a plane without —"

Alec cut him off in mid-sentence again. "You're wasting my time," he said, looking at his watch.

"But —"

"There's no but. Do I have to make a call?" Alec said, furrowing his dark brows. He was serious. "If I do —"

Special Agent Douglas acquiesced, sensing the obvious. "Well, doctor." Hesitating for a moment, he continued, "Let us say that I have no idea what you are talking about." *Alec had just trumped him again and he didn't like it.*

"Boys, get in," came the order from Alec, as he summoned his men.

Special Agent Douglas turned the other way in an effort to make a case for *plausible deniability* should his superiors question him about how and why Alec took his vehicle and the law into his own hands.

The black, tinted-windowed Suburban screeched out from in front of the Willis Tower. Alec drove through the first police barricade and then the second. Police officers scattered like bowling pins as he stepped hard on the accelerator. In a few minutes, he was rocketing west down the I-290 headed to O'Hare. Billowy, gray clouds occluded the sun's last rays of the day as the Suburban continued down the Eisenhower Expressway with its red and blue grill lights flashing. Cars slowed down and quickly pulled to the side. Suddenly, two state troopers on motorcycles drew up on the Suburban, their lights and sirens on. Alec refused to pull over. One motorcycle came up closer on the passenger side and motioned for him to pull over. Bobby put the window down and tried his best to speak to the trooper, but the wind and expressway noise made it impossible. By now, the second trooper had approached the driver's side. He too tried to tell Alec to pull over, but to no avail.

Alec continued to push the Suburban to its limit. He was grateful that the FBI had ordered the vehicle with the police interceptor option that included a stiffer suspension and a more powerful engine. As the airport came into view, the motorcycle troopers were still trying to force Alec to stop. At the entrance to O'Hare, Alec saw two local police cruisers blocking the entrance. "Well boys, shall we?" he said with an impish grin on his face. The Suburban jumped the curb, hit a light pole, and then plowed through a three-foot high hedgerow. The landing was hard, but the Suburban kept moving. The motorcycle troopers skidded to an abrupt stop in front of the police cruisers.

"When I pull up to the entrance," Alec said loudly to Bobby, "you jump out and go directly to the airport authorities and tell them that I have an FBI order to detain Raissi's plane!"

Bobby knew there was no FBI order, but he did not care. He would have said the same thing to stop the plane from leaving.

The black Suburban rolled up close to the main entrance. A dozen police cruisers and several of the airport's security detail had blocked it. Alec suddenly slowed to about five miles per hour and Bobby jumped out. He instantly darted toward a side entrance before anyone could stop him. Alec then brought the Suburban to a skidding stop, as police cruisers and officers with their guns drawn, encircled him.

"Get the hell out of the vehicle. All of you. Hands in the air now, assholes," an angry police officer ordered.

Alec and his men stepped out of the Suburban with their hands in the air, laughing under their breaths.

"What in the fuck are you shitheads doing?" another officer asked.

As Alec was about to explain, Special Agent Douglas arrived in another black Suburban, red lights flashing. Approaching the state troopers and airport security now congregated around OS9, he said sharply, "Stand down." Waving his FBI badge in the air, he repeated, "Stand down. Holster your weapons."

State Trooper Pete Gall exclaimed, "What is this?"

Special Agent Douglas answered, "I'm Special Agent Douglas of the FBI's Hostage Rescue team and these men are —"

"Wait," State Trooper Gall interrupted over the sounds of a jet taking off. He removed his hat and scratched his hairless head several times. "Just before I came on duty, I heard that officers were needed at the Willis Tower because of a bomb, and now I see an unidentified man jump out of a blacked-out SUV and race into the airport terminal to do what? This is post 9/11, sir," he added sternly. "What am I supposed to think?"

"Like I was about to say Trooper Gall, these men are part of a team that was hunting the bomber at the Willis Tower. Now that he's been captured, I mean dead, they are in pursuit of his accomplices that are believed to be aboard a private aircraft here at the airport," Special Agent Douglas said with urgency.

"Yeah. So, walk me through this, Special Agent Douglas," State Trooper Gall demanded, grinding his teeth loudly.

"We need to get into the airport and stop the plane," Alec interrupted.

As Special Agent Douglas turned to answer the police officer, Alec and the rest of OS9 rushed into the airport.

The very moment Alec entered the busy terminal, Bobby came running back toward him, a look of disappointment on his face. "Bobby, what's up?"

With labored breath, he said, "Sir, Raissi's plane was rolling down the runway as I got to TSA's security office. We missed it by seconds, sir. By seconds," he said with frustration.

"Did you ask why they let the plane leave?"

"The conning tower gave them a priority take-off," Bobby said, still gasping for air to fill his burning lungs.

"Why?" Alec demanded to know.

"Didn't say, sir."

Alec ran outside and gazed upward into the approaching dusk. Focusing his eyes, then refocusing, he caught a glimpse of the arctic-white Global Petroleum Resources Boeing 767 banking northward. Emblazoned on its tail was the silhouette of a gigantic, black raven.

Even in death, Raissi made a statement.

CHAPTER NINETY

Massive klieg lights illuminated the area around the Willis Tower as if it were a three-ring circus under the *big top*. A continuous din of ambulance and police sirens continued to pollute the air, as police helicopters moved across the airspace looking for anything out of the ordinary. People were running about in peripatetic fashion searching for loved ones; journalists were hunting for the next hot story; and the roar of city buses moving others out of the police zone served only to add to the chaos. Special Agent Douglas, fighting to be heard above the sirens, spoke into Alec's ear, "Dr. Hakimian. Listen, my men will finish up here, but you and your men have been called to meet with the president and then later to be debriefed by the suits at the NSA."

"What did you say?" Alec asked with incredulity.

"I said that Homeland Security just informed me a few minutes ago that the President of the United States wants to see you and your men, pronto. A plane's waiting at Meigs Field. Sounds very important. Very secret," he intoned, with a suggestion of jealousy in his voice.

Alec had anticipated the debriefing by the NSA, *but the President of the United States...and now!*

CHAPTER NINETY-ONE

The Air Force designated Gulfstream 100, courtesy of the 201st Airlift Squadron, had just arrived from Andrews Air Force Base in Maryland, when the two FBI black Suburbans carrying the members of Operation Star 9 suddenly rolled onto the Meigs Field tarmac.

The Chicago Department of Public Works had converted Meigs Field, formerly known as Northerly Island, into a local airport in 1946. Although the runaway was short for a G100, the pilot had landed there many times before, and knew he had to push it to get lift-off. The Department of Homeland Security chose Meigs Field because of its controlled accessibility. It was essentially an island unto itself just off Chicago's Lake Shore Drive opposite Burnham Park.

After refueling, the twin Honeywell TFE 731-40R jet engines spooled up again, emitting an ear splitting, growing whine. OS9 exited the Suburban and walked straight toward the aircraft. Air Force Lieutenant Colonel Val Kozlow stood at the stairs leading up to the main cabin, flagged by two junior officers. Saluting Alec and his men, the lieutenant colonel said with military clarity, "Gentlemen, I am Lieutenant Colonel Val Kozlow."

Alec and the others returned the lieutenant colonel's salute.

"Please, get onboard. Once we are wheels up, you'll be briefed. As you have probably surmised by now, this flight is *top-secret* on the orders of POTUS," he said without expression.

Lt. Colonel Kozlow, a thirty-two year veteran of the Air Force and three wars, was hardtack hard. He was the kind of military officer who bled red, white, and blue, and never questioned a direct order.

Once inside, Bobby rushed to stake his claim to a corner of the small sofa in the rear of the cabin. Alec and the others took their places in the oversized seats that lined both sides of the cabin. The décor was rather bland, but it was their final leg of a very long and arduous journey and all they wanted was to get home, home to their families and friends…at least for a while.

The Gulfstream G100 began to roll down the runway, eating up foot after foot of concrete with the engines at full throttle. While the others relaxed in their seats, Bobby was wide-awake, staring out the window at Lake Michigan in the dark. He was waiting for lift-off, but nothing. He began to wonder if the aircraft would ever get off the ground, but then, lift-off was achieved, with no runway to spare. The G100 knifed through the cold night air, as it veered east. Once it reached its cruising speed of Mach 0.85, the pilot set the autopilot for a course that would take them to Andrews Air Force Base, home to the presidential air fleet maintained by the 89th Airlift Wing.

As the G100 raced across the lower reaches of Michigan, the cockpit door opened and out stepped Lt. Colonel Kozlow. He was short in stature, an advantage when moving about the low-ceiling cabins of smaller military jet aircraft. He took a seat next to Alec and began. "Dr. Hakimian, once we arrive at Andrews you and your men will have the opportunity to clean-up and eat a good meal. You will then spend the night at the Distinguished Visitors Quarters. The next morning I hear that you and your men go by helo to the White House for a meeting with the president. Must be important."

Alec did not respond.

"What's the meeting with the president about, sir?" Bobby asked impulsively.

"That is well above my pay grade. However, there will be a presidential assistant from the White House waiting for you at Andrews. He will walk you through the rest of it. Oh, and by the way, Dr. Hakimian, the president has ordered a plane to pick your wife up and return her to your home in California to be with your daughter."

A smile formed on Alec's face. It was yet another sign that his long, dangerous journey had ended, and he would soon be where he wanted to be, with his family.

The men of Operation Star 9 sat back and tried to slow down. They had spent what seemed like eternity trekking across the Middle East, facing everything that the deadly terrorists and torturous environment could throw at them. They would always lament the loss of their comrade, DEVGRU Team Specialist Bernard Riemann, in the firefight in southern Lebanon that destroyed the Hezbollah's encampment. However, they all understood that it was for a cause far greater than any one of them.

CHAPTER NINETY-TWO

In less than two hours, the G100 was wheels-down at Andrews Air Force Base. It was 10:00 P.M. The G100 taxied to a stop at the opening of a gargantuan hangar. Inside was parked Marine One, the presidential helicopter.

The middle of the night at Andrews was always very active, with military personnel scurrying about, performing their scheduled tasks, tasks that were never truly completed, only repeated, because the moment they were done, the process started over again. Earlier in the evening, the president had returned aboard Air Force One from a weekend summit on global security in Edinburgh, Scotland. As such, the area was humming, for the presidential air force was in a constant state of readiness.

Andrews Air Force Base's origins dated back to the American Civil War, when Union troops bivouacked at a small church in Camp Springs, Maryland. Today the very same church, called Chapel Two, was still in use. The base was named in honor of fallen World War II Air Force Lieutenant General Frank M. Andrews, and became officially operational as a military installation in 1943.

"Damn, I stink," Bobby said, as he winced a bit while smelling his armpits.

"What was your first clue?" Nutworth said laughingly. "Was it the fact that no one wants to stand next to you?"

With OS9 now on solid ground again, the base commander arranged for refreshments in the officers' lounge, after which the men cleaned up in the DVQ and changed into fresh gear before dinner.

CHAPTER NINETY-THREE

As usual, Mackay asked for a wee dram, but the base commander had not anticipated they would be catering to a connoisseur of fine, single malt Scotch whiskey. However, Mackay quickly befriended an aide, who was able to rustle some up from the private bar of a brigadier general who was out of the country. Nutworth wanted a juicy hamburger, fries, and a Pepsi, while Josiah longed for a thick lamb chop and baked potato. Bobby remained the constant amongst the team, requesting a full rack of ribs and a longneck beer. Pratt would eat just about anything placed in front of him, while Alvarado dreamed of a flame-broiled Porterhouse steak with a side of creamed spinach. Alec asked for a rare filet and baked potato.

The hour passed quickly, with every member of OS9 seated in the officers' secure dining hall awaiting their meals. They had been given military fatigues, each selected to reflect their individual branch of service. Alec received gray sweats supplied by the base PX.

A television was on in the corner of the room. The men were watching a National League baseball game when a *news alert* interrupted play. "Good evening. I'm Heidi Carter and this is a FOX News Alert." With a movie star smile, she continued, "This afternoon a spokesperson for the Department of Homeland Security in Washington announced that the dirty bomb found in Chicago at the Willis Tower earlier today contained three kilograms of Plutonium-239. Scientists say that if the bomb had exploded, thousands of Chicagoans would have been killed instantly and tens of thousands more would have contracted cancer from the exposure to high doses of radiation. An unnamed group of military personnel discovered the dirty bomb and killed three of the men responsible. One of the men was Dr. Raymond Raissi, Chairman of Global Petroleum Resources and a world-renowned philanthropist. The spokesperson indicated that Dr. Raissi was suspected to have been the leader of the international terrorist organization known as Khamsin. We will have further details as they become available. Now back to our regular programming."

Alec and his men paid scant attention to the announcement. They were tired, hungry, and just wanted to watch some baseball. As for Alec, all he wanted to do was to be with his wife and daughter.

The quiet of dinner was broken when a tall man, dressed in the ubiquitous dark blue suit and red tie, entered the officers' dining hall and introduced himself as Brett McCullers, Deputy Assistant to the President. He ended his self-introduction when he said, "Gentlemen, thank-you for being here. On behalf of the President of the United States, Secretaries Drummond of DHS and Trucker of Defense, and NSA Director Caccavale, your service to your country has exceeded all expectations. I am not at liberty to discuss what will transpire tomorrow other than to say you will be meeting with the president in the White House at 10:00 A.M. Dress uniforms will be ready for you at 7:30 A.M., so get some shuteye."

CHAPTER NINETY-FOUR

0730 hours, Alec awoke from a restless sleep. He had been reliving, in flashbacks, the past months since OS9 was deployed on its *black ops mission*. From his first few days in Baghdad and OS9's trek across the vast expanse of the Middle East, to when he had learned of the kidnapping of his wife on the eve of the mission in southern Lebanon that cost the life of Sergeant Riemann, he knew that OS9 had done its job well. The deaths of Raymond and Raja Raissi, and Ali as-Saffah, had dealt a mortal blow to the Khamsin, but did nothing to bring back his friend William Francis. That said, he felt the albatross of revenge had been lifted.

The knock on the door brought Alec back to the moment. "Dr. Hakimian," came a voice from the other side of the door.

"Yes."

"I have your clothes for you, sir," he replied.

Alec opened the door to find a bright-eyed, young protocol airman holding a zippered garment bag and a box containing size ten dress shoes, Alec's size. "Thank-you," he said, taking the clothes and shutting the door.

He threw the garment bag down on the twin bed and set the shoebox on a side table. A quick, warm shower brightened his senses and washed away the feelings that he knew were certain to return. The base had supplied the room with all manner of toiletries, which made his getting ready to meet the president rather simple. Unzipping the garment bag revealed a black suit that had to have been a last minute purchase by the quartermaster at a local men's store. It was a little more stylish than what he would have expected from the military, and the fit worked. The white, long-sleeve dress shirt, red power tie, and black leather belt rounded out the ensemble. Given that his feet had been in exoskeleton combat boots for weeks on end, the black leather slip-ons were a welcomed change for his tired and sore feet.

Alec met the others in the officers' social hall a building away. Pratt, Josiah, Nutworth, and Mackay were there, with Nutworth having coffee and Mackay still waiting for his Earl Grey tea and milk. Bobby and Alvarado entered a few minutes later. Each man was dressed in his military branch's dress uniform.

A huge feeling of pride and gratitude welled up in Alec, as he looked at each of his men. They fought the agents of evil together, and now they were about to meet the President of the United States together.

"Gentlemen," Brett McCullers exclaimed from the doorway. The helicopter is waiting to take you to the White House." Looking at Alec, he said, "Dr. Hakimian, if you and your men will follow me."

The men followed McCullers out to the hangar that housed Marine One. Once inside, Bobby said, "Where's the helo?"

"Sir, here it is," McCullers answered, pointing to Marine One. "The president requested that you meet him at the White House and he wanted you to travel there aboard Marine One."

Marine One was usually a Sikorsky VH-3D Sea King. HMX-1, Marine Helicopter Squadron One, operated the president's heliocopter. The helicopter's call sign was *Marine One* "only" when the president was onboard, hence, today's flight required a different tail number designation.

Alec and his men entered the helicopter and took their seats, followed by McCullers. As soon as the door closed and everyone was belted in, it was rolled out of its hangar. A few minutes later, the pilot pulled back on the cyclic stick and they were airborne for the very short hop to the south lawn of the White House.

Flying over Washington, D.C., was always an awe-inspiring experience, even for the most jaded of individuals. In no time at all the eighteen acres of the most famous place on earth came into view. The sun was strong, and it was a windless day. *It was perfect*, Alec thought.

In 1792, the cornerstone for the White House was laid, and even though George Washington supervised the grand residence's construction, it was not until 1800 that John Adams, the second president, moved in as its first occupant with his wife Abigail.

The pilot deftly set the huge, dark green-colored Sikorsky helicopter down on the manicured south lawn. Two Marines stood at attention as the helicopter came to a rest; they lowered the steps and awaited its passengers.

Alec was the first to exit, followed by Nutworth in his Navy dress uniform. The rest of OS9 emerged, each taking a long, close-up look at the spectacular White House grounds. Two Marines and a Secret Service agent escorted Alec and his men to a side entrance of the "people's house." There McCullers said, "Gentlemen, if you'll follow the Secret Service agent, he'll take you to a waiting room. There you can relax for a few minutes before your audience with the president. I'll be with you shortly." McCullers turned on his heels and left.

The centurion-looking Secret Service agent said without a hint of emotion, "If you'll come with me gentlemen." The men followed him, as he whispered into his cuff mike, into the Map Room near the South Portico.

President Franklin D. Roosevelt used the Map Room as his situation room during the Second World War. It was tastefully decorated with Chippendale-style furniture, much of it dating back to the 1760s. Rococo, Oriental, and Gothic themes embellished the impressive room. Above a sandstone mantel hanged the last situation map Roosevelt used to prosecute World War II. On the east wall was displayed an exceptional 1755 French version of a surveyor's map prepared by early colonial surveyors Peter Jefferson, Thomas's father, and Joshua Fry.

Everyone quietly milled about, anxious to meet the president and hear what he had to say. Not used to dress uniforms, they felt uneasy standing about in such formal attire and surroundings. After all, they were a highly trained black ops team who knew nothing more than *to fight for the cause of freedom in the trenches and to die if need be.*

The anticipation of what was about to happen came to an end as Brett McCullers, Deputy Assistant to the President, accompanied by two Secret Service agents, said politely, "Dr. Hakimian, would you and your men please come with me?" Adjusting their jackets and caps, the men followed McCullers out of the Map Room.

"Gentlemen, you are about to meet the president in the East Room, the largest room in the residence. As you may know," he said jokingly, "the East Room was once used as a laundry room by Abigail Adams. President Jefferson used one end of the grand room as an office while his personal aide Meriwether Lewis slept at the other end. During the Civil War Union troops camped in the East Room, and Teddy Roosevelt's children used it to roller skate when the weather was bad. Today the room is used for formal occasions and large parties, but frankly, my favorite bit of history about the East Room hangs on one wall. It is the Gilbert Stuart state portrait of George Washington you will see when you enter. It is also the only object that has been in the White House since it opened in 1800. It even survived the War of 1812 when the British set fire to the White House."

The expression on McCullers's face demonstrated that he truly enjoyed giving a short history lesson of the White House whenever the opportunity presented itself.

Bobby raised his hand like a student trying to get his teacher's attention and asked, "Is all that true?"

"Every word. It's all true," McCullers said emphatically.

"Cool," Bobby said excitedly.

McCullers then motioned for them to follow. He led them on a path through the grand entrance and ornate cross-halls of the White House and to the entrance of the East Room. There, two Marine guards stood sentry at the west doorway.

The room was festooned with immense chandeliers, floor-to-ceiling draperies, antique carpets, highly polished parquet-oak floors, elaborate sconces, and an exquisite grand piano. "Now gentlemen, please," McCullers said, motioning for them to enter and take their seats.

As they walked into the awe-inspiring room, those already seated turned around and looked. In attendance were the vice-president and his lovely wife, the Directors of the NSA, CIA, FBI, as well as Homeland Security, the Chairman of the Joint Chiefs of Staff, the Director of National Intelligence, and numerous others of the president's inner circle.

Alec spotted Lt. General Meade of CENTCOM-Baghdad, and

seated next to him, Mica Seddons. Both smiled proudly, as the men of OS9 took their seats in the front row. The two were already in Washington, D.C., for OS9's debriefing that was scheduled to take place in the next few days.

Missing were the wives and families of the men of OS9, except for Riemann's wife. Everything happened so fast that there was no time to assemble family members for the auspicious occasion. In reality, it was a meeting with the president that the outside world would never know about. After all, *Operation Star 9 never existed.…*

Alec noticed that there were no photographers in the room, no press of any kind. *No photo opportunities for this president*, he thought. The room felt uncommonly still, even secretive in nature. Then, the silence was broken when the president's Assistant Chief of Staff, Mitchell Markham, entered the room and announced, "Ladies and gentlemen, the President of the United States and the First Lady." Everyone stood at attention as they gracefully and quietly made their entrance, sans *Hail to the Chief.* An aide seated the First Lady, attired in a pink Chanel suit, next to Alec. The two exchanged cordialities, as the president took to the podium.

The president smiled, nodded his acknowledgment of the vice-president and others, and then began his remarks. "Good morning ladies and gentlemen. I'm pleased to see all of you here on such short notice. I apologize for that, but as you know, we are here to recognize the very successful efforts of our country's most secret special operations team, Operation Star 9, and it simply can't wait. OS9, lead by Dr. Alexander Hakimian, is made up of select members from various branches of the U.S. Military. They are the best of the best. And I can't stress enough that their names must remain a secret…for their safety and the nation's security depend on it."

Smiles rolled over the faces of Mica Seddons and Lt. General Meade.

The vice-president stood to clap and everyone followed. Once seated again, the president continued.

"These men spent the past several months in the Middle East, charged with finding the leader of the Khamsin and his lieutenants, and they did just that. They also found WMD in Syria, Jordan, and Lebanon. I don't have to tell any of you here this morning what that means. Hopefully, this will lead to a bipartisan support of the overall war on terror. After this gathering to honor these brave patriots this morning, I will give a brief press conference in the Rose Garden. There I will announce the success of an operation that was responsible for finding WMD and the deaths of the Ankabut, leader of the Khamsin, and Ali as-Saffah."

The president paused for applause, then continued, "Certainly these findings are what I and many others have been waiting for. The region is better off now that these terrorists and the WMD are no longer a threat to human lives. However, let me disabuse you of the notion that the threat of terrorism is over. It is not! And you should also know that Operation Star 9's mission did not end in the Middle East, but rather right here at home. It was the brave men of Operation Star 9 who discovered the lethal dirty bomb in the Willis Tower yesterday." Everyone's face showed instant shock. The president continued, "Yes, Dr. Hakimian and his men were able to eliminate the leader of the Khamsin and defuse the dirty bomb just seconds before its detonation. Several other members of the Khamsin were killed or apprehended as well."

The president paused to let his words sink in and then continued, "But I must warn you that we need to be ever vigilant because the Khamsin itself is not dead. History teaches us that evil organizations of this type often reconstitute themselves for an even more evil purpose."

The president took a long look around the room, eyeing each person in attendance. He knew that his persona at a personal level was very powerful and convincing. Setting his eyes directly on Alec, he continued, "On a personal note, Dr. Hakimian. I am aware that the success of Operation Star 9 did not come without great cost to you and your men."

Everyone in the East Room looked to the members of OS9 as they held their heads high. Mica Seddons, sitting directly behind Alec, touched him on the shoulder as a gesture of pride and gratitude.

The president stood silent for a long pause, then said, "Ladies and gentlemen, of all the duties of a president, what I am about to say always proves the most difficult. The loss of any one of our brave men or women in uniform never gets easier, but a hard truth is that freedom has always come at the highest cost, the loss of human life. Days ago in southern Lebanon, during the most intense of firefights, DEVGRU Specialist Bernard Riemann lost his life. I am grateful that his wife Rita Riemann is here with us today. And Mrs. Riemann, know that your loss is the nation's loss."

Rita Riemann began to tear up and was comforted by the vice president's wife seated next to her.

The room fell silent again. The president's revelation overwhelmed every person in attendance.

Now looking to the members of OS9 seated in the front row, the president continued, "I personally, and we as a nation, are deeply grateful to Dr. Alexander Hakimian and his team of patriots who risked it all in service to their country. As is always the case, special black operations are forever classified. The public will never know of Operation Star 9, which, on my orders, was deactivated as of this morning. To the outside world, it never existed. Yet, its successes will forever be known anonymously because we are freer today than yesterday. And although I cannot publicly acknowledge you by name, a special Congressional decree has ordered that each of you be awarded the Congressional Medal of Honor." Bobby, Alvarado, Mackay, Nutworth, Josiah, Pratt, and Riemann's wife just stared at each other with looks of astonishment on their faces.

The Congressional Medal of Honor, first awarded during the American Civil War, was America's highest military decoration bestowed upon those who distinguished themselves "conspicuously by gallantry and intrepidity at the risk of his life above and beyond the call of duty while engaged in an action against an enemy of the United States...."

"I have also ordered the Service Secretaries of your respective branches to give each of you a raise in rank. Again, I thank-you for your service to the cause of freedom."

The president paused for a long beat. With great pride evident in his eyes, he continued, "Dr. Hakimian, the Presidential Medal of Freedom is our nation's highest civilian honor, but it does not begin to reflect your contribution to the preservation of freedom for every American. Doctor, because of your personal sacrifices, the seeds of freedom will continue to grow and flourish, not only in the Middle East, but throughout the world."

He took a deep breath, giving the audience time to absorb his every word.

"Therefore, Congress has established the *American Medal of Honor*, to be given to those civilians who have risked their lives in selfless acts of bravery under fire for the cause of freedom we all cherish." Looking directly to Alec, he added, "Dr. Alexander Hakimian, it is my privilege to present you with the 'first' American Medal of Honor. Your courage in leading Operation Star 9 is why America is still the '*land of the free and the home of the brave.*'"

The new American Medal of Honor was a large, gold disk with a wide lanyard of red, white, and blue tri-colored ribbon. The medal's obverse showed a five-pointed American star in high relief. Atop the star, an American bald eagle with wings spread wide. In the eagle's left talon, a bundle of arrows, and in its right talon, an olive branch. The perimeter held the words "United States of America." On the reverse was displayed an American flag, also in high relief. The words "American Medal of Honor" were above the flag. Below the flag appeared the phrase "Courage, Honor, Sacrifice."

Without hesitation, the president walked from behind the podium and approached Alec, who instantly stood up. With the decorative medal in hand, he said proudly, "Dr. Hakimian, I present you with the first American Medal of Honor. I thank-you and America thanks-you." Alec leaned over as the president placed it around his neck. He then shook his hand as those in attendance began to applaud.

The president proceeded to move down the front row, followed by an aide, as he draped the Congressional Medal of Honor around the neck of each of the remaining members of OS9 and Specialist Riemann's wife.

The room erupted in applause once again, as the president called OS9 around him to shake hands and exchange a few words with each of them. Then the president leaned into Alec and whispered, "Doctor, can I call on you again?"

Alec answered the president with a wink.

EPILOGUE

"Suction. Aneurysm clip. Needle."

Alec was in the last hour of a delicate surgery when he gingerly advanced the long spinal needle along the skull base to aspirate the blood within the aneurysm sac and collapse it. Suddenly, in a nanosecond the unthinkable happened, the aneurysm ruptured and its bloody contents spewed out into the brain. Without hesitation, he went into crisis mode, only to realize that the clip had held. Looking up at Roxy, his other surgical nurse, he said with a tight smile, "Well, that's over."

Alec pondered the thought. *Only weeks before he had his hands on a dirty bomb that would have killed thousands if he hadn't found it and defused it.*

One hour later the double doors to the recovery room opened and Alec gleefully walked in carrying Faith, the four-month old baby girl who had been named so because of her parents' *faith* in one man.

Tears flowed from her mother's bright blue eyes as Alec gently placed Faith in her arms. Despite the lasting effects of general neuroanesthesia, Meghan could not control her emotions, nor could anyone else in the room, including *The Doctor* himself.

"Meghan my dear, she's beautiful," Alec said happily, but with a tight jaw. He reached down to kiss her on the forehead and then turned to shake Martin's hand. "Now, if you'll excuse me. I'll leave the two of you with your daughter."

"Dr. Hakimian," Meghan's husband Martin said, his voice tight with emotion, "you are a miracle worker." Hugging Alec, he added, "We are blessed doctor. We are truly blessed."

Leaving the room, Alec stopped at the elevator and thought, *he was glad to be a doctor again…saving lives. And he too felt blessed.*

His walk back to his office from the hospital was a pleasant change. He had returned to his quotidian life, and he knew that it was where he wanted to be. His medical practice was flourishing and his family was happy.

From the moment he met the lovely and very pregnant Meghan and her husband Martin several months ago in his office, he had always believed that she would not only live to see this day, but live to see her daughter Faith give her grandchildren.

Still in his scrubs, Alec opened the private entrance to his suite of offices. Once inside the tasteful surroundings his assistant Lara, a woman in her late thirties, who made every effort to see to it that Alec was never distracted by the mundane issues of office life, called out to him. "Dr. Hakimian, remember, you have a conference call with Drs. Topalian and Javahi in about an hour."

"Very good, Lara," Alec said. He reached over the secretary's desk and scanned his messages. Putting them back down on the desk, he then walked into his private office and closed the door. With the bright Southern California morning sun shining intensely through the large, tinted window behind his desk, he turned on his Bose stereo. Handel's *Water Music* began to flow from its acoustically tuned speakers. He then leaned back in his Herman-Miller Aeron swivel chair, kicked off his Merrells, put his feet on the top of his mahogany desk, expelled a deep breath of air, and relaxed.

A few minutes later, Alec reached for the remote control to change the music selection when suddenly his *private line* began ringing. Picking it up, he had anticipated hearing his wife Leyla's delightful voice. "*Hamov*, my delicious one," he said, waiting for a response.

"Well, Dr Hakimian. You remembered. How sweet," the peculiar sounding voice said.

"Who is this?" Alec asked, trying to place the strange voice.

"Don't you remember me, doctor?" the voice said calmly.

Alec could not place the voice. It sounded almost mechanical, electronically altered. Still puzzled, he said sharply, "Listen, I don't have time for this. Please tell me who you are."

"Now, now, Dr. Hakimian," the mysterious voice said slowly. "Be patient. Think. Think very hard, and it will come to you. I know you are a very intelligent man. Just try."

Alec put his feet on the ground and sat up in his chair. He reached for a memo pad and slid it across the desk. Picking up his Montblanc fountain pen, he said, "Who gave you my private number?"

"This is a private call, doctor. I thought it was most appropriate that we speak on your private line. Don't you agree?" the voice said, in a casual manner.

Alec did not answer.

"So, doctor. Tell me about Leyla. She is very attractive. You must love her. Is she good to you? And how about your daughter Karina? She is awfully cute. How old is she now? She must be about two."

Alec felt violated. *How did the caller know about Leyla, Karina?* He looked down and saw line three blinking. "One moment, I have another call," Alec said.

"Certainly doctor, I have all the time in the world," the voice replied slowly.

Picking up line three, he said, "Yes, this is Dr. Hakimian, may I —?"

"*Hamov*, it's me. I tried your private line, but it was busy."

"Leyla, my dearest. Can I call you back?" he asked hastily.

Pausing for a second, she answered, "Yes. But is there anything wrong?"

"No, no, nothing is wrong," he answered in a dismissive tone.

"Okay darling, but don't forget that Karina has her first swimming lesson this afternoon, and you promised her you'd be home to see it," she said plaintively.

Alec pushed his private line again and said with heat in his voice, "Enough. What do you want?"

"Patience. Patience," came the reply.

Alec struggled to divine the mysterious voice. He now detected a slight change of pitch. It was much higher now than when he first took the call. It sounded less male and more female in inflection and volume.

He was convinced that some type of voice changer was electronically modifying the voice. *But why? Why was the caller toying with him?*

"All right, stop the game playing and get to it," Alec demanded, clenching his teeth to contain his anger and impatience.

"Alexander," the voice said, now creamy smooth, sexy in its intonation. *"Ana kont malekatak.* I was your queen," came out softly.

It stunned him, but before he could process the words *I was your queen*, she continued. "I was your queen in Palmyra."

A collage of memories instantly riddled his body, each fighting to get his undivided attention.

He fell mute.

Sensing his silence, Sahar continued, "Oh, now. Did I upset you, my dear Alexander? Did I say something you did not like?" she questioned, as the anger in her voice began to rise.

Alec was transfixed by her words.

"Alec, my dear. Do you remember Robert Tishermann?"

He immediately asked himself, *why would she ask about him?*

She drew in a deep breath and slowly expelled the words, "He was my brother!"

The air in Alec's office stood still.

The music went silent.

Everything stopped.

The voice was now very intense. "You stopped one bomb, but you cannot stop them all. *Allahu Akbar!*"

Alec began to speak but —

"Alexander. I am the Ankabut."

CLICK.

DIAL TONE.

□ □ □

ABOUT THE AUTHORS

MARKO PERKO

(PHOTO CREDIT: HEATHER MACKAY)

Marko Perko is a graduate of the University of Southern California. He has always had an insatiable thirst for knowledge of all types, and as such, he is highly regarded as a modern-day Renaissance man, historian, and polemicist. He is the author of the critically acclaimed and wildly popular book entitled Did You Know That...? an uncommon compendium of knowledge. He is also the founder of the Marko Perko Online Web site, and the creator of the Cultural Enrichment Programs™.

Perko has written for and edited numerous publications, and has worked as a lecturer, columnist, speechwriter, composer, and playwright. He is a member of The Authors Guild and other professional societies.

Presently, he is lecturing and at work on his next book.

Marko Perko lives in California with his wife Heather and their two children, Marko III and Skye Mackay.

Visit his Web sites:
www.MarkoPerko.com
www.KhamsinTheBook.com

HRAYR SHAHINIAN

(PHOTO CREDIT: LESLIE SHAHINIAN)

Hrayr Shahinian M.D. was born in Lebanon to Armenian parents and is a graduate of the American University of Beirut, where he received his Bachelor and Medical degrees, both with Distinction. He continued his postgraduate education at prestigious medical centers, including the University of Chicago, Vanderbilt University, and New York University. He is a member of the Alpha Omega Alpha Honor Society, author of eighty peer reviewed articles and book chapters and senior author of the textbook *Endoscopic Skull Base Surgery*.

Dr. Shahinian is the founder of the Skull Base Institute. He is regarded as a pioneer in the field of skull base brain surgery and has lead a paradigm shift by shunning traditional open brain surgery techniques in favor of high definition, fiberoptic endoscopic technology that enables the safe and skillful removal of brain tumors, while at the same time dramatically reducing operating and recovery times.

Dr. Shahinian is currently working with NASA's Jet Propulsion Laboratory (JPL) to design and introduce the next generation of endoscopic microsurgical instruments. He lives in California with his wife Leslie and their two children, Alexander and Karina.

Visit his Web sites:
www.SkullBaseInstitute.com
www.KhamsinTheBook.com

LaVergne, TN USA
17 November 2010
205267LV00002B/1/P

9 781450 238885